STORM FRONT

'Someone killed two people with sorcery last night, Dresden. I think it was you. And when I find how you did it and can trace it back to you, don't think you're going to live long enough to cast the same spell at me.' Morgan swiped at the blood with one big fist.

It was my turn to blink. I tried to shift mental gears, to keep up with the change in subject. Morgan thought I was the killer. And since Morgan didn't do too much of his own thinking, that meant that the White Council thought I was the killer. Holy shit.

Of course, it made sense, from Morgan's narrow and single-minded point of view. A wizard had killed someone. I was a wizard who had already been convicted of killing another with magic, even if the self-defense clause had kept me from being executed. Cops looked for people who had already committed crimes before they started looking for other culprits. Morgan was just another kind of cop, as far as I was concerned.

And, as far as he was concerned, I was just one more dangerous con.

By Jim Butcher

The Dresden Files

Storm Front
Fool Moon
Grave Peril
Summer Knight
Death Masks
Blood Rites
Dead Beat
Proven Guilty
White Night
Small Favour
Turn Coat
Changes
Ghost Story
Cold Days
Skin Game

Side Jobs: Stories from the Dresden Files

The Codex Alera

Furies of Calderon
Academ's Fury
Cursor's Fury
Captain's Fury
Princeps' Fury
First Lord's Fury

JIM BUTCHER

THE DRESDEN FILES
STORM FRONT

orbit

www.orbitbooks.net

ORBIT

First published in Great Britain in 2005 by Orbit
Published by arrangement with Signet,
a member of Penguin Group (USA) Inc.
This paperback edition published in 2011 by Orbit
Reprinted 2012 (three times), 2013 (twice), 2014

A CIP catalogue record for this book
is available from the British Library.

ISBN 978-0-356-50027-0

Typeset in Garamond 3 by Palimpsest Book Production Limited,
Falkirk, Stirlingshire
Printed and bound by CPI Group (UK) Ltd, Croydon, CR0 4YY

Papers used by Orbit are from well-managed forests
and other responsible sources.

MIX
Paper from
responsible sources
FSC® C104740

Orbit
An imprint of
Little, Brown Book Group
100 Victoria Embankment
London EC4Y 0DY

An Hachette UK Company
www.hachette.co.uk

www.orbitbooks.net

For Debbie Chester, who taught me everything I really needed to know about writing. And for my father, who taught me everything I really needed to know about living. I miss you, Dad.

Acknowledgments

Special thanks go out to Caroline, Fred, Debra, Tara, and Corin: the original Harry Dresden fans. Without the perverse desire to make you guys scream at me to write the next chapter, Harry would never have gotten into so much trouble. More thanks are due to Ricia Mainhardt and to A. J. Janschewitz, great agents and good people, and to Chris Ely, who is just an all around neat person.

Super special thanks to my son, J. J., who believed his dada had written a good book even if he couldn't read it.

And thank you, Shannon, for too many things to list. You're my angel. One day, I will learn to turn my socks rightside out before throwing them on the bedroom floor.

1

I heard the mailman approach my office door, half an hour earlier than usual. He didn't sound right. His footsteps fell more heavily, jauntily, and he whistled. A new guy. He whistled his way to my office door, then fell silent for a moment. Then he laughed.

Then he knocked.

I winced. My mail comes through the mail slot unless it's registered. I get a really limited selection of registered mail, and it's never good news. I got up out of my office chair and opened the door.

The new mailman, who looked like a basketball with arms and legs and a sunburned, balding head, was chuckling at the sign on the door glass. He glanced at me and hooked a thumb toward the sign. 'You're kidding, right?'

I read the sign (people change it occasionally), and shook my head. 'No, I'm serious. Can I have my mail, please.'

'So, uh. Like parties, shows, stuff like that?' He looked past me, as though he expected to see a white tiger, or possibly some skimpily clad assistants prancing around my one-room office.

I sighed, not in the mood to get mocked again, and reached for the mail he held in his hand. 'No, not like that. I don't do parties.'

He held on to it, his head tilted curiously. 'So what? Some kinda fortune-teller? Cards and crystal balls and things?'

'No,' I told him. 'I'm not a psychic.' I tugged at the mail.

He held on to it. 'What are you, then?'

'What's the sign on the door say?'

'It says "Harry Dresden. Wizard."'

'That's me,' I confirmed.

'An actual wizard?' he asked, grinning, as though I should let him in on the joke. 'Spells and potions? Demons and incantations? Subtle and quick to anger?'

'Not so subtle.' I jerked the mail out of his hand and looked pointedly at his clipboard. 'Can I sign for my mail please.'

The new mailman's grin vanished, replaced with a scowl. He passed over the clipboard to let me sign for the mail (another late notice from my landlord), and said, 'You're a nut. That's what you are.' He took his clipboard back, and said, 'You have a nice day, sir.'

I watched him go.

'Typical,' I muttered, and shut the door.

My name is Harry Blackstone Copperfield Dresden. Conjure by it at your own risk. I'm a wizard. I work out of an office in midtown Chicago. As far as I know, I'm the only openly practicing professional wizard in the country. You can find me in the yellow pages, under 'Wizards'. Believe it or not, I'm the only one there. My ad looks like this:

HARRY DRESDEN – WIZARD
Lost Items Found. Paranormal Investigations.
Consulting. Advice. Reasonable Rates.
No Love Potions, Endless Purses, Parties, or Other
Entertainment

You'd be surprised how many people call just to ask me if I'm serious. But then, if you'd seen the things I'd seen, if you knew half of what I knew, you'd wonder how anyone could *not* think I was serious.

The end of the twentieth century and the dawn of the new millennium had seen something of a renaissance in the public awareness of the paranormal. Psychics, haunts, vampires – you name it. People still didn't take them seriously, but all the things Science had promised us hadn't come to pass. Disease was still a problem. Starvation was still a problem. Violence and crime and war were still problems. In spite of the advance of technology, things just hadn't changed the way everyone had hoped and thought they would.

Science, the largest religion of the twentieth century, had become somewhat tarnished by images of exploding space shuttles, crack babies, and a generation of complacent Americans who had allowed the television to raise their children. People were looking for something – I think they just didn't know what. And even though they were once again starting to open their eyes to the world of magic and the arcane that had been with them all the while, they still thought I must be some kind of joke.

Anyway, it had been a slow month. A slow pair of months, actually. My rent from February didn't get paid until the tenth of March, and it was looking like it might be even longer until I got caught up for this month.

My only job had been the previous week, when I'd gone down to Branson, Missouri, to investigate a country singer's possibly haunted house. It hadn't been. My client hadn't been happy with that answer, and had been even less happy when I suggested he lay off of any intoxicating substances and try to get some exercise and sleep, and see if that didn't help things more than an exorcism. I'd gotten travel expenses plus an hour's pay, and gone away feeling I had done the honest, righteous, and impractical thing. I heard later that he'd hired a shyster psychic to come in and perform a ceremony with a lot of incense and black lights. Some people.

I finished up my paperback and tossed it into the DONE box. There was a pile of read and discarded paperbacks in a cardboard box on one side of my desk, the spines bent and the pages mangled. I'm terribly hard on books. I was eyeing the pile of unread books, considering which to start next, given that I had no real work to do, when my phone rang.

I stared at it in a somewhat surly fashion. We wizards are terrific at brooding. After the third ring, when I thought I wouldn't sound a little too eager, I picked up the receiver and said, 'Dresden.'

'Oh. Is this, um, Harry Dresden? The, ah, wizard?' Her tone was apologetic, as though she were terribly afraid she would be insulting me.

No, I thought. It's Harry Dresden the, ah, lizard. Harry the wizard is one door down.

It is the prerogative of wizards to be grumpy. It is not, however, the prerogative of freelance consultants who are late on their rent, so instead of saying something smart, I told the woman on the phone, 'Yes, ma'am. How can I help you today?'

'I, um,' she said. 'I'm not sure. I've lost something, and I think maybe you could help me.'

'Finding lost articles is a specialty,' I said. 'What would I be looking for?'

There was a nervous pause. 'My husband,' she said. She had a voice that was a little hoarse, like a cheerleader who'd been working a long tournament, but had enough weight of years in it to place her as an adult.

My eyebrows went up. 'Ma'am, I'm not really a missing-persons specialist. Have you contacted the police or a private investigator?'

'No,' she said, quickly. 'No, they can't. That is, I haven't. Oh dear, this is all so complicated. Not something someone can talk about on the phone. I'm sorry to have taken up your time, Mr Dresden.'

'Hold on now,' I said quickly. 'I'm sorry, you didn't tell me your name.'

There was that nervous pause again, as though she were checking a sheet of written notes before answering. 'Call me Monica.'

People who know diddly about wizards don't like to give us their names. They're convinced that if they give a wizard their name from their own lips it could be used against them. To be fair, they're right.

I had to be as polite and harmless as I could. She was about to hang up out of pure indecision, and I needed the job. I could probably turn hubby up, if I worked at it.

'Okay, Monica,' I told her, trying to sound as melodious and friendly as I could. 'If you feel your situation is of a sensitive nature, maybe you could come by my office and talk about it. If it turns out that I can help you best, I will, and if not, then I can direct you to someone I think can help you better.' I gritted my teeth and pretended I was smiling. 'No charge.'

It must have been the no charge that did it. She agreed to come right out to the office, and told me that she would be there in an hour. That put her estimated arrival at about two-thirty. Plenty of time to go out and get some lunch, then get back to the office to meet her.

The phone rang again almost the instant I put it down, making me jump. I peered at it. I don't trust electronics. Anything manufactured after the forties is suspect – and doesn't seem to have much liking for me. You name it: cars, radios, telephones, TVs, VCRs – none of them seem to behave well for me. I don't even like to use automatic pencils.

I answered the phone with the same false cheer I had summoned up for Monica Husband-Missing. 'This is Dresden, may I help you?'

'Harry, I need you at the Madison in the next ten minutes. Can you be there?' The voice on the other end of the line was also a woman's, cool, brisk, businesslike.

'Why, Lieutenant Murphy,' I gushed, overflowing with saccharine, 'It's good to hear from you, too. It's been so long. Oh, they're fine, fine. And your family?'

'Save it, Harry. I've got a couple of bodies here, and I need you to take a look around.'

I sobered immediately. Karrin Murphy was the director of Special Investigations out of downtown Chicago, a de facto appointee of the Police Commissioner to investigate any crimes dubbed *unusual*. Vampire attacks, troll maraudings, and faery abductions of children didn't fit in very neatly on a police report – but at the same time, people got attacked, infants got stolen, property was damaged or destroyed. And someone had to look into it.

In Chicago, or pretty much anywhere in Chicagoland, that person was Karrin Murphy. I was her library of the supernatural on legs, and a paid consultant for the police department. But two bodies? Two deaths by means unknown? I hadn't handled anything like that for her before.

'Where are you?' I asked her.

'Madison Hotel on Tenth, seventh floor.'

'That's only a fifteen-minute walk from my office,' I said.

'So you can be here in fifteen minutes. Good.'

'Um,' I said. I looked at the clock. Monica No-Last-Name would be here in a little more than forty-five minutes. 'I've sort of got an appointment.'

'Dresden, I've sort of got a pair of corpses with no leads and no suspects, and a killer walking around loose. Your appointment can wait.'

My temper flared. It does that occasionally. 'It can't, actually,' I said. 'But I'll tell you what. I'll stroll on over and take a look around, and be back here in time for it.'

'Have you had lunch yet?' she asked.

'What?'

She repeated the question.

'No,' I said.

'Don't.' There was a pause, and when she spoke again, there was a sort of greenish tone to her words. 'It's bad.'

'How bad are we talking here, Murph?'

Her voice softened, and that scared me more than any images of gore or violent death could have. Murphy was the original tough girl, and she prided herself on never showing weakness. 'It's bad, Harry. Please don't take too long. Special Crimes is itching to get their fingers on this one, and I know you don't like people to touch the scene before you can look around.'

'I'm on the way,' I told her, already standing and pulling on my jacket.

'Seventh floor,' she reminded me. 'See you there.'

'Okay.'

I turned off the lights to my office, went out the door, and locked up behind me, frowning. I wasn't sure how long it was going to take to investigate Murphy's scene, and I didn't want to miss out on speaking with Monica Ask-Me-No-Questions. So I opened the door again, got out a piece of paper and a thumbtack, and wrote:

Out briefly. Back for appointment at 2:30. Dresden

That done, I started down the stairs. I rarely use the elevator, even though I'm on the fifth floor. Like I said, I don't trust machines. They're always breaking down on me just when I need them.

Besides which. If I were someone in this town using magic to kill people two at a time, and I didn't want to get caught, I'd make sure that I removed the only practicing wizard the police department kept on retainer. I liked my odds on the stairwell a lot better than I did in the cramped confines of the elevator.

Paranoid? Probably. But just because you're paranoid doesn't mean that there isn't an invisible demon about to eat your face.

2

Karrin Murphy was waiting for me outside the Madison. Karrin and I are a study in contrasts. Where I am tall and lean, she's short and stocky. Where I have dark hair and dark eyes, she's got Shirley Temple blonde locks and baby blues. Where my features are all lean and angular, with a hawkish nose and a sharp chin, hers are round and smooth, with the kind of cute nose you'd expect on a cheerleader.

It was cool and windy, like it usually is in March, and she wore a long coat that covered her pantsuit. Murphy never wore dresses, though I suspected she'd have muscular, well-shaped legs, like a gymnast. She was built for function, and had a pair of trophies in her office from aikido tournaments to prove it. Her hair was cut at shoulder length and whipped out wildly in the spring wind. She wasn't wearing earrings, and her makeup was of sufficient quality and quantity that it was tough to tell she had on any at all. She looked more like a favorite aunt or a cheerful mother than a hard-bitten homicide detective.

'Don't you have any other jackets, Dresden?' she asked, as I came within hailing distance. There were several police cars parked illegally in front of the building. She glanced at my eyes for a half second and then away, quickly. I had to give her credit. It was more than most people did. It wasn't really dangerous unless you did it for several seconds, but I was used to anyone who knew I was a wizard making it a point not to glance at my face.

I looked down at my black canvas duster, with its heavy mantling and waterproof lining and sleeves actually long enough for my arms. 'What's wrong with this one?'

'It belongs on the set of *El Dorado*.'

'And?'

She snorted, an indelicate sound from so small a woman, and spun on her heel to walk toward the hotel's front doors.

I caught up and walked a little ahead of her.

She sped her pace. So did I. We raced one another toward the front door, with increasing speed, through the puddles left over from last night's rain.

My legs were longer; I got there first. I opened the door for her and gallantly gestured for her to go in. It was an old contest of ours. Maybe my values are outdated, but I come from an old school of thought. I think that men ought to treat women like something other than just shorter, weaker men with breasts. Try and convict me if I'm a bad person for thinking so. I enjoy treating a woman like a lady, opening doors for her, paying for shared meals, giving flowers – all that sort of thing.

It irritates the hell out of Murphy, who had to fight and claw and play dirty with the hairiest men in Chicago to get as far as she has. She glared up at me while I stood there holding open the door, but there was a reassurance about the glare, a relaxation. She took an odd sort of comfort in our ritual, annoying as she usually found it.

How bad was it up on the seventh floor, anyway?

We rode the elevator in a sudden silence. We knew one another well enough, by this time, that the silences were not uncomfortable. I had a good sense of Murphy, an instinctual grasp for her moods and patterns of thought – something I develop whenever I'm around someone for any length of time.

Whether it's a natural talent or a supernatural one I don't know.

My instincts told me that Murphy was tense, stretched as tight as piano wire. She kept it off her face, but there was something about the set of her shoulders and neck, the stiffness of her back, that made me aware of it.

Or maybe I was just projecting it onto her. The confines of the elevator made me a bit nervous. I licked my lips and looked around the interior of the car. My shadow and Murphy's fell on the floor, and almost looked as though they were sprawled there. There was something about it that bothered me, a nagging little instinct that I blew off as a case of nerves. Steady, Harry.

She let out a harsh breath just as the elevator slowed, then sucked in another one before the doors could open, as though she were planning on holding it for as long as we were on the floor and breathing only when she got back in the elevator again.

Blood smells a certain way, a kind of sticky, almost metallic odor, and the air was full of it when the elevator doors opened. My stomach quailed a little bit, but I swallowed manfully and followed Murphy out of the elevator and down the hall past a couple of uniform cops, who recognized me and waved me past without asking to see the little laminated card the city had given me. Granted, even in a big-city department like Chicago P.D., they didn't exactly call in a horde of consultants (I went down in the paperwork as a psychic consultant, I think), but still. Unprofessional of the boys in blue.

Murphy preceded me into the room. The smell of blood grew thicker, but there wasn't anything gruesome behind door number one. The outer room of the suite looked like some kind of a sitting room done in rich tones of red and gold, like a set from an old movie in the thirties – expensive-looking, but somehow faux, nonetheless. Dark, rich leather covered the chairs, and my feet sank into the thick, rust-colored shag of the carpet. The velvet velour curtains had been drawn, and though the lights were all on, the place still seemed a little too dark, a little too sensual in its textures and colors. It wasn't the kind of room where you sit and read a book. Voices came from a doorway to my right.

'Wait here a minute,' Murphy told me. Then she went through the door to the right of the entryway and into what I supposed was the bedroom of the suite.

I wandered around the sitting room with my eyes mostly closed, noting things. Leather couch. Two leather chairs. Stereo and television in a black glossy entertainment center. Champagne bottle warming in a stand holding a brimming tub of what had been ice the night before, with two empty glasses set beside it. There was a red rose petal on the floor, clashing with the carpeting (but then, in that room, what didn't?).

A bit to one side, under the skirt of one of the leather recliners, was a little piece of satiny cloth. I bent at the waist and lifted the skirt with one hand, careful not to touch anything. A pair of black-satin panties, a tiny triangle with lace coming off the points, lay there, one strap snapped as though the thong had simply been torn off. Kinky.

The stereo system was state of the art, though not an expensive brand. I took a pencil from my pocket and pushed the PLAY button with the eraser. Gentle, sensual music filled the room, a low bass, a driving drumbeat, wordless vocals, the heavy breathing of a woman as background.

The music continued for a few seconds more, and then

it began to skip over a section about two seconds long, repeating it over and over again.

I grimaced. Like I said, I have this effect on machinery. It has something to do with being a wizard, with working with magical forces. The more delicate and modern the machine is, the more likely it is that something will go wrong if I get close enough to it. I can kill a copier at fifty paces.

'The love suite,' came a man's voice, drawing the word *love* out into *luuuuuuv*. 'What do you think, Mister Man?'

'Hello, Detective Carmichael,' I said, without turning around. Carmichael's rather light, nasal voice had a distinctive quality. He was Murphy's partner and the resident skeptic, convinced that I was nothing more than a charlatan, scamming the city out of its hard-earned money. 'Were you saving the panties to take home yourself, or did you just overlook them?' I turned and looked at him. He was short and overweight and balding, with beady, bloodshot eyes and a weak chin. His jacket was rumpled, and there were food stains on his tie, all of which served to conceal a razor intellect. He was a sharp cop, and absolutely ruthless at tracking down killers.

He walked over to the chair and looked down. 'Not bad, Sherlock,' he said. 'But that's just foreplay. Wait'll you see the main attraction. I'll have a bucket waiting for you.' He turned and killed the malfunctioning CD player with a jab from the eraser end of his own pencil.

I widened my eyes at him, to let him know how terrified I was, then walked past him and into the bedroom. And regretted it. I looked, noted details mechanically, and quietly shut the door on the part of my head that had started screaming the second I entered the room.

They must have died sometime the night before, as rigor mortis had already set in. They were on the bed; she was astride him, body leaned back, back bowed like a dancer's, the curves of her breasts making a lovely outline. He stretched beneath her, a lean and powerfully built man, arms reaching out and grasping at the satin sheets, gathering them in his fists. Had it been an erotic photograph, it would have made a striking tableau.

Except that the lovers' rib cages on the upper left side of their torsos had expanded outward, through their skin, the ribs jabbing out like ragged, snapped knives. Arterial blood had sprayed out of their bodies, all the way to the mirror on the ceiling, along with pulped, gelatinous masses of flesh that had to be what remained of their hearts. Standing over them, I could see into the upper cavity of the bodies. I noted the now greyish lining around the motionless left lungs and the edges of the ribs, which apparently were forced outward and snapped by some force within.

It definitely cut down on the erotic potential.

The bed was in the middle of the room, giving it a subtle emphasis. The bedroom followed the decor of the sitting room – a lot of red, a lot of plush fabrics, a little over the top unless viewed in candlelight. There were indeed candles in holders on the wall, now burned down to the nubs and extinguished.

I stepped closer to the bed and walked around it. The carpet squelched as I did. The little screaming part of my brain, safely locked up behind doors of self-control and strict training, continued gibbering. I tried to ignore it. Really I did. But if I didn't get out of that room in a hurry, I was going to start crying like a little girl.

So I took in the details fast. The woman was in her

twenties, in fabulous condition. At least I thought she had been. It was hard to tell. She had hair the color of chestnuts, cut in a pageboy style, and it seemed dyed to me. Her eyes were only partly open, and I couldn't quite guess at their color beyond not-dark. Vaguely green?

The man was probably in his forties, and had the kind of fitness that comes from a lifetime of conditioning. There was a tattoo on his right bicep, a winged dagger, that the pull of the satin sheets half concealed. There were scars on his knuckles, layers deep, and across his lower abdomen was a vicious, narrow, puckered scar that I guessed must have come from a knife wound.

There were discarded clothes around – a tux for him, a little sheath of a black dress and a pair of pumps for her. There were a pair of overnight bags, unopened and set neatly aside, probably by a porter.

I looked up. Carmichael and Murphy were watching me in silence.

I shrugged at them.

'Well?' Murphy demanded. 'Are we dealing with magic here, or aren't we?'

'Either that or it was really incredible sex,' I told her.

Carmichael snorted.

I laughed a little, too – and that was all the screaming part of my brain needed to slam open the doors I'd shut on it. My stomach revolted and heaved, and I lurched out of the room. Carmichael, true to his word, had set a stainless-steel bucket outside the room, and I fell to my knees throwing up.

It only took me a few seconds to control myself again – but I didn't want to go back in that room. I didn't need to see what was there anymore. I didn't want to see the two dead people, whose hearts had literally exploded out of their chests.

And someone had used magic to do it. They had used magic to wreak harm on another, violating the First Law. The White Council was going to go into collective apoplexy. This hadn't been the act of a malign spirit or a malicious entity, or the attack of one of the many creatures of the Nevernever, like vampires or trolls. This had been the premeditated, deliberate act of a sorcerer, a wizard, a human being able to tap into the fundamental energies of creation and life itself.

It was worse than murder. It was twisted, wretched perversion, as though someone had bludgeoned another person to death with a Botticelli, turned something of beauty to an act of utter destruction.

If you've never touched it, it's hard to explain. Magic is created by life, and most of all by the awareness, intelligence, emotions of a human being. To end such a life with the same magic that was born from it was hideous, almost incestuous somehow.

I sat up again and was breathing hard, shaking and tasting the bile in my mouth, when Murphy came back out of the room with Carmichael.

'All right, Harry,' Murphy said. 'Let's have it. What do you see happening here?'

I took a moment to collect my thoughts before answering. 'They came in. They had some champagne. They danced for a while, made out, over there by the stereo. Then went into the bedroom. They were in there for less than an hour. It hit them when they were getting to the high point.'

'Less than an hour,' Carmichael said. 'How do you figure?'

'CD was only an hour and ten long. Figure a few minutes

for dancing and drinking, and then they're in the room.
Was the CD playing when they found them?'

'No,' Murphy said.

'Then it hadn't been set on a loop. I figure they wanted
music, just to make things perfect, given the room and all.'

Carmichael grunted, sourly. 'Nothing we hadn't already
figured out for ourselves,' he said to Murphy. 'He'd better
come up with more than this.'

Murphy shot Carmichael a look that said 'Shut up,' then
said, softly, 'I need more, Harry.'

I ran one of my hands back over my hair. 'There's only
two ways anyone could have managed this. The first is by
evocation. Evocation is the most direct, spectacular, and
noisy form of expressed magic, or sorcery. Explosions, fire,
that sort of thing. But I doubt it was an evocator who did
this.'

'Why?' Murphy demanded. I heard her pencil scritching
on the notepad she always kept with her.

'Because you have to be able to see or touch where you
want your effect to go,' I told her. 'Line of sight only. The
man or woman would have had to be there in the room
with them. Tough to hide forensic evidence with something like that, and anyone who was skilled enough to pull
off a spell like that would have had the sense to use a gun
instead. It's easier.'

'What's the other option?' Murphy asked.

'Thaumaturgy,' I said. 'As above, so below. Make something happen on a small scale, and give it the energy to
happen on a large scale.'

Carmichael snorted. 'What bullshit.'

Murphy's voice sounded skeptical. 'How would that
work, Harry? Could it be done from somewhere else?'

I nodded. 'The killer would need to have something to connect him or her to the victims. Hair, fingernails, blood samples. That sort of thing.'

'Like a voodoo doll?'

'Exactly the same thing, yes.'

'There's fresh dye in the woman's hair,' Murphy said.

I nodded. 'Maybe if you can find out where she got her hair styled, you could find something out. I don't know.'

'Is there anything else you could tell me that would be of use?'

'Yes. The killer knew the victims. And I'm thinking it was a woman.'

Carmichael snorted. 'I don't believe we got to sit here and listen to this. Nine times out of ten the killer knows the victim.'

'Shut up, Carmichael,' Murphy said. 'What makes you say that, Harry?'

I stood up, and rubbed at my face with my hands. 'The way magic works. Whenever you do something with it, it comes from inside of you. Wizards have to focus on what they're trying to do, visualize it, believe in it, to make it work. You can't make something happen that isn't a part of you, inside. The killer could have murdered them both and made it look like an accident, but she did it this way. To get it done this way, she would have had to want them dead for very personal reasons, to be willing to reach inside them like that. Revenge, maybe. Maybe you're looking for a lover or a spouse.

'Also because of when they died – in the middle of sex. It wasn't a coincidence. Emotions are a kind of channel for magic, a path that can be used to get to you. She picked a time when they'd be together and be charged up with lust. She got samples to use as a focus, and she planned it out in advance. You don't do that to strangers.'

'Crap,' Carmichael said, but this time it was more of an absentminded curse than anything directed at me.

Murphy glared at me. 'You keep saying "she",' she challenged me. 'Why the hell do you think that?'

I gestured toward the room. 'Because you can't do something that bad without a whole lot of hate,' I said. 'Women are better at hating than men. They can focus it better, let it go better. Hell, witches are just plain *meaner* than wizards. This feels like feminine vengeance of some kind to me.'

'But a man could have done it,' Murphy said.

'Well,' I hedged.

'Christ, you are a chauvinist pig, Dresden. Is it something that *only* a woman could have done?'

'Well. No. I don't think so.'

'You don't *think* so?' Carmichael drawled. 'Some expert.'

I scowled at them both, angry. 'I haven't really worked through the specifics of what I'd need to do to make somebody's heart explode, Murph. As soon as I have occasion to I'll be sure to let you know.'

'When will you be able to tell me something?' Murphy asked.

'I don't know.' I held up a hand, forestalling her next comment. 'I can't put a timer on this stuff, Murph. It just can't be done. I don't even know if I can do it at all, much less how long it will take.'

'At fifty bucks an hour, it better not be too long,' Carmichael growled. Murphy glanced at him. She didn't exactly agree with him, but she didn't exactly slap him down, either.

I took the opportunity to take a few long breaths, calming

myself down. I finally looked back at them. 'Okay,' I asked.
'Who are they? The victims.'

'You don't need to know that,' Carmichael snapped.

'Ron,' Murphy said. 'I could really use some coffee.'

Carmichael turned to her. He wasn't tall, but he all but
loomed over Murphy. 'Aw, come on, Murph. This guy's
jerking your chain. You don't really think he's going to be
able to tell you anything worth hearing, do you?'

Murphy regarded her partner's sweaty, beady-eyed face
with a sort of frosty hauteur, tough to pull off on someone six
inches taller than she. 'No cream, two sugars.'

'Dammit,' Carmichael said. He shot me a cold glance
(but didn't quite look at my eyes), then jammed his hands
into his pants pockets and stalked out of the room.

Murphy followed him to the door, her feet silent, and
shut it behind him. The sitting room immediately became
darker, closer, with the grinning ghoul of its former chintzy
intimacy dancing in the smell of the blood and the memory
of the two bodies in the next room.

'The woman's name was Jennifer Stanton. She worked
for the Velvet Room.'

I whistled. The Velvet Room was a high-priced escort
service run by a woman named Bianca. Bianca kept a flock
of beautiful, charming, and witty women, pandering them
to the richest men in the area for hundreds of dollars an
hour. Bianca sold the kind of female company that most
men only see on television and the movies. I also knew
that she was a vampiress of considerable influence in the
Nevernever. She had Power with a capital P.

I'd tried to explain the Nevernever to Murphy before.
She didn't really comprehend it, but she understood that
Bianca was a badass vampiress who sometimes squabbled

for territory. We both knew that if one of Bianca's girls was involved, the vampiress must have been involved somehow, too.

Murphy cut right to the point. 'Was this part of one of Bianca's territorial disputes?'

'No,' I said. 'Unless she's having it with a human sorcerer. A vampire, even a vamp sorcerer, couldn't have pulled off something like this outside of the Nevernever.'

'Could she be at odds with a human sorcerer?' Murphy asked me.

'Possible. But it doesn't sound like her. She isn't that stupid.' What I didn't tell Murphy was that the White Council made sure that vampires who trifled with mortal practitioners never lived to brag about it. I don't talk to regular people about the White Council. It just isn't done. 'Besides,' I said, 'if a human wanted to take a shot at Bianca by hitting her girls, he'd be better off to kill the girl and leave the customer healthy, to let him spread the tale and scare off business.'

'Mmph,' Murphy said. She wasn't convinced, but she made notes of what I had said.

'Who was the man?' I asked her.

Murphy looked up at me for a moment, and then said, evenly, 'Tommy Tomm.'

I blinked at her to let her know she hadn't revealed the mystery of the ages. 'Who?'

'Tommy Tomm,' she said. 'Johnny Marcone's bodyguard.'

Now it made sense. 'Gentleman' Johnny Marcone had been the thug to emerge on top of the pile after the Vargassi family had dissolved into internal strife. The police department saw Marcone as a mixed blessing, after years of merciless struggle and bloody exchanges with the Vargassis.

Gentleman Johnny tolerated no excesses in his organization, and he didn't like freelancers operating in his city. Muggers, bank robbers, and drug dealers who were not a part of his organization somehow always seemed to get ratted out and turned in, or else simply went missing and weren't heard from again.

Marcone was a civilizing influence on crime – and where he operated, it was more of a problem in terms of scale than ever before. An extremely shrewd businessman, he had a battery of lawyers working for him that kept him fenced in from the law behind a barricade of depositions and papers and tape recordings. The cops never said it, but sometimes it seemed like they were almost reluctant to chase him. Marcone was better than the alternative – anarchy in the underworld.

'I remember hearing he had an enforcer,' I said. 'I guess he doesn't anymore.'

Murphy shrugged. 'So it would seem.'

'So what will you do next?'

'Run down this hairstylist angle, I guess. I'll talk to Bianca and to Marcone, but I can already tell you what they'll tell me.' She flicked her notebook closed and shook her head, irritated.

I watched her for a minute. She looked tired. I told her so.

'I am tired,' she replied. 'Tired of being looked at like I'm some sort of nutcase. Even Carmichael, my own partner, thinks I've gone over the edge in all of this.'

'The rest of the station think so too?' I asked her.

'Most of them just scowl and spin their index fingers around their temples when they think I'm not looking, and file my reports without ever reading them. The rest are the ones who have run into something spooky out there, and they're scared shitless. They don't want to believe in anything they didn't see on *Mister Science* when they were kids.'

'How about you?'

'Me?' Murphy smiled, a curving of her lips that was a vibrantly feminine expression, making her look entirely too pretty to be such a hardass. 'The world's falling apart at the seams, Harry. I guess I just think people are pretty arrogant to believe we've learned everything there is to know in the past century or so. What the hell. I can buy that we're just now starting to see the things around us in the dark again. It appeals to the cynic in me.'

'I wish everyone thought like you do,' I said. 'It would cut down on my crank calls.'

She continued to smile at me, impish. 'But could you imagine a world where all the radio stations played ABBA?'

We shared a laugh. God, that room needed a laugh.

'Hey, Harry,' Murphy said, grinning. I could see the wheels spinning in her head.

'Yeah?'

'What you said about being able to figure out how the killer did this. About how you're not sure you can do it.'

'Yeah?'

'I know it's bullshit. Why did you lie to me about it?'

I stiffened. Christ, she was good. Or maybe I'm just not much of a liar. 'Look, Murph,' I said. 'There's some things you just don't do.'

'Sometimes I don't want to get into the head of the slime I go after, either. But you do what needs to be done to finish the job. I know what you mean, Harry.'

'No,' I said, shortly. 'You don't know.' And she didn't.

She didn't know about my past, or the White Council, or the Doom of Damocles hanging over my head. Most days, I could pretend I didn't know about it, either.

All the Council needed now was an excuse, just an excuse, to find me guilty of violating one of the Seven Laws of Magic, and the Doom would drop. If I started putting together a recipe for a murder spell, and they found out about it, that might be all the excuse they needed.

'Murph,' I told her, 'I *can't* try figuring this spell out. I *can't* go putting together the things I'd need to do it. You just don't understand.'

She glared at me, without looking at my eyes. I hadn't ever met anyone else who could pull that one off. 'Oh, I understand. I understand that I've got a killer loose that I can't catch in the act. I understand that you know something that can help, or you can at least find out something. And I understand that if you dry up on me now, I'm tearing your card out of the department Rolodex and tossing it in the trash.'

Son of a bitch. My consulting for the department paid a lot of my bills. Okay, most of my bills. I could sympathize with her, I supposed. If I was operating in the dark like she was, I'd be nervous as hell, too. Murphy didn't know anything about spells or rituals or talismans, but she knew human hatred and violence all too well.

It wasn't as though I was actually going to be doing any black magic, I told myself. I was just going to be figuring out how it was done. There was a difference. I was helping the police in an investigation, nothing more. Maybe the White Council would understand that.

Yeah, right. And maybe one of these days I'd go to an art museum and become well rounded.

Murphy set the hook a second later. She looked up at my eyes for a daring second before she turned away, her face tired and honest and proud. 'I need to know everything you can tell me, Harry. Please.'

Classic lady in distress. For one of those liberated, professional women, she knew exactly how to jerk my old-fashioned chains around.

I gritted my teeth. 'Fine,' I said. 'Fine. I'll start on it tonight.' Hoo boy. The White Council was going to love this one. I'd just have to make sure they didn't find out about it.

Murphy nodded and let out a breath without looking at me. Then she said, 'Let's get out of here,' and walked toward the door. I didn't try to beat her to it.

When we walked out, the uniform cops were still lazing around in the hall outside. Carmichael was nowhere to be seen. The guys from forensics were there, standing around impatiently, waiting for us to come out. Then they gathered up their plastic bags and tweezers and lights and things and filed past us into the room.

Murphy was brushing at her windblown hair with her hand while we waited for the ancient elevator to take its sweet time getting up to the seventh floor. She was wearing a gold watch, which reminded me. 'Oh, hey,' I asked her. 'What time is it?'

She checked. 'Two twenty-five. Why?'

I breathed out a curse, and turned for the stairs. 'I'm late for my appointment.'

I fairly flew down the stairs. I've had a lot of practice at them, after all, and I hit the lobby at a jog. I managed to dodge a porter coming through the front doors with an armload of luggage, and swung out onto the sidewalk at a lope. I have long legs that eat a lot of ground. I was running into the wind, my black duster billowing out behind me.

It was several blocks to my building, and after covering half of them I slowed to a walk. I didn't want to arrive at my appointment with Monica Missing-Man puffing like a bellows, with my hair windblown and my face streaming with sweat.

Blame it on being out of shape from an inactive winter season, but I was breathing hard. It occupied enough of my attention that I didn't see the dark blue Cadillac until it had pulled up beside me, and a rather large man had stepped out of it onto the sidewalk in front of me. He had bright red hair and a thick neck. His face looked like someone had smashed it flat with a board, repeatedly, when he was a baby – except for his jutting eyebrows. He had narrow little blue eyes that got narrower as I sized him up.

I stopped, and backed away, then turned around. Two more men, both of them as tall as me and a good deal heavier, were slowing down from their own jog. They had apparently been following me, and they looked annoyed. One was limping slightly, and the other wore a buzz cut that had been spiked up straight with some kind of styling gel. I felt like I was in high school again, surrounded by bullying members of the football team.

'Can I help you gentlemen?' I asked. I looked around for a cop, but they were all over at the Madison, I supposed. Everyone likes to gawk.

'Get in the car,' the one in front of me said. One of the others opened the rear door.

'I like to walk. It's good for my heart.'

'You don't get in the car, it isn't going to be good for your legs,' the man growled.

A voice came from inside the car. 'Mister Hendricks, please. Be more polite. Mister Dresden, would you join me for a moment? I'd hoped to give you a lift back to your office, but your abrupt exit made it somewhat problematic. Perhaps you will allow me to convey you the rest of the way.'

I leaned down to look into the backseat. A man of handsome and unassuming features, dressed in a casual sports jacket and Levi's, regarded me with a smile. 'And you would be?' I asked him.

His smile widened, and I swear it made his eyes twinkle.

'My name is John Marcone. I would like to discuss business with you.'

I stared at him for a moment. And then my eyes slid aside to the very large and very overdeveloped Mister Hendricks. The man growled under his breath, and it sounded like Cujo just before he jumped at the woman in the car. I didn't feel like duking it out with Cujo and his two buddies.

So I got into the back of the Caddy with Gentleman Johnny Marcone.

It was turning out to be a very busy day. And I was still late for my appointment.

3

Gentleman Johnny Marcone didn't look like the sort of man who would have my legs broken or my jaw wired shut. His salt-and-pepper hair was cut short, and there were lines from sun and smiling etched into the corners of his eyes. His eyes were the green of well-worn dollar bills. He seemed more like a college football coach: good-looking, tanned, athletic, and enthusiastic. The impression was reinforced by the men he kept with him. Cujo Hendricks hulked like an all-pro player who had been ousted for extreme unnecessary roughness.

Cujo got in the car again, glowered at me in the rearview mirror, then pulled out into the street, driving slowly toward my office. The steering wheel looked tiny and delicate in his huge hands. I made a mental note: Do not let Cujo put his hands around your throat. Or hand. It looked almost like one of them could manage it.

The radio was playing, but as I got in the car it fouled up, squealing feedback out over the speakers. Hendricks scowled and thought about it for a second. Maybe he had to relay the message through his second brain or something. Then he reached out and fiddled with the knobs before finally turning the radio off. At this rate I hoped the car would make it all the way to my office.

'Mister Dresden,' Marcone said, smiling, 'I understand that you work for the police department, from time to time.'

'They throw the occasional tidbit my way,' I agreed.

'Hey, Hendricks. You should really wear your seat belt. Statistics say you're fifty or sixty percent safer.'

Cujo growled at me in the rearview mirror again, and I beamed at him. Smiling always seems to annoy people more than actually insulting them. Or maybe I just have an annoying smile.

Marcone seemed somewhat put off by my attitude. Maybe I was supposed to be holding my hat in my hand, but I had never really liked Francis Ford Coppola, and I didn't have a Godfather. (I *do* have a Godmother, and she is, inevitably perhaps, a faery. But that's another story.) 'Mister Dresden,' he said. 'How much would it cost to retain your services?'

That made me wary. What would someone like Marcone want me for? 'My standard fee is fifty dollars an hour plus travel expenses,' I told him. 'But it can vary, depending on what you need done.'

Marcone nodded along with my sentences, as if encouraging me to speak. He wrinkled up his face as if carefully considering what he would say, and taking my well-being into account with grandfatherly concern. 'How much would it set me back to have you not investigate something?'

'You want to pay me to not do something?'

'Let's say I pay you your standard fee. That comes out to fourteen hundred a day, right?'

'Twelve hundred, actually,' I corrected him.

He beamed at me. 'An honest man is a rare treasure. Twelve hundred a day. Let's say I pay you for two weeks worth of work, Mister Dresden, and you take some time off. Go catch a few movies, get some extra sleep, that sort of thing.'

I eyed him. 'And for more than a thousand dollars a day, you want me to . . . ?'

'Do nothing, Mister Dresden,' Marcone smiled. 'Nothing at all. Just relax, and put your feet up. And stay out of Detective Murphy's way.'

Ah-hah. Marcone didn't want me looking into Tommy Tomm's murder. Interesting. I looked out the window and squinted my eyes, as though thinking about it.

'I've got the money with me,' Marcone said. 'Cash on the spot. I'll trust you to fulfill your end of the deal, Mister Dresden. You come highly recommended for your honesty.'

'Mmmm. I don't know, John. I'm kind of busy to be accepting any more accounts right now.' The car was almost to my office building. The car door was still unlocked. I hadn't worn my seat belt, either — just in case I needed to throw the door open and jump out. See how I think ahead? It's that wizardly intellect — and paranoia.

Marcone's smile faltered. His expression became earnest. 'Mister Dresden, I am quite eager to establish a positive working relationship, here. If it's the money, I can offer you more. Let's say double your usual fee.' He steepled his hands in front of him as he talked, half-turning toward me. My God, I kept expecting him to tell me to go out there and win one for the Gipper. He smiled. 'How does that sound?'

'It isn't the money, John,' I told him. I lazily locked my eyes onto his. 'I just don't think it's going to work out.'

To my surprise, he didn't look away.

Those who deal in magic learn to see the world in a slightly different light than everyone else. You gain a perspective you had never considered before, a way of thinking that would just never have occurred to you without exposure to the things a wizard sees and hears.

When you look into someone's eyes, you see them in

that other light. And, for just a second, they see you in the same way. Marcone and I looked at one another.

He was a soldier, a warrior, behind that relaxed smile and fatherly manner. He was going to get what he wanted and he was going to get it in the most efficient way possible. He was a dedicated man – dedicated to his goals, dedicated to his people. He never let fear affect him. He made a living on human misery and suffering, peddling in drugs and flesh and stolen goods, but he took steps to minimize that suffering because it was simply the most efficient means of running his business. He was furious over Tommy Tomm's death – a cold and practical kind of fury that his rightful dominion had been invaded and challenged. He intended to find those responsible and deal with them in his own way – and he didn't want the police interfering. He had killed before, and would again, and it would all mean nothing more to him than a business transaction, than paying for groceries in the checkout line. It was a dry and cool place, inside Gentleman Johnny Marcone. Except for one dim corner. There, hidden away from his everyday thoughts, there lurked a secret shame. I couldn't quite see what it was. But I knew that, somewhere in the past there was something that he would give anything to undo, would spill blood to erase. It was from that dark place that he drew his resolve, his strength.

That was the way I saw him when I looked inside, past all his pretenses and defenses. And I was, on some instinctual level, certain that he had been aware of what I would see if I looked – that he had deliberately met my gaze, knowing what he would give away. That was his purpose in getting me alone. He wanted to take a peek at my soul. He wanted to see what sort of man I was.

When I look into someone's eyes, into their soul, their innermost being, they can see mine in return – the things I had done, the things I was willing to do, the things I was capable of doing. Most people who did that got really pale, at least. One woman had passed out entirely. I didn't know what they saw when they looked in there – it wasn't a place I poked around much, myself.

John Marcone wasn't like the other people who had seen my soul. He didn't even blink an eye. He just looked and assessed, and after the moment had passed, he nodded at me as though he understood something. I got the uncomfortable impression that he had duped me. That he had found out more about me than I had about him. The first thing I felt was anger, anger at being manipulated, anger that he should presume to soulgaze upon me.

Just a second later, I felt scared to death of this man. I had looked on his soul and it had been as solid and barren as a stainless-steel refrigerator. It was more than unsettling. He was strong, inside, savage and merciless without being cruel. He had a tiger's soul.

'All right, then,' he said, smoothly, and as though nothing had happened. 'I won't try to force my offer on you, Mister Dresden.' The car was slowing down as it approached my building, and Hendricks pulled over in front of it. 'But let me offer you some advice?' He had dropped the father-talking-to-son act, and spoke in a calm and patient voice.

'If you don't charge for it.' Thank God for wise-cracks. I was too rattled to have said anything intelligent.

Marcone almost smiled. 'I think you'll be happier if you come down with the flu for a few days. This business that Detective Murphy has asked you to look into doesn't need to be dragged out into the light. You won't like what you see. It's on my side of the fence. Just let me deal with it, and it won't ever trouble you.'

'Are you threatening me?' I asked him. I didn't think he was, but I didn't want him to know that. It would have helped if my voice hadn't been shaking.

'No,' he said, frankly. 'I have too much respect for you to resort to something like that. They say that you're the real thing, Mister Dresden. A real magus.'

'They also say I'm nutty as a fruitcake.'

'I choose which "they" I listen to very carefully,' Marcone said. 'Think about what I've said, Mister Dresden? I do not think our respective lines of work need overlap often. I would as soon not make an enemy of you over this matter.'

I clenched my jaw over my fear, and spat words out at him quick and hard. 'You don't want to make an enemy of me, Marcone. That wouldn't be smart. That wouldn't be smart at all.'

He narrowed his eyes at me, lazy and relaxed. He could meet my eyes by then without fear. We had taken a measure of one another. It would not happen in such a way again. 'You really should try to be more polite, Mister Dresden,' he said. 'It's good for business.'

I didn't give him an answer to that: I didn't have one that wouldn't sound frightened or stupidly macho. Instead, I told him, 'If you ever lose your car keys, give me a call. Don't try offering me money or threats again. Thanks for the ride.'

He watched me, his expression never changing, as I got out of the car and shut the door. Hendricks pulled out and drove away, after giving me one last dirty look. I had soul-gazed on several people before. It wasn't the sort of thing you forgot. I had never run into someone like that, someone so cool and controlled – even the other practitioners I had met gazes with had not been that way. None of them had simply assessed me like a column of numbers and filed it away for reference in future equations.

I stuck my hands in the pockets of my duster and shivered as the wind hit me. I was a wizard, throwing around real magic, I reminded myself. I was not afraid of big men in big cars. I do not get rattled by corpses blasted from life by magic more intense than anything I could manage. Really. Honest.

But those dollar-bill-colored eyes, backed by that cool and nearly passionless soul, had me shaking as I took the stairs back up to my office. I had been stupid. He had surprised me, and the sudden intimacy of the soulgaze had startled and frightened me. All added together, it had caused me to fall apart, throwing threats at him like a frightened schoolkid. Marcone was a predator. He practically smelled my fear. If he got to thinking I was weak, I had a feeling that polite smile and fatherly facade would vanish as thoroughly and as quickly as it had appeared.

What a rotten first impression.

Oh, well. At least I was going to be on time for my appointment.

4

Monica No-Last-Name was standing outside of my office when I got there, writing on the back of the note I had left taped to my office door.

I walked toward her, and she was too intent upon her writing to look up. She was a good-looking woman, in her mid-thirtysomethings. Ash-blonde hair that I thought must be natural, after a morbid and involuntary memory of the dead woman's dye job. Her makeup was tasteful and well applied, and her face was fair, friendly, with enough round-ness of cheek to look fresh-faced and young, enough fullness of mouth to look very feminine. She was wearing a long, full skirt of palest yellow with brown riding boots, a crisp white blouse, and an expensive-looking green cardigan over it, to ward off the chill of early spring. She had to be in good shape to pull off a color combination like that, and she did it. Overall, it was a naggingly familiar look, something like Annette Funicello or Barbara Billingsley, maybe – wholesome and all-American.

'Monica?' I asked. I put on my most innocent and friendly smile.

She blinked at me as I approached. 'Oh. Are you, um, Harry . . .'

I smiled and offered her my hand. 'Harry Dresden, ma'am. That's me.'

She took my hand after a tiny pause and kept her eyes firmly focused on my chest. At this point, I was just as glad to be dealing with someone who was too nervous to risk looking at my eyes. I gave her a firm, but gentle handshake, and let go of her, brushing past her to unlock the office door and open it up. 'I apologize for being late. I got a call from the police that I had to look in on.'

'You did?' she asked. 'You mean, the police, um . . .' She waved her fingers instead of finishing the sentence and entered when I held the door open for her.

'Sometimes,' I nodded. 'They run into something and want my take on it.'

'What sorts of things?'

I shrugged and swallowed. I thought of the corpses at the Madison, and felt green. When I looked up at Monica, she was studying my face, chewing on her lip nervously. She hurriedly averted her gaze.

'Can I get you some coffee?' I asked her. I shut the door behind us, flicked on the lights.

'Oh. No, thank you. I'm fine.' She stood there, looking at my box of discarded paperbacks and holding her purse over her tummy with both hands. I thought she might scream if I said *boo* so I made sure to move carefully and slowly, making myself a cup of instant coffee. I breathed in and out, going through the familiar motions, until I had calmed down from my encounter with Marcone. By the time I was done, so was my coffee. I went to my desk, and invited her to have a seat in one of the two chairs across from me.

'Okay, Monica,' I said. 'What can I do for you today?'

'Well, um. I told you that my husband was . . . was . . .' She nodded at me, gesturing.

'Missing?' I supplied.

'Yes,' she said with an exhalation of almost relief. 'But

he's not mysteriously missing or anything. Just gone.' She flushed and stammered. 'Like he just packed up a few things and left. But he didn't say anything to anyone. And he hasn't showed up again. I'm concerned about him.'

'Uh-huh,' I said. 'How long has he been gone?'

'This is the third day,' she said.

I nodded. 'There must be some reason why you're coming to me, rather than a private investigator or the police.'

She blushed again. She had a good face for blushing, fair skin that colored girlishly. It was quite fetching, really. 'Yes, um. He had been interested in . . . in . . .'

'Magic?'

'Yes. He had been buying books on it in the religion section at the bookstore. Not like those Dungeons and Dragons games. The real thing. He bought some of those tarot cards.' She pronounced it like *carrot*. Amateurs.

'And you think his disappearance might have had something to do with this interest?'

'I'm not sure,' she confessed. 'But maybe. He was very upset. He had just lost his job and was under a lot of pressure. I'm worried about him. I thought whoever found him might need to be able to talk to him about all of this stuff.' She took a deep breath, as if the effort of completing so many sentences without a single *um* had tired her.

'I'm still not clear on this. Why me? Why not the police?'

Her knuckles whitened on her purse. 'He packed a bag, Mr Dresden. I think the police will just assume he left his wife and his children. They won't really look. But he didn't. He's not like that. He only wants to make a good life for us, really, that's all he wants.'

I frowned at her. Nervous that maybe hubby has run out on you after all, dear? 'Even so,' I said, 'why come to me? Why not a private investigator? I know a reliable man if you need one.'

'Because you know about . . .' She gestured, fitfully.

'About magic,' I said.

Monica nodded. 'I think it might be important. I mean, I don't know. But I think it might.'

'Where did he work?' I asked her. While I spoke, I got a pad of paper out of my pocket and jotted down a few notes.

'SilverCo,' she told me. 'They're a trading company. They locate good markets for products and then advise companies where they can best spend their money.'

'Uh-huh,' I said. 'What is his name, Monica?'

She swallowed, and I saw her twitching, trying to think of something to tell me other than his real name. 'George,' she supplied at last.

I looked up at her. She was staring furiously down at her hands.

'Monica,' I said. 'I know this must be really hard for you. Believe me, ma'am, there are plenty of people who are nervous when they come into my office. But please, hear me out. I am not out to hurt you or anyone else. What I do, I do to help people. It's true that someone with the right skills could use your names against you, but I'm not like that.' I borrowed a line from Johnny Marcone. 'It isn't good business.'

She gave a nervous little laugh. 'I feel so silly,' she confessed. 'But there's so many things that I've heard about . . .'

'Wizards. I see.' I put my pencil down and steepled my fingers in wizardly fashion. The woman was nervous and had certain expectations. I might ease her fears a little if I fulfilled some of them. I tried not to look over her shoulder at the calendar I had hanging on the wall, and the red circle around the fifteenth of last month. Late rent. Need money. Even with the fee from today and what I would make in the future, it would take the city forever to pay up.

Besides. I could never resist going to the aid of a lady in distress. Even if she wasn't completely, one hundred percent sure that she wanted to be rescued by me.

'Monica,' I told her. 'There are powers in the universe that most people don't even know about. Powers that we still don't fully understand. The men and women who work with these powers see things in a different light than regular people. They come to understand things in a slightly different way. This sets them apart. Sometimes it breeds unwarranted suspicion and fear. I know you've read books and seen movies about how horrible people like me are, and that whole "suffer not a witch to live" part of the Old Testament hasn't made things all roses. But we really aren't any different from anyone else.' I gave her my best smile. 'I want to help you. But if I'm going to do that, you're going to have to give me a little trust. I promise. I give you my word that I won't disappoint you.'

I saw her take this in and chew on it for a while, while staring down at her hands.

'Victor,' she said at last. 'Victor Sells.'

'All right,' I said, picking up my pencil and duly noting it. 'Is there anyplace he might have gone that you can think of, offhand?'

She nodded. 'The lake house. We have a house down by . . .' She waved her hand.

'The lake?'

She beamed at me, and I reminded myself to be patient. 'In Lake Providence, over the state line, around Lake Michigan. It's beautiful up there in the autumn.'

'Okay, then. Are you aware of any friends he might have run off to see, family he might have visited, anything like that?'

'Oh, Victor wasn't on speaking terms with his family. I never knew why. He didn't talk about them, really. We've been married for ten years, and he never once spoke to them.'

'Okay,' I said, noting that down, too. 'Friends, then?'

She fretted her lip, a gesture that seemed familiar to her. 'Not really. He was friends with his boss, and some people at work, but after he was fired . . .'

'Uh-huh,' I said. 'I understand.' I continued writing things down, drawing bold lines between thoughts to separate them. I spilled over onto the next page before I was finished writing down the facts and my observations about Monica. I like to be thorough about this kind of thing.

'Well, Mr Dresden?' she asked. 'Can you help me?'

I looked over the page and nodded. 'I think so, Monica. If possible, I'd like to see these things your husband collected. Which books and so on. It would help if I had a picture of him, too. I might like to take a look around your house at Lake Providence. Would that be all right?'

'Of course,' she said. She seemed relieved, but at the same time even more nervous than before. I noted down the address of the lake house and brief directions.

'You're aware of my fees?' I asked her. 'I'm not cheap. It might be less costly for you to hire someone else.'

'We've got quite a bit of savings, Mr Dresden,' she told me. 'I'm not worried about the money.' That seemed an odd statement from her, at the time – out of tune with her generally nervous manner.

'Well, then,' I told her. 'I charge fifty dollars an hour, plus expenses. I'll send you an itemized list of what I do, so you'll have a good idea what I'm working on. A retainer is customary. I'm not going to guarantee that I work exclusively on your case. I try to handle each of my customers with respect and courtesy, so I can't put any one of them before another.'

She nodded to me, emphatically, and reached into her purse. She drew out a white envelope and passed it over to me. 'There's five hundred inside,' she told me. 'Is that enough for now?'

Cha-ching. Five hundred dollars would take care of last month's rent and a good bit of this month's, too. I could get into this bit with nervous clients wanting to preserve the anonymity of their checking accounts from my supposed sorcerous might. Cash always spends.

'That will be fine, yes,' I told her. I tried not to fondle the envelope. At least I wasn't crass enough to dump the money on my desk and count it out.

She drew out another envelope. 'He took most of his things with him,' she said. 'At least, I couldn't find them where he usually keeps them. But I did find this.' There was something in the envelope, making it bulge, an amulet, ring, or charm of some kind, I was betting. A third envelope came out of her purse — the woman must be compulsively well organized. 'There's a picture of him in here, and my phone number inside. Thank you, Mr Dresden. When will you call?'

'As soon as I know something,' I told her. 'Probably by tomorrow afternoon or Saturday morning. Sound good?'

She almost looked at my eyes, caught herself, and smiled directly at my nose instead. 'Yes. Yes, thank you so much for your help.' She glanced up at the wall. 'Oh, look at the time. I need to go. School's almost out.' She closed her teeth over her words and flushed again, as though embarrassed that she had let such an important fact about her slip out.

'I'll do whatever I can, ma'am,' I assured her, rising, and walking her to the door. 'Thank you for your business. I'll be in touch soon.'

She said her good-byes, never looking me in the face, and fled out the door. I shut it behind her and went back to the envelopes.

First, the money. It was all in fifties, which always look new even when they're years old because they get so little circulation. There were ten of them. I put them in my wallet, and trashed the envelope.

The envelope with the photo in it was next. I took it out and regarded a picture of Monica and a man of lean and handsome features, with a wide forehead and shaggy eyebrows that skewed his handsomeness off onto a rather eccentric angle. His smile was whiter-than-white, and his skin had the smooth, dark tan of someone who spends a lot of time in the sun, boating maybe. It was a sharp contrast against Monica's paleness. Victor Sells, I presume.

The phone number was written on a plain white index card that had been neatly trimmed down to fit inside the envelope. There was no name or area code, just a seven-digit number. I got out my cross-listing directory and looked it up.

I noted that down as well. I wondered what the woman had expected to accomplish by only giving out first names, when she had been going to hand me a dozen other ways of finding out in any case. It only goes to show that people are funny when they're nervous about something. They say screwy things, make odd choices which, in retrospect, they feel amazingly foolish for making. I would have to be careful not to say anything to rub that in when I spoke to her again.

I trashed the second envelope and opened the last one, turning it upside down over my desk.

The brown husk of a dead, dried scorpion, glistening with some sort of preservative glaze, clicked down onto my desk. A supple, braided leather cord led off from a ring set through the base of its tail, so that if it was worn, it would hang head down, tail up and curled over the dried body to point at the ground.

I shuddered. Scorpions were symbolically powerful in certain circles of belief. They weren't usually symbols of anything good or wholesome, either. A lot of petty, mean spells could be focused around a little talisman like that. If you wore it next to your skin, as such things are supposed to be worn, the prickly legs of the thing would be a constant poking and agitation at your chest, a continual reminder that it was there. The dried stinger at the tail's tip might actually pierce the skin of anyone who tried to give the wearer a hug. Its crablike pincers would catch in a man's chest hair, or scratch at the curves of a woman's breasts. Nasty, unpleasant thing. Not evil, as such – but you sure as hell weren't likely to do happy shiny things with magic with such an item around your neck.

Maybe Victor Sells had gotten involved in something real, something that had absorbed his attention. The Art could do that to a person – particularly the darker aspects of it. If he had turned to it in despair after losing his job, maybe that would explain his sudden absence from his home. A lot of sorcerers or wanna-be sorcerers secluded themselves in the belief that isolation would increase their ability to focus on their magic. It didn't – but it did make it easier for a weak or untrained mind to avoid distractions.

Or maybe it wasn't even a true talisman. Maybe it was just a curiosity, or a souvenir from some visit to the Southwest. There wasn't any way for me to tell if it was indeed a device used to improve the focus and direction of magical energies, short of actually using it to attempt a spell – and I really didn't want to be using such a dubious article, for a variety of good reasons.

I would have to keep this little un-beauty in mind as I tried to run this man down. It might well mean nothing. On the other hand, it might not. I looked up at the clock. A quarter after three. There was time to check with the local morgues to see if they had turned up any likely John Does – who knew, my search might be over before the day's end – and then to get to the bank to deposit my money and fire off a check to my landlord.

I got out my phone book and started calling up hospitals – not really my routine line of work, but not difficult, either, except for the standard problems I had using the telephone: static, line noise, other people's conversations being louder than mine. If something can go wrong, it will.

Once I thought I saw something out of the corner of my eye, a twitch of motion from the dried scorpion that sat on my desk. I blinked and stared at it. It didn't move. Cautiously, I extended my senses toward it like an invisible hand, feeling about for any traces of enchantment or magical energy.

Nothing. It was as dry of enchantment as it was of life.

Never let it be said that Harry Dresden is afraid of a dried, dead bug. Creepy or not, I wasn't going to let it ruin my concentration.

So I scooped it up with the corner of the phone book and popped it into the middle drawer of my desk. Out of sight, out of mind.

So I have a problem with creepy, dead, poisonous things. So sue me.

5

McAnally's is a pub a few blocks from my office. I go there when I'm feeling stressed, or when I have a few extra bucks to spend on a nice dinner. A lot of us fringe types do. Mac, the pub's owner, is used to wizards and all the problems that come along with us. There aren't any video games at McAnally's. There are no televisions or expensive computer trivia games. There isn't even a jukebox. Mac keeps a player piano instead. It's less likely to go haywire around us.

I say *pub* in all the best senses of the word. When you walk in, you take several steps down into a room with a deadly combination of a low clearance and ceiling fans. If you're tall, like me, you walk carefully in McAnally's. There are thirteen stools at the bar and thirteen tables in the room. Thirteen windows, set up high in the wall in order to be above ground level, let some light from the street into the place. Thirteen mirrors on the walls cast back reflections of the patrons in dim detail, and give the illusion of more space. Thirteen wooden columns, carved with likenesses from folktales and legends of the Old World, make it difficult to walk around the place without weaving a circuitous route – they also quite intentionally break up the flow of random energies, dispelling to one degree or another the auras that gather around broody, grumpy wizards and keeping them from manifesting in unintentional and colorful ways. The colors are all muted, earth browns and sea greens. The first time I entered McAnally's,

I felt like a wolf returning to an old, favorite den. Mac makes his own beer, ale really, and it's the best stuff in the city. His food is cooked on a wood-burning stove. And you can damn well walk your own self over to the bar to pick up your order when it's ready, according to Mac. It's my sort of place.

Since the calls to the morgues had turned up nothing, I kept a few bills out of Monica Sells's retainer and took myself to McAnally's. After the kind of day I'd had, I deserved some of Mac's ale and someone else's cooking. It was going to be a long night, too, once I went home and started trying to figure out how whoever it was had pulled off the death spell used on Johnny Marcone's hatchet man, Tommy Tomm, and his girlfriend, Jennifer Stanton.

'Dresden,' Mac greeted me, when I sat down at the bar. The dim, comfortable room was empty, but for a pair of men I recognized by sight at a back table, playing chess. Mac is a tall, almost gangly man of indeterminate age, though there's a sense to him that speaks of enough wisdom and strength that I wouldn't venture that he was less than fifty. He has squinty eyes and a smile that is rare and mischievous when it manifests. Mac never says much, but when he does it's almost always worth listening to.

'Hey there, Mac,' I hailed him. 'Been one hell of a day. Give me a steak sandwich, fries, ale.'

'Ungh,' Mac said. He opened a bottle of his ale and began to pour it warm, staring past me, into the middle distance. He does that with everyone. Considering his clientele, I don't blame him. I wouldn't chance looking them in the face, either.

'You hear about what happened at the Madison?'

'Ungh,' he confirmed.

'Nasty business.'

Such an inane comment apparently didn't merit even a grunted reply. Mac set my drink out and turned to the stove behind the bar, checking the wood and raking it back and forth to provide even heating for it.

I picked up a prethumbed newspaper nearby and scanned the headlines. 'Hey, look at this. Another ThreeEye rampage. Jesus, this stuff is worse than crack.' The article detailed the virtual demolition of a neighborhood grocery store by a pair of ThreeEye junkies who were convinced that the place was destined to explode and wanted to beat destiny to the punch.

'Ungh.'

'You ever seen anything like this?'

Mac shook his head.

'They say the stuff gives you the third sight,' I said, reading the article. Both junkies had been admitted to the hospital and were in critical condition, after collapsing at the scene. 'But you know what?'

Mac looked back at me from the stove, while he cooked.

'I don't think that's possible. What a bunch of crap. Trying to sell these poor kids on the idea that they can do magic.'

Mac nodded at me.

'If it was serious stuff, the department would have already called me by now.'

Mac shrugged, turning back to the stove. Then he squinted up and peered into the dim reflection of the mirror behind the bar.

'Harry,' he said, 'you were followed.'

I had been too tense for too much of the day to avoid feeling my shoulders constrict in a sudden twinge. I put both hands around my mug and brought a few phrases of quasi-Latin to mind. It never hurt to be ready to defend myself, in case someone was intending to hurt me. I watched someone approach, a dim shape in the reflection cast by the ancient, worn mirror. Mac went on with cooking, unperturbed. Nothing much perturbed Mac.

I smelled her perfume before I turned around. 'Why, Miss Rodriguez,' I said. 'It's always pleasant to see you.'

She came to an abrupt stop a couple of paces from me, apparently disconcerted. One of the advantages of being a wizard is that people always attribute anything you do to magic, if no other immediate explanation leaps to mind. She probably wouldn't think about her perfume giving her identity away when she could assign my mysterious, blind identification of her to my mystical powers.

'Come on,' I told her. 'Sit down. I'll get you a drink while I refuse to tell you anything.'

'Harry,' she admonished me, 'you don't know I'm here on business.' She sat down on the barstool next to me. She was a woman of average height and striking, dark beauty, wearing a crisp business jacket and skirt, hose, pumps. Her dark, straight hair was trimmed in a neat cut that ended at the nape of her neck and was parted off of the dark skin of her forehead, emphasizing the lazy appeal of her dark eyes.

'Susan,' I chided her, 'you wouldn't be in this place if you weren't. Did you have a good time in Branson?'

Susan Rodriguez was a reporter for the Chicago *Arcane*, a yellow magazine that covered all sorts of supernatural and paranormal events throughout the Midwest. Usually, the events they covered weren't much better than: 'Monkey Man Seen With Elvis's Love Child,' or 'JFK's Mutant Ghost

Abducts Shape-shifting Girl Scout.' But once in a great, great while, the *Arcane* covered something that was real. Like the Unseelie Incursion of 1994, when the entire city of Milwaukee had simply vanished for two hours. Gone. Government satellite photos showed the river valley covered with trees and empty of life or human habitation. All communications ceased. Then, a few hours later, there it was, back again, and no one in the city itself the wiser.

She had also been hanging around my investigation in Branson the previous week. She had been tracking me ever since interviewing me for a feature story, right after I'd opened up my business. I had to hand it to her – she had instincts. And enough curiosity to get her into ten kinds of trouble. She had tricked me into meeting her eyes at the conclusion of our first interview, an eager young reporter investigating an angle on her interviewee. She was the one who had fainted after we'd soulgazed.

She smirked at me. I liked her smirk. It did interesting things to her lips, and hers were already attractive. 'You should have stayed around for the show,' she said. 'It was pretty impressive.' She put her purse on the bar and slid up onto the stool beside me.

'No thanks,' I told her. 'I'm pretty sure it wasn't for me.'

'My editor loved the coverage. She's convinced it's going to win an award of some kind.'

'I can see it now,' I told her. '"Mysterious Visions Haunt Drug-Using Country Star." Real hard-hitting paranormal journalism, that.' I glanced at her, and she met my eyes without fear. She didn't let me see if my jibe had ruffled her.

'I heard you got called in by the S.I. director today,' she told me. She leaned toward me, enough that a glance down would have afforded an interesting angle to the V of her white shirt. 'I'd love to hear you tell me about this one, Harry.' She quirked a smile at me that promised things.

I almost smiled back at her. 'Sorry,' I told her. 'I have a standard nondisclosure agreement with the city.'

'Something off the record, then?' she asked. 'Rumor has it that these killings were pretty sensational.'

'Can't help you, Susan,' I told her. 'Wild horses couldn't drag it out of me, et cetera.'

'Just a hint,' she pressed. 'A word of comment. Something shared between two people who are very attracted to one another.'

'Which two people would that be?'

She put an elbow on the counter and propped her chin in her hand, studying me through narrowed eyes and thick, long lashes. One of the things that appealed to me about her was that even though she used her charm and femininity relentlessly in pursuit of her stories, she had no concept of just how attractive she really was – I had seen that when I looked within her last year. 'Harry Dresden,' she said, 'you are a thoroughly maddening man.' Her eyes narrowed a bit further. 'You didn't look down my blouse even once, did you,' she accused.

I took a sip of my ale and beckoned Mac to pour her one as well. He did. 'Guilty.'

'Most men are off balance by now,' she complained. 'What does it take with you, anyway, Dresden?'

'I am pure of heart and mind,' I told her. 'I cannot be corrupted.'

She stared at me in frustration for a moment. Then she tilted back her head to laugh. She had a good laugh, too, throaty and rich. I *did* look down at her chest when she did that, just for a second. A pure heart and mind only takes you so far – sooner or later the hormones have their say, too. I mean, I'm not a teenager or anything, anymore, but I'm not exactly an expert in things like this, either. Call it an overwhelming interest in my professional career, but I've never had much time for dating or the fair sex in general. And when I have, it hasn't turned out too well.

Susan was a known quantity – she was attractive, bright, appealing, her motivations were clear and simple, and she was honest in pursuing them. She flirted with me because she wanted information as much as because she thought I was attractive. Sometimes she got it. Sometimes she didn't. This one was way too hot for Susan or the *Arcane* to touch, and if Murphy heard I'd tipped someone off about what had happened, she'd have my heart between two pieces of bread for lunch.

'I'll tell you what, Harry,' she said. 'How about if I ask some questions, and you just answer them with a yes or a no?'

'No,' I said promptly. Dammit. I am a poor liar, and it didn't take a reporter with Susan's brains to tell it.

Her eyes glittered with cheerfully malicious ambition. 'Was Tommy Tomm murdered by a paranormal being or means?'

'No,' I said again, stubbornly.

'No, he wasn't?' Susan asked, 'Or no, it wasn't a para-normal being.'

I glanced at Mac as though to appeal for help. Mac ignored me. Mac doesn't take sides. Mac is wise.

'No, I'm not going to answer questions,' I said.

'Do the police have any leads? Any suspects?'

'No.'

'Are you a suspect yourself, Harry?'

Disturbing thought. 'No,' I said, exasperated. 'Susan—'

'Would you mind having dinner with me Saturday night?'

'No! I—' I blinked at her. 'What?'

She smiled at me, leaned over, and kissed me on the cheek. Her lips, that I'd admired so much, felt very, very nice. 'Super,' she said. 'I'll pick you up at your place. Say around nine?'

'Did I just miss something?' I asked her.

She nodded, dark eyes sparkling with humor. 'I'm going to take you to a fantastic dinner. Have you ever eaten at the Pump Room? At the Ambassador East?'

I shook my head.

'Steaks you wouldn't believe,' she assured me. 'And the most romantic atmosphere. Jackets and ties required. Can you manage?'

'Um. Yes?' I said, carefully. 'This is the answer to the question of whether or not I'll go out with you, right?'

'No,' Susan said, with a smile. 'That was the answer I tricked out of you, so you're stuck, there. I just want to make sure you own something besides jeans and button-down Western shirts.'

'Oh. Yes,' I said.

'Super,' she repeated, and kissed me on the cheek once more as she stood up and gathered her purse. 'Saturday, then.' She drew back and quirked her smirky little smile at me. It was a killer look, sultry and appealing. 'I'll be there. With bells on.'

She turned and walked out. I sort of turned to stare after her. My jaw slid off the bar as I did and landed on the floor.

Had I just agreed to a date? Or an interrogation session?

'Probably both,' I muttered.

Mac slapped my steak sandwich and fries down in front of me. I put down some money, morosely, and he made change.

'She's going to do nothing but try to trick information out of me that I shouldn't be giving her, Mac,' I said.

'Ungh,' Mac agreed.

'Why did I say yes?'

Mac shrugged.

'She's pretty,' I said. 'Smart. Sexy.'

'Ungh.'

'Any red-blooded man would have done the same thing.'

'Hngh,' Mac snorted.

'Well. Maybe not you.'

Mac smiled a bit, mollified.

'Still. It's going to make trouble for me. I must be crazy to go for someone like that.' I picked up my sandwich and sighed.

'Dumb,' Mac said.

'I just said she was smart, Mac.'

Mac's face flickered into that smile, and it made him look years younger, almost boyish. 'Not her,' he said. 'You.'

I ate my dinner. And had to admit that he was right.

This threw a wrench into my plans. My best idea for poking around the Sells lake house and getting information had to be carried out at night. And I already had tomorrow night slated for a talk with Bianca, since I had a feeling Murphy and Carmichael would fail to turn up any cooperation from the vampiress. That meant I would have to drive out to Lake Providence tonight, since Saturday night was now occupied by the date with Susan — or at least the premidnight portion was.

My mouth went dry when I considered that maybe the rest of the night might be occupied, too. One never knew. She had dizzied me and made me look like an idiot, and she was probably going to try every trick she knew to drag more information out of me for the Monday morning release of the *Arcane*. On the other hand, she was sexy, intelligent, and at least a little attracted to me. That indicated that more might happen than just talk and dinner. Didn't it?

The question was, did I really want that to happen?

I had been a miserable failure in relationships, ever since my first love went sour. I mean, a lot of teenage guys fail in their first relationships.

Not many of them murder the girl involved.

I shied away from that line of thought, lest it bring up too many old memories.

I left McAnally's, after Mac had handed me a doggy bag with a grunt of 'Mister,' by way of explanation. The chess game in the corner was still in progress, both players puffing up a sweet-smelling smog cloud from their pipes. I tried to figure out how to deal with Susan, while I walked out to my car. Did I need to clean up my apartment? Did I have all the ingredients for the spell I would cast at the lake house later tonight? Would Murphy go through the roof when I talked to Bianca?

I could still feel Susan's kiss lingering on my cheek as I got in the car.

I shook my head, bewildered. They say we wizards are subtle. But believe you me, we've got nothing, nothing at all, on *women*.

6

Mister was nowhere to be seen when I got home, but I left the food in his dish anyway. He would eventually forgive me for getting home late. I collected the things I would need from my kitchen – fresh-baked bread with no preservatives, honey, milk, a fresh apple, a sharp silver penknife, and a tiny dinner set of a plate, bowl, and cup that I had carved myself from a block of teakwood.

I went back out to my car. The Beetle isn't really blue anymore, since both doors have been replaced, one with a green clone, one with a white one, and the hood of the storage trunk in front had to be replaced with a red duplicate, but the name stuck anyway. Mike is a super mechanic. He never asked questions about the burns that slagged a hole in the front hatch or the claw marks that ruined both the doors. You can't pay for service like that.

I revved up the Beetle and drove down I-94, around the shore of Lake Michigan, crossing through Indiana, briefly, and then crossing over the state line into Michigan itself. Lake Providence is an expensive, high-class community with big houses and sprawling estates. It isn't cheap to own land there. Victor Sells must have been doing well in his former position at SilverCo to afford a place out that way.

The lakeshore drive wound in and out among thick, tall trees and rolling hills down to the shore. The properties were well spread out, several hundred yards between them.

Most of them were fenced in and had gates on the right side of the road, away from the lake as I drove north. The Sells house was the only one I saw on the lake side of the drive.

A smooth gravel lane, lined by trees, led back from the lakeshore drive to the Sells house. A peninsula jutted out into the lake, leaving enough room for the house and a small dock, at which no boats were moored. The house was not a large one, by the standards of the rest of the Lake Providence community. Built on two levels, it was a very modern dwelling – a lot of glass and wood that was made to look like something more synthetic than wood by the way it had been smoothed and cut and polished. The drive curved around to the back of the house, where a driveway big enough to host a five-on-five game of basket-ball around a backboard erected to one side was overlooked by a wooden deck leading off the second level of the house.

I drove the Blue Beetle around to the back of the house and parked there. My ingredients were in a black-nylon backpack, and I picked that up and brought it with me as I got out of the car and stretched my legs. The breeze coming up from the lake was cool enough to make me shiver a little, and I drew my mantled duster closed across my belly.

First impressions are important, and I wanted to listen to what my instincts said about the house. I stopped for a long moment and just stared up at it.

My instincts must have been holding out for another bottle of Mac's ale. They had little to say, other than that the place looked like a pricy little dwelling that had hosted a family through many a vacation weekend. Well, where instinct fails, intellect must venture. Almost everything was fairly new. The grass around the house had not grown

long enough, this winter, to require a cutting. The basketball net was stretched out and loose enough to show that
it had been used fairly often. The curtains were all drawn.

On the grass beneath the deck something red gleamed,
and I went beneath the deck to retrieve it. It was a plastic
film canister, red with a grey cap, the kind you keep a roll
of film in when you send it in to the processors. Film
canisters were good for holding various ingredients I used,
sometimes. I tucked it in my duster's pocket and continued
my inspection.

The place didn't look much like a family dwelling, really.
It looked like a rich man's love nest, a secluded little getaway
nestled back in the trees of the peninsula and safe from
spying eyes. Or an ideal location for a novice sorcerer to
come to try out his fledgling abilities, safe from interrup-
tions. A good place for Victor Sells to set up shop and
practice.

I made a quick circuit of the house, tried the front and
rear doors, and even the door up on the deck that led,
presumably, to a kitchen. All were locked. Locks really
weren't an obstacle, but Monica Sells hadn't invited me
actually to take a look inside the house, just around it. It's
bad juju to go tromping into people's houses uninvited.
One of the reasons vampires, as a rule, don't do it – they
have enough trouble just holding themselves together,
outside of the Nevernever. It isn't harmful to a human
wizard, like me, but it can really impair anything you try
to do with magic. Also, it just isn't polite. Like I said, I'm
an old-fashioned sort of guy.

Of course, the TekTronic Securities control panel that I
could see through the front window had some say in my
decision – not that I couldn't hex it down to a useless

bundle of plastic and wires, but a lot of security systems will cause an alarm with their contact company if they abruptly stop working without notice. It would be a useless exercise, in any case – the real information was to be had elsewhere.

Still, something nagged at me, a sense of not-quite-emptiness to the house. On a hunch, I knocked on the front door, several times. I even rang the bell. No one came to answer the door, and no lights were on, inside. I shrugged and walked back to the rear of the house, passing a number of empty trash cans as I did.

Now that was a bit odd. I mean, I would expect a little something in the trash, even if someone hadn't been there in a while. Did the garbage truck come all the way down the drive to pick up the trash cans? That didn't seem likely. If the Sellses came out to the house for the weekend and wanted the trash emptied, it would stand to reason that they'd have to leave it out by the drive near the road as they left. Which would seem to imply that the garbage men would leave the empty trash cans out by the road. Someone must have brought them back to the house.

Of course, it needn't have been Victor Sells. It could have been a neighbor, or something. Or maybe he tipped the garbagemen to carry the cans back away from the road. But it was something to go on, a little hint that maybe the house hadn't been empty all week.

I left the house behind me and walked out toward the lake. The night was breezy but clear, and a bit cool. The tall old trees creaked and groaned beneath the wind. It was still early for the mosquitoes to be too bad. The moon was waxing toward full overhead, with the occasional cloud slipping past her like a gauzy veil.

It was a perfect night for catching faeries.

I swept an area of dirt not far from the lakeshore clear of leaves and sticks, and took the silver knife from the backpack. Using the handle, I drew a circle in the earth, then covered it up with leaves and sticks again, marking the location of the circle's perimeter in my head. I was careful to focus in concentration on the circle, without actually letting any power slip into it and spoil the trap. Then, working carefully, I prepared the bait by setting out the little cup and bowl. I poured a thimbleful of milk into the cup and daubed the bowl full of honey from the little plastic bear in my backpack.

Then I tore a piece of bread from the loaf I had brought with me and pricked my thumb with the knife. In the silver light of the moon, a bit of dark blood welled up against the skin, and I touched it daintily to the underside of the coarse bread, letting it absorb the blood. Then I set the bread, bloody side down, on the tiny plate.

My trap was set. I gathered up my equipment and retreated to the cover of the trees.

There are two parts of magic you have to understand to catch a faery. One of them is the concept of true names. Everything in the whole world has its own name. Names are unique sounds and cadences of words that are attached to one specific individual – sort of like a kind of theme music. If you know something's name, you can associate yourself with it in a magical sense, almost in the same way a wizard can reach out and touch someone if he possesses a lock of their hair, or fingernail clippings, or blood. If you know something's name, you can create a magical link to it, just as you can call someone up and talk to them if you know their phone number. Just knowing the name isn't good enough, though; you have to know exactly how to say it. Ask two John Franklin Smiths to say their names for you, and you'll get subtle differences in tone and pronunciation, each one unique to its owner. Wizards tend to collect names of creatures, spirits, and people like some kind of huge Rolodex. You never know when it will come in handy.

The other part of magic you need to know is magic-circle theory. Most magic involves a circle of one kind or another. Drawing a circle sets a local limit on what a wizard is trying to do. It helps him refine his magic, focus and direct it more clearly. It does this by creating a sort of screen, defined by the perimeter of the circle, that keeps random magical energy from going past it, containing it within the circle so that it can be used. To make a circle, you draw it out on the ground, or close hands with a bunch of people, or walk about spreading incense, or any of a number of other methods, while focusing on your purpose in drawing it. Then, you invest it with a little spark of energy to close the circuit, and it's ready.

One other thing such a circle does: it keeps magical creatures, like faeries, or even demons, from getting past it. Neat, huh? Usually, this is used to keep them out. It's a bit trickier to set up a circle to keep them *in*. That's where the blood comes into play. With blood comes power. If you take in some of someone else's blood, there is a metaphysical significance to it, a sort of energy. It's minuscule if you aren't really trying to get energy that way (the way vampires do), but it's enough to close a circle.

Now you know how it's done. But I don't recommend that you try it at home. You don't know what to do when something goes wrong.

I retreated to the trees and called the name of the particular faery I wanted. It was a rolling series of syllables, quite beautiful, really – especially since the faery went by the name of Toot-toot every time I'd encountered him before. I pushed my will out along with the name, just made it a call, something that would be subtle enough to make him wander this way of his own accord. Or at least, that was the theory.

What was his name? Please, do you think wizards just *give* information like that away? You don't know what I went through to get it.

About ten minutes later, Toot came flickering in over the water of Lake Michigan. At first I mistook him for a reflection of the moon on the side of the softly rolling waves of the lake. Toot was maybe six inches tall. He had silver dragonfly's wings sprouting from his back and the pale, beautiful, tiny humanoid form that echoed the splendor of the fae lords. A silver nimbus of ambient light surrounded him. His hair was a shaggy, silken little mane, like a bird of paradise's plumes, and was a pale magenta.

Toot loved bread and milk and honey – a common vice of the lesser fae. They aren't usually willing to take on a nest of bees to get to the honey, and there's been a real dearth of milk in the Nevernever since hi-tech dairy farms took over most of the industry. Needless to say, they don't grow their own wheat, harvest it, thresh it, and then mill it into flour to make bread, either.

Toot alighted on the ground with caution, scanning around the trees. He didn't see me. I saw him wipe at his mouth and walk in a slow circle around the miniature dining set, one hand rubbing greedily at his stomach. Once he took the bread and closed the circle, I'd be able to bargain information for his release. Toot was a lesser spirit in the area, sort of a dockworker of the Nevernever. If anyone had seen anything of Victor Sells, Toot would have, or would know someone who had.

Toot dithered for a while, fluttering back and forth around the meal, but slowly getting closer. Faeries and honey. Moths and flame. Toot had fallen for this several times before, and it wasn't in the nature of the fae to keep memories for very long, or to change their essential natures. All the same, I held my breath.

The faery finally hunkered down, picked up the bread, dipped it in the honey, then greedily gobbled it down. The circle closed with a little *snap* that occurred just at the edge of my hearing.

Its effect on Toot was immediate. He screamed a shrill little scream, like a trapped rabbit, and took off toward the lake in a buzzing flurry of wings. At the perimeter of the circle, he smacked into something as solid as a brick wall, and a little puff of silver motes exploded out from him in a cloud. Toot grunted and fell onto his little faery ass on the earth.

'I should have known!' he exclaimed, as I approached from the trees. His voice was high-pitched, but more like a little kid's than the exaggerated kind of faery voices I'd heard in cartoons. 'Now I remember where I've seen those plates before! You ugly, sneaky, hamhanded, big-nosed, flat-footed mortal worm!'

'Hiya, Toot,' I told him. 'Do you remember our deal from last time, or do we need to go over it again?'

Toot glared defiantly up at me and stomped his foot on the ground. More silver faery dust puffed out from the impact. 'Release me!' he demanded. 'Or I will tell the Queen!'

'If I don't release you,' I pointed out, 'you *can't* tell the Queen. And you know just as well as I do what she would say about any dewdrop faery who was silly enough to get himself caught with a lure of bread and milk and honey.'

Toot crossed his arms defiantly over his chest. 'I warn you, mortal. Release me now, or you will feel the awful, terrible, irresistible might of the faery magic! I will rot your teeth from your head! Take your eyes from their sockets! Fill your mouth with dung and your ears with worms!'

'Hit me with your best shot,' I told him. 'After that, we can talk about what you need to do to get out of the circle.'

I had called his bluff. I always did, but he probably wouldn't remember the details very well. If you live a few hundred years, you tend to forget the little things. Toot sulked and kicked up a little spray of dirt with one tiny foot. 'You could at least *pretend* to be afraid, Harry.'

'Sorry, Toot. I don't have the time.'

'Time, time,' Toot complained. 'Is that all you mortals can ever think about? Everyone's complaining about *time*! The whole city rushes left and right screaming about being late and honking horns! You people *used* to have it right, you know.'

I bore the lecture with good nature. Toot could never keep his mind on the same subject long enough to be really trying, in any case.

'Why, I remember the folk who lived here before you pale, wheezy guys came in. And they *never* complained about ulcers or—' Toot's eyes wandered to the bread and milk and honey again, and glinted. He sauntered that way, then snatched the remaining bread, sopping up all the honey with it and eating it with greedy, birdlike motions.

'This is good stuff, Harry. None of that funny stuff in it that we get sometimes.'

'Preservatives,' I said.

'Whatever.' Toot drank down the milk, too, in a long pull, then promptly fell down on his back, patting at his rounded tummy. 'All right,' he said. 'Now, let me out.'

'Not yet, Toot. I need something first.'

Toot scowled up at me. 'You wizards. Always needing something. I really could do the thing with the dung, you know.' He stood up and folded his arms haughtily over his chest, looking up at me as though I weren't a dozen times taller than he. 'Very well,' he said, his tone lofty. 'I have deigned to grant you a single request of some small nature, for the generous gift of your cuisine.'

I worked to keep a straight face. 'That's very kind of you.'

Toot sniffed and somehow managed to look down his little pug nose at me. 'It is my nature to be both benevolent and wise.'

I nodded, as though this were a very great wisdom. 'Uh-huh. Look, Toot. I need to know if you were around this place for the past few nights, or know someone who was. I'm looking for someone, and maybe he came here.'

'And if I tell you,' Toot said, 'I take it you will disassemble this circle which has, by some odd coincidence no doubt, made its way around me?'

'It would be only reasonable,' I said, all seriousness.

Toot seemed to consider it, as though he might be inclined not to cooperate, then nodded. 'Very well. You will have the information you wish. Release me.'

I narrowed my eyes. 'Are you sure? Do you promise?'

Toot stamped his foot again, scattering more silver dust motes. 'Harry! You're ruining the drama!'

I folded my arms. 'I want to hear you promise.'

Toot threw up his hands. 'Fine, fine, *fine*! I promise, I promise, I promise! I'll dig up what you want to know!' He started to buzz about the circle in great agitation, wings lifting him easily into the air. 'Let me out! Let me out!'

A promise thrice made is as close to absolute truth as you can get from a faery. I went quickly to the circle and scuffed over the line drawn in the dirt with my foot, willing the circle to part. It did, with a little hiss of released energy.

Toot streaked out over Lake Michigan's waters again, a miniature silver comet, and vanished in a twinkling, just like Santa Claus. Though I should say that Santa is a *much* bigger and more powerful faery than Toot, and I don't know his true name anyway. You'd never see me trying to nab Saint Nick in a magic circle, even if I did. I don't think anyone has stones that big.

I waited around, walking about to keep from falling asleep. If I did that, Toot would be perfectly within his rights as a faery to fulfill his promise by telling me the information while I was sleeping. And, given that I had just now captured and humiliated him, he'd probably do something to even the scales — two weeks from now he wouldn't even remember it, but if I let him have a free shot at me tonight, I might wake up with an ass's head, and I didn't think that would be good for business.

So I paced, and I waited. Toot usually took about half an hour to round up whatever it was I wanted to know.

Sure enough, half an hour later he came sparkling back in and buzzed around my head, drizzling faery dust from his blurring wings at my eyes. 'Hah, Harry!' he said. 'I did it!'

'What did you find out, Toot?'

'Guess!'

I snorted. 'No.'

'Aw, come on. Just a little guess?'

I scowled, tired and irritated, but tried not to let it show. Toot couldn't help being what he was. 'Toot, it's late. You promised to tell me.'

'No fun at *all*,' he complained. 'No wonder you can't get a date unless someone wants to know something from you.'

I blinked at him, and he chortled in glee. 'Hah! I love it! We're watching you, Harry Dresden!'

Now that was disconcerting. I had a sudden image of a dozen faery voyeurs lingering around my apartment's windows and peering inside. I'd have to take precautions to make sure they couldn't do that. Not that I was afraid of them, or anything. Just in case.

'Just tell me, Toot,' I sighed.

'Incoming!' he shrilled, and I held out my hand, fingers flat and palm up. He alighted in the center of my palm. I could barely feel his weight, but the sense, the aura of him ran through my skin like a tiny electric current. He stared fearlessly at my eyes – the fae have no souls to gaze upon, and they could not fathom a mortal's soul, even if they could see it.

'Okay!' Toot said. 'I talked to Blueblossom, who talked to Rednose, who talked to Meg O' Aspens, who said that Goldeneyes said that he was riding the pizza car when it came here last night!' Toot thrust out his chest proudly.

'Pizza car?' I asked, bewildered.

'Pizza!' Toot cried, jubilant. 'Pizza! Pizza! Pizza!' His wings fluttered again, and I tried to blink the damned faery dust out of my eyes before I started sneezing.

'Faeries like pizza?' I asked.

'Oh, Harry,' Toot said breathlessly. 'Haven't you ever had pizza before?'

'Of course I have,' I said.

Toot looked wounded. 'And you didn't share?'

I sighed. 'Look. Maybe I can bring you guys some pizza sometime soon, to thank you for your help.'

Toot leapt about in glee, hopping from one fingertip to the other. 'Yes! Yes! Wait until I tell them! We'll *see* who laughs at Toot-toot next time!'

'Toot,' I said, trying to calm him, 'did he see anything else?'

Toot tittered, his expression sly and suggestive. 'He said that there were mortals sporting and that they needed pizza to regain their strength!'

'Which delivery place, Toot?'

The faery blinked and stared at me as though I were hopelessly stupid. 'Harry. *The* pizza truck.' And then he darted off skyward, vanishing into the trees above.

I sighed and nodded. Toot wouldn't know the difference between Domino's and Pizza Hut. He had no frame of reference, and couldn't read – most faeries were studiously averse to print.

So, I had two pieces of information. One, someone had ordered a pizza to be delivered here. That meant two things. First, that someone was here last night. Second, that someone had seen them and talked to them. Maybe I could track down the pizza driver, and ask if he had seen Victor Sells.

The second piece of information had been Toot's reference to sporting. Faeries didn't think too much of mortals' idea of 'sporting' unless there was a lot of nudity and lust involved. They had a penchant for shadowing necking teenagers and playing tricks on them. So Victor had been here with a lover of some kind, for there to be any 'sport' going on.

I was beginning to think that Monica Sells was in denial. Her husband wasn't wandering around learning to be a sorcerer, spooky scorpion talismans notwithstanding. He was lurking about his love nest with a girlfriend, like any other husband bored with a timid and domestic wife might do under pressure. It wasn't admirable, but I guess I could understand the motivations that could cause it.

The only problem was going to be telling Monica. I had a feeling that she wasn't going to want to listen to what I had found out.

I picked up the little plate and bowl and cup and put them back into my black-nylon backpack, along with the silver knife. My legs ached from too much walking and standing about. I was looking forward to getting home and getting some sleep.

The man with the naked sword in his hands appeared out of the darkness without a warning rustle of sound or whiff of magic to announce his presence. He was tall, like me, but broad and heavy-chested, and he carried his weight with a ponderous sort of dignity. Perhaps fifty years old, his listless brown hair going grey in uneven patches, he wore a long, black coat, a lot like mine but without the mantle, and his jacket and pants, too, were done in dark colors – charcoal and a deep blue. His shirt was crisp, pure white, the color that you usually only see with tuxedos. His eyes were grey, touched with crow's-feet at the corners, and dangerous. Moonlight glinted off those eyes in the same shade it did from the brighter silver of the sword's blade. He began to walk deliberately toward me, speaking in a quiet voice as he did.

'Harry Blackstone Copperfield Dresden. Irresponsible use of true names for summoning and binding others to your will violates the Fourth Law of Magic,' the man intoned. 'I remind you that you are under the Doom of Damocles. No further violations of the Laws will be tolerated. The sentence for further violation is death, by the sword, to be carried out at once.'

7

Have you ever been approached by a grim-looking man, carrying a naked sword with a blade about ten miles long in his hand, in the middle of the night, beneath the stars on the shores of Lake Michigan? If you have, seek professional help. If you have not, then believe you me, it can scare the bejeezus out of you.

I took in a quick breath, and had to work not to put it into a quasi-Latin phrase on the exhale, one that would set the man's body on fire and reduce him to a mound of ashes. I react badly to fear. I don't usually have the good sense to run, or hide – I just try to smash whatever it is that is making me afraid. It's a primitive sort of thing, and one I don't question too much.

But reflex-based murder seemed a tad extreme, so rather than setting him on fire, I nodded instead. 'Evening, Morgan. You know as well as I do that those laws apply to mortals. Not faeries. Especially for something as trivial as I just did. And I didn't break the Fourth Law. He had the choice whether to take my deal or not.'

Morgan's sour, leathery face turned a bit more sour, the lines at the corners of his mouth stretching and becoming deeper. 'That's a technicality, Dresden. A pair of them.' His hands, broad and strong, resettled their grip upon the sword he held. His unevenly greying hair was tied into a ponytail in the back, like Sean Connery's in some of his movies, except that Morgan's face was too pinched and thin to pull off the look.

'Your point being?' I did my best to keep from looking nervous or impressed. Truth be told, I was both. Morgan was my Warden, assigned to me by the White Council to make sure I didn't bend or break any of the Laws of Magic. He hung about and spied on me, mostly, and usually came sniffing around after I'd cast a spell of some kind. I would be damned if I was going to let the White Council's guard dog see any fear out of me. Besides, he would take it as a sign of guilt, in the true spirit of paranoid fanatics everywhere. So, all I had to do was keep a straight face and get out before my weariness made me slip up and do or say something he could use against me.

Morgan was one of the deadliest evocators in the world. He wasn't bright enough to question his loyalties to the Council, and he could do quick-and-dirty magic like few others could.

Quick and dirty enough to rip the hearts out of Tommy Tomm and Jennifer Stanton's chests, in fact, if he wanted to.

'My point,' he said, scowling, 'is that it is my assigned duty to monitor your use of your power, and to see to it that you do not abuse it.'

'I'm on a missing-persons case,' I said. 'All I did was call up a dewdrop faery to get some information. Come on, Morgan. Everybody calls up faeries now and then. There's no harm in it. It's not as though I'm mind-controlling the things. Just leaning on them a little.'

'Technicality,' Morgan growled.

I stuck out my chin at him belligerently. We were of a height, though he outweighed me by about a hundred pounds. I could pick better people to antagonize, but he'd really gotten under my skin. 'A technicality I'm prepared to hide wildly behind. So, unless you want to convene a meeting of the Council to call me on it, we can just drop the discussion right here. I'm pretty sure it will only take them about two days to cancel all their plans, make travel arrangements, and then get here. I can put you up until then. I mean, you'd be dragging a bunch of really crotchety old men away from their experiments and things for nothing, but if you really think it's necessary . . .'

Morgan scowled at me. 'No. It isn't worth it.' He opened his dark trench coat and slid the sword away into its scabbard. I relaxed a little. The sword wasn't the most dangerous thing about him, not by a long shot, but it was his symbol of the authority given to him by the White Council, and if rumors were true, it was enchanted to cut through the magical spells of anyone resisting him. I didn't want things ever to go far enough for me to find out if the rumors were true.

'I'm glad we agree about something,' I said. 'Nice seeing you again.' I started to walk past him.

Morgan put one of those big hands on my arm as I went by, and his fingers closed around it. 'I'm not finished with you, Dresden.'

I didn't dare mess around with Morgan when he was acting in his role as a Warden of the White Council. But he wasn't wearing that hat, now. Once he'd put the sword away, he was acting on his own, without any more official authority than any other man — or at least, that was the technical truth. Morgan was big on technicalities. He had scared the heck out of me and annoyed the heck out of me, in rapid succession. Now he was trying to bully me. I hate bullies.

So I took a calculated risk, used my free hand, and hit him as hard as I could in the mouth.

I think the blow startled him more than anything. He took a step back, letting go of my arm in surprise, and just blinked at me. He put one hand to his mouth, and when he drew his fingers away, there was blood on them.

I planted my feet and faced him, without meeting his eyes. 'Don't touch me.'

Morgan continued to stare at me. And then I saw anger creep over his face, set his jaw, make the veins at his temple stand out.

'How dare you,' he said. 'How dare you strike me.'

'It wasn't so hard,' I said. 'If you've got Council business with me, I'm willing to give you whatever respect is your due. When you come on strong to me on personal business, I don't have to put up with it.'

I saw the steam coming out of his ears as he mulled it over. He looked for a reason to come after me, and realized that he didn't have one, according to the Laws. He wasn't too bright – did I mention that already? – and he was a big one for following the Laws. 'You're a fool, Dresden,' he sputtered finally. 'An arrogant little fool.'

'Probably,' I told him. I tensed myself to move quickly if necessary. I may not like to run away from what scares me, but I try not to fight hopeless battles, either, and Morgan had me by years of experience and a hundred pounds, at least. There was no Law of Magic that protected *me* from *him* and his fists, either, and if that occurred to him, he might decide to do something about it. That punch I'd landed had been lucky, coming out of the blue. I wouldn't get away with it again.

'Someone killed two people with sorcery last night,

Dresden. I think it was you. And when I find how you did it and can trace it back to you, don't think you're going to live long enough to cast the same spell at me.' Morgan swiped at the blood with one big fist.

It was my turn to blink. I tried to shift mental gears, to keep up with the change in subject. Morgan thought I was the killer. And since Morgan didn't do too much of his own thinking, that meant that the White Council thought I was the killer. Holy shit.

Of course, it made sense, from Morgan's narrow and single-minded point of view. A wizard had killed someone. I was a wizard who had already been convicted of killing another with magic, even if the self-defense clause had kept me from being executed. Cops looked for people who had already committed crimes before they started looking for other culprits. Morgan was just another kind of cop, as far as I was concerned.

And, as far as he was concerned, I was just one more dangerous con.

'You're not serious,' I told him. 'You think I did it?'

He sneered at me. His voice was contemptuous, confident, and seethed with absolute conviction. 'Don't try to hide it, Dresden. I'm sure you think you're clever enough to come up with something innovative that we hidebound old men won't be able to trace. But you're wrong. We'll determine how you did it, and we'll follow it back to you. And when we do, I'll be there to make sure you never hurt anyone again.'

'Knock yourself out,' I told him. It was hard, really hard, to keep my voice as blithe as I wanted it to sound. 'I didn't do it. But I'm helping the police find the man who did.'

'The police?' Morgan asked. He narrowed his eyes, as

though gauging my expression. 'As if they could have any authority on this matter. They won't do you any good. Even if you do set someone up to take the fall for you under mortal law, the White Council will still see that justice is done.' His eyes glittered, fanatic-bright underneath the stars.

'Whatever. Look, if you find something out about the killer, anything that could help the cops out, would you give me a call?'

Morgan looked at me with profound distaste. 'You ask me to warn you when we are closing in on you, Dresden? You are young, but I never thought you stupid.'

I bit back the obvious comment that leapt to mind. Morgan was on the edge of outrage already. If I'd realized how rabid he was to catch me slipping, I wouldn't have added more fuel to his fire by hitting him in the mouth.

Okay. I probably still would have hit him in the mouth. But I wouldn't have done it quite so hard.

'Good night, Morgan,' I told him. I started to walk away again, before I could let my mouth get me into more trouble.

He moved faster than I would have given a man his age credit for. His fist went across my jaw at approximately a million miles an hour, and I spun down to the dirt like a string-cut puppet. For several long moments, I was unable to do anything at all, even breathe. Morgan loomed over me.

'We'll be watching you, Dresden.' He turned and started walking away, the shadows of the evening quickly swallowing up his black coat. His voice drifted back to me. 'We'll find out what really happened.'

I didn't dare spout out a snappy comeback. I felt my jaw with my fingers, and made sure it wasn't broken, before

I stood up and walked back to the Beetle, my legs feeling loose and watery. I fervently hoped that Morgan would find out what had really happened. It would keep the White Council from executing me for breaking the First Law, for one thing.

I could feel his eyes on my back, all the way to the Beetle. Damn that Morgan. He didn't have to take quite so much pleasure in being assigned to spy on me. I had a sinking feeling that anywhere I went over the next few days, he would be likely to turn up, watching. He was like this big, cartoon tomcat waiting outside the mousehole for the little mouse to stick its nose out so he could smash it flat with one big paw. I was feeling a lot like that little mouse.

I let that analogy cheer me up a bit. The cartoon cats always seemed to get the short end of the stick, in the final analysis. Maybe Morgan would, too.

Part of the problem was that seeing Morgan always brought up too many memories of my angsty teenage days. That was when I'd started to learn magic, when my mentor had tried to seduce me into Black wizardry, and when he had attempted to kill me when he failed. I killed him instead, mostly by luck – but he was just as dead, and I'd done it with sorcery. I broke the First Law of Magic: *Thou Shalt Not Kill*. There is only one sentence, if someone is found guilty, and one sword that they use to carry it out.

The White Council commuted the death sentence, because tradition demands that a wizard can resort to the use of deadly force if he is defending his own life, or the lives of the defenseless, and my claim that I had been attacked first could not be contested by my master's corpse. So instead, they'd stuck me on a kind of accelerated probation: one strike and I was out. There were some wizards who thought that the judgment against me was a ludicrous injustice (I happened to be one of them, but my vote didn't really count), and others who thought that I should have been executed regardless of extenuating circumstances. Morgan belonged to that latter group. Just my luck.

I was feeling more than a bit surly at the entire White Council, benevolent intentions aside. I guess it only made sense that they'd suspect me, and God knows I'd been a thorn in their side, flying in the face of tradition by practicing my art openly. There were plenty of people on the Council who might well want me dead. I would have to start being more careful.

I rolled down the Beetle's windows on the way back to Chicago to help me stay awake. I was exhausted, but my mind was racing around like a hamster on an exercise wheel, working furiously, getting nowhere.

The irony was thick enough to make my tongue curl. The White Council suspected me of the killings, and if no other suspect came forward, I was going to take the rap. Murphy's investigation had just become very, very important to me. But to pursue the investigation, I would have to try to figure out how the killer had pulled off that spell, and to do *that*, I would have to indulge in highly questionable research that would probably be enough to get me a death sentence all by itself. Catch twenty-two. If I had any respect at all for Morgan's intelligence, I would have suspected him of pulling off the killings himself and setting me up to take the blame.

But that just didn't track. Morgan might twist and bend the rules, to get what he saw as justice, but he'd never blatantly violate them. But if not Morgan, then who could have done it? There just weren't all that many people who could get enough power into that kind of spell to make it work – unless there was some flaw in the quasiphysics that governed magic that let hearts explode more easily than other things; and I wouldn't know that until I had pursued the forbidden research.

Bianca would have more information on who might have done it – she had to. I had already planned on talking to the vampiress, but Morgan's visit had made it a necessity, rather than merely a priority. Murphy was not going to be thrilled that I was thrusting myself into her side of this investigation. And, better and better, because White Council business was all hush-hush to nonwizards, I wouldn't be able to explain to her why I was doing it. Further joy.

You know, sometimes I think Someone up there really hates me.

8

By the time I got home, it was after two o'clock in the morning. The clock in the Beetle didn't work (of course), but I made a pretty good guess from the position of the stars and the moon. I was strung out, weary, and my nerves were stretched as tight as guitar strings.

I didn't think sleep was likely, so I decided to do a little alchemy to help me unwind.

I've often wished that I had some suave and socially acceptable hobby that I could fall back on in times like this. You know, play the violin (or was it the viola?) like Sherlock Holmes, or maybe twiddle away on the pipe organ like the Disney version of Captain Nemo. But I don't. I'm sort of the arcane equivalent of a classic computer geek. I do magic, in one form or another, and that's pretty much it. I really need to get a life, one of these days.

I live in a basement apartment beneath a big, roomy old house that has been divided up into lots of different apartments. The basement and the subbasement below it are both mine, which is sort of neat. I'm the only tenant living on two floors, and my rent is cheaper than all the people who have whole windows.

The house is full of creaks and sighs and settling boards, and time and lives have worn their impressions into the wood and the brick. I can hear all the sounds, all the character of the place, above and around me all through the night. It's an old place, but it sings in the darkness and is, in its own quirky little way, alive. It's home.

Mister was waiting for me at the bottom of the stairs that led down to the apartment's front door. Mister is an enormous grey cat. I mean, enormous. There are dogs smaller than Mister. He weighs in at just over thirty pounds, and there isn't an undue amount of fat on his frame. I think maybe his father was a wildcat or a lynx or something. I had found Mister in a garbage can about three years before, a mewling kitten, with his tail torn off by a dog or a car – I was never sure which, but Mister hated both, and would either attack or flee from them on sight.

Mister had recovered his dignity over the next few months, and shortly came to believe that he was the apartment's tenant, and I was someone he barely tolerated to share the space with him. Right now he looked up and mrowed at me in an annoyed tone.

'I thought you had a hot date,' I told him.

He sauntered over to me and rammed one shoulder playfully against my knee. I wavered, recovered my balance, and unlocked the door. Mister, as was his just due, entered before I did.

My apartment is a studio, one not-too-large room with a kitchenette in the corner and a fireplace to one side. There's a door that leads to the other room, my bedroom and bathroom, and then there's the hinged door in the floor that goes down to the subbasement, where I keep my lab. I've got things pretty heavily textured – there are multiple carpets on the floor, tapestries on the walls, a collection of knickknacks and oddities on every available surface, my staff and my sword cane in the corner, and several bulging bookshelves which I really will organize one day.

Mister went to his spot before the fireplace and demanded that it be made warm. I obliged him with a fire and lit a lamp as well. Oh, I have lights and so on, but they foul up so often it almost isn't worth turning them on. And I'm not even about to take chances with the gas heater. I stick with the simple things, the fireplace and my candles and lamps. I have a special charcoal stove and a vent to take most of the smoke out, though the whole place smells a little of woodsmoke and charcoal, no matter what I do.

I took off my duster and got out my heavy flannel robe before I went down into the lab. That's why wizards wear robes, I swear to you. It's just too damned cold in the lab to go without one. I clambered down the ladder to the lab, carrying my candle with me, and lit a few lamps, a pair of burners, and a kerosene heater in the corner.

The lights came up and revealed a long table in the center of the room, other tables against three of the walls around it, and a clear space at one end of the room where a brass circle had been laid out on the floor and fastened into the cement with U-shaped bolts. Shelves over the tables were crowded with empty cages, boxes, Tupperware, jars, cans, containers of all descriptions, a pair of unusual antlers, a couple of fur pelts, several musty old books, a long row of notebooks filled with my own cramped writing, and a bleached white human skull.

'Bob,' I said. I started clearing space off of the center table, dumping boxes and grocery sacks and plastic tubs over the brass circle on the floor. I needed room to work. 'Bob, wake up.'

There was a moment of silence, while I started getting

some things down from the shelves. 'Bob!' I said, louder. 'Come on, lazybones.'

A pair of lights came up in the empty sockets of the skull, orangish, flickering like candle flames. 'It isn't enough,' the skull said, 'that I have to wake up. I have to wake up to bad puns. What is it about you that you have to make the bad puns?'

'Quit whining,' I told him, cheerfully. 'We've got work to do.'

Bob the Skull grumbled something in Old French, I think, though I got lost when he got to the anatomical improbabilities of bullfrogs. He yawned, and his bony teeth rattled when his mouth clicked closed again. Bob wasn't really a human skull. He was a spirit of air – sort of like a faery, but different. He made his residence inside the skull that had been prepared for him several hundred years ago, and it was his job to remember things. For obvious reasons, I can't use a computer to store information and keep track of the slowly changing laws of quasiphysics. That's why I had Bob. He had worked with dozens of wizards over the years, and it had given him a vast repertoire of knowledge – that, and a really cocky attitude. 'Blasted wizards,' he mumbled.

'I can't sleep, so we're going to make a couple of potions. Sound good?'

'Like I have a choice,' Bob said. 'What's the occasion?'

I brought Bob up to speed on what had happened that day. He whistled (no easy trick without lips), and said, 'Sounds sticky.'

'Pretty sticky,' I agreed.

'Tell you what,' he said. 'Let me out for a ride, and I'll tell you how to get out of it.'

That made me wary. 'Bob, I let you out once. Remember?'

He nodded dreamily, scraping bone on wood. 'The sorority house. I remember.'

I snorted, and started some water to boiling over one of the burners. 'You're supposed to be a spirit of intellect. I don't understand why you're obsessed with sex.'

Bob's voice got defensive. 'It's an academic interest, Harry.'

'Oh yeah? Well maybe I don't think it's fair to let your academia go peeping in other people's houses.'

'Wait a minute. My academia doesn't *just* peep—'

I held up a hand. 'Save it. I don't want to hear it.'

He grunted. 'You're trivializing what getting out for a bit means to me, Harry. You're insulting my masculinity.'

'Bob,' I said, 'you're a *skull*. You don't *have* any masculinity to insult.'

'Oh yeah?' Bob challenged me. 'Pot kettle black, Harry! Have you gotten a date yet? Huh? Most men have something better to do in the middle of the night than play with their chemistry sets.'

'As a matter of fact,' I told him, 'I'm set up for Saturday night.'

Bob's eyes fluttered from orange to red. 'Oooooo,' he leered. 'Is she pretty?'

'Dark skin,' I said. 'Dark hair, dark eyes. Legs to die for. Smart, sexy as hell.'

Bob chortled. 'Think she'd like to see the lab?'

'Get your mind out of the gutter.'

'No, seriously,' Bob said. 'If she's so great, what's she doing with you? You aren't exactly Sir Gawain, you know.'

It was my turn to get defensive. 'She likes me,' I said. 'Is that such a shock?'

'Harry,' Bob drawled, his eye lights flickering smugly, 'what you know about women, I could juggle.'

I stared at Bob for a moment, and realized with a somewhat sinking feeling that the skull was probably right. Not that I would admit that to him, not in a million years, but he was.

'We're going to make an escape potion,' I told him. 'I don't want to be all night, so can we get to work? Huh? I can only remember about half the recipe.'

'There's always room to make two if you're making one, Harry. You know that.'

That much was true. The process of mixing up an alchemical potion is largely stirring, simmering, and waiting. You can always get another one going and alternate between them. Sometimes you can even do three, though that's pushing it. 'Okay, so, we'll make a copy.'

'Oh, come on,' Bob chided me. 'That's dull. You should stretch yourself. Try something new.'

'Like what?'

Bob's eye sockets twinkled cheerfully. 'A love potion, Harry! If you won't let me out, at least let me do that! Spirits know you could use it, and—'

'No,' I said, firmly. 'No way. No love potion.'

'Fine,' he said. 'No love potion, no escape potion either.'

'Bob,' I said, warningly.

Bob's eye lights winked out.

I growled. I was tired and cranky, and under the best of circumstances I am not exactly a type A personality. I stalked over, picked up Bob by the jaws and shook him.

'Hey!' I shouted. 'Bob! You come out of there! Or I'm going to take this skull and throw it down the deepest well I can find! I swear to you, I'll put you somewhere where no one can ever let you out ever again!'

Bob's eyes winked on for a moment. 'No you won't. I'm far too valuable.' Then they winked out again.

I gritted my teeth and tried not to smash the skull to little pieces on the floor. I took deep breaths, summoning years of wizardly training and control to not throw a tantrum and break the nice spirit to little pieces. Instead, I put the skull back on the shelf and counted slowly to thirty.

Could I make the potion by myself? I probably could. But I had the sinking feeling that it might not have precisely the effect I wanted. Potions were a tricky business, and a lot more relied upon precise details than upon intent, like in spells. And just because I made a love potion didn't mean I had to use it. Right? It would only be good for a couple of days, in any case – surely not through the weekend. How much trouble could it cause?

I struggled to rationalize the action. It would appease Bob, and give him some kind of vicarious thrill. Love potions were about the cheapest things in the world to make, so it wouldn't cost me too much. And, I thought, if Susan should ask me for some kind of demonstration of magic (as she always did), I could always—

No. That would be too much. That would be like admitting I couldn't get a woman to like me on my own, and it would be unfair, taking advantage of the woman. What I wanted was the escape potion. I might need it at Bianca's place, and I could always use it, if worse came to worst, to make a getaway from Morgan and the White

Council. I would feel a lot better if I had the escape potion.

'Okay, Bob. Fine. You win. We'll do them both. All right?'

Bob's eye lights came up warily. 'You're sure? You'll do the love potion, just like I say?'

'Don't I always make the potions like you say, Bob?'

'What about that diet potion you tried?'

'Okay. That one was a mistake.'

'And the antigravity potion, remember that?'

'We *fixed* the floor! It was no big deal!'

'And the—'

'Fine, fine,' I growled. 'You don't have to rub it in. Now cough up the recipes.'

Bob did so, in fine humor, and for the next two hours we made potions. Potions are all made pretty much the same way. First you need a base to form the essential liquid content; then something to engage each of the senses, and then something for the mind and something else for the spirit. Eight ingredients, all in all, and they're different for each and every potion, and for each person who makes them. Bob had centuries of experience, and he could extrapolate the most successful components for a given person to make into a potion. He was right about being an invaluable resource – I had never even heard of a spirit with Bob's experience, and I was lucky to have him.

That didn't mean I didn't want to crack that skull of his from time to time, though.

The escape potion was made in a base of eight ounces of Jolt cola. We added a drop of motor oil, for the smell of it, and cut a bird's feather into tiny shavings for the tactile value. Three ounces of chocolate-covered espresso beans, ground into powder, went in next. Then a shredded bus ticket I'd never used, for the mind, and a small chain which I broke and then dropped in, for the heart. I unfolded a clean white cloth where I'd had a flickering shadow stored for just such an occasion, and tossed it into the brew, then opened up a glass jar where I kept my mouse scampers and tapped the sound out into the beaker where the potion was brewing.

'You're sure this is going to work, Bob?' I said.

'Always. That's a super recipe, there.'

'Smells terrible.'

Bob's lights twinkled. 'They usually do.'

'What's it doing? Is this the superspeed one, or the teleportation version?'

Bob coughed. 'A little of both, actually. Drink it, and you'll be the wind for a few minutes.'

'The wind?' I eyed him. 'I haven't heard of that one before, Bob.'

'I am an air spirit, after all,' Bob told me. 'This'll work fine. Trust me.'

I grumbled, and set the first potion to simmering, then started on the next one. I hesitated, after Bob told me the first ingredient.

'Tequila?' I asked him, skeptically. 'Are you sure on that one? I thought the base for a love potion was supposed to be champagne.'

'Champagne, tequila, what's the difference, so long as it'll lower her inhibitions?' Bob said.

'Uh. I'm thinking it's going to get us a, um, sleazier result.'

'Hey!' Bob protested. 'Who's the memory spirit here! Me or you?'

'Well—'

'Who's got all the experience with women here? Me or you?'

'Bob—'

'Harry,' Bob lectured me, 'I was seducing shepherdesses when you weren't a twinkle in your great-grandcestor's eyes. I think I know what I'm doing.'

I sighed, too tired to argue with him. 'Okay, okay. Sheesh. Tequila.' I got down the bottle, measured eight ounces into the beaker, and glanced up at the skull.

'Right. Now, three ounces of dark chocolate.'

'Chocolate?' I demanded.

'Chicks are into chocolate, Harry.'

I muttered, more interested in finishing than anything else, and measured out the ingredients. I did the same with a drop of perfume (some name-brand imitation that I liked), an ounce of shredded lace, and the last sigh at the bottom of the glass jar. I added some candlelight to the mix, and it took on a rosy golden glow.

'Great,' Bob said. 'That's just right. Okay, now we add the ashes of a passionate love letter.'

I blinked at the skull. 'Uh, Bob. I'm fresh out of those.'

Bob snorted. 'How did I guess. Look on the shelf behind me.'

I did, and found a pair of romance novels, their covers filled with impossibly delightful flesh. 'Hey! Where did you get these?'

'My last trip out,' Bob answered blithely. 'Page one seventy-four, the paragraph that starts with, "Her milky-white breasts." Tear that page out and burn it and add those ashes in.'

I choked. 'That will work?'

'Hey, women eat these things up. Trust me.'

'Fine,' I sighed. 'This is the spirit ingredient?'

'Uh-huh,' Bob said. He was rocking back and forth on his jawbones in excitement. 'Now, just a teaspoon of powdered diamond, and we're done.'

I rubbed at my eyes. 'Diamond. I don't have any diamonds, Bob.'

'I figured. You're cheap, that's why women don't like you. Look, just tear up a fifty into real little pieces and put that in there.'

'A fifty-dollar bill?' I demanded.

'Money,' Bob opined. 'Very sexy.'

I muttered and got the remaining fifty out of my pocket, shredding it and tossing it in to complete the potion.

The next step was where the effort came in. Once all the ingredients are mixed together, you have to force enough energy through them to activate them. It isn't the actual physical ingredients that are important — it's the meaning that they carry, too, the significance that they have for the person making the potion, and for those who will be using it.

The energy from magic comes from a lot of places. It can come from a special place (usually some spectacular natural site, like Mount St Helens, or Old Faithful), from a focus of some kind (like Stonehenge is, on a large scale), or from inside of people. The best magic comes from the inside. Sometimes it's just pure mental effort, raw willpower. Sometimes it's emotions and feelings. All of them are viable tinder to be used for the proverbial fire.

I had a lot of worry to use to fuel the magic, and a lot of annoyance and one hell of a lot of stubbornness. I murmured the requisite quasi-Latin litany over the potions, over and over, feeling a kind of resistance building, just out of the range of the physical senses, but there, nonetheless. I gathered up all my worry and anger and stubbornness and threw them all at the resistance in one big ball, shaping them with the strength and tone of my words. The magic left me in a sudden wave, like a pitcher abruptly emptied out.

'I love this part,' Bob said, just as both potions exploded into puffs of greenish smoke and began to froth up over the lips of the beakers.

I sagged onto a stool, and waited for the potions to fizz down, all the strength gone out of me, the weariness building up like a load of bricks on my shoulders. Once the frothing had settled, I leaned over and poured each potion into its own individual sports bottle with a squeeze-top, then labeled the containers with a permanent Magic Marker – very clearly. I don't take chances in getting potions mixed up anymore, ever since the invisibility/hair tonic incident, from when I was trying to grow out a decent beard.

'You won't regret this, Harry,' Bob assured me. 'That's the best potion I've ever made.'

'I made it, not you,' I growled. I really was exhausted, now – way too tired to let petty concerns like possible execution keep me from bed.

'Sure, sure,' Bob agreed. 'Whatever, Harry.'

I went around the room putting out all the fires and the kerosene heater, then climbed the ladder back to the basement without saying good night. Bob was chortling happily to himself as I did.

I stumbled to my bed and fell into it. Mister always climbs in and goes to sleep draped over my legs. I waited for him, and a few seconds later he showed up, settling down and purring like a miniature outboard motor.

I struggled to put together an itinerary for the next couple of days through the haze of exhaustion. Talk to the vampire. Locate missing husband. Avoid the wrath of the White Council. Find the killer.

Before he found me.

An unpleasant thought – but I decided that I wasn't going to let that bother me, either, and curled up to go to sleep.

9

Friday night, I went to see Bianca, the vampiress.

I didn't just leap out of bed and go see her, of course. You don't go walking into the proverbial lion's den lightly. You start with a good breakfast.

My breakfast took place around three in the afternoon, when I woke up to hear my phone ringing. I had to get out of bed and pad into the main room to answer it.

'Mmmrrmmph,' I grumbled.

'Dresden,' Murphy said, 'what can you tell me?'

Murphy sounded stressed. Her voice had that distinct edge that she got whenever she was nervous, and it rankled me, like fingernails scraping on bones. The investigation into Tommy Tomm's murder must not be going well. 'Nothing yet,' I said. Then I lied to her, a little. 'I was up most of the night working, but nothing to show yet.'

She answered me with a swear word. 'That's not good enough, Harry. I need answers, and I need them yesterday.'

'I'll get to it as quick as I can.'

'Get to it faster,' she snarled. She was angry. Not that this was unusual for Murphy, but it told me that something else was going on. Some people panic when things get rough, harried. Some people fall apart. Murphy got pissed.

'Commissioner riding your back again?' City Police Commissioner Howard Fairweather used Murphy and her team as scapegoats for all sorts of unsolvable crimes that he had dumped in her lap. Fairweather was always lurking around, trying for an opportunity to make Murphy look bad, as though by doing so he could avoid being crucified himself.

'Like a winged monkey from *The Wizard of Oz*. Kind of makes you wonder who's leaning on *him* to get things done.' Her voice was sour as ripe lemons. I heard her drop an Alka-Seltzer into a glass of liquid. 'I'm serious, Harry. You get me those answers I need, and you get them to me fast. I need to know if this was sorcery, and, if so, how it was done and who could have done it. Names, places – I need to know everything.'

'It isn't that simple, Mur—'

'Then *make* it simple. How long before you can tell me? I need an estimate for the Commissioner's investigative committee in fifteen minutes or I might as well turn in my badge today.'

I grimaced. If I was able to get something out of Bianca, I might be able to help Murph on the investigation – but if it proved fruitless, I was going to have spent the entire evening doing nothing productive, and Murphy needed her answers now. Maybe I should have made a stay-awake potion. 'Does the committee work weekends?'

Murphy snorted. 'Are you kidding?'

'We'll have something by Monday, then.'

'You can have it figured out by then?' she asked.

'I don't know how much good it will do you, even if I can puzzle it out. I hope you've got more to go on than this.'

I heard her sigh into the phone and drink the fizzy drink. 'Don't let me down, Harry.'

Time to change the subject, before she pinned me down

and smelled me lying. I had no intention of doing the forbidden research if I could find a way out of doing it. 'No luck with Bianca?'

Another swear word. 'That bitch won't talk to us. Just smiles and nods and blows smoke, makes small talk, and crosses her legs. You should have seen Carmichael drooling.'

'Well. Tough to blame him, maybe. I hear she's cute. Listen, Murph. What if I just—'

'No, Harry. Absolutely not. You will not go over to the Velvet Room, you will *not* talk to that woman, and you will not get involved in this.'

'Lieutenant Murphy,' I drawled. 'A little jealous, are we?'

'Don't flatter yourself. You're a civilian, Dresden, even if you do have your investigator's license. If you get your ass laid out in the hospital or the morgue, it'll be me that suffers for it.'

'Murph, I'm touched.'

'I'll touch your head to a brick wall a few times if you cross me on this, Harry.' Her voice was sharp, vehement.

'Hey, wind down, Murph. If you don't want me to go, no problem.' Whups. A lie. She'd be all over that like a troll on a billy goat.

'You're a lousy liar, Harry. Godammit, I ought to take you down to lockup just to keep you from—'

'What?' I said, loudly, into the receiver. 'Murph, you're breaking up. I can't hear you. Damn phone again. Call me back.' Then I hung up on her.

Mister padded over to me and batted at my leg. He watched me with serious green eyes as I leaned down and unplugged the phone as it started to ring again.

'Okay, Mister. You hungry?'

I got us breakfast. Leftover steak sandwich for him,

SpaghettiOs heated up on the wood stove for me. I rationed out my last can of Coke, which Mister craves at least as badly as I do, and by the time I was done eating and drinking and petting, I was awake and thinking again — and getting ready for sundown.

Daylight savings time hadn't cut in yet, and dark would fall around six. I had about two hours to get set to go.

You might think you know a thing or two about vampires. Maybe some of the stuff you've heard is accurate. Likely, it's not. Either way, I wasn't looking forward to the prospect of going into Bianca's lair to demand information from her. I was going to assume that things were going to get ugly before all was said and done, just to make sure I didn't get caught with my staff down.

Wizardry is all about thinking ahead, about being prepared. Wizards aren't really superhuman. We just have a leg up on seeing things more clearly than other people, and being able to use the extra information we have for our benefit. Hell, the word *wizard* comes from the same root as *wise*. We know things. We aren't any stronger or faster than anyone else. We don't even have all that much more going in the mental department. But we're God-awful sneaky, and if we get the chance to get set for something, we can do some impressive things.

As a wizard, if you're ready to address a problem, then it's likely that you'll be able to come up with something that will let you deal with it. So, I got together all the things I thought I might need: I made sure my cane was polished and ready. I put my silver knife in a sheath that hung just under my left arm. I put the escape potion in its plastic squeeze-bottle into my duster's pocket. I put on my favorite talisman, a silver pentacle on a silver chain – it had been my mother's. My father had passed it down to me. And I put a small, folded piece of white cloth into my pocket.

I had several enchanted items around – or half-enchanted items, anyway. Carrying out a full enchantment is expensive and time-consuming, and I just couldn't afford to do it very much. We blue-collar wizards just have to sling a few spells out where we can and hope they don't go stale at the wrong time. I would have been a lot more comfortable if I had been carrying my blasting rod or my staff, but that would be like showing up at Bianca's door in a tank, walking in carrying a machine gun and a flamethrower, while announcing my intention to fight.

I had to maintain a fine balance between going in ready for trouble and going in asking for trouble.

Not that I was afraid, mind you. I didn't think Bianca would be willing to cause problems for a mortal wizard. Bianca wouldn't want to piss off the White Council by messing with me.

On the other hand, I wasn't exactly the White Council's favorite guy. They might even look the other way if Bianca decided to take me quietly out of the picture.

Careful, Harry, I warned myself. Don't get entirely para-noid. If you get like that, you'll be building your little apartment into a Basement of Solitude.

'What do you think?' I asked Mister, once I was decked out in what paraphernalia I was willing to carry.

Mister went to the door and batted at it insistently.

'Everyone's a critic. Fine, fine.' I sighed. I let him out, then I went out, got into my car and drove down to the Velvet Room in its expensive lakeside location.

Bianca runs her business out of a huge old mansion from the early days of the Roaring Twenties. Rumor has it that the infamous Al Capone had it built for one of his mistresses.

There was a gate with an iron fence and a security guard. I pulled the Beetle up into the little swath of driveway that began at the street and ended at the fence. There was a hiccoughing rattle from back in the engine as I brought the machine to a halt. I rolled down the window and stuck my head out, peering back. Something went *whoomph*, and then black smoke poured out from the bottom of the car and scuttled down the slope of the drive and into the street.

I winced. The engine gave an almost apologetic rattle and shuddered to its death. Great. Now I had no ride home. I got out of the Beetle, and stood mourning it for a moment.

The security guard on the other side of the gate was a blocky man, not overly tall but overly muscled and hiding it under an expensive suit. He studied me with attack-dog eyes, and then said, through the gate, 'Do you have an appointment?'

'No,' I told him. 'But I think Bianca will want to see me.'

He looked unimpressed. 'I'm sorry,' he said. 'Bianca is out for the evening.'

Things are never simple anymore. I shrugged at him, folded my arms, and leaned on the hood of the Beetle. 'Suit yourself. I'll just stay until a tow truck comes by, then, until I can get this thing out of the drive for you.'

He stared at me, his eyes narrowed down to tiny slits with the effort of thinking. Eventually, the thoughts got to his brain, got processed, and sent back out with a message to 'pass the buck'. 'I'll call your name in,' he said.

'Good man,' I approved. 'You won't be sorry.'

'Name,' he growled.

'Harry Dresden.'

If he recognized my name, it didn't show on his face. He glared at me and the Beetle then walked a few paces off, lifting a cellular phone from his pocket and to his ear.

I listened. Listening isn't hard to do. No one has practice at it, nowadays, but you can train yourself to pay attention to your senses if you work at it long enough.

'I've got a guy down here says that Bianca will want to talk to him,' the guard said. 'Says his name is Harry Dresden.' He was silent for a moment. I couldn't quite make out the buzz of the other voice, other than that it was female. 'Uh-huh,' he said. He glanced back at me. 'Uh-huh,' he said again. 'Sure. Sure, I will. Of course, ma'am.'

I reached in through the window of the Beetle and got out my cane. I rested it on the concrete beside my boots and tapped it a few times, as though impatient.

The guard turned back to me, leaned over to one side, and pushed a button somewhere. The gate buzzed and clicked open.

'Come on in, Mr Dresden,' he said. 'I can have someone come tow your car, if you like.'

'Super,' I told him. I gave him the name of the wrecker Mike has a deal with and told him to tell the guy that it was Harry's car again. Fido the Guard dutifully noted this down, writing on a small notebook he drew from a pocket. While he did, I walked past him toward the house, clicking my cane on the concrete with every pace.

'Stop,' he told me, his voice calm and confident. People don't speak with that kind of absolute authority unless they have a gun in their hands. I stopped.

'Put the cane down,' he told me, 'And put your arms up. You are to be searched before you are allowed inside.'

I sighed, did what he said, and let him pat me down. I didn't turn around to face him, but I could smell the metal of his gun. He found the knife and took it. His fingers brushed the nape of my neck, felt the chain there.

'What's this?' he said.

'Pentacle,' I told him.

'Let me see it. Use one hand.'

I used my left to draw it out of my shirt and show it to him, a silver five-pointed star within a circle, all smooth geometry. He grunted, and said, 'Fine.' The search went on, and he found the plastic squeeze-bottle. He took it out of my pocket, opened it, and sniffed at it.

'What's this?'

'A health cola,' I told him.

'Smells like shit,' he said, capped it, and put it back in my pocket.

'What about my cane?'

'Returned when you leave,' he said.

Damn. My knife and my cane had been my only physical lines of defense. Anything else I did would have to rely wholly upon magic and that could be dicey on the best of days. It was enough to rattle me.

Of course, Fido the Guard had missed a couple of things. First, he'd overlooked the clean white handkerchief in my pocket. Second, he'd passed me on with my pentacle still upon my neck. He probably figured that since it wasn't a crucifix or a cross, that I couldn't use it to keep Bianca away from me.

Which wasn't true. Vampires (and other such creatures) don't respond to symbols as such. They respond to the power that accompanies an act of faith. I couldn't ward off a vampire mosquito with my faith in the Almighty – He and I have just never seemed to connect. But the pentacle was a symbol of magic itself, and I had plenty of faith in that.

And, of course, Fido had overlooked my getaway potion. Bianca really ought to trust her guards with more awareness of the supernatural and what sort of things to look for.

The house itself was elegant, very roomy, with the high ceilings and the broad floors that they just don't make anymore. A well-groomed young woman with a short, straight haircut greeted me in the enormous entry hall. I was passing polite to her, and she showed me to a library, its walls lined with old books in leather bindings, similar to the leather-cushioned chairs around the enormous old dogfoot table in the room's center.

I took a seat and waited. And waited. And waited. More than half an hour went by before Bianca finally arrived.

She came into the room like a candle burning with a cold, clear flame. Her hair was a burnished shade of auburn that was too dark to cast back any ruddy highlights, but did anyway. Her eyes were dark, clear, her complexion flawlessly smooth and elegantly graced with cosmetics. She was not a tall woman, but shapely, wearing a black dress with a plunging neckline and a slash in one side that showed off a generous portion of pale thigh. Black gloves covered her hands to above the elbows, and her three-hundred-dollar shoes were a study in high-heeled torture devices. She looked too good to be true.

'Mister Dresden,' she greeted me. 'This is an unexpected pleasure.'

I rose when she entered the room. 'Madame Bianca,' I replied, nodding to her. 'We meet at last. Hearsay neglected to mention how lovely you are.'

She laughed, lips shaping the sounds, head falling back just enough to show a flash of pale throat. 'A gentleman, they said. I see that they were correct. It is a charmingly passé thing to be a gentleman in this country.'

'You and I are of another world,' I said.

She approached me and extended her hand, a motion oozing feminine grace. I bowed over her hand briefly, taking it and brushing my lips against the back of her glove. 'Do you really think I'm beautiful, Mister Dresden?' she asked me.

'As lovely as a star, Madame.'

'Polite and a pretty one, too,' she murmured. Her eyes flickered over me, from head to toe, but even she avoided meeting gazes with me, whether from a desire to avoid inadvertently directing her power at me, or being on the receiving end of mine, I couldn't tell. She continued into the room, and stopped beside one of the comfortable chairs. As a matter of course, I stepped around the table, and drew out the chair for her, seating her. She crossed her legs, in that dress, in those shoes, and made it look good. I blinked for just a moment, then returned to my own seat.

'So, Mister Dresden. What brings you to my humble house? Care for an evening of entertainment? I quite assure you that you will never have another experience like it.' She placed her hands in her lap, smiling at me.

I smiled at her, and put one hand into my pocket, onto the white handkerchief. 'No, thank you. I came to talk.'

Her lips parted in a silent *ah*. 'I see. About what, if I might ask?'

'About Jennifer Stanton. And her murder.'

I had all of a second's warning. Bianca's eyes narrowed, then widened, like those of a cat about to spring. Then she was coming at me over the table, faster than a breath, her arms extended toward my throat.

I toppled over backward in my chair. Even though I'd started to move first, it almost wasn't enough to get away from her reaching nails in time. One grazed my throat with a hot sensation of pain, and she kept coming, following me down to the floor, those rich lips drawn back from sharp fangs.

I jerked my hand out of my pocket, and flapped open my white hanky at her, releasing the image of sunlight I'd been storing for use in potions. It lit up the room for a moment, brilliant.

The light smashed into Bianca, hurled her back across the old table into one of the shelves, and tore pieces of flesh away from her like bits of rotten meat being peeled off a carcass by a sandblaster. She screamed, and the flesh around her mouth sloughed and peeled away like a snake's scales.

I had never seen a real vampire before. I would have time to be terrified later. I took in the details as I tugged my talisman off over my neck. It had a batlike face, horrid and ugly, the head too big for its body. Gaping, hungry jaws. Its shoulders were hunched and powerful. Membranous wings stretched between the joints of its almost skeletal arms. Flabby black breasts hung before it, spilling out of the black dress that no longer looked feminine. Its eyes were wide, black, and staring, and a kind of leathery, slimy hide covered its flesh, like an inner tube lathered with Vaseline, though there were tiny holes corroded in it by the sunlight I had brought with me.

It recovered quickly, crouching and spreading long arms that ended in claw-tipped fingers to either side with a hiss of rage.

I drew my pentacle into my fist, raised it like every vampire slayer you ever saw does it, and said, 'Jesus Christ, lady. I just came here to talk.'

The vampire hissed and started toward me with a gangling, weirdly graceful step. Its clawed feet were still wearing the three-hundred-dollar black pumps.

'Back,' I said, taking a step towards it, myself. The pentacle began to burn with the cold, clear light of applied will and belief — my faith, if you will, that it could turn such a monster aside.

It hissed, and turned its face aside, lifting its membranous arms to shield its eyes from the light. It took one step back, and then another, until its hunched back was pressed against a wall of books.

Now what did I do? I wasn't going to go try to put a stake through her heart. But if I lowered my will, she might come at me again — and I didn't think I had anything, even the quickest evocations, that I could get out of my mouth before she tore it off of my head. And even if I got past her, she probably had mortal lackies, like the security guard at the gate, who would be happy to kill me if they saw me trashing their mistress.

'You killed her,' the vampire snarled, and its voice was exactly the same, sultry and feminine, even though twisted by rage and coming from that horrid mouth. It was unsettling. 'You killed Jennifer. She was *mine*, mageling.'

'Look,' I told her. 'I didn't come here for any of this. And the police know I'm here. Save yourself a lot of trouble. Sit down, talk with me, and then we'll both go away happy.

Christ, Bianca, do you think that if I'd killed Jennifer and Tommy Tomm that I'd just be waltzing in here like this?'

'You expect me to believe that you didn't? You will never leave this house alive.'

I was feeling angry myself, and frightened. Christ, even the *vampire* thought I was the bad guy. 'What'll it take to convince you that I didn't do it?'

Black, bottomless eyes stared at me through the burning fire of my faith. I could feel some sort of power there, trying to get at me, and held off by the force of my will, just as the creature itself was. The vampire snarled, 'Lower the amulet, wizard.'

'If I do, are you going to come at my throat again?'

'If you do not, I most certainly will.'

Shaky logic, that. I tried to work through the situation from her point of view. She had been scared when I showed up. She'd had me searched and divested of weapons as best she could. If she thought that I was Jennifer Stanton's murderer, would the mere mention of that name have brought that sudden violence out of her? I began to get that sinking feeling you get when you realize that not everything is as it appears.

'If I put this down,' I told her, 'I want your word that you'll sit down and talk to me. I swear to you, by fire and wind, that I had nothing to do with her death.'

The vampire hissed at me, shielding its eyes from the light with one taloned hand. 'Why should I believe you?'

'Why should I believe *you*?' I countered.

Yellowed fangs showed in its mouth. 'If you do not trust my word, wizard, then how can I trust yours?'

'Then you give it?'

The vampire stiffened, and though its voice was still harsh with rage and pain, still sexy as a silk shirt without any buttons, I thought I heard the ring of truth in its words. 'You have my promise. Lower your talisman, and we will talk.'

Time for another calculated risk. I tossed the pentacle onto the table. The cold light drained away, leaving the room lit by mere electricity once more.

The vampire slowly lowered its arms, blinking its too-big eyes at me and then at the pentacle upon the table. A long, pink tongue flickered out nervously over its jaws and lower face, then slipped back into its mouth. It was surprised, I realized. Surprised that I had done it.

My heart was racing, but I forced my fear back down out of my forebrain and into the background. Vampires are like demons, like wolves, like sharks. You don't let them think that you are potential food and get their respect at the same time. The vampire's true appearance was grotesque – but it wasn't as bad as some of the things I had seen in my day. Some demons were a lot worse, and some of the Elder Things could rip your mind apart just by letting you look at them. I regarded the creature with a level gaze.

'How about it?' I said. 'Let's talk. The longer we sit around staring at one another, the longer Jennifer's killer stays free.'

The vampire stared at me for a moment more. Then it shuddered, drawing its wing membranes about itself. Black slime turned into patches of pale, perfect flesh that spread over the vampire's dark skin like a growth of fungus. The flabby black breasts swelled into softly rounded, rosy-tipped perfection once more.

Bianca stood before me a moment later, settling her dress

back into modesty again, her arms crossed over her as though she was cold, her back stiff and her eyes angry. She was no less beautiful than she had been a few moments before, not a line or a curve any different. But for me, the glamour had been ruined. She still had the same eyes, dark and fathomless and alien. I would always remember what she truly looked like, beneath her flesh mask.

I stooped and picked up my chair, righting it. Then I went around the table, turned my back on her, and stood hers up as well. Then I held it out for her, just as I had when I had entered the room.

She stared at me for a long minute. Some expression flickered across her face. She was disconcerted by my apparent lack of concern about the way she looked, and it told. Then she lifted her chin, proud, and settled gracefully into the chair again, regal as any queen, every line stiff with anger. The Old World rules of courtesy and hospitality were holding – but for how long?

I returned to my seat and leaned over to pick up my white handkerchief, toying with it. Bianca's angry eyes flickered down to it, and once again she repeated the nervous gesture of licking her teeth and lips, though this time her tongue looked human.

'So. Tell me about Jennifer and Tommy Tomm,' I said.

She shook her head, almost sneering. 'I can tell you what I told the police. I don't know who could have killed them.'

'Come on, Bianca. We don't have to hide things from one another. We're not a part of the mortal world.'

Her eyebrows slanted down, revealing more anger. 'No. You're the only one in the city with the kind of skill required to cast that sort of spell. If you didn't do it, I have no idea who else could have.'

'You don't have any enemies? Anyone who might have been wanting to make an impression on you?'

A bitter little line appeared at the corner of her lips, something that was not quite a smile. 'Of course. But none of them could have managed what happened to Tommy and Jenny.' She drummed her fingernails over the tabletop, leaving little score marks in the wood. 'I don't let any enemies that dangerous run around alive. At least, not for long.'

I settled back in my chair, frowning, and did my damnedest not to let her see how scared I was. 'How did you know Tommy Tomm?'

She shrugged, her shoulders gleaming like porcelain, and just as brittle. 'You may have thought he was just a bruiser for Johnny Marcone, Mister Dresden. But Tommy was a very gentle and considerate man, underneath. He was always good to his women. He treated them like real people.' Her gaze shifted from side to side, not lifting. 'Like human beings. I wouldn't take on a client if I thought he wouldn't be a gentleman, but Tommy was better than most. I met him years ago, elsewhere. I always made sure he had someone to take care of him when he wanted an evening of company.'

'You sent Jennifer out to him that night?'

She nodded, her expression bleak. Her nails drummed the tabletop again, gouging out more wood.

'Was there anyone else he saw on a regular basis? Maybe someone who would have talked to him, known what was going on in his life?'

Bianca shook her head. 'No,' she said. But then she frowned.

I just watched her, and absently tossed the handkerchief on the tabletop. Her eyes flicked to it, then up to mine.

I didn't flinch. I met her bottomless gaze and quirked my mouth up in a little smile, as though I had something more, and worse, to pull out of my hat if she wanted to come after me again. I saw her anger, her rage, and for just a moment I got a peek inside, saw the source of it. She was furious that I had seen her true form, horrified and embarrassed that I had stripped her disguise away and seen the creature beneath. And she was afraid that I could take away even her mask, forever, with my power.

More than anything else, Bianca wanted to be beautiful. And tonight, I had destroyed her illusion. I had rattled her gilded little world. She sure as hell wasn't going to let me forget that.

She shuddered and jerked her eyes away, furious and frightened at the same time, before I could see any deeper into her – or she into me. 'If I had not given you my word, Dresden,' she whispered, 'I would kill you this instant.'

'That would be unfortunate,' I said. I kept my voice hard. 'You should know the risks in a wizard's death curse. You've got something to lose, Bianca. And even if you could take me out, you can bet your pretty ass I'd be dragging you into hell with me.'

She stiffened, then turned her head to one side, and let her fingers go limp. It was a silent, bitter surrender. She didn't move quickly enough for me to miss seeing a tear streak down one cheek.

I'd made the vampire cry. Great. I felt like a real superhero. Harry Dresden, breaker of monsters' hearts.

'There may be one person who might know something,' she said, her lovely voice dull, flat, lifeless. 'I had a woman who worked for me. Linda Randall. She and Jennifer went out on calls together, when customers wanted that sort of thing. They were close.'

'Where is she now?' I asked.

'She's working as a driver for someone. Some rich couple who wanted a servant that would do more than windows. She wasn't the type I usually keep around in any case. I think Jennifer had her phone number. I can have someone fetch it for you, Mister Dresden.' She said my name as though it were something bitter and poisonous that she wanted to spit out.

'Thank you. That would be very kind.' I kept my tone carefully formal, neutral. Formality and a good bluff were all that was keeping her from my throat.

She remained quiet, controlling her evident emotions, before she started to look up again, at last. Her eyes froze, then widened when they came to my throat. Her expression went perfectly, inhumanly still.

I grew tense. Not just tense, but steel-tight, wire-bound, spring-coiled. I was out of tricks and weapons. If she came after me now, I wasn't going to get the chance to defend myself. There was no way I would be able to drink the potion before she tore me apart. I gripped the arms of my chair hard, to keep myself from bolting. Do not show fear. Do not run away. It would only make her chase me, snap her instincts into the reaction of pursing the prey.

'You're bleeding, Mister Dresden,' she whispered.

I lifted my hand, slowly, to my throat, where her nails had scored me, earlier. My fingertips came away slick with my own blood.

Bianca kept on staring. Her tongue flickered around her mouth again. 'Cover it,' she whispered. A strange, mewling sound came out of her mouth. '*Cover* it, Dresden.'

I picked up my handkerchief, and pressed it over my throat. Bianca blinked her eyes closed, slowly, and then turned away, half-hunched over her stomach. She didn't stand up.

'Go,' she told me. 'Go now. Paula's coming. I'll send her down to the gate with the phone number in a little while.'

I walked toward the door, but then stopped, glancing back at her. There was a sort of horrid fascination to it, to knowing what was beneath the alluring exterior, the flesh mask, but seeing it twist and writhe with need.

'Go,' Bianca whimpered. Fury, hunger, and some emotion I couldn't even begin to fathom made her voice stretched out, thinner. 'Go. And do not think that I will not remember this night. Do not think that I will not make you regret it.'

The door to the library opened, and the straight-haired young woman who had greeted me earlier entered the room. She gave me a passing glance, then walked past me, kneeling at Bianca's side. Paula, I presumed.

Paula murmured something too soft to hear, gently brushing Bianca's hair back from her face with one hand. Then she unbuttoned the sleeve of her blouse, rolled it up past her elbow, and pressed her wrist to Bianca's mouth.

I had a good view of what happened. Bianca's tongue flashed out, long and pink and sticky, smearing Paula's wrist with shining saliva. Paula shuddered at the touch, her breath coming quicker. Her nipples stiffened beneath the thin fabric of the blouse, and she let her head fall slowly backwards. Her eyes were glazed over with a narcotic langour, like a junkie who had just shot up.

Bianca's fangs extended and slashed open Paula's pale,

pretty skin. Blood welled. Bianca's tongue began to flash in and out, faster than could really be seen, lapping the blood up as quickly as it appeared. Her dark eyes were narrowed, distant. Paula was gasping and moaning in pleasure, her entire body shivering.

I felt a little sick and withdrew step by step, not turning my back on the scene. Paula toppled slowly to the floor, writhing her way toward unconsciousness with an evident glee. Bianca followed her down, unladylike now, a creature of bestial hunger. She crouched over the supine woman, and in the hunch of her pale shoulders I could see the batlike thing beneath the flesh mask, lapping up Paula's blood.

I got out of there, fast, shutting the door behind me. My heart was hammering, too quickly. The scene with Paula might have aroused me, if I hadn't seen what was underneath Bianca's mask. Instead, it only made me sick to my stomach, afraid. The woman had given herself to that thing, as quickly and as willingly as any woman to her lover.

The saliva, some part of me rationalized, desperate to latch on to something cold and logical and detached. The saliva was probably narcotic, perhaps even addictive. It would explain Paula's behavior, the need to have more of her drug. But I wondered if Paula would have been so eager, had she known Bianca's true face.

Now I understood why the White Council was so hardnosed with vampires. If they could get that kind of control over a mortal, what would happen if they could get their hooks into a wizard? If they could addict a wizard to them as thoroughly as Bianca had the girl I'd just seen? Surely, it wasn't possible.

But if it wasn't, why would the Council be so nervous about them?

Do not think I will not make you regret it, she had said.

I felt cold as I hurried down the dark driveway toward the gate.

Fido the security guard was waiting for me at the front gate, and passed back my knife and my cane without a word. A tow truck was out front, latching itself to the Beetle. I put one hand on the cold metal of the gate and kept the other, with its handkerchief, pressed to my throat, as I watched George the towtruck guy work. He recognized me and waved, flashing a grin that showed the white teeth in his dark face. I nodded back. I wasn't up to answering the smile.

A few minutes later, the guard's cellular phone beeped at him. He withdrew several paces, repeated several affirmatives, then took a notebook from his pocket, writing something down. He put the phone away and walked back over to me, offering me the piece of paper.

'What's this?' I said.

'The phone number you were looking for. And a message.'

I glanced at the paper, but avoided reading it just then. 'I thought Bianca was going to send Paula down with it.'

He didn't say anything. But his jaw tightened, and I saw his eyes flick toward the house, where his mistress was. He swallowed. Paula wasn't coming out of the house, and Fido was afraid.

I took the paper. I kept my hand from shaking as I looked at it.

On it was a phone number. And a single word: *Regret*.

I folded the piece of paper in half and put it away into

the pocket of my duster. Another enemy. Super. At least with my hands in my pockets, Fido couldn't see them shaking. Maybe I should have listened to Murphy. Maybe I should have stayed home and played with some nice, safe, forbidden black magic instead.

10

I departed Bianca's place in George's loaner, a wood-panel
Studebaker that grumbled and growled and squealed everywhere it went. I stopped at a pay phone, a short distance
from the house, and called Linda Randall's number.

The phone rang several times before a quiet, dusky
contralto answered, 'Beckitts', this is Linda.'

'Linda Randall?' I asked.

'Mmmm,' she answered. She had a furry, velvety voice,
something tactile. 'Who's this?'

'My name is Harry Dresden. I was wondering if I could
talk to you.'

'Harry who?' she asked.

'Dresden. I'm a private investigator.'

She laughed, the sound rich enough to roll around naked
in. 'Investigating my privates, Mr Dresden? I like you
already.'

I coughed. 'Ah, yes. Ms Randall—'

'Miss,' she said, cutting in. 'Miss Randall. I'm not occupied. At the moment.'

'Miss Randall,' I amended. 'I'd like to ask you some
questions about Jennifer Stanton, if I could.'

Silence on the other end of the line. I could hear some
sounds in the background, a radio playing, perhaps, and a
recorded voice talking about white zones and red zones and
loading and unloading of vehicles.

'Miss Randall?'

'No,' she said.

'It won't take long. And I assure you that you aren't the subject of anything I'm doing. If you could just give me a few moments of your time.'

'No,' she told me. 'I'm on duty, and will be the rest of the night. I don't have time for this.'

'Jennifer Stanton was a friend of yours. She's been murdered. If there's anything you could tell me that might help—'

She cut me off again. 'There isn't,' she said. 'Good-bye, Mr Dresden.'

The line went dead.

I scowled at the phone, frustrated. That was it, then. I had gone through all the preparation, the face-off with Bianca, and possible future trouble for nothing.

No way, I thought. No way in hell.

Bianca had said that Linda Randall was working as a driver for someone, the Beckitts, I presumed, whoever they were. I'd recognized the voice in the background as a recorded message that played outside the concourses at O'Hare airport. So she was in a car at the airport, maybe waiting to pick up the Beckitts, and definitely not there for long.

With no time to lose, I kicked the wheezing old Studebaker into gear and drove to O'Hare. It was far easier to blow off someone over the phone than it was to do it in person. There were several concourses, but I had to trust to luck – luck to guide me to the right one, and luck to get me there before *Miss* I-am-not-occupied Randall had the opportunity to pick up her employers and leave. And a little more luck to keep the Studebaker running all the way to O'Hare.

The Studebaker did make it all the way there, and on the second concourse I came across a silver baby limo, idling in a parking zone. The interior was darkened, so I couldn't see inside very well. It was a Friday evening, and the place was busy, business folk in their sober suits returning home from long trips about the country. Cars continually purred in and out of the semicircular drive. A uniformed cop was directing traffic, keeping people from doing brainless things like parking in the middle of one of the traffic lanes in order to load up the car.

I swerved the old Studebaker into a parking place, racing a Volvo for it and winning by dint of driving the older and heavier vehicle and having the more suicidal attitude. I kept an eye on the silver limo as I got out of the car and strode over to a bank of pay phones. I plopped my quarter in, and once more dialed the number provided by Bianca.

The phone rang. In the silver limo, someone stirred.

'Beckitts', this is Linda,' she purred.

'Hello, Linda,' I said. 'This is Harry Dresden again.'

I could almost hear her smirk. There was a flicker of light from inside the car, the silhouette of a woman's face, then the orange glow of a cigarette being lit. 'I thought I told you I didn't want to talk to you, Mr Dresden.'

'I like women who play hard to get.'

She laughed that delicious laugh. I could see her head move in the darkened car when she did. 'I'm getting harder to get by the second. Good-bye again.' She hung up on me.

I smiled, hung up the phone, walked over to the limo, and rapped on the window.

It buzzed down, and a woman in her mid-twenties arched an eyebrow at me. She had beautiful eyes the color of rain clouds, a little too much eye shadow, and brilliant scarlet lipstick on her cupid's-bow lips. Her hair was a medium brown, drawn back into a tight braid that made her cheeks look almost sharp, severe, except for her forelocks, which hung down close to her eyes in insolent disarray. She had a predatory look to her, harsh, sharp. She wore a crisp white shirt, grey slacks, and held a lit cigarette in one hand. The smoke curled up around my nose, and I exhaled, trying to push it away.

She looked me up and down, frankly assessing. 'Don't tell me. Harry Dresden.'

'I really need to talk to you, Miss Randall. It won't take long.'

She glanced at her watch and then at the terminal doors. Then back up at me. 'Well. You've got me cornered, don't you? I'm at your mercy.' Her lips quirked. She took a drag of her cigarette. 'And I like a man who just won't stop.'

I cleared my throat again. The woman was attractive, but not unduly so. Yet there was something about her that revved my engines, something about the way she held her head or shaped her words that bypassed my brain and went straight to my hormones. Best to head directly to the point and minimize my chances of looking moronic. 'How did you know Jennifer Stanton?'

She looked up at me through long lashes. 'Intimately.'

Ahem. 'You, uh. Worked for Bianca with her.'

Linda blew more smoke. 'That prissy little bitch. Yes, I worked with Jen. We were even roommates for a while. Shared a bed.' She wrapped her lips around the last word, drawing it out with a little tremor that dripped wicked, secret laughter.

'Did you know Tommy Tomm?' I asked.

'Oh, sure. Fantastic in bed.' She lowered her eyes and

shifted on the car's seat, lowering one of her hands out of sight, and making me wonder where it had gone. 'He was a regular customer. Maybe twice a month Jen and I would go over to his place, have a little party.' She leaned toward me. 'He could do things to a woman that would turn her into a real animal, Harry Dresden. You know what I mean? Growling and snarling. In heat.'

She was driving me crazy. That voice of hers inspired the kinds of dreams you wish you could remember more clearly in the morning. Her expression promised to show me things that you don't talk about with other people, if I would give her half a chance. Your job, Harry. Think about your job.

Some days I really hate my job.

'When was the last time you talked to her?'

She took another drag, and this time I saw a small shake to her fingers, one she quickly hid. Just not quickly enough. She was nervous. Nervous enough to be shaking, and now I could see what she was up to. She was wearing the alley-cat mask, appealing to my glands instead of my brain, and trying to distract me with it, trying to keep me from finding something out.

I'm not inhuman. I can be distracted by a pretty face, or body, like any other youngish man. Linda Randall was damned good at playing the part. But I do not like to be made the fool.

So, Miss Sex Goddess. What are you hiding?

I cleared my throat, and asked, mildly, 'When was the last time you spoke to Jennifer Stanton, Miss Randall?'

She narrowed her eyes at me. She wasn't dumb, whatever else she was. She'd seen me reading her, seeing through her pretense. The flirting manner vanished. 'Are you a cop?' she demanded.

I shook my head. 'Scout's honor. I'm just trying to find out what happened to her.'

'Dammit,' she said, softly. She flicked the butt of the cigarette out onto the concrete and blew out a mouthful of smoke. 'Look. I tell you anything and see a cop coming around, I never saw you before. Got it?'

I nodded.

'I talked to Jen on Wednesday evening. She called me. It was Tommy's birthday. She wanted to get together again.' Her mouth twisted. 'Sort of a reunion.'

I glanced about and leaned down closer to her. 'Did you?'

Her eyes were roving about now, nervous, like a cat who has found herself shut into a small room. 'No,' she said. 'I had to work. I wanted to, but—'

'Did she say anything unusual? Anything that might have made you suspect she was in danger?'

She shook her head again. 'No, nothing. We hadn't talked much for a while. I didn't see her as much after I split from the Velvet Room.'

I frowned at her. 'Do you know what else she was doing? Anything she might have been involved with that could have gotten her hurt?'

She shook her head. 'No, no. Nothing like that. That wasn't her style. She was sweet. A lot of girls get like— They get pretty jaded, Mr Dresden. But it never really touched her. She made people feel better about themselves somehow.' She looked away. 'I could never do that. All I did was get them off.'

'There's nothing you can tell me? Nothing you can think of?'

She pressed her lips together and shook her head. She

shook her head, and she lied to me as she did it. I was just sure of it. She was closing in, tightening up, and if there was nothing to tell me, she wouldn't be trying to hide it. She must know something – unless she was just shutting down because I'd stomped all over her feelings, as I had Bianca's. Either way, she wasn't telling me anything else.

I tightened my fist, frustrated. If Linda Randall had no information for me, I was at a dead end. And I'd romped all over another woman's feelings – two in one night. You are on a roll, Dresden. Even if one of them had been something not-human.

'Why?' I asked her, the words slipping out before I thought about them. 'Why the slut act?'

She looked up at me again, and smirked. I saw the subtle shifting in her, magnifying that sort of animal appeal she had, once more, as she had been doing when I first approached her – but it didn't hide the self-loathing in her eyes. I looked away, quickly, before I had to see any more of it. I got the feeling that I didn't want to see Linda Randall's soul. 'Because it's what I do, Mr Dresden. For some people it's drugs. Booze. For me, orgasms. Sex. Passion. Just another addict. City's full of them.' She glanced aside. 'Next best thing to love. And it keeps me in work. Excuse me.'

She swung open the door. I took a quick step back and out of her way as she moved to the back of the limo, long legs taking long steps, and opened the trunk.

A tall couple, both wearing glasses and dressed in stylish grey business clothes, emerged from the terminal and approached the limo. They had the look of lifestyle professionals, the kind that have a career and no kids, with enough money and time to spend on making themselves look good – a NordicTrack couple. He was carrying an overnight bag over his shoulder and a small suitcase in one hand, while she bore only a briefcase. They wore no jewelry, not even watches or wedding rings. Odd.

The man slung the luggage items into the limo's trunk and looked from Linda to me. Linda avoided his eyes. He tried to speak quietly enough not to be heard, but I have good ears.

'Who's this?' he asked. His voice had a strained note to it.

'Just a friend, Mr Beckitt. A guy I used to see,' she answered him.

More lies. More interesting.

I looked across the limo to the woman, presumably Mrs Beckitt. She regarded me with a calm face, entirely void of emotion. It was a little spooky. She had the look I'd seen in films, on the faces of prisoners released from the German *stalags* at the end of World War II. Empty. Numb. Dead, and just didn't know it yet.

Linda opened the back door and let Mr and Mrs Beckitt into the car. Mrs Beckitt briefly put a hand on Linda's waist in passing, a gesture that was too intimate and possessive for the hired help. I saw Linda shiver, then close the door. She walked back around the car to me.

'Get out of here,' she said, quietly. 'I don't want to get in any trouble with my boss.'

I reached for her hand, grabbed it, and held it between both of mine, as an old lover might, I supposed. My business card was pressed between our palms. 'My card. If you think of anything else, give me a call. Okay?'

She turned away from me without answering, but the card vanished into a pocket before she got back into the limo.

Mrs Beckitt's dead eyes watched me through the side window as the limo went by me. It was my turn to shiver. Like I said, spooky.

I went on into the airport. The monitors displaying flight times flickered to fuzz when I walked by. I went to one of the cafés inside, sat down, and ordered myself a cup of coffee. I had to pay for it with change. Most of my money had gone into paying off last month's rent and into the love potion I'd let Bob talk me into making. Money. I needed to get to work on Monica Sells's case, finding her husband. I didn't want to get out of hot water with the White Council only to lose my office and apartment because I couldn't pay the bills.

I sipped coffee and tried to organize my thoughts. I had two areas of concern. The most important was finding who had killed Tommy Tomm and Jennifer Stanton. Not only to catch the killer before any more corpses turned up, but because if I didn't, the White Council would probably use the opportunity to have me put to death.

And, while tracking down killers and avoiding execution squads, I had to do some work for someone who would pay me. Tonight's excursion wasn't something I could charge Murphy for – she'd have my ass in a sling if she knew I was running around asking questions, poking my nose in where it shouldn't be. So, if I wanted money from Chicago P.D., I would have to spend time doing the research Murphy wanted – the black-magic research that could get me killed all by itself.

Or, I could work on Monica Sells's missing husband case. I thought I had that one pretty well pegged down, but it wouldn't hurt to get it fleshed out fully. I could spend time working on it, fill out the hours on the retainer, maybe even get a few more added on. That appealed to me a lot more than trying to work out some black magic.

So, I could follow up on the lead Toot-toot had given me. There'd been pizza delivered out to the Lake Providence home that night. Time to talk to the deliveryman, if possible.

I left the café, went out to the pay phones, and dialed directory assistance. There was only one place near the Lake Providence address that delivered pizza. I got the number and dialed through.

'Pizza 'Spress,' someone with his mouth full said. 'What'll it be tonight?'

'Hey there,' I said. 'I wonder if you can help me out. I'm looking for the driver who took an order out to an address on Wednesday night.' I told him the address, and asked if I could speak to the driver.

'Another one,' he snorted. 'Sure, hang on. Jack just got in from a run.' The voice on the other end of the line called out to someone, and a minute later the high baritone of a young man spoke tentatively into my ear.

'H-hello?'

'Hello,' I answered. 'Are you the driver who took pizza to—'

'*Look*,' he said, his voice exasperated and nervous. 'I *said* I was sorry already. It won't happen again.'

I blinked for a minute, off balance. 'Sorry for what?'

'Jeezus,' he said. I heard him move across a room, with a lot of music and loud talk in the background, and then the background noise cut off, as though he had stepped into another room and shut the door behind him. 'Look,' he said in a half whine. 'I told you I'm not gonna say anything to anyone. I was only looking. You can't blame me, right? No one answered the door, what was I supposed to do?' His voice cracked in the middle of his sentences. 'Hell of a party, but hey. That's your business. Right?'

I struggled to keep up with the kid. 'What, exactly, did you see, Jack?' I asked him.

'No one's face,' he assured me, his voice growing more nervous. He gave a jittery little laugh and tried to joke. 'Better things to look at than faces, right? I mean, I don't give a damn what you do in your own house. Or your friends, or whoever. Don't worry about me. Never going to say a thing. Next time I'll just leave the pizza and run a tab, right?'

Friends, plural. Interesting. The kid was awfully nervous. He must have gotten an eyeful. But I had a gut instinct that he was hiding something else, keeping it back.

'What else?' I asked him. I kept my voice calm and neutral. 'You saw something else. What was it?'

'None of my business,' he said, instantly. 'None of my business. Look, I gotta get off this line. We have to keep it open for orders. It's Friday night, we're busy as hell.'

'What,' I said, separating my words, keeping them clipped, 'else?'

'Oh, shit,' he breathed, his voice shaking. 'Look, I wasn't with that guy. Didn't know anything about him. I didn't tell him you were having an orgy out there. Honest. Jeezus, mister, I don't want any trouble.'

Victor Sells seemed to have a real good idea of how to party – and of how to frighten teenagers. 'One more question, and I'll let this go,' I told him. 'Who was it you saw? Tell me about him.'

'I don't know. I don't know him, didn't recognize him. Some guy, with a camera, that's all. I went around the back of the house to try the back door, got up on your deck, and just saw inside. I didn't keep on looking. But he was up there, all in black, with this camera, taking pictures.' He paused as someone pounded on the door he had closed earlier. 'Oh, God, I have to go, mister. I don't know you. I don't know nothing.' And then there was a scrambling of feet, and he hung up the phone.

I hung up the phone myself and ambled back to George's loaner. I worked out the details I had just learned on the way back to my apartment.

Someone else had called Pizza 'Spress, evidently just before I had. Someone else had gone asking after the pizza boy. Who?

Why, Victor Sells, of course. Tracing down people who might have information about him, his possible presence in the lake house. Victor Sells, who had been having some sort of get-together out there that night. Maybe he'd been drunk, or one of his guests had, and ordered the pizza – and now Victor was trying to cover his tracks.

Which implied that Victor knew someone was looking for him. Hell, as far as I knew, he'd been *in* the house when I'd gone out there last night. This made things a lot more interesting. A missing man who doesn't want to be found could get dangerous if someone came snooping after him.

And a photographer? Someone lurking around outside of windows and taking pictures? I rummaged in my duster pocket and felt the round plastic film canister. That explained where the canister had come from, at any rate. But why would someone be out there at the house, taking pictures of Victor and his friends? Maybe because Monica had hired someone else, a PI, without telling me. Maybe just a neighbor with the hots for taking dirty pictures. No way to tell, really. More mysteries.

I pulled the Studebaker into my drive and killed the engine. I tallied the score for the evening. Enigmas: lots. Harry: zero.

My investigation for Monica Sells had netted me one husband throwing wild parties in his beach house after losing his job, and working hard not to be found. Probably an advanced case of male menopause. Monica didn't seem to be the kind of woman who would take such a thing with good grace – more like the kind who would close her eyes and call me a liar if I told her the truth. But at least it merited a little more looking into – I could log a few more hours in on the case, maybe earn some more money out of it before I gave her the bill. But I still didn't really *know* anything.

The angle with Bianca had come to a dead end at Linda Randall. All I had were more questions for Miss Randall, and she was as closed as a bank on Sunday. I didn't have anything solid enough to hand to Murphy to let her pursue the matter. Dammit. I was going to have to do that research after all. Maybe it *would* turn up something helpful, some kind of clue to help lead me and the police to the murderer.

And maybe dragons would fly out my butt. But I had to try.

So I got out of the car to go inside and get to work.

He was waiting for me behind the trash cans that stood next to the stairs leading down to my front door. The baseball bat he swung at me took me behind the ear and pitched me to the bottom of the stairs in a near-senseless heap. I could hear his footsteps, but couldn't quite move, as he came down the stairs toward me.

It figured. It was just the kind of day I was having.

I felt his foot on the back of my neck. Felt him lift the baseball bat. And then it came whistling down toward my skull with a mighty crack of impact.

Except that it missed my motionless head, and whacked into the concrete next to my face, right by my eyes, instead.

'Listen up, Dresden,' my attacker said. His voice was rough, low, purposefully hoarse. 'You got a big nose. Stop sticking it where it doesn't belong. You got a big mouth. Stop talking to people you don't need to talk to. Or we're going to shut that mouth of yours.' He waited a melodramatically appropriate moment, and then added, 'Permanently.'

His footsteps retreated up the stairs and vanished.

I just lay there watching the stars in front of my eyes for a while. Mister appeared from somewhere, probably drawn by the groaning noises, and started licking at my nose.

I eventually regained my mobility and sat up. My head was spinning, and I felt sick to my stomach. Mister rubbed up against me, as though he sensed something was wrong, purring in a low rumble. I managed to stand up long enough to unlock my apartment door, let Mister and myself in, and lock it behind me. I staggered over to my easy chair in the darkness and sat down with a *whuff* of expelled breath.

I sat motionless until the spinning slowed down enough to allow me to open my eyes again, and until the pounding of my head calmed down. Pounding head. Someone could have been pounding on my head with a baseball bat just then, pounding my head into new and interesting shapes that were inconducive to carrying on businesslike pursuits. Someone could have been pounding Harry Dresden right into the hereafter.

I cut off that line of thought. 'You are not some poor

rabbit, Dresden!' I reminded myself, sternly. 'You are a
wizard of the old school, a spellslinger of the highest caliber.
You're not going to roll over for some schmuck with a
baseball bat because he tells you to!'

Galvanized by the sound of my own voice, or maybe
only by the somewhat unsettling realization that I had
begun talking to myself, I stood up and built up the fire
in the fireplace, then walked unsteadily back and forth in
front of it, trying to think, to work out the details.

Had this evening's visits triggered the warning? Who
had reason to threaten me? What were they trying to keep
me from finding? And, most importantly, what was I going
to do about it?

Someone had seen me talking to Linda Randall, maybe.
Or, more likely, someone had seen me showing up at
Bianca's place, asking questions. The Blue Beetle may not
be glitzy, but it is sort of difficult to mistake for anyone
else's car. Who would have reason to have me watched?

Why, hadn't Gentleman Johnny Marcone followed me
so that he could have a word with me? So he could ask
me to keep out of this business with Tommy Tomm's
murder? Yes he had. Maybe this had been another reminder
from the mob boss. It had that kind of mafioso feel to it.

I staggered to my kitchenette and fixed myself a tisane
tea for the headache, then added in some aspirin. Herbal
remedies are well and good, but I don't like to take chances.

Working on that same principle, I got my Smith &
Wesson .38 Chief's Special out of its drawer, took the cloth
covering off of it, and made sure it was loaded. Then I
stuck the revolver in my jacket pocket.

Wizardry aside, it's tough to beat a gun for discouraging
men with baseball bats. And I sure as hell wasn't going to

roll over for the tiger-souled Johnny Marcone, let him push me around, let him know that it was all right to walk all over me whenever he felt like it. No way in hell or on earth, either.

My head was throbbing, and my hands were shaking, but I went down the ladder to my workroom – and started figuring out how to rip someone's heart out of his chest from fifty miles away.

Who says I never do anything fun on a Friday night?

11

It took me the rest of the night and part of the morning, but I worked out how I could murder someone in the same manner that Tommy Tomm and Jennifer Stanton had been killed. After the fifth or sixth time I'd checked the figures, I stared at my calculations.

It didn't make any *sense*. It was *impossible*.

Or maybe we were all underestimating just how dangerous this killer was.

I grabbed my duster, and headed out without bothering to check my looks. I don't keep any mirrors in my home. Too many things can use mirrors as windows – or doors – but I was pretty sure I looked like a wreck. The Studebaker's rearview mirror confirmed this. My face was haggard, with a shadow of a beard, deep circles under bloodshot eyes, and hair that looked as though it had been riding a speeding motorcycle through a cloud of greasy smoke. Smoothing your hair back with sweaty palms as a study habit will do that to you. Especially if you do it for twelve or fourteen hours straight.

It didn't matter. Murphy wanted this information, and she needed to have it. Things were bad. They were very, very bad.

I made quick time down to the station, knowing Murphy would want to hear this from me face-to-face. The police station Murphy worked in was one in an aged complex of buildings that housed the metro police department. It was run-down, sagging in places like an old soldier who nonetheless stood at attention and struggled to hold in his gut. There was graffiti along one wall that the janitor wouldn't come to scrub off until Monday morning.

I parked in the visitors' parking – easy to do on a Saturday morning – and headed up the steps and into the building. The desk sergeant wasn't the usual moustached old warhorse who I had run into before, but a greying matron with steely eyes who disapproved of me and my lifestyle in a single glance, then made me wait while she called up Murphy.

While I waited, a pair of officers came in, dragging a handcuffed man between them. He wasn't resisting them – just the opposite, in fact. His head was down, and he was moaning in an almost musical way. He was on the thin side, and I got the impression that he was young. His denim jeans and jacket were battered, unkempt, as was his hair. The officers dragged him past the desk, and one of them said, 'That DUI we called in. We're going to take him up to holding until he can see straight.'

The desk sergeant passed a clipboard over, and one of the officers took it under his arm, before the two of them dragged the young man up the stairs. I waited, rubbing at my tired eyes, until the sergeant managed to get through to someone upstairs. She gave a rather surprised 'Hmph,' and then said, 'All right, Lieutenant. I'll send him on up.' She waved a hand at me to go on past. I could feel her eyes on me as I went by, and I smoothed my palm self-consciously over my head and jaw.

Special Investigations kept a little waiting area just within the door at the top of the staircase. It consisted of four wooden chairs and a sagging old couch that would probably kill your back if you tried to sleep on it. Murphy's office was at the end of a double row of cubicles.

Murphy stood just inside her office with a phone pressed to her ear, wearing a martyred expression. She looked like a teenager having a fight with an out-of-town boyfriend, though she'd tear my head off if she heard me saying any such thing. I waved my hand, and she nodded back at me. She pointed at the waiting area, then shut her office door.

I took a seat in one of the chairs and leaned my head back against a wall. I had just closed my eyes when I heard a scream from behind me in the hallway. There was a struggling sound, and a few startled exclamations, before the scream repeated itself, closer this time.

I acted without thinking − I was too tired to think. I rose and went into the hall, towards the source of the sound. To my left was the staircase, and to my right the hallway stretched ahead of me.

A figure appeared, the silhouette of a running man, moving toward me with long strides. It was the man who had hung so limply between the two officers, humming, a few minutes before. He was the one screaming. I heard a scrabbling sound, and then the pair of officers I had seen downstairs a few moments before came around the corner. Neither of them was a young man anymore, and they both ran with their bellies out, puffing for breath, holding their gun belts against their hips with one hand.

'Stop!' one of the officers shouted, panting. 'Stop that man!'

The hair on the back of my neck prickled. The man running toward me kept on screaming, high and terrified, his voice a long and uninterrupted peal of . . . something. Terror, panic, lust, rage, all rolled up into a ball and sent spewing out into the air through his vocal cords.

I had a quick impression of wide, staring eyes, a dirty face, a denim jacket, and old jeans as he came down the shadowy hallway. His hands were behind his back, presumably held there by cuffs. He wasn't seeing the hall he was running through. I don't know what he *was* looking at, but I got the impression that I didn't want to know. He came hurtling toward me and the stairs, blind and dangerous to himself.

It wasn't any of my business, but I couldn't let him break himself apart in a tumble down the stairs. I threw myself toward him as hard as I could, attempting to put my shoulder into his stomach and drive him backward in a football-style tackle.

There is a reason I got cut every year during high school. I rammed into him, but he just *whuffed* out a breath and spun to one side, into a wall. It was as though he hadn't seen me coming and had no realization that I was there. He just kept staring blindly and screaming, careening off the wall and continuing on his way, toward the stairs. I went down to the floor, my head abruptly throbbing again where the unknown tough had rapped me with a baseball bat last night.

One good thing about being as tall as I am – I have long arms. I rolled back toward him and lashed out with one hand, fingers clutching. I caught his jeans at the cuff and gave his leg a solid sideways tug.

That did it. He spun, off-balance, and went down to the tile floor. The scream stopped as the fall took the wind from him. He slid to the top of the stairs and stopped, feebly struggling. The officers pounded past me toward him, one going to either side.

And then something strange happened.

The young man looked up at me, and his eyes rounded and dilated, until I thought they had turned into huge black coins dotted onto his bloodshot eyeballs. His eyes rolled back into his head until he could hardly have been able to see, and he started to shout in a clarion voice.

'Wizard!' he trumpeted. 'Wizard! I see you! I see you, wizard! I see the things that follow, those who walk before and He Who Walks Behind! They come, they come for you!'

'Jesus Christ on a crutch,' the shorter, rounder officer said, as they took the man by his arms and started dragging him back down the hall. 'Junkies. Thanks for the assist, buddy.'

I stared at the man, stunned. I caught the sleeve of the taller officer. 'What's going on, sir?' I asked him.

He stopped, letting the prisoner hang between him and his partner. The prisoner's head was bowed forward, and his eyes were still rolled back, but he had his head turned toward me and was grinning a horrible, toothy grin. His forehead was wrinkled oddly, almost as though he were somehow focusing on me through the bones of his browridges and the frontal lobes of his brain.

'Junkie,' the taller officer said. 'One of those new ThreeEye punks. Caught him down by the lake in his car with nearly four grams of the stuff. Probably more in him.' He shook his head. 'You okay?'

'Fine, fine,' I assured him. 'ThreeEye? That new drug?'

The shorter officer snorted. 'One that's supposed to make them see the spirit world, that kind of crap.'

The taller one nodded. 'Stuff hooks harder than crack. Thanks for the help. Didn't know you were a civilian, though. Didn't expect anyone but police down here this time of day.'

'No problem,' I assured him. 'I'm fine.'

'Hey,' the stouter one said. He squinted at me and shook his finger. 'Aren't you the guy? That psychic consultant Carmichael told me about?'

'I'll take the fifth,' I said to him with a grin that I didn't feel. The two officers chuckled and turned back to their business, quickly shouldering me aside as they dragged their prisoner away.

He whispered in a mad little voice, all the way down the hall. 'See you, see you, wizard. See He Who Walks Behind.'

I returned to my chair in the waiting area at the end of the row of cubicles and sat down, my head throbbing, my stomach rolling uncomfortably. He Who Walks Behind. I had never seen the junkie before. Never been close to him. I hadn't sensed the subtle tension of power in the air around him that signified the presence of a magical practitioner.

So how the hell had he seen the shadow of He Who Walks Behind flowing in my wake?

For reasons I don't have time to go into now, I am marked, indelibly, with the remnants of the presence of a hunter-spirit, a sort of spectral hit man known as He Who Walks Behind. I had beaten long odds in surviving the enemy of mine who had called up He Who Walks Behind and sent him after me – but even though the hunter-spirit had never gotten to me, the mark could still be seen upon me by those who knew how, by using the Third Sight, stretching out behind me like a long and horribly shaped shadow. Sort of a spiritual scar to remind me of the encounter.

But only a wizard had that kind of vision, the ability to sense the auras and manifestations of magical phenomena. And that junkie had been no wizard.

Was it possible that I had been wrong in my initial assessment of ThreeEye? Could the drug genuinely grant to its users the visions of the Third Sight?

I shuddered at the thought. The kind of things you see when you learn how to open your Third Eye could be blindingly beautiful, bring tears to your eyes – or they could be horrible, things that made your worst nightmares seem ordinary and comforting. Visions of the past, the future, of the true natures of things. Psychic stains, troubled shades, spirit-folk of all description, the shivering power of the Nevernever in all its brilliant and subtle hues – and all going straight into your brain: unforgettable, permanent. Wizards quickly learn how to control the Third Eye, to keep it closed except in times of great need, or else they go mad within a few weeks.

I shivered. If the drug was real, if it really did open the Third Eye in mortals instead of just inflicting ordinary hallucinations upon its users, then it was far more dangerous than it seemed, even with the deleterious effects demonstrated by the junkie I had tackled. Even if a user didn't go mad from seeing too many horrible or otherworldly things, he might see through the illusions and disguises of any of a number of beings that passed among mankind regularly, unseen – which could compel such creatures to act in defense, for fear of being revealed. Double jeopardy.

'Dresden,' Murphy snapped, 'wake up.'

I blinked. 'Not asleep,' I slurred. 'Just resting my eyes.'

She snorted. 'Save it, Harry,' and pushed a Styrofoam cup into my hands. She'd made me coffee with a ton of sugar in it, just the way I like, and even though it was a little stale, it smelled like heaven.

'You're an angel,' I muttered. I took a sip, then nodded

down the row of cubicles. 'You want to hear this one in your office.'

I could feel her eyes on me as I drank. 'All right,' she said. 'Let's go. And the coffee's fifty cents, Harry.'

I followed her to her office, a hastily assembled thing with cheap plywood walls and a door that wasn't hung quite straight. The door had a paper sign taped to it, neatly lettered in black Magic Marker with LT. KARRIN MURPHY. There was a rectangle of lighter wood where a plaque had once held some other hapless policeman's name. That the office never bothered to put up a fresh plaque was a not-so-subtle reminder of the precarious position of the Special Investigations director.

Her office furniture, the entire interior of the office, in fact, was a contrast with the outside. Her desk and chair were sleek, dark, and new. Her PC was always on and running on its own desk set immediately to her left. A bulletin board covered most of one little wall, and current cases were neatly organized on it. Her college diploma, the aikido trophies, and her marksman's awards were on the wall to one's immediate right as you entered the office, and sitting there right next to your face if you were standing before her desk or sitting in the chair in front of it. That was Murphy – organized, direct, determined, and just a little bit belligerent.

'Hold it,' Murphy told me. I stopped outside of her office, as I always did, while she went inside and turned off, then unplugged her computer and the small radio on her desk. Murphy is used to the kind of mayhem that happens whenever I get around machinery. After she was done, I went on in.

I sat down and slurped more coffee. She slid up onto

the edge of her desk, looking down at me, her blue eyes narrowed. She was dressed no less casually on a Saturday than she was on a workday – dark slacks, a dark blouse, set off by her golden hair, and bright silver necklace and earrings. Very stylish. I, in my rumpled sweats and T-shirt, black duster, and mussed hair, felt very slouchy.

'All right, Harry,' she said. 'What have you got for me.'

I took one last drink of coffee, stifled a yawn, and put the cup down on her desk. She slipped a coaster under it as I started speaking. 'I was up all night working on it,' I said, keeping my voice soft. 'I had a hell of a time figuring out the spell. And as near as I can figure it, it's almost impossible to do it to one person, let alone two at once.'

She glared at me. 'Don't tell me almost impossible. I've got two corpses that say otherwise.'

'Keep your shirt on,' I growled at her. 'I'm just getting started. You've got to understand the whole thing if you're going to understand any of it.'

Her glare intensified. She put her hands on the edge of her desk, and said in a deadly, reasonable tone, 'All right. Why don't you explain it to me.'

I rubbed at my eyes again. 'Look. Whoever did this did it with a thaumaturgic spell. That much I'm sure of. He or she used some of Tommy Tomm and Jennifer Stanton's hair or fingernails or something to create a link to them. Then they ripped out a symbolic heart from some kind of ritual doll or sacrificial animal and used a whale of an amount of energy to make the same thing happen to the victims.'

'This doesn't tell me anything new, Harry.'

'I'm getting there, I'm getting there,' I said. 'The amount of energy you need to do this is staggering. It would be a lot easier to manage a small earthquake than to affect a living being like that. Best-case scenario, I might be able to do it without killing myself. To one person who had really, really pissed me off.'

'You're naming yourself as a suspect?' Murphy's mouth quirked at the corner.

I snorted. 'I said I was strong enough to do it to one person. I think it would kill me to try two.'

'You're saying that some sort of wizard version of Arnold Schwarzenegger pulled this off?'

I shrugged. 'It's possible, I suppose. More likely, someone who's just really good pulled it off. Raw power doesn't determine all that you can do with magic. Focus matters, too. The better your focus is, the better you are at putting your power in one place at the same time, the more you can get done. Sort of like when you see some ancient little Chinese martial-arts master shatter a tree trunk with his hands. He couldn't lift a puppy over his head, but he can focus what power he does have with incredible effect.'

Murphy glanced at her aikido trophies and nodded. 'Okay,' she said, 'I can understand that, I think. So we're looking for the wizard version of Mister Miyagi.'

'Or,' I said, lifting a finger, 'more than one wizard worked on this at the same time. Pooled their power together and used it all at once.' My pounding head, combined with the queasy stomach and the caffeine, was making me a little woozy. 'Teamwork, teamwork, that's what counts.'

'Multiple killers,' Murphy drawled. 'I don't have one, and you're telling me there might be fifty.'

'Thirteen,' I corrected her. 'You can never use more than thirteen. But I don't think that's very likely. It's a bitch to do. Everyone in the circle has to be committed to the spell, have no doubts, no reservations. And they have to trust one another implicitly. You don't see that kind of thing from your average gang of killers. It just isn't something that's going to happen, outside of some kind of fanaticism. A cult or political organization.'

'A *cult*,' Murphy said. She rubbed at her eyes. 'The *Arcane* is going to have a field day with this one, if it gets out. So Bianca is involved in this, after all. Surely she's got enough enemies out there who could do this. She could inspire that kind of effort to get rid of her.'

I shook my head. The pain was getting worse, heavier, but pieces were falling into place. 'No. You're thinking the wrong angle here. The killer wasn't taking out the hooker and Tommy Tomm to get at Bianca.'

'How do you know?'

'I went to see her,' I responded.

'Dammit, Harry!'

I didn't react to her anger. 'You know she wasn't going to talk to you, Murph. She's an old-fashioned monster girl. No cooperation with the authorities.'

'But she *did* talk to you?' Murphy demanded.

'I said pretty please.'

'I would beat you to crap if you didn't already look like it,' Murphy said. 'What did you find out?'

'Bianca wasn't in on it. She didn't have a clue who it could have been. She was nervous, scared.' I didn't mention that she'd been scared enough to try to take me to pieces.

'So someone was sending a message – but not to Bianca?'

'To Johnny Marcone,' I confirmed.

'Gang war in the streets,' Murphy said. 'And now the outfit is bringing sorcery into it as well. Mafioso magic spells. Jesus Christ.' She drummed her heels on the edge of the desk.

'Gang war. ThreeEye suppliers versus conventional narcotics. Right?'

She stared at me for a minute. 'Yeah,' Murphy said. 'Yeah, it is. How did you know? We've been holding out details from the papers.'

'I just ran into this guy who was stoned out of his mind on ThreeEye. Something he said makes me think that stuff isn't a bunch of crap. It's for real. And you would have to be one very, very badass wizard to manufacture a large quantity of this kind of drug.'

Murphy's blue eyes glittered. 'So, whoever is the one supplying the streets with ThreeEye—'

'—is the one who murdered Jennifer Stanton and Tommy Tomm. I'm pretty sure of it. It feels right.'

'I'd tend to agree,' Murphy said, nodding. 'All right, then. How many people do you know of who could manage the killing spell?'

'Christ, Murphy,' I said, 'you can't ask me to just hand you a list of names of people to drag downtown for questioning.'

She leaned down closer to me, blue eyes fierce. 'Wrong, Harry. I can ask you. I can *tell* you to give them to me. And if you don't, I can haul you in for obstruction and complicity so quick it will make your head spin.'

'My head's already spinning,' I told her. A little giggle slipped out. Throbbing head, pound, pound, pound. 'You wouldn't do that, Murph. I know you. You know damned well that if I had anything you could use, I would give it to you. If you'd just let me in on the investigation, give me the chance to—'

'No, Harry,' she said, her voice flat. 'Not a chance. I am ass deep in alligators already without you getting difficult on me. You're already hurt, and don't ask me to buy some line about falling down the stairs. I don't want to have to scrape you off the concrete. Whoever did Tommy Tomm is going to get nasty when someone comes poking around, and it isn't your job to do it. It's mine.'

'Suit yourself,' I told her. 'You're the one with the deadline.'

Her face went pale, and her eyes blazed. 'You're such an incredible shit, Harry.'

I started to answer her, I really did – but my skull got loose and shaky on my neck, and things spun around, and my chair sort of wobbled up onto its back legs and whirled about precariously. I thought it was probably safest to slide my way along to the floor, rubbery as a snake. The tiles were nice and cool underneath my cheek and felt sort of comforting. My head went boom, boom, boom, the whole time I was down there, spoiling what would have otherwise been a pleasant little nap.

12

I woke up on the floor of Murphy's office. The clock on the wall said that it was about twenty minutes later. Something soft was underneath my head, and my feet were propped up with several phone books. Murphy was pressing a cool cloth against my forehead and throat.

I felt terrible. Exhausted, achy, nauseous, my head throbbing. I wanted to do nothing so much as curl up and whimper myself to sleep. Given that I would never live *that* down, I made a wisecrack instead. 'Do you have a little white dress? I've had this deep-seated nurse fantasy about you, Murphy.'

'A pervert like you would. Who hit your head?' she demanded.

'No one,' I mumbled. 'Fell down the stairs to my apartment.'

'Bullshit, Harry,' she said, her voice hard. Her hands were no less gentle with the cool cloth, though. 'You've been running around on this case. That's where you got the bump on the head. Isn't it?'

I started to protest.

'Oh, save it,' she said, letting out a breath. 'If you didn't already have a concussion, I'd tie your heels to my car and drive through traffic.' She held up two fingers. 'How many fingers am I holding up?'

'Fifty,' I said, and held up two of my own. 'It's not a concussion. Just a little bump on the head. I'll be fine.' I started to sit up. I needed to get home, get some sleep.

Murphy put her hand on my neck and pressed me back down on the pillow beneath my head, which was, apparently, her jacket, because she wasn't wearing it. 'Stay down,' she growled. 'How did you get here? Not in that heap of a car, I hope.'

'The Beetle is doing its phoenix impression,' I told her. 'I've got a loaner. Look, I'll be fine. Just let me out of here, and I'll go home and get some sleep.'

'You aren't in any shape to drive,' Murphy said. 'You're a menace. I'd have to arrest myself if I let you behind a wheel in your condition.'

'Murph,' I said, annoyed, 'unless you can pay up what you owe me already, right now, I can't exactly afford a cab.'

'Dream on, Harry,' Murphy said. 'And save your breath. I'll give you a ride home.'

'I don't need a—' I began, but she got up from her knees and stalked out of her office.

Foolishness, I thought. Stupidity. I was perfectly capable of moving myself around. So I sat up and heaved myself to my feet.

Or tried to. I actually managed to half sit up. And then I just heaved.

Murphy came back in to find me curled on my side, her office stinking from where I'd thrown up. She didn't, for a change, say anything. She just knelt by me again, cleaned off my mouth, and put another cool cloth over the back of my neck.

I remember her helping me out to her car. I remember little pieces of the drive back to my apartment. I remember giving her the keys to the loaner, and mumbling something about Mike and the tow-truck driver.

But mostly I remember the way her hand felt on

mine – cold with a little bit of nervousness to the soft fingers, small beneath my great gawking digits, and strong. She scolded and threatened me the entire way back to the apartment, I think. But I remember the way she made sure she held my hand, as though to assure herself that I was still there. Or to assure me that she was, that she wasn't going anywhere.

There's a reason I'll go out on a limb to help Murphy. She's good people. One of the best.

We got back to my apartment sometime before noon. Murphy helped me down the stairs and unlocked the door for me. Mister came running up and hurled himself against her legs in greeting. Maybe being short gives her better leverage or something, since she didn't really wobble when Mister rammed her, like I do. Or maybe it's the aikido.

'Christ, Harry,' she muttered. 'This place is dark.' She tried the light switch, but the bulbs had burnt out last week, and I hadn't had the cash to replace them. So she sat me down on the couch and lit some candles off of the glowing coals in the fireplace. 'All right,' she said. 'I'm putting you in bed.'

'Well. If you insist.'

The phone rang. It was in arm's reach so I picked it up. 'Dresden,' I mumbled.

'Mister Dresden, this is Linda. Linda Randall. Do you remember me?'

Heh. Do men remember the scene in the movie with Marilyn standing over the subway grating? I found myself remembering Linda Randall's eyes and wondering things a gentleman shouldn't.

'Are you naked?' I said. It took me a minute to register what I'd said. Whoops.

Murphy gave me an arch look. She stood up and walked into my bedroom, and busied herself straightening the covers and giving me a modicum of privacy. I felt cheered. My slip had thrown Murphy off better than any lie I could have managed. Maybe a woozy Harry was not necessarily a bad Harry.

Linda purred laughter into the phone. 'I'm in the car right now, honey. Maybe later. Look, I've come up with a few things that might help you. Can you meet me tonight?'

I rubbed at my eyes. It was Saturday. Tonight was Saturday night. Wasn't there something I was supposed to do tonight?

To hell with it, I thought. It couldn't have been all that important if I couldn't even remember it. 'Sure,' I told her. 'Fine.'

She mmmmed into the phone. 'You're such a gentleman. I like that, once in a while. I get off at seven. All right? Do you want to meet me? Say at eight?'

'My car exploded,' I said. My tongue felt fuzzy. 'I can meet you at the 7-Eleven down the street from my apartment.'

She poured that rich, creamy laughter into my ear again. 'Tell you what. Give me an extra hour or so to go home, get a nice hot bath, make myself all pretty, and then I'll be there in your arms. Sound good to you?'

'Well. Okay.'

She laughed again, and didn't say good-bye before disconnecting.

Murphy appeared again as soon as I hung up the phone. 'Tell me you didn't just make a date, Dresden.'

'You're just jealous.'

Murphy snorted. 'Please. I need more of a man than you to keep me happy.' She started to get an arm beneath me to help me up. 'You'd break like a dry stick, Dresden. You'd better get to bed before you get any more delusions.'

I put a hand against her shoulder to push her back. I didn't have that kind of strength, but she backed off, frowning. 'What?'

'Something,' I said. I rubbed at my eyes. Something was bothering me. I was forgetting something, I was sure of it. Something I said I would do on Saturday. I struggled to push thoughts of drug wars and people driven mad by the Third Sight visions given them by the ThreeEye drug, and tried to concentrate.

It didn't take long to click. Monica. I had told her I would get in contact with her. I patted at my duster pockets until I found my notepad, and took it out. Fumbled it open, and waved at Murphy.

'Candle. Need to read something.'

'Christ, Dresden. I swear you're at least as bad as my first husband. He was stubborn enough to kill himself, too.' She sighed, and brought a candle over. The light hurt my eyes for a moment. I made out Monica's number and I dialed her up.

'Hello?' a male child's voice asked.

'Hi,' I said. 'I need to speak to Monica, please.'

'Who's this?'

I remembered I was working for her on the sly and answered, 'Her fourth cousin, Harry, from Vermont.'

''Kay,' the kid said. 'Hold on.' Then he screamed, without lowering the mouthpiece of the phone from his lips, 'MOM! YOUR COUSIN HARRY FROM VERMONT IS ON THE PHONE LONG-DISTANCE!'

Kids. You gotta love them. I adore children. A little salt, a squeeze of lemon − perfect.

I waited for the pounding in my head to resolve into mere agony as the kid dropped the phone and ran off, feet thumping on a hardwood floor.

A moment later, there was the rattle of the phone being picked up, and Monica's quiet, somewhat nervous voice said, 'Um. Hello?'

'It's Harry Dresden,' I told her. 'I just wanted to call to let you know what I'd been able to find out for y—'

'I'm sorry,' she interrupted me. 'I don't, um . . . need any of those.'

I blinked. 'Uh, Monica Sells?' I read her the phone number.

'Yes, yes,' she said, her voice hurried, impatient. 'We don't need any help, thank you.'

'Is this a bad time?'

'No. No, it's not that. I just wanted to cancel my order. Discontinue the service. Don't worry about me.' There was an odd quality to her voice, as though she were forcing a housewife's good cheer into it.

'Cancel? You don't want me looking for your husband anymore? But ma'am, the money—' The phone began to buzz and static made the line fuzzy. I thought I heard a voice in the background, somewhere, and then the sound went dead except for the static. For a moment, I thought I'd lost the connection entirely. Blasted unreliable phones. Usually, they messed up on my end, not on the receiving end. You can't even trust them to foul up dependably.

'Hello? Hello?' I said, cross and grumpy.

Monica's voice returned. 'Don't worry about that. Thank you *so* much for all of your help. Good day, bye-bye, thank you.' Then she hung up on me.

I took the phone away from my ear and stared at it. 'Bizarre,' I said.

'Come on, Harry,' Murphy said. She took the phone from my hand and planted it firmly in its cradle.

'Aww, Mom. It's not even dark yet.' I made the lame joke to try to think about something besides how terribly my head was going to hurt when Murphy helped me up. She did. It did. We hobbled into the bedroom and when I stretched out on the cool sheets I was reasonably certain I was going to set down roots.

Murphy took my temperature and felt my scalp with her fingers, careful around the goose egg on the back of my skull. She shined a penlight into my eyes, which I did not like. She also got me a drink of water, which I did like, and had me swallow a couple of aspirin or Tylenol or something.

I only remember two more things about that morning. One was Murphy stripping me out of my shirt, boots, and socks, and leaning down to kiss my forehead and ruffle my hair. Then she covered me up with blankets and put out the lights. Mister crawled up and lay down across my legs, purring like a small diesel engine, comforting.

The second thing I remember was the phone ringing again. Murphy was just about to leave, her car keys rattling in her hand. I heard her turn back to pick up the phone, and say, 'Harry Dresden's residence.'

There was a silence.

'Hello?' Murphy said.

After another pause Murphy appeared in the doorway, a small shadow, looking down at me. 'Wrong number. Get some rest, Harry.'

'Thanks, Karrin.' I smiled at her, or tried to. It must have looked ghastly. She smiled back, and I'm sure hers was nicer than mine.

She left then. The apartment got dark and quiet. Mister continued to rumble soothingly in the dark.

It kept nagging at me, even as I fell asleep. What had I forgotten? And another, less sensible question – who had been on the line who hadn't wanted to speak to Murphy? Had Monica Sells tried to call me back? Why would she call me off the case and tell me to keep the money?

I pondered that, and baseball bats and other matters until Mister's purring put me to sleep.

13

I woke up when thunder rattled the old house above me.

True dark had fallen. I had no idea of what time it was. I lay in bed for a moment, confused and a little dizzy. There was a warm spot on my legs, where Mister must have been until a few moments before, but the big grey cat was nowhere to be seen. He was a chicken about thunderstorms.

Rain was coming down in sheets. I could hear it, on the concrete outside and on the old building above me. It creaked and swayed in the spring thunderstorm and the wind, timbers gently flexing, wise enough with age to give a little, rather than put up stubborn resistance until they broke. I could probably stand to learn something from that.

My stomach was growling. I got out of bed, wobbled a little, and rooted about for my robe. I couldn't find it in the dark, but came across my duster where Murphy had left it on a chair, neatly folded. Lying on top of it was a scattering of cash, along with a napkin bearing the words 'You will pay me back. —Murphy.' I scowled at the money and tried to ignore the flash of gratitude I felt. I picked up my duster and tugged it on over my bare chest. Then I padded on naked feet out into the living room.

Thunder rumbled again, growling outside. I could feel the storm, in a way that a lot of people can't, and that most of those who can put down to nerves. It was raw energy up there, naked and pulsing through the clouds. I could feel the water in the rain and clouds, the moving air blowing the droplets in gusts against the walls of the house above. I could sense, waiting, the fire of the deadly lightning, leaping from cloud to cloud above and seeking a path of least resistance to the patient, timeless earth that bore the brunt of the storm's attack. All four elements, interacting, moving, energy flashing from place to place in each of its forms. There was a lot of potential in storms, that a sorcerer could tap into if he was desperate or stupid enough. A lot of energy to be used, up there, where the forces of ancient nature brawled and tumbled.

I frowned, thinking about that. It hadn't occurred to me before. Had there been a storm on Wednesday night? Yes, there had. I remember thunder waking me for a few moments in the hours before dawn. Could our killer have tapped into it to fuel his spells? Possibly. It bore looking into. Such tapped magic was often too unstable or volatile to use in such a carefully directed fashion.

Lightning flashed again, and I counted three or four seconds before the rumble reached me. If the killer *was* using the storms, it would make sense that if he or she were to strike again, it would happen tonight. I shivered.

My stomach growled, and more mundane matters took my attention. My head was feeling somewhat better. I wasn't dizzy anymore. My stomach was furious with me – like a lot of tall, skinny men, I eat endlessly, but it never stays on. I have no idea why. I shambled into the kitchen and started building up the grill.

'Mister?' I called. 'You hungry, bud? I'm gonna fry up some burgers, mmm, mmm, mmm.'

Lightning flashed again, closer this time, the thunder following right on its heels. The flash was bright enough to sear through my half-sunken windows and make me wince against it. But, in the flash of light, I caught sight of Mister.

The cat was up on the top of my bookshelf, in the far corner of the apartment – as far as it was possible to get away from my front door. He was watching it, his eyes luminous in the half dark, and though he had the cat-lazy look of any lounging feline, his ears were tilted forward, and his gaze focused unwaveringly upon the door. If he'd had a tail, it would have been twitching.

There came a knocking, a rapping, at my chamber door.

Maybe it was the storm making me nervous, but I quested out with my senses, feeling for any threat that might have been there. The storm made a mess of things, and all of that noise, both physical and spiritual, kept me from being able to tell anything more than that there was someone outside my door.

I felt in the pocket of my duster for the gun – but I remembered that I had set it aside in the lab last night and not taken it with me down to the police station. Police don't take kindly to anyone but police toting firearms inside the station, don't ask me why. In any case, it was out of easy reach now.

And then I remembered that Linda Randall was supposed to be showing up. I berated myself for getting spooked so easily, and then again for sleeping so long, and then again for looking and smelling like I hadn't showered in a couple of days or combed my hair or shaved or anything else that might have made me marginally less unappealing. Ah, well. I got the impression that with Linda, that sort of thing didn't seem to matter too much. Maybe she was into *eau des hommes*.

I walked over to the door and opened it, smoothing back my hair with one hand and trying to keep a sheepish grin off of my face.

Susan Rodriguez waited outside in the rain, her black umbrella held above her. She wore a khaki trench coat and an expensive black dress beneath it, with heels. Pearls shone at her throat and ears. She blinked at me when I appeared in the door. 'Harry?'

I stared at her. Oh my gosh. I had forgotten my date with Susan. How in the world could I have forgotten that? I mean, the White Council, the police, vampires, concussions, junkies, mob bosses, and baseball-bat-swinging thugs notwithstanding—

Well, no. There probably weren't any women incredible enough to make me keep my mind on them through all of that. But all the same, it seemed a little rude of me.

'Hi, Susan,' I said, lamely. I peered past her. When had Susan said she was going to show up? Nine? And when had Linda said? Eight – no, wait. She'd said eight o'clock at first, and then said she'd be by in another hour after that. At nine. Hooboy. This was not going to be pretty.

Susan read me like a book and glanced back behind her in the rain, before looking back up at me. 'Expecting someone, Harry?'

'Not exactly,' I told her. 'Uh, well. Maybe. Look, come on in. You're getting drenched.' Which wasn't exactly true. *I* was getting drenched, my bare feet soaked, standing there in the open door, the wind blowing rain down the stairway at me.

Susan's mouth quirked in a malicious, predatory little smile, and she came in, folding down her umbrella and brushing past me. 'This is your apartment?'

'Nah,' I told her. 'This is my summer home in Zurich.' She eyed me as I closed the door, took her coat, and hung it up on a tall old wooden hat stand near the doorway.

Susan turned away from me as I hung up her coat. Her dress showed her back, the long curve of her spine, all the way down to her waist. It had a fairly tame hemline, and long, tight sleeves. I liked it. A lot. She let me see her back for a while as she walked away from me, toward the fireplace, then slowly turned to face me, smirking, leaning one smooth hip on the couch. Her midnight hair was bound up on top of her head, displaying a long and slender neck, her skin an advertisement for something smooth and wonderful. Her lips quirked up at the corners, and she narrowed her dark, flashing eyes at me. 'The police having you put in overtime, Harry?' she drawled. 'The killings must be sensational. Major crime figure, murdered with magic. Care to make a statement?'

I winced. She was still hunting for an angle for the *Arcane*. 'Sure,' I told her. Her eyes widened in surprise. 'I need a shower,' I said. 'I'll be right back. Mister, keep an eye on the lady, eh?'

Susan gave me a little roll of her eyes, then glanced up and studied Mister on his perch on the bookcase. Mister, for his part, flicked an ear and continued staring at the door.

More thunder rumbled overhead.

I lit a few candles for her, then took one with me into the bathroom. Think, Harry. Get awake, and get your head clear. What to do?

Get clean, I told myself. You smell like a horse. Get some cool water over your head and work this out. Linda Randall is going to be here in a minute, and you need to figure out how to keep Susan from prying her nose into the murders.

So advised, I agreed with myself and hurriedly got undressed and into the shower. I don't use a water heater, and consequently I am more than used to cold showers. Actually, given how often I, and wizards in general, get to date actual real women, maybe that's just as well.

I was just lathering up with shampoo when the lightning got a lot worse, the thunder a lot louder, the rain a lot harder. The height of the storm had hit the old house and hit it hard. It was almost possible to see clearly in the violent electrical discharge. Almost impossible to hear over the thunder. But I caught a flicker of motion out of the corner of my eye, a shadow that moved across the sunken window (covered by modest curtains) in the bathroom. Someone was moving toward the stairs down to my apartment.

Did I mention how I haven't had a ton of success with women? Nights like this are one reason why. I panicked, hard. I leapt out of the shower, my head all a-sudsy, wrapped a towel around my waist, and headed out into the front room.

I couldn't let Linda just come to the door and have Susan answer it. *That* would be the cattiest thing you've ever seen, and I would be the one to get all the scratches and bites, too.

I rounded the corner from my bedroom into the main room and saw Susan reaching for the doorknob. Lightning flashed again, and thunder kept me from hearing the knob's *click-clack*. I heard something else, though, a snarling, spitting sound, and saw Mister, on his feet now, his back arched up and all his fur fluffed out, teeth bared, his no-longer-sleepy eyes fastened on the door.

The thunder passed as Susan swung the door open. I could see her face in profile. One hand was on her hip, and there was an amused, dangerous little smile on her pretty mouth.

As the door opened, I felt it, the cloud of energies that accompanies a spirit-being when it comes into the mortal world, disguised until now by the background clutter of the storm. A figure stood in the doorway, rather squat, less than five feet tall, dressed in a plain brown trench coat, illuminated by blue lightning overhead. There was something *wrong* to the shape, something that just wasn't a part of good old Mother Earth. It's 'head' turned to look at me, and sudden twin points of fire, as blue as the lightning dancing above, flared up, illuminating the leathery, inhuman curves of a face that most closely resembled that of a large and warty toad.

Susan got a good look at the demon's eyes and face from two feet away and screamed.

'Susan!' I shouted, already moving toward the couch. 'Get out of the way!' I threw myself to the floor behind the couch, landed with a *whumph* of hard floor hitting my ribs.

The demon's jaws parted in a silent hiss, and its throat constricted weirdly as I vanished behind the couch. There was a hissing sound, and a heart-sized section of the couch just *dissolved* in a cloud of mist and foul stench. Droplets of liquid spattered through, onto the floor near me, and where they touched little holes corroded outward in the space of two seconds. I rolled away from the couch and the demon's acid.

'Susan!' I shouted. 'Get back toward the kitchen! Don't get between it and me!'

'What is it?' she screamed back at me.

'A bad guy.' I poked my head up and peered through the smoking hole in the couch, ready to duck back down at a moment's notice. The demon, squat and bulkier than a human, was standing in the doorway, both long-fingered, pad-tipped hands leaning forward toward the inside of the house. It paused as though resting against a light screen.

'Why isn't it coming in?' Susan asked from the far corner, near the door. Her back was pressed to the wall, and her eyes were wide and terrified. My God, I thought, just don't pass out on me, Susan.

'Homestead laws,' I said. 'It isn't a mortal creature. It has to gather its energy to push through the barrier around a home.'

'Can it get in?' she said. Her voice was thin, reedy. She was asking questions, gathering information, data, falling back on her ingrained career instincts – because, I suspected, her rational brain had short-circuited. That happens to people who get a good hard look at a demon for the first time.

I hurried over to her and grabbed her arm, dragging her back toward the door leading down to my lab. 'Get down there,' I shouted, jerking the door up and revealing the folding ladder-staircase.

'It's *dark*,' Susan protested. 'Oh, God.' She blinked down at my waist. 'Harry? Why are you naked?'

I looked down. And blushed. The towel must have fallen off while I was dancing around. Looking down made the shampoo suds still in my hair runnel down into my eyes, making them sting and burn. Could this evening get any worse?

There was a tearing sound from the doorway, and the

toad-demon sort of surged forward a stumbling step. It was now in my house. Lightning still danced in the sky behind it, and I could only see it in ugly, hunchbacked outline, except for the electric light of its wide, round, googly eyes as it came toward me. Its throat was working in little, undulating motions.

'Crap,' I said. I'm quite eloquent in times of crisis. I shoved Susan toward the stairs, and turned toward the demon, tips of my thumbs touching, fingers spread, palms out toward it.

The demon's mouth opened again, and it made a slick, spittooning sound.

'*Vento Riflittum*,' I shouted, willing my fear and anxiety into a tangible shape, throwing it down from my pounding heart through my shoulders and arms, directed at the foe. The globule of demonacid sped toward my face.

My terror and adrenaline roared out of my fingertips in the form of wind, gathering up speed enough to tear the hair from a man's head. It caught the blob of acid and flung it back at the demon in a fine spray, stopped the thing dead in its tracks, and even drove it back several feet, its claw-tipped feet sliding on my smooth floor, catching on the rugs.

The acid sizzled and spat little electric blue sparks on its skin, but it didn't seem to harm the demon. It did, however, dissolve the trench coat to shreds in less time than it takes to draw a breath and wreaked havoc on my rugs and furniture.

The demon shook its head, gathering its wits. I turned to the far corner, near the door, and extended my hand, trumpeting, '*Vento servitas!*' The pale, smooth wood of my wizard's staff all but glowed in the darkness as it flew toward me, driven by a gentler, finer blast of the same wind. I caught it in my hand and spun it toward the demon, calling on the lines of power and force deep within the long, unbroken grains of wood in the staff. I extended the staff toward it, horizontally like a bar, and shouted, 'Out! Out! Out! You are not welcome here!' A touch dramatic in any other circumstance, maybe – but when you've got a demon in your living room, nothing seems too extreme.

The toad-demon hunched its shoulders, planted its broad feet, and grunted as a wave of unseen force swept out from my staff like a broom whisking along the floor. I could feel the demon resist me, pressing against the strength of the staff, as though I were leaning the wood against a vertical steel bar and attempting to snap it across that length.

We strained silently for several seconds until I realized that this thing was just too strong for me. I wasn't going to be able to brush it off like a minor imp or a niggling poltergeist. It wouldn't take me long to exhaust myself, and once the demon could move again it was either going to dissolve me with its acid or else just waddle up to me and rip me into pieces. It would be stronger than a mortal, a hell of a lot faster, and it was not going to stop until I was dead or the sun had come up or one of any of a number of other unlikely conditions were met.

'Susan!' I shouted, my chest heaving. 'Are you down there?'

'Yes,' she said. 'Is it gone?'

'Not exactly, no.' I felt my palms get sweaty, the smooth wood of the staff begin to slip. The burning of the soap suds in my eyes increased, and the lights of the demon's eyes brightened.

'Why don't you set it on fire? Shoot it! Blow it up!' Her

voice had a searching quality to it, as though she were looking around, down there in the lab.

'I *can't*,' I said to her. 'I can't pump enough juice into it to *hurt* the thing without blowing us up along with it. You've got to get out of there.' My mind was racing along, calculating possibilities, numbers, my reserves of energy, cold and rational. The thing was here for me. If I drew it off to one side, into my bedroom and bathroom, Susan might be able to escape. On the other hand, it might be under orders to kill me and any witnesses, in which case after it had finished me it would simply go after her as well. There had to be another way to get her out of here. And then I remembered it.

'Susan!' I shouted. 'There's a sports bottle on my table down there. Drink what's in it, and think about being away from here. Okay? Think about being far away.'

'I found it,' she called up a second later. 'It smells bad.'

'Dammit, it's a potion. It'll get you out of here. Drink it!'

There was a gagging noise, and then a moment later she said, 'Now what?'

I blinked and looked at the stairs going down. 'It should have work—' I broke off as the toad thing leaned forward, reached out a clawed foot, and in that stride gained three feet of ground toward me. I was able to stop it again, barely, but I knew that it was going to be coming for my throat in a few more seconds.

'Nothing happened,' she said. 'Dammit, Harry, we have to do something.' And then she came pounding up the ladder, dark eyes flashing, my .38 revolver in her hand.

'No!' I told her. 'Don't!' I felt the staff slip more. The demon was getting ready to come through all my defenses.

Susan raised the gun, face pale, her hands shaking, and

started shooting. A .38 Chief's Special carries six rounds, and I use a medium-speed load, rather than armor-piercing or explosive bullets or anything fancy like that. Fewer chances that something will go wrong in the presence of a lot of magic.

A gun is a pretty simple machine. A revolver approaches *very* simple. Wheels, gears, and a simple lever impact to ignite the powder. It's tough for magic to argue with physics, most of the time.

The revolver roared six times.

The first two shots must have gone wide and hit somewhere else. The next two struck the demon's hide and made deep dents in it before springing off and rebounding wildly around the room, as I had feared they would, more of a threat to us than to it. Fortunately, neither of us was injured or killed by the ricochets. The fifth shot went between its long, oddly shaped legs and past it.

The sixth hit the thing square between its lightning-lantern eyes, knocked it off-balance, and sent it tumbling over with a toady hiss of frustration.

I gasped and grabbed at Susan's wrist. 'Basement,' I wheezed, as she dropped the gun. We both scrambled down the ladder. I didn't bother to shut it behind me. The thing could just tear its way through the floor, if it needed to. This way, I would at least know where it would come down, rather than have it tunnel through the floor and come out on top of my head.

At my will, the tip of the staff I still held burst into light, illuminating the room.

'Harry?' Bob's voice came from the shelf. The skull's eyelights came on, and he swiveled around to face me. 'What the hell is going on? Woo woo, who is the babe?'

Susan jumped. 'What is *that?*'

'Ignore him,' I said, and followed my own advice. I went to the far end of my lab table and started kicking boxes, bags, notebooks, and old paperbacks off the floor. 'Help me clear this floor space. Hurry!'

She did, and I cursed the lack of cleaning skills that had left this end of the lab such a mess. I was struggling to get to the circle I had laid in the floor, a perfect ring of copper, an unbroken loop in the concrete that could be empowered to hold a demon in − or out.

'Harry!' Bob gulped as we worked. 'There's, a, um. A seriously badass toad-demon coming down the ladder.'

'I *know* that, Bob.' I heaved a bunch of empty cardboard boxes aside as Susan frantically tossed some papers away, exposing the entirety of the copper ring, about three feet across. I took her hand and stepped into the circle, drawing her close to me.

'What's happening?' Susan asked, her expression bewildered and terrified.

'Just stay close,' I told her. She clung tightly to me.

'It sees you, Harry,' Bob reported. 'It's going to spit something at you, I think.'

I didn't have time to see if Bob was right. I leaned down, touched the circle with the tip of my staff, and willed power into it, to shut the creature out. The circle sprang up around us, a silent and invisible tension in the air.

Something splattered and hissed against the air a few inches from my face. I looked up to see dark, sputtering acid slithering off the invisible shield the circle's power provided us. Half a second earlier and it would have eaten my face off. Cheery thought.

I tried to catch my breath, stand straight, and not let

any part of me extend outside the circle, which would break its circuit and negate its power. My arms were shaking and my legs felt weak. Susan, too, was visibly trembling.

The demon stalked over to us. I could see it clearly in the light of my staff, and I wished that I couldn't. It was horribly ugly, misshapen, foul, heavily muscled, and I compared it to a toad only because I knew of nothing else that even remotely approached a description of it. It glared at us and drove a fist at the circle's shield. It rebounded in a shower of blue sparks, and the thing hissed, a horrible and windy sound.

Outside, the storm continued to rumble and growl, muffled by the thick walls of the subbasement.

Susan was holding close to me, and almost crying. 'Why isn't it killing us? Why isn't it getting us?'

'It can't,' I said, gently. 'It can't get through, and it can't do anything to break the circle. So long as neither of us crosses that line, we'll be safe.'

'Oh, God,' Susan said. 'How long do we have to stand here?'

'Dawn,' I said. 'Until dawn. When the sun rises, it has to go.'

'There's no sun down here,' she said.

'Doesn't work that way. It's got a sort of power cord stretching back to whoever summoned it. A fuel line. As soon as the sun comes up, that line gets cut, and he goes away, like a balloon with no air.'

'When does the sun come up?' she asked.

'Oh, well. About ten more hours.'

'Oh,' she said. She laid her head against my bare chest and closed her eyes.

The toad-demon paced in a slow circuit around the circle,

searching for a weakness in the shield. It would find none.
I closed my eyes and tried to think.

'Uh, Harry,' Bob began.

'Not now, Bob.'

'But Harry—' Bob tried again.

'Dammit, Bob. I'm trying to think. If you want to be
really useful, you could try to figure out why that escape
potion you were so confident of didn't work for Susan.'

'Harry,' Bob protested, 'that's what I'm trying to tell you.'

Susan murmured, against my chest, 'Is it getting warm
in here? Or is it just me?'

A terrible suspicion struck me. I looked down at Susan
and got a sinking feeling. Surely not. No. It couldn't be.

She looked up at me, her dark eyes smoky. 'We're going
to die, aren't we Harry? Have you ever thought you'd want
to die making love?'

She kissed my chest, almost absently.

It felt nice. Really, really nice. I tried not to notice all
the bare, lovely back that was naked underneath my hand.

'I've thought that, many times,' she said, against my skin.

'Bob,' I began, my voice getting furious.

'I *tried* to tell you,' Bob wailed. 'I did! She grabbed the
wrong potion and just chugged it down.' Bob's skull turned
toward me a bit, and the lights brightened. 'You've got to
admit, though. The love potion works *great.'*

Susan was kissing my chest and rubbing her body up
against me in a fashion that was unladylike and extremely
pleasant and distracting. 'Bob, I swear, I am going to lock
you in a wall safe for the next two hundred years.'

'It's not my *fault!'* Bob protested.

The demon watched what was happening in the circle
with froggy eyes and kicked a section of floor clear enough

of debris for it to squat down on its haunches and stare, restless and ready as a cat waiting for a mouse to stick its head out of its hole. Susan stared up at me with sultry eyes and tried to wrench me to the floor, and consequently out of the circle's protective power. Bob continued to wail his innocence.

Who says I don't know how to show a lady a good time?

14

Susan tugged at my neck and jerked my head down to hers for a kiss. As kisses went, well. It was, um, extremely interesting. Perfectly passionate, abandoned, not a trace of self-consciousness or hesitation to it. Or at any rate not from her. I came up for air a minute later, my lips itching with the intensity of it, and she stared up at me with burning eyes. 'Take me, Harry. I need you.'

'Uh, Susan. That's not really a good idea right now,' I said. The potion had taken hold of her hard. No wonder she had recovered from her terror enough to come back up the stairs and fire my gun at the demon. It had lowered her inhibitions to a sufficient degree that it must also have dulled her fears.

Susan's fingers wandered, and her eyes sparkled. 'Your mouth says no,' she purred, 'but *this* says yes.'

I went up on my toes, and swallowed, trying to keep my balance and get her hand off me at the same time. 'That thing is *always* saying something stupid,' I told her. She was beyond reason. The potion had kicked her libido into suicidal overdrive. 'Bob, help me out here!'

'I'm stuck in the skull,' Bob said. 'If you don't let me out, I can't do much of anything, Harry.'

Susan stood up on tiptoe to gnaw at my ear, wrapped her shapely thigh around one of mine, and started whimpering and pulling me toward the floor. My balance wavered. A three-foot circle was not enough to perform wrestling or gymnastics or . . . anything else in, without leaving something sticking out for the waiting demon to chew on.

'Is the other potion still there?' I asked.

'Sure,' Bob said. 'I can see it where it fell on the floor. Could throw it to you, too.'

'Okay,' I said, growing excited – well. More excited. I might yet get out of this basement alive. 'I'm going to let you out for five minutes. I want you to help me by throwing me the potion.'

'No, boss,' Bob said, his voice maddeningly cheerful.

'No? No?!'

'I get a twenty-four-hour leave, or nothing.'

'Dammit, Bob! I'm responsible for what you do if I let you out! You know that!'

Susan whispered, into my ear, 'I'm not wearing any underwear,' and tried something approximating a pro-wrestling takedown to drop me to the floor. I wavered in balance and barely managed to stave her off. The demon's frog-eyes narrowed, and it came to its feet, ready to leap on us.

'Bob!' I yelled. 'You slimy jerk!'

'You try living in a bony old skull for a few hundred years, Harry! You'd want to get a night off once in a while, too!'

'Fine!' I shouted, my heart leaping into my throat as my balance wavered again. 'Fine! Just make sure you get me the potion! You have twenty-four hours.'

'Just make sure you catch it,' Bob replied. And then a flood of orangish light flowed out of both of the skull's eye sockets and into the room. The lights swooped down in an elongated cloud over the potion bottle that lay on the floor at the far side of the lab, gathered it up, and hurled it through the air toward me. I reached up with my spare hand and caught it, bobbled it for a minute, and then secured it again.

The orange lights that were Bob's spirit-form danced a little jig, then whizzed up the ladder and out of the lab, vanishing.

'What's that?' Susan murmured, eyes dazed.

'Another drink,' I said. 'Drink this with me. I think I can cover us both in the focus department, get us out of here.'

'Harry,' she said. 'I'm not *thirsty*.' Her eyes smoldered. 'I'm *hungry*.'

I hit upon an idea. 'Once we drink this, I'll be ready, and we can go to bed.'

She looked up at me hazily and smiled, wicked and delighted. 'Oh, Harry. Bottoms up.' Her hands made a sort of silent commentary on her words, and I jumped, almost dropping the bottle. More shampoo from my hair trailed down my already burning eyes, and I squeezed them closed.

I slugged away about half the potion, trying to ignore the flat-cola taste, and quickly passed the rest to Susan. She smiled lazily and drank it down, licking her lips.

It started in my guts — a sort of fluttery, wobbly feeling that moved out, up through my lungs and out along my shoulders, down my arms. It also went down, over my hips and into my legs. I began to shake and quiver uncontrollably.

And then I just flew apart into a cloud of a million billion tiny pieces of Harry, each one with its own perspective and view. The room wasn't just a square, cluttered basement to me, but a pattern of energies, grouped into specific shapes and uses. Even the demon was only a cloud of particles, slow and dense. I flowed around that cloud, up through the opening in the ceiling pattern, and outside of the apartment and into the raging nonpattern of the storm.

It took maybe five seconds, and then the power of the potion faded. I felt all the little pieces of me abruptly rush back together and slam into one another at unthinkable speed. It hurt, and made me nauseous, a sort of heavy-duty thump of impact that didn't come from any one direction, but from every direction at once. I staggered, planted my staff on the ground, and felt the rain wash down over me.

Susan appeared next to me a heartbeat later, and promptly sat down on her butt on the ground, in the rain. 'Oh, God. I feel terrible.'

Inside the apartment, the demon screamed, a raging, voiceless hiss. I could hear it madly rampaging around inside. 'Come on,' I told her. 'We've got to get out of here before it gets smart and starts looking outside for us.'

'I'm sick,' she said. 'I'm not sure I can walk.'

'The mixed potions,' I said. 'They can do that to you. But we have to go now. Come on, Susan. Up and at 'em.' I bent down and got her up on her feet and moving away from my apartment.

'Where are we going?' she asked.

'Do you have your car keys?'

She patted the dress, as if looking for pockets, and then shook her head dazedly. 'They were in my coat pocket.'

'We walk, then.'

'Walk where?'

'Over to Reading Road. It always floods when there's this much rain. It'll be enough water to ground that thing if it tries to follow us.' It was only a couple of blocks away. The cold rain came down in buckets. I was shaking, shivering, and naked, and more soap was getting into my eyes. But hey. At least I was clean.

'Wha?' she mumbled. 'What will the rain do to it?'

'Not rain. Running water. It kills him if he tries to go over it after us,' I explained to her, patiently. I hoped the potions mixing together in her stomach hadn't done anything irreversible. There had been accidents before. We were moving at good speed, all things considered, and had covered maybe forty yards in the pouring rain. Not much farther to go.

'Oh. Oh, that's good,' she said. And then she convulsed and pitched to the ground. I tried to hold her, but I was just too tired, my arms too weak. I nearly went down with her. She rolled to her side and lay that way, retching horribly, vomiting herself empty.

Thunder and lightning raged around us again, and I heard the sharp crack of the storm's power touching a tree nearby. I saw a bright flash of contact and then the subdued glow of burning branches. I looked in the direction we had been heading. The flooding Reading Road, safety from the demon, was still thirty yards away.

'I didn't think you'd last this long,' someone said.

I almost jumped out of my skin. I picked my staff up in both hands and turned in a slow circle, searching for the source of the voice. 'Who's there?' There, to one side, a spot of cold – not physical cold, but something deeper and darker that my other senses detected. A pooling of shadows, an illusion in the darkness between lights, gone when lightning flashed and back again when it had passed.

'Do you expect me to give you my name?' the shadows

scorned. 'Suffice to say that I am the one who has killed you.'

'You're an underachiever,' I shot back, still turning, eyes searching. 'The job's not done.'

In the darkness underneath a broken streetlight, then, maybe twenty feet away, I could make out the shape of a person. Man or woman, I couldn't tell, nor could I distinguish from the voice. 'Soon,' the shape said. 'You can't last much longer. My demon will finish you before another ten minutes have passed.' The voice was supremely confident.

'You called that demon here?'

'Indeed,' the shadowy shape confirmed.

'Are you *crazy?*' I demanded, stunned. 'Don't you know what could happen to you if that thing gets loose?'

'It won't,' the shape assured me. 'It is mine to control.'

I extended my senses toward the shape, and found that what I had suspected was true. It wasn't a real person, or an illusion masking a real person. It was only the seeming of one, a phantasm of shape and sound, a hologram that could see and hear and speak for its creator, wherever he or she was.

'What are you doing?' it demanded. It must have sensed me feeling it out.

'Checking your credentials,' I said, and sent some of my remaining will toward it, the sorcerous equivalent of a slap in the face.

The image cried out in surprise and reeled back. 'How did you *do* that?' it snarled.

'I went to school.'

The hologram growled, then raised up its voice, calling out in rolling syllables. I tried to hear what had been said, but another peal of thunder blocked out the middle half of what was undoubtedly the demon's name.

From within my apartment, the distant, faint sound of the demon's smashing ruckus came to an abrupt halt.

'Now,' the image said, a sneer to its voice. 'Now you will pay.'

'Why are you doing this?' I demanded.

'You're in my way.'

'Let the woman go.'

'Sorry,' the image said. 'She's seen too much. She's in the way, too, now. My demon will kill you both.'

'You bastard,' I snarled.

It laughed at me.

I looked over my shoulder, back toward the apartment. Through the rain I heard a dry and raspy hiss, underlaid with a sort of clicking growl. Blue frog-eyes, reflecting the storm's lightning, came up the stairs from my basement apartment. It focused on me immediately and started forward. The back fender of Susan's car, which she had parked outside my apartment, got in its way, and with the pad-tipped fingers of one skinny, soft-looking hand, it picked up the back end of the car and tossed it to one side, where it landed with a heavy crunch.

I tried not to think about those fingers around my throat.

'You see?' the image said. 'Mine to call. Time for you to die, Mr Dresden.'

Another flash of lightning showed the demon falling to all fours and scrambling toward me like an overweight lizard scuttling across hot sand to shade, in an exaggerated wagging motion that looked ridiculous but brought it closer and closer at deceptive speed.

'Deposit another quarter to continue your call, asshole,'

I said. I thrust my staff toward the shadowy image, this time, focusing my will into a full-fledged attack. '*Stregallum finitas.*'

Scarlet light abruptly flooded over it, devouring its edges and moving inward.

The image snarled, then gasped in pain. 'Dresden! My demon will roll in your bones!' And then it broke off into a scream of anguish as my counterspell began to tear the image-sending apart. I was better than whoever had made the image, and they couldn't hold the spell in the face of my counter. The image and the scream alike faded slowly into the distance until both were gone. I allowed myself the smallest touch of satisfaction, and then turned to the woman on the ground.

'Susan,' I said, crouching by her, keeping my eyes on the onrushing demon. 'Susan, get up. We have to go.'

'I can't,' she sobbed. 'Oh, God,' and she threw up some more. She tried to rise but collapsed back to the ground, moaning piteously.

I looked back at the water, gauging the thing's speed. It was coming, fast, but not quite as fast as a man could run. I could still escape it, if I ran, full out. I could get across the water. I could be safe.

But I couldn't carry Susan there. I'd never make it, with her slowing me down. But if I didn't go, both of us would die. Wouldn't it be better for one of us, at least, to live?

I looked back at the demon. I was exhausted, and it had caught me unprepared. The heavy rain would keep fire, man's ancient weapon against the darkness and the things it hid, from being effective in holding it back. And I didn't have enough left in me to do anything else. It would be as good as suicide to stand against it.

Susan sobbed on the ground, helpless in the rain, sick from my potions, unable to rise.

I leaned my head back and let the rain wash the last traces of shampoo from my eyes, my hair. Then I turned, took a step toward the oncoming demon. I couldn't leave Susan to that thing. Not even if it meant dying. I'd never be able to live with myself afterward.

The demon squalled something at me in its hissing, toady voice, and raised both its hands toward me, coming up onto its hind legs. Lightning flashed overhead, blinding bright. Thunder came hard on its heels, deep enough to shake the street beneath my bare feet.

Thunder.

Lightning.

The storm.

I looked up at the boiling clouds overhead, lit by the dancing lightning moving among them, deadly beautiful and luminous. Power seethed and danced in the storm, mystic energies as old as time, enough power to shatter stones, superheat air, boil water to steam, burn anything it touched to ashes.

At this point, I think it is safe to say, I was desperate enough to try anything.

The demon howled and waddled forward, clumsy and quick. I raised my staff to the sky with one hand, and with the other pointed a finger at the demon. This was dangerous work, tapping the storm. There was no ritual to give it shape, no circle to protect me, not even words to shield my mind from the way the energies of magic would course through it. I sent my senses coursing upward, toward the storm, taking hold of the formless powers and drawing them into patterns of raw energy that began to surge toward me, toward the tip of my staff.

'Harry?' Susan said. 'What are you doing?' She huddled on the ground in her evening dress, shuddering. Her voice was weak, thready.

'You ever form a line of people holding hands when you were a kid, and scuff your feet across the carpeting together, and then have the last person in the line touch someone on the ear to zap them?'

'Yeah,' she said, confused.

'I'm doing that. Only bigger.'

The demon squalled again and drove itself into the air with its powerful toad-legs, hurtling toward me, sailing through the air with a frightening and unnatural grace.

I focused what little I had left of my will on the staff, and the clouds and raging power above. '*Ventas!*' I shouted, '*Ventas fulmino!*'

At my will, a spark leapt up from the tip of my staff toward the clouds above. It touched the rolling, restless belly of the storm.

Hell roared down in response.

Lightning, white-hot fury, with a torrent of wind and rain, all fell upon me, centered around the staff. I felt the power hit the end of the soaking wet wood with a jolt like a sledgehammer. It coursed down the staff and into my hand, making my muscles convulse, bowing my naked body with the strain. It took everything I had to hold the image of what I wanted in my mind, to keep my hand pointed at the demon as it came for me, to keep the energy surging through me to wreak its havoc on flesh less tender than mine.

The demon was maybe six inches away when the storm's fury boiled down my body and out through my arm, out of my pointing finger, and took it in the heart. The force of it threw the thing back, back and up, into the air, and held it there, wreathed in a corona of blinding energy.

The demon struggled, screamed, toad-hands flailing, toad-legs kicking.

And then it exploded in a wash of blue flame. The night was lit once more, bright as day. I had to shield my eyes against it. Susan cried out in fear, and I think I must have been screaming along with her.

Then the night grew quiet again. Flaming bits of something that I didn't want to think about were raining down around us, landing with little, wet, plopping sounds upon the road, the sidewalk, the yards of the houses around me, burning quickly to little briquettes of charcoal and then hissing into sputtering coolness. The wind abruptly died down. The rain slowed to a gentle patter, the storm's fury spent.

My legs gave out, and I sat down shakily on the street, stunned. My hair was dry, and standing on end. There was smoke curling up from the blackened ends of my toenails. I just sat there, happy to be alive, to be breathing in and out again. I felt like I could crawl back in bed and go to sleep for a few days, even though I'd gotten up not half an hour ago.

Susan sat up, blinking, her face blank. She stared at me.

'What are you doing next Saturday?' I asked her.

She just kept on staring for a minute. And then quietly lay down again on her side.

I heard the footsteps approach from the darkness off to one side. 'Summoning demons,' the sour voice said, disgusted.

'In addition to the atrocities you have already committed. I knew I smelled black magic on the winds tonight. You are a blight, Dresden.'

I sort of rolled my head over to one side to regard Morgan, my warden, tall and massive in his black trench coat. The rain had plastered his greying hair down to his head, and coursed down the lines of his face like channels in a slab of stone.

'I didn't call that thing,' I said. My voice was slurred with fatigue. 'But I damn well sent it back to where it belongs. Didn't you see?'

'I saw you defend yourself against it,' Morgan said. 'But I didn't see anyone else summon it. You probably called it up yourself and lost control of it. It couldn't have taken me anyway, Dresden. It wouldn't have done you any good.'

I laughed, weakly. 'You're flattering yourself,' I said. 'I sure as hell wouldn't risk calling up a demon just to get to *you*, Morgan.'

He narrowed his already-narrow eyes. 'I have convened the Council,' he said. 'They will be here two dawns hence. They will hear my testimony, Dresden, and the evidence I have to present to them against you.' There was another, more subdued flash of lightning, and it gave his eyes a wild, madman's gleam. 'And then they will order you put to death.'

I just stared at him for a moment, dully. 'The Council,' I said. 'They're coming here. To Chicago.'

Morgan smiled at me, the kind of smile sharks reserve for baby seals. 'Dawn, on Monday, you will be brought before them. I don't usually enjoy my position as executioner, Harry Blackstone Copperfield Dresden. But in your case, I am proud to fulfill that role.'

I shuddered when he pronounced my full name. He did

it almost exactly right – maybe by accident, and maybe not, too. There were those on the White Council who knew my name, knew how to say it. To run from the Council convened, to avoid them, would be to admit guilt and invite disaster. And because they knew my name, they could find me. They could get to me. Anywhere.

Susan moaned and stirred. 'H-H-Harry?' she mumbled. 'What happened?'

I turned to her, to make sure she was all right. When I glanced back over my shoulder, Morgan was gone. Susan sneezed and huddled against me. I put an arm around her, to share what little warmth I had.

Monday morning.

Monday morning, Morgan would bring his suspicions and level his accusations, and it would likely be enough to get me voted dead. Whoever Mister or Miss Shadows was, I had to find him, her, it, or them before Monday morning, or I was as good as dead.

I was reflecting on what a miserable date I was, when the squad car pulled up, turned its spotlights on us, and the officer said, over the loudspeaker, 'Set the stick down and put your hands up. Don't make any sudden moves.'

Perfectly natural, I thought, embracing a sort of exhausted stoicism, for the officer to arrest a naked man and a woman dressed in an evening gown, sitting on a sidewalk in the pouring rain like a couple of drunks fresh off a bender.

Susan shielded her eyes and then looked at the spotlight. All the throwing up she'd done must have gotten rid of the potion in her, ended its amorous effects. 'This,' she said, in a calm and dispassionate voice, 'is the worst night of my life.' The officers got out of the car and started toward us.

I grunted. 'That's what you get for trying to go out with a wizard.'

She glanced aside at me, and her eyes glittered darkly for a moment. She almost smiled, and there was a sort of vindictive satisfaction to her tone when she spoke.

'But it's going to make a *fantastic* story.'

15

As it turned out, Linda Randall had a darn good reason for skipping out on our appointment Saturday night.

Linda Randall was dead.

I sneezed as I ducked under the yellow police tape in the sweatpants and T-shirt I had been allowed to pluck from the mess of my place before the police car had brought me across town to Linda Randall's apartment. And cowboy boots. Mister had dragged one of my sneakers off, and I hadn't had time to find it, so I wore what I had. Freaking cat.

Linda had died a bit earlier that evening. After getting to the scene, Murphy had tried to phone me, failed to get through, and then sent a squad car down to pick me up and bring me in to do my consultant bit. The dutiful patrolmen sent to collect me had stopped to check out the crazy naked guy a block away from my apartment, and had been surprised and more than a little suspicious when I turned out to be the very same man they were supposed to pick up and bring to the crime scene.

Dear Susan had come to my rescue, explaining away what had happened as 'Just one of those things, tee-hee,' and assuring the officers that she was all right and would be fine to drive home. She got a little pale around the edges when she saw once more the ruins of my apartment and the enormous dent the demon had put in the side of her car, but she made a bold face of it and eventually left the scene with that 'I have a story to write' gleam in her eye. She stopped and gave me a kiss on the cheek on her way out, and whispered, 'Not bad, Harry,' in my ear. Then she patted my bare ass and got in her car.

I blushed. I don't think the cops noticed it, in the rain and the dark. The patrolmen had looked at me askance, but were more than happy to let me go put on some fresh clothes. The only things I had clean were more sweats and another T-shirt, this one proclaiming in bold letters over a little cartoon graveyard, 'EASTER HAS BEEN CANCELED – THEY FOUND THE BODY.'

I put those on, and my duster, which had somehow survived the demon attack, and my utterly inappropriate cowboy boots, and then I had gotten in the patrol car and been driven across town. I clipped my little ID card to my coat's lapel and followed the uniforms in. One of them led me to Murphy.

On the way, I took in little details. There were a lot of people standing around gawking. It was still fairly early, after all. The rain came down in a fine mist and softened the contours of the scene. There were several police cars parked in the apartment building's parking lots, and one on the lawn by the door leading out to the little concrete patio from the apartment in question. Someone had left his bulbs on, and blue lights flashed over the scene in alternating swaths of shadow and cold light. There was a lot of yellow police tape around.

And right in the middle of it all was Murphy.

She looked terrible, like she hadn't eaten anything that didn't come out of a vending machine or drunk anything but stale coffee since I had seen her last. Her blue eyes were tired, and bloodshot, but still sharp. 'Dresden,' she said. She peered up at me. 'You planning on having King Kong climb your hair?'

I tried to smile at her. 'We still need to cast our screaming damsel. Interested?'

Murphy snorted. She snorts really well for someone with such a cute nose. 'Come on.' She spun on one heel and walked up to the apartment, as though she wasn't exhausted and at the end of her rope.

The forensics team was already there, so we got some nifty plastic booties to put over our shoes and loose plastic gloves for our hands from an officer standing beside the door. 'I tried to call earlier,' Murphy said, 'but your phone was out of service. Again, Harry.'

'Bad night for it,' I responded, wobbling as I slipped the booties on. 'What's the story?'

'Another victim,' she said. 'Same M.O. as Tommy Tomm and the Stanton woman.'

'Jesus,' I said. 'They're using the storms.'

'What?' Murphy turned and fixed her eyes on me.

'The storm,' I repeated. 'You can tap storms and other natural phenomena to get things done. All natural fuel for the mojo.'

'You didn't say anything about that before,' Murphy accused.

'I hadn't thought of it until tonight.' I rubbed at my face. It made sense. Hell's bells, that was how the Shadowman had been able to do all of that in one night. He'd called the demon and been able to send it after me, as well as appearing in the shadow he'd projected. And he'd been able to kill again.

'Have you got an ID on the victim?' I asked.

Murphy turned to go inside as she answered. 'Linda Randall. Chauffeur. Age twenty-nine.'

It was a good thing Murphy had turned away, or the way my jaw dropped would have told her that I knew the deceased, and she would have had all sorts of uncomfortable questions. I stared after Murphy for a second, then hurriedly veiled my expression and followed her inside the apartment.

Linda Randall's one-room apartment looked like the trailer of a rock band that did little besides play concerts, host parties, and fall into a stupor afterward. Dirty clothes were strewn on one side of a king-size bed. There was a disproportionate amount of clothing that looked as though it had been purchased from a Frederick's of Hollywood catalog — lacy and silky and satiny colors, all bright, designed to attract the eye. There were many candles around the bed, on shelves and dressers and a night table, most burned halfway down. The drawer of the night table was partly open, revealing a number of personal amusements — Linda Randall had, apparently, liked her toys.

The kitchenette, off to one side, looked largely unused, except for the coffeepot, the microwave, and the trash can, in which several pizza boxes were crammed. Maybe it was the pizza boxes that did it, that gave me a sudden pang of understanding and empathy for Linda. My own kitchen looked the same, a lot of the time, minus the microwave. Here had lived someone else who knew that the only thing waiting at home was a sense of loneliness. Sometimes it is comforting. Most often, it isn't. I'll bet Linda would have understood that.

But I'd never have the chance to know. The forensics team was gathered around the bed, concealing whatever was there, like a cluster of buzzards around the exposed head of the outlaws they used to bury up to their necks in the Old West. They spoke among themselves in low, calm voices, dispassionate as skilled dinner chatter, calling little details to the attention of their companions, complimenting one another on their observations.

'Harry?' Murphy said, quietly. Her tone of voice suggested that it wasn't the first time she'd said it. 'Are you sure you're all right for this?'

My mouth twitched. Of course I wasn't all right for this. No one should ever be all right for this sort of thing. But instead of saying that, I told her, 'My head's just aching. Sorry. Let's just get it over with.'

She nodded and led me over toward the bed. Murphy was a lot shorter than most of the men and women working around the bed, but I had almost a head of height on all of them. So I didn't have to ask anyone to move, just stepped up close to the bed and looked.

Linda had been on the phone when she died. She was naked. Even this early in the year, she had tan lines around her hips. She must have gone to a tanning booth during the winter. Her hair was still damp. She lay on her back, her eyes half-closed, her expression tranquil as it hadn't been any time I'd seen her.

Her heart had been torn out. It was lying on the king-size bed about a foot and a half from her, pulped and squashed and slippery, sort of a scarlet and grey color. There was a hole in her chest, too, showing where bone had been splintered outward by the force that had removed her heart.

I just stared for a few moments, noting details in a sort of detached way. Again. Again someone had used magic to end a life.

I had to think of her as she sounded on the phone. Joking, a quick wit. A sort of sly sensuality, in the way she said her words and phrased her sentences. A little hint of insecurity around the edges, vulnerability that magnified the other parts of her personality. Her hair was damp because she'd been taking a bath before she came to see me. Whatever anyone said of her, she had been passionately, vitally alive. Had been.

Eventually, I realized how quiet the room was.

The men and women of the forensics team, all five of them, were looking up at me. Waiting. As I looked around, they all averted their gazes, but you didn't have to be a wizard to see what was in their faces. Fear, pure and simple. They had been faced with something that science couldn't explain. It rattled them, shook them to their cores, this sudden, violent, and bloody evidence that three hundred years of science and research was no match for the things that were still, even after all this time, lurking in the dark.

And I was the one who was supposed to have the answers.

I didn't have any for them, and I felt like shit for remaining silent as I stepped back and turned away from Linda's body, then walked across the room to the small bathroom. The tub was still full of water. A bracelet and earrings were laid out on the counter in front of a mirror, plus a little makeup, a bottle of perfume.

Murphy appeared beside me and stood with me, looking at the bathroom. She seemed a lot smaller than she usually does.

'She called us,' Murphy said. 'Nine one one has the call recorded. That's how we knew to come out here. She called and said that she knew who had killed Jennifer Stanton and Tommy Tomm and that now they were coming for her. Then she started screaming.'

'That's when the spell hit her. The phone probably went out right after.'

Murphy frowned up at me and nodded. 'Yeah. It did. But it was working fine when we got here.'

'Magic disrupts technology sometimes. You know that.' I rubbed at one eye. 'Have you talked to any relatives, anything like that?'

Murphy shook her head. 'There aren't any relatives in town. We're looking, now, but it might take some time. We tried to reach her boss, but he wasn't available. A Mr Beckitt?' She studied my face, waiting for me to say something. 'You ever heard of him?' she asked, after a moment.

I didn't look back at Murphy. I shrugged.

Murphy's jaw tensed, little motions at the corners of her face. Then she said, 'Greg and Helen Beckitt. Three years ago, their daughter, Amanda, was killed in a cross fire. Johnny Marcone's thugs were shooting it out with some of the Jamaican gang that was trying to muscle in on the territory back then. One of them shot the little girl. She lived for three weeks in intensive care and died when they took her off life support.'

I didn't say anything. But I thought of Mrs Beckitt's numb face and dead eyes.

'The Beckitts attempted to lodge a wrongful death suit against Johnny Marcone, but Marcone's lawyers were too good. They got it thrown out before it even went to court. And they never found the man who shot the little girl. Word has it that Marcone offered to pay them blood money. Make reparation. But they turned him down.'

I didn't say anything. Behind us, they were putting Linda in a body bag, sealing her in. I heard men count to three and lift her, put her onto a gurney of some kind, and wheel her out. One of the forensics guys told Murphy they were going to take a break and would be back in ten minutes. She nodded and sent them out. The room got even more quiet.

'Well, Harry,' she said. Her voice was hushed, like she didn't want to disturb the apartment's new stillness. 'What can you tell me?' There was a subtle weight to the question. She might as well have asked me what I wasn't telling her. That's what she meant. She took her hand out of her jacket pocket and handed me a plastic bag.

I took it. Inside was my business card, the one I'd given to Linda. It was still curled a little, where I'd had to palm it. It was also speckled with what I presumed was Linda's blood. I looked at the part of the bag where you write the case number and the identification of the piece of evidence. It was blank. It wasn't on the records. It wasn't official. Yet.

Murphy was waiting for my answer. She wanted me to tell her something. I just wasn't sure if she was waiting for me to tell her that a lot of people have my card, and that I didn't know how it had gotten here, or if she wanted me to say how I had known the victim, how I had been involved with her. Then she would have to ask me questions. The kinds of questions you ask suspects.

'If I tell you,' I said, 'that I was having a psychic premonition, would you take me seriously?'

'What kind of premonition?' she said. She didn't look up at me.

'I sense . . .' I paused, thinking of my words. I wanted them to be very clear. 'I sense that this woman will have a police record, probably for possession of narcotics and solicitation. I sense that she used to work at the Velvet

Room for Madame Bianca. I sense that she used to be close friends and lovers with Jennifer Stanton. I sense that if she had been approached, yesterday, and asked about those deaths, that she would have claimed to know nothing.'

Murphy mulled over my words for a moment. 'You know, Dresden,' she said, and her voice was tight, cool, furious, 'if you'd *sensed* these things yesterday, or maybe even this morning, it's possible that we could have talked to her. It's possible that we could have found out something from her. It's even *possible*' – and she turned to me and slammed me against the doorway with one forearm and the weight of her body, suddenly and shockingly hard – 'it's even possible,' she snarled, 'that she'd still be *alive*.' She stared up at my face, and she didn't look at all like a cutesy cheerleader, now. She looked like a mother wolf standing over the body of one of her cubs and getting ready to make someone pay for it.

This time I was the one to look away. 'A lot of people have my card,' I said. 'I put them up all over the place. I don't know how she got it.'

'Godammit, Dresden,' she said. She stepped back from me and walked away, toward the bloodstained sheets. 'You're holding out on me. I know you are. I can get a warrant for your arrest. I can have you brought in for questioning.' She turned back to me. 'Someone's killed three people already. It's my *job* to stop them. It's what I do.'

I didn't say anything. I could smell the soap and shampoo from Linda Randall's bath.

'Don't make me choose, Harry.' Her voice softened, if not her eyes or her face. 'Please.'

I thought about it. I could bring everything to her. That's what she was asking – not half the story, not part of the information. She wanted it all. She wanted all the pieces in front of her so she could puzzle them together and bring the bad guys in. She didn't want to work the puzzle knowing that I was keeping some of the pieces in my pocket.

What could it hurt? Linda Randall had called me earlier that evening. She had planned on coming to me, to talk to me. She was going to give me some information and someone had shut her up before she could.

I saw two problems with telling Murphy that. One, she would start thinking like a cop. It would not be hard to find out that Linda wasn't exactly a high-fidelity piece of equipment. That she had numerous lovers on both sides of the fence. What if she and I were closer than I was admitting? What if I'd used magic to kill her lovers in a fit of jealous rage and then waited for another storm to kill her, too? It sounded plausible, workable, a crime of passion – Murphy had to know that the DA would have a hell of a time proving magic as a murder weapon, but if it had been a gun instead, it would have flown.

The second problem, and the one that worried me a lot more, was that there were already three people dead. And if I hadn't gotten lucky and creative, there would have been two more dead people, back at my apartment. I still didn't know who the bad guy was. Telling Murphy what little more I knew wouldn't give her any helpful information. It would only make her ask more questions, and she wanted answers.

If the voice in the shadows knew that Murphy was heading the investigation to find him, and was on the right track, he would have no qualms about killing her, too. And there was nothing she could do to protect herself against it. She might have been formidable to your average criminal, but all the aikido in the world wouldn't do her any good against a demon.

Then, too, there was the White Council. Men like Morgan and his superiors, secure in their own power, arrogant and considering themselves above the authority of any laws but their own, wouldn't hesitate to remove one police lieutenant who had discovered the secret world of the White Council.

I looked at the bloodstained sheets and thought of Linda's corpse. I thought of Murphy's office, and what it would look like with her sprawled on the floor, her heart torn from her chest, or her throat torn out by some creeping thing from beyond.

'Sorry, Murph,' I said. My voice came out in a rasping whisper. 'I wish I could help you. I don't know anything useful.' I didn't try to look up at her, and I didn't try to hide that I was lying.

I sensed, more than saw, the hardening around her eyes, the little lines of hurt and anger. I'm not sure if a tear fell, or if she really just raised a hand to brush back some of her hair. Then she turned to the front door, and shouted, 'Carmichael! Get your ass in here!'

Carmichael looked equally as slobbish as he had a few days ago, as though the passage of time hadn't changed him — it certainly hadn't changed his jacket, only the food stains on his tie and the particular pattern of rumplement to his hair. There had to be something comforting, I reflected, in that kind of stability. No matter how bad things got, no matter how horrible or sickening the scene, you could count on Carmichael to look like the same quality of crap. He glared at me as he came in. 'Yeah?'

She tossed the plastic bag to him, and he caught it.

'Mark that and log it,' she said. 'Hang around for a minute. I want a witness.'

Carmichael looked down at the bag and saw my card. His beady eyes widened. He looked back up at me, and I saw the shift in gears in his head, reclassifying me from *annoying ally* to *suspect*.

'Mr Dresden,' Murphy said. She kept her tone frosty, polite. 'There are some questions we'd like to ask you. Do you think you could come down to the station and make a statement?'

Questions to be asked. The White Council would convene and execute me in a little more than thirty hours. I didn't have time for questions. 'I'm sorry, Lieutenant. I've got to comb my hair tonight.'

'Tomorrow morning, then,' she said.

'We'll see,' I said.

'If you aren't there in the morning,' Murphy said, 'I'm going to ask for a warrant. We'll come and find you and by God, Harry, I'll get some answers to this.'

'Suit yourself,' I told her, and I started for the door. Carmichael took a step forward and stood in my way. I stopped and looked at him, and he kept his eyes focused on the center of my chest. 'If I'm not under arrest,' I told her, 'then I presume I'm free to go.'

'Let him go, Ron,' Murphy said. Her tone of voice was disgusted, but I could hear the hurt underneath it. 'I'll talk to you again soon, Mr Dresden.' She stepped closer and said, in a perfectly even tone, 'And if it turns out that you're the one behind all this, rest assured. Whatever you can do and whatever you can pull, I will find you and I will bring you down. Do you understand me?'

I did understand, really. I understood the pressure she

was under, her frustration, her anger, and her determination to stop the killing from happening again. If I was some kind of hero from a romance novel, I'd have said something brief and eloquent and heartrending. But I'm just me, so I said, 'I do understand, Karrin.'

Carmichael stepped out of my way.

And I walked away from Murphy, who I couldn't talk to, and from Linda, who I couldn't protect, my head aching, weary to my bones, and feeling like a total piece of shit.

16

I walked down the block from Linda Randall's apartment building, my thoughts and emotions a far more furious thunderstorm than the one now rolling away from the city, out over the vastness of the lake. I called a cab from the pay phone outside a gas station and stood about with my back resting against the wall of the building in the misting rain, scowling and waiting.

I had lost Murphy's trust. It didn't matter that I had done what I had to protect both her and myself. Noble intentions meant nothing. It was the results that counted. And the results of my actions had been telling a bald-faced lie to one of the only people I could come close to calling a friend. And I wasn't sure that, even if I found the person or persons responsible, even if I worked out how to bring them down, even if I did Murphy's job for her, that what had happened between us could ever be smoothed over.

My thoughts were on that topic and similar issues of doom and gloom when a man with a hat pulled low over his face began to walk past me, stopped halfway, then turned and drove his fist into my belly.

I had time to think, *Not again*, and then he struck me a second, and third time. Each blow drove into my guts, thrust me back against the unyielding wall, made me sick. My breath flew out of my mouth in a little, strangling gasp, and even if I'd had a spell already in mind, I wouldn't have had the breath to speak it.

I sort of sagged when he stopped hitting me, and he threw me to the ground. We were at a well-lit gas station, just before midnight on a Friday night, and anything he did was in full view of any cars going by. Surely, God, he didn't plan on killing me. Though at the moment, I was too tired and achy to care.

I lay there for a moment, dazed. I could smell my attacker's sweat and cologne. I could tell it was the same person who had jumped me the night before. He grabbed my hair, jerked my head up, and, with an audible snip of steel scissors, cut off a big lock of my hair. Then let me go.

My blood went cold.

My hair. The man had cut off my hair. It could be used in almost any kind of magic, any kind of deadly spell, and there wouldn't be a damned thing I could do to stop it.

The man turned away, walking quickly, but not running. In a flood of panic and desperation, I leapt at his leg, got him around the knee, and yanked hard. I heard a distinctive little *pop*, and then the man screamed, 'Son of a bitch!' and fell heavily to earth. One fist, one very large and knob-knuckled fist, was clutched around my hair. I tried to suck in a breath, and leapt for that hand.

My attacker's hat had fallen off, and I recognized him – one of Johnny Marcone's men who had followed me from the hotel on Thursday afternoon, the one who had begun limping after jogging after me for several blocks. Apparently, Gimpy had a trick knee, and I had just made it jump through its hoop.

I grabbed his wrist and held on with both hands. I'm not a particularly strong man, but I'm made out of wire, and stubborn as hell. I curled up around his wrist and hung on, trying to pry at his thick fingers. Gimpy tried to jerk his arm away. He was carrying a lot of muscle on that arm, but it wasn't enough to move the weight of my whole body. He shoved at me with his other arm, trying to push me off of him, then started pounding at me with one fist.

'Let go of me, dammit,' Gimpy shouted. 'Get off of me!'

I hunched my head down, my shoulders up, and hung on. If I could dig my thumbs into his tendons for long enough, his hand would have to open, no matter how strong he was. I tried to imagine his wrist as Play-Doh and my thumbs as solid steel, pushing into him, and held on for everything I was worth. I felt his fingers start to loosen. I could see the dark, thin strands of my hair.

'Jesus Christ,' someone shouted. 'Hey, Mike, come on!'

There were running footsteps.

And then a couple of young guys dressed in jogging suits and sneakers came over and dragged me off Gimpy. I screamed, incoherently, as my hands slipped from Gimpy's wrist. Some of my hair spilled out, onto the wet concrete, but more stayed in his grip as his fingers closed over it again.

'Easy, easy, man,' one of the guys was saying as they dragged me off. 'Take it easy.'

There wasn't any use struggling against the pair of them. Instead, I dragged in a breath and managed to gasp, 'Wallet. He's got my wallet.'

Considering the way I was dressed, compared to Gimpy's suit and coat, that was one lie that was never going to get off the ground. Or at least, it wouldn't have, if Gimpy hadn't turned and started hurrying away. The two men let me go, confused. Then, taking the cautious route, they started away, walking hurriedly back to their car.

I struggled to my feet and after Gimpy, wheezing like

a leaky accordion. Gimpy headed across the street to a car, and was already in it and leaving by the time I got there. I shambled to a halt in a cloud of his exhaust, and stared dully after his taillights as he drove off into the misting rain.

My heart pounded in my chest and didn't slow down even after I recovered my breath. My hair. Johnny Marcone now had a lock of my hair. He could give it to someone who used magic, and use it to do whatever they damn well pleased to me.

They could use my hair to tear my heart from my chest, rip it right out, like they had done to Jennifer Stanton, Tommy Tomm, and poor Linda Randall. Marcone had warned me to stop, twice, and now he was going to take me out once and for all.

My weariness, fear, and fatigue were abruptly burned away by anger. 'Like hell,' I snarled. 'Like hell you will!'

All I had to do was to find them, find Johnny Marcone, find Gimpy, and find Marcone's wizard, whoever he or she was. Find them, get my hair back, lay them out like ninepins, and send in Murphy to round them up.

By God, I wasn't going to take this lying down. These assholes were serious. They'd already tried to kill me once, and they were coming after me again. Marcone and his boys—

No, I thought. Not Marcone. That didn't make any sense, unless it had been Marcone's gang dealing the ThreeEye from the very beginning. If Marcone had a wizard in residence, why would he have tried to bribe me away? Why not just swipe a lock of hair from me when he'd sent the thug with the bat, and then kill me when I didn't pay attention?

Could it be Marcone? Or could his thug be playing two sides of the street?

I decided that ultimately it didn't matter. One thing was clear: Someone had a lock of my hair. Some wizard, somewhere, meant to kill me.

Whoever this wizard was, he wasn't much good – I'd seen that when I'd wiped out his shadow-sending spell. He couldn't stand up to me if I could force him into a direct confrontation – he might have a lot of moxie, and a lot of raw power, to harness the storms as he had and to slap a demon into servitude. But he was like a big, gawky teenager, new to his strength. I had more than just strength, more than just moxie. I had training, experience, and savvy on my side.

Besides. At the moment I was mad enough to chew up nails and spit out paper clips.

The Shadowman couldn't take a shot at me yet. He didn't have that kind of strength. He needed to wait for the storms that came each spring, and to use them to kill me. I had time. I had time to work. If I could just find out where they were, where Gimpy had taken my hair, I could go after him.

The answer came to me in a flash, and it seemed simple. If the hair could be used as a link to the rest of me, I should be able to reverse it – to create a link from me back to the hair. Hell, maybe I could just set it on fire, burn it all up from my apartment. The formula for a spell like that would be screwy as hell, though. I needed Bob. Bob could help me work out a spell, figure out a formula like that in minutes instead of hours or days.

I grimaced. Bob was gone, and would be for almost another twenty-four hours. There was no way I could work out that formula in less than ten or twelve hours by myself, and I didn't think my brain was coherent enough to come up with solid calculations at the moment, anyway.

I could have called Murphy. Murphy would have known where Marcone was lurking, and Gimpy would probably be nearby. She could have given me an idea, at least, of how to find Gentleman Johnny, Gimpy, and the Shadowman. But she never would, now. And even if she did, she'd demand to know the whole story, and after I'd told it to her, she'd try to take me into protective custody or something ridiculous like that.

I clenched my fists, hard, and my nails dug into my palms. I should trim them sometime—

I looked down at my nails. Then hurriedly crossed the street to stand under the gas station's lights, and stared at my hands.

There was blood under my fingernails, where they'd bitten into Gimpy's wrists. I threw back my head and laughed. I had everything I needed.

I moved back out of the misting rain and squatted down on the concrete sidewalk. I used a bit of chalk I keep in my duster pocket to sketch out a circle on the concrete, surrounding me. Then I scraped the blood out from under my nails and put it onto the concrete between my feet. It glistened in the fine, misty fall of rain.

The next part took me a moment to figure out, but I settled for using the tracking spell I already knew rather than trying to modify it to something a little more dignified. I plucked out a couple of nose hairs and put them in the circle, too, on top of the bits of Gimpy's skin and blood. Then I touched a finger to the chalk circle and willed energy into it, closing it off.

I gathered up my energy, from my anger, my renewed fear, my aching head and queasy stomach, and hurled it into the spell. '*Segui votro testatum.*'

There was a rush of energy that focused on my nostrils and made me sneeze several times in a row. And then it came to me, quite strongly, the scent of Gimpy's cologne. I stood up, opened the circle again with a swipe of my foot, and walked out of it. I turned in a slow circle, all the way around. Gimpy's scent came to me strongly from the southwest, out toward some of the richer suburbs of Chicago.

I started laughing again. I had the son of a bitch. I could follow him back to Marcone, or whoever he was working for, but I had to do it now. I hadn't had enough blood to make it last long.

'Hey, buddy!' The cabby leaned out the window and glared at me, the engine running at an idle, the end of his cheroot glowing orange.

I stared at him for a second. 'What?'

He scowled. 'What, are you deaf? Did someone call for a cab?'

I grinned at him, still angry, still a little light-headed, still eager to go kick Gimpy and the Shadowman's teeth in. 'I did.'

'Why do I get all the nuts?' he said. 'Get in.'

I did, closing the door behind me. He eyed me suspiciously in the mirror and said, 'Where to?'

'Two stops,' I told him. I gave him my apartment's address, and sat back in the seat, my head automatically drawn toward the southwest, toward where the men who wanted to kill me were.

'That's one,' he said. 'Where's number two?'

I narrowed my eyes. I needed a few things from my apartment. My talismans, my blasting rod, my staff, a fetish that should still be vital. And after that, I was going to have a serious talk with one of Chicago's biggest gangsters.

'I'll tell you when we get there.'

17

We ended up at the Varsity, a club Marcone owned in a Chicago suburb. It was a busy place, catering to much of the college-age crowd to be found on this side of the city, and even at one-thirty in the morning it was still fairly crowded for someplace so isolated, alone in a strip mall, the only business open at this time of the evening, the only lit windows in sight.

'Loony,' the cabby muttered as he drove away, and I had to pause for a moment and agree with him. I had directed him about in a meandering line, the spell I'd cast letting me literally follow my nose along Gimpy's trail. The spell had begun fading almost the moment I'd cast it − I didn't have enough blood to make a more lasting enchantment − but it had held long enough for me to zero in on the Varsity, and to identify Gimpy's car in the parking lot. I walked past the windows and, sure enough, in a large, circular booth in the back I saw Johnny Marcone, the bull-necked Mr Hendricks, Gimpy, and Spike, sitting together and talking. I ducked out of sight in a hurry, before one of them noticed me. Then walked back into the parking lot to consider exactly what I had at my disposal.

A bracelet on each wrist. A ring. My blasting rod. My staff.

I thought of all the subtle and devious means by which I might tilt the situation in my favor − clever illusions, conveni-ent faltering of electricity or water, a sudden invasion of rats or cockroaches. I could have managed any of them. Not many people who use magic are that versatile, but very few have the kind of experience and training it takes to put such spells together on the fly.

I shook my head, irritated. I didn't have time to bother with subtlety.

Power into the talismans, then. Power into the ring. I reached for the power in both the staff and rod, cool strength of wood and seething anger of fire, and stepped up to the front door of the Varsity.

Then I blew it off its hinges.

I blew it out, rather than in. Pieces flew toward me and bounced off the shield of air I held in front of me, while others rained back behind me, into the parking lot. It wouldn't do to injure a bunch of innocent diners on the other side. You only get one chance to make a first impression.

Once the door was off, I pointed my blasting rod inside and spoke a command. The jukebox slammed back against the wall as though a cannonball had impacted it, and then melted into a puddle of liquid-plastic goo. The music squealed out the speakers and stopped. I stepped into the doorway and released a pent-up wave of energy from my ring. Starting at the door and then circling throughout the room, the lightbulbs began to explode with sharp little detonations and showers of powdered glass and glowing bits of filament. People at the bar and at all the wooden tables scattered around the room reacted as people tend to do in this sort of situation. They started screaming and shouting, rising to their feet or ducking beneath their tables in confusion. A few ducked out the fire door at the back of one side of the room. Then there was an abrupt and profound silence. Everyone stood stock-still and stared at the doorway – they stared at me.

At the back table, Johnny Marcone regarded the doorway with his passionless, money-colored eyes. He was not smiling. Mr Hendricks, beside him, was glaring at me, his single eyebrow lowered far enough to threaten him with blinding. Spike was tight-lipped and pale. Gimpy stared at me in pure horror. None of them made any moves or any sound. I guess seeing a wizard cut loose can do that to you.

'Little pig, little pig, let me in,' I said, into the silence. I planted my staff on the ground and narrowed my eyes at Marcone. 'I'd really like to talk to you for a minute, John.'

Marcone stared at me for a moment, then his lips twitched up at the corners. 'You have a singular manner of persuasion, Mr Dresden.' He stood up and spoke aloud to the room without ever taking his eyes off me. He must have been angry, but the icy exterior concealed it. 'Ladies and gentlemen, the Varsity is closing early, it would seem. Please make an orderly exit through the door nearest you. Don't worry about your bills. Mr Dresden, if you would step out of the doorway and allow my customers to leave?'

I stepped out of the doorway. The place cleared out fast, customers and staff alike, leaving me alone in the room with Marcone, Hendricks, Spike, and Gimpy. None of them moved as they waited for the customers, the witnesses, to leave. Gimpy started sweating. Hendricks's expression never changed. The big man was as patient as a mountain lion, ready to leap out on the unsuspecting deer.

'I want my hair back,' I said, as soon as the last college-age couple had hustled out the door.

'Beg pardon?' Marcone said. His head tilted to one side, and he seemed genuinely puzzled.

'You heard me,' I said. 'This piece of trash of yours' – I swung my blasting rod up and pointed it at Gimpy – 'just jumped me outside a gas station across town and cut off some of my hair. I want it back. I'm not going to go out like Tommy Tomm did.'

Marcone's eyes abruptly shone with a terrible, cold, money-colored anger. He turned his head, deliberately, to Gimpy.

Gimpy's broad face went a bit more pasty. He blinked a trickle of sweat out of his eyes. 'I don't know what he's talking about, boss.'

Marcone's gaze never wavered. 'I presume, Mr Dresden,' he said, 'that you have some kind of proof?'

'Look at his left wrist,' I said. 'He's got several finger-nail marks on his skin where I grabbed him.'

Marcone nodded, those cold, tiger's eyes on Gimpy's, and said, almost gently, 'Well?'

'He's lying, boss,' Gimpy protested. He licked at his lips. 'Hell, I got some fingernail marks from my girl. He knew that. You know what you said, he's for real, he knows things.'

The pieces of the puzzle fell into place. 'Whoever killed Tommy Tomm knows that I'm on his trail,' I said. 'Your rival, whoever it is selling the ThreeEye. Gimpy here must have gotten a sweet deal from him to turn on you. He's been providing your rival with information all along, running errands for him.'

Gimpy couldn't have played a game of poker to save his life. He stared at me in horror, shook his head in protest.

'There's an easy way to settle this,' Marcone said, his voice smooth and even. 'Lawrence. Show me your wrist.'

'He's lying, boss,' Gimpy Lawrence said again, but his voice was shaking. 'He's just trying to mess with your head.'

'Lawrence,' Marcone said, his tone the gentle reproof of parent to child.

Gimpy Lawrence knew it was over. I saw the desperate decision in his face before he actually moved. 'Liar!' he howled at me. He got up, lifting his hand from underneath the table. I had time to realize he held a revolver, virtually a twin to my own .38, in his fist, before he started shooting.

Several things happened at the same time. I lifted my hand, focusing my will on the bracelet of tiny medieval-style shields around my left wrist, and hardened the protective energies around me. Bullets hammered against it with whining noises, striking sparks in the near dark of the restaurant.

Spike leapt clear of the table, staying low, a small Uzi-style automatic now in his hand. Hendricks was more ruthless and direct, reacting with the mindlessly violent instincts of a savage. With one hand, the big bodyguard hauled Marcone back, putting his own bulk between the mob boss and Gimpy Lawrence. With the other hand, he produced a compact semiautomatic.

Gimpy Lawrence turned his head and saw Hendricks and his gun. He panicked, turning his own weapon toward the larger man.

Hendricks shot him with a ruthless efficiency, three sharp claps of sound, three flashes of muzzle light. The first two shots hit Gimpy in the middle of his chest, driving him back a pair of steps. The third hit him over the right eyebrow, jerked his head back, and toppled him to the ground.

Gimpy Lawrence had dark eyes, like mine. I could see them. His head turned toward me as he lay there on the floor. I saw him blink, once. Then the lights went out of them, and he was gone.

I stood there for a moment, stunned. Grand entrance or not, this wasn't what I had wanted to happen. I didn't want to kill anyone. Hell, I didn't want anyone to die, not me and not them. I felt sick. It had been a sort of game, a macho contest of showmanship I had been determined to win. All of a sudden, it wasn't a game anymore, and I just wanted to walk away from it alive.

We all stood there, no one moving. Then Marcone said, from beneath Hendricks, 'I wanted him alive. He could have answered several questions, first.'

Hendricks frowned and got up off of Marcone. 'Sorry, boss.'

'That's all right, Mr Hendricks. Better to err on the side of caution, I suppose.' Marcone stood up, straightened his tie, then went and knelt by the body. He felt the man's throat, then wrist, and shook his head. 'Lawrence, Lawrence. I would have paid you twice what they offered you, if you'd come to me with it. You never were very smart, were you?' Then, his face showing no more emotion than it had the entire evening, Marcone peeled back Gimpy Lawrence's left sleeve, and studied the man's wrist. He frowned, and lowered the arm again, his expression pensive.

'It would seem, Mr Dresden,' he said, 'that we have a common enemy.' He turned to focus his gaze on me. 'Who is it?'

I shook my head. 'I don't know. If I did, I wouldn't be here. I thought maybe it was you.'

Marcone lifted his eyebrows. 'You should have known me better than that, Mr Dresden.'

It was my turn to frown. 'You're right. I should have.'

The killings had been more vicious, savage than Marcone would have cared to use. Competitors might have to be removed, but there would be no sense in making a production of it. Certainly, there was no reason to murder bystanders, like Linda, like Jennifer Stanton. It was inefficient, bad for business.

'If he has something of yours, you are welcome to take it, Mr Dresden,' Marcone said. He looked around the room and sighed. 'Better hurry. I think the Varsity has seen its last crowd. A shame.'

It was hard, but I walked over to Gimpy Lawrence's body. I had to set aside my staff, my rod, to rifle the corpse's pockets. I felt like a ghoul, crouched over the body of a dead man, picking what was valuable to me off of it, out of his pockets.

I didn't find my hair anywhere. I looked up at Marcone, and he regarded me, my eyes, without any readable emotion.

'Nothing,' I told him.

'Interesting. He must have passed the material in question to someone else before he came here,' Marcone said.

'Someone after he got here, maybe?'

Marcone shook his head. 'I am quite sure he did not do that. I would have noticed.'

'I believe you,' I told him, and I did. 'But who?'

'Our enemy,' Marcone said. 'Obviously.'

I closed my eyes, suddenly sagging with weariness. 'Dammit.'

Marcone said nothing. He stood up, and issued a few quiet orders to Hendricks and Spike. Hendricks wiped down his gun with a napkin, then left it lying on the floor. Spike went over behind the bar and started to do something involving a power cord and a bottle of whiskey.

I gathered up my staff and rod, stood up, and turned to Marcone. 'Tell me what else you know. I need everything you have if I'm going to catch this guy.'

Marcone considered that, and nodded. 'Yes, you do. Unfortunately, you chose a public forum for this discussion. You have set yourself up in the eyes of anyone who cared to watch as my enemy. As understandable as your reasons might have been, the fact that you have publicly defied me remains. I cannot let that go without response, regardless of my personal feelings, without inviting more of the same. I must maintain control. It isn't personal, Mr Dresden. It's business.'

I tightened my jaw, and my grip on my blasting rod, and made sure my shield was still there, ready to go. 'So what are you going to do about it?'

'Nothing,' he said. 'I need do nothing. Either our enemy will kill you, in which case I need not risk myself or my people in removing you, or you will find him in time and bring him down. If you do defeat him, I will let it be understood to any who ask that you did so at my behest, after which I will be inclined to forget this evening. Either way, it profits me best to wait and see.'

'If he kills me,' I pointed out, 'if I'm the next one to have my heart ripped out, you still won't know where he is. You won't be any closer to removing him and protecting your business.'

'True,' Marcone said. Then he smiled, an expression that lasted for only a fraction of a second. 'But I think you will not be such easy prey. I think that even if he kills you, he will reveal himself in some way. And since our encounter the other day, I think I have a better feel for what sorts of things to look for.'

I scowled at him and turned to go, moving briskly toward the door.

'Harry,' he said. I stopped and turned back around.

'On a personal note – I know nothing that would profit you in any case. All of his people we managed to take revealed nothing. They were that afraid of him. No one seems to know just where the drug comes from, from what it is made, or where this person does business. Shadows, they say. That he is always in the shadows. That is all that I have learned.'

I regarded Johnny Marcone for a moment, and then nodded, once. 'Thank you.'

He shrugged. 'Good luck. I think it would be best if you and I did not encounter one another in the future. I cannot tolerate any more interference in my affairs.'

'I think that's a good idea, too,' I said.

'Excellent. It is good to have someone who understands.' And then he turned back toward his remaining two men, leaving the corpse of Gimpy Lawrence on the floor behind him.

I turned and trudged out of the place, into the night and the cold and the misty rain. I still felt sick, could still see Gimpy Lawrence's eyes as he died. I could still hear Linda Randall's husky laughter in my head. I still regretted lying to Murphy, and I still had no intentions of telling her any more than I already had. I still didn't know who was trying to kill me. I still had no defense to present to the White Council.

'Let's face it, Harry,' I told myself. 'You're still screwed.'

18

Have you ever felt despair? Absolute hopelessness? Have you ever stood in the darkness and known, deep in your heart, in your spirit, that it was never, ever going to get better? That something had been lost, forever, and that it wasn't coming back?

That's what it felt like, walking out of the Varsity, walking out into the rain. When I'm in turmoil, when I can't think, when I'm exhausted and afraid and feeling very, very alone, I go for walks. It's just one of those things I do. I walk and I walk and sooner or later something comes to me, something to make me feel less like jumping off a building.

So I walked. It was pretty stupid, in retrospect, walking around Chicago late on a Saturday night. I didn't look up very often. I walked and let things roll around in my head, my hands in the pockets of my duster, which flapped around my long legs while the light rain gradually plastered my hair to my head.

I thought about my father. I usually do, when I get that low. He was a good man, a generous man, a hopeless loser. A stage magician at a time when technology was producing more magic than magic, he had never had much to give his family. He was on the road most of the time, playing run-down houses, trying to scratch out a living for my mother. He wasn't there when I was born.

He wasn't there when she died.

He showed up more than a day after I'd been born. He

gave me the names of three magicians, then took me with him, on the road, entertaining children and retirees, performing in school gymnasiums and grocery stores. He was always generous, kind – more kind and more generous than we could afford, really. And he was always a little bit sad. He would show me pictures of my mother, and talk about her, every night. It got to where I almost felt that I knew her, myself.

As I got older, the feeling increased. I saw my father, I think, as she must have – as a dear, sweet, gentle man. A little naive, but honest and kind. Someone who cared for others, and who didn't value material gain over all else. I can see why she would have loved him.

I never got to be old enough to be his assistant, as he had promised me. He died in his sleep one night. An aneurism, the doctors said. I found him, cold, smiling. Maybe he'd been dreaming of Mother when he went. And as I looked at him, I suddenly felt, for the very first time in my life, utterly, entirely alone. That something was gone that would never return, that a little hole had been hollowed out inside of me that wasn't ever going to be filled again.

And that was how I felt, that rainy spring night in Chicago, walking along the streets, my breath pluming into steam, my right boot creaking with every step, dead people occupying all of my thoughts.

I shouldn't have been surprised, I suppose, when after hours of walking, my steps carried me back to Linda Randall's apartment. The police were all gone, now, the lights all off, all the gawking neighbors cozy in their beds. It was quiet in the apartment complex. Dawn wasn't yet brushing the sky, but somewhere, on a window ledge or in a rooftop nest, a bird was twittering.

I was at the end of my strength, my resources. I hadn't thought of anything, hadn't come up with any brilliant ideas. The killer was going to get a spell together to kill me the next time he had a storm to draw on, and from the way the air felt that could be anytime. If he didn't kill me, Morgan would certainly have the White Council set to execute me at dawn on Monday. The bastard was probably out lobbying votes, already. If the matter came before the Council, I wouldn't stand a chance.

I leaned against the door to Linda's apartment. It was striped with POLICE LINE – DO NOT CROSS yellow-and-black tape. I didn't really realize what I was doing until I had already worked a spell that opened the door, unfastened the lowest strip of yellow tape, and walked into her apartment.

'This is stupid, Harry,' I told myself. I guess I wasn't in the mood to listen. I walked around Linda's apartment, smelling her perfume and her blood. They hadn't come to clean up the blood, yet. The apartment manager would probably have to handle that, later. They never really show you details like that at the movies.

I eventually found myself lying on the floor, on the carpeting next to Linda Randall's large bed. I was curled on my side, my back to her bed, my face toward the sliding glass doors that led out to her little concrete patio. I didn't feel like moving, like going anywhere, like doing anything. Useless. It had all been useless. I was going to die in the next two days.

The worst part was that I wasn't sure that I cared. I was just so tired, exhausted from all the magic I'd had to use, from the walking, from the bruises and punches and lack of sleep. It was dark. Everything was dark.

I think I must have fallen asleep. I needed it, after everything that had happened. I don't remember anything else, until the sun was too bright in my eyes.

I blinked and lifted a hand against the light, keeping my eyes closed. Mornings had never been my best time, and the sun had risen above the tops of the buildings across the street, cheerful springtime sunshine that dashed down through Linda Randall's curtains, through my eyelids and into my brain. I grumbled something, and rolled over, face to the cool darkness under Linda's bed, back to the warm sunlight.

But I didn't go back to sleep. Instead, I started to get disgusted with myself.

'What the hell are you doing, Harry?' I demanded, out loud.

'Lying down to die,' I told myself, petulantly.

'Like hell,' my wiser part said. 'Get off the floor and get to work.'

'Don't wanna. Tired. Go away.'

'You're not too tired to talk to yourself. So you're not too tired to bail your ass out of the alligators, either. Open your eyes,' I told myself, firmly.

I hunched my shoulders, not wanting to obey, but against my better judgment, I did open my eyes. The sunlight had turned Linda Randall's apartment into an almost cheerful place, overlaid with a patina of gold – empty still, to be sure, but warm with a few good memories. I saw a high-school yearbook lying nearby, underneath the bed, several photographs serving as bookmarks. There was also a framed picture of a much-younger Linda Randall, smiling brightly, none of the jaded weariness I had seen in her in evidence, standing in her graduation robes between a kind-looking couple in their late fifties. Her parents, I presumed. She looked happy.

And, lying just in the edge of a stray little beam of sunlight, one that was already retreating as the sun rose above the edge of the buildings, was a small, red plastic cylinder with a grey cap.

My salvation.

I snatched it out from under the bed. I was shaking. I shook the canister, and it rattled. A roll of film was inside. I opened up the canister and dumped the film into my hand. The plastic leader had been retracted into the case – there were pictures on the film, but they hadn't been developed yet. I closed the film up again and reached into the pocket of my duster and drew out another canister, the one I'd found at Victor Sells's lake house. The two were a match.

My mind spun around, taking off down a whole new track. An entirely new realm of possibility had opened up to me, and somewhere in it might be my opportunity, my chance to get out of this alive, to catch the killer, to salvage everything that had started going to hell.

But it still wasn't clear. I couldn't be sure what was going on, but I had a possible link now, a link between the murder investigation and Monica Sells's aborted inquiry into the disappearance of her husband, Victor. I had another lead to follow, but there wasn't much time to follow it. I had to get up, to get on my feet, and get going, fast. You can't keep a good wizard down.

I stood up, grabbed my staff and rod, and started toward the door. The last thing I needed was to get caught trespassing on a crime scene. It could get me arrested and stuck in holding, and I'd be dead before I could get bail.

My mind was already rolling ahead, working out the next step, trying to find this photographer who had been at Victor's beach house, and getting these pictures developed and seeing if there was anything in them that was worth Linda Randall's death.

It was then that I heard a sound, and stopped. It came again, a quiet scraping.

Somcone turned the key in the dead bolt of the apartment's front door and swung it open.

19

There was no time to flee beneath the bed, or into the bathroom, and I didn't want to be limited in mobility in any case. I leapt forward and stood behind the door as it opened, keeping very still.

A man entered – slim, short, harried-looking. His hair, a listless shade of brown, was drawn back into a ponytail. He wore dark cotton pants, a dark jacket, and carried a pouch on a strap at his side. He shut the door, most of the way, and looked around with great agitation. But, like most people who are too nervous to be thinking clearly, he was seeing less than he should have been, and though his head swept over where I would have been in his peripheral vision, he didn't notice me. He was a good-looking man, or so it seemed, with strong lines to his jaw and cheekbones.

He crossed the room and stopped short when he saw the bloodstained bed. I saw him clench his hands into fists. He made a strange, cawing little sound, then hurried forward, to throw himself down on the floor by the bed and start pawing underneath it. After a few seconds, his pawing grew more frantic, and I heard him curse out loud.

I slid my fingers over the smooth surface of the film canister in my pocket. So. The mysterious photographer lurking outside of Victor Sells's lake house was here looking for the film. I had a feeling in my stomach like I get when I finish a particularly difficult jigsaw puzzle – a peculiar satisfaction mingled with a touch of smugness.

I settled my staff and rod silently into the corner by the door and flipped my official police consultant's badge, complete with my photograph on it, out of my duster, so that it showed against the black canvas. I covered my ratty old T-shirt with the coat and hoped that the man would be too rattled and nervous to notice that I was wearing sweatpants and cowboy boots beneath the duster.

I kept my hands in my pockets, pushed the door shut with a little nudge of my boot, and just as it closed, said, 'So. Returning to the scene of the crime. I knew we'd catch you if I just waited.'

The man's reaction would have had me rolling in laughter on any other day. He jerked, slammed his head against the bottom of the bed, yelped, drew himself back from the bed, turned to look at me, and all but leapt back over the bed in surprise when he saw me. I revised my opinion of his looks — his mouth was too pinched, his eyes too small and too close together, giving him the intent, predatory look of a ferret.

I narrowed my eyes and stalked toward him one slow pace at a time. 'Just couldn't stay away, could you?'

'No!' he said, 'Oh, God! You don't understand. I'm a photographer. See? See?' He fumbled with the case at his side and produced a camera from it. 'Taking pictures. For the papers. That's what I'm doing here, just trying to get a good look around.'

'Save it,' I told him. 'We both know you aren't here to take pictures. You were looking for this.' And I pulled the film canister out of my pocket, held it up, and showed it to him.

His babbling stopped, and he stood stock-still, staring

at me. Then at the canister. He licked his lips and started trying to say something.

'Who are you?' I asked. I kept my voice gruff, demanding. I tried to think of what Murphy would sound like, if I was downtown with her right now, waiting for her to ask me questions.

'Uh, Wise. Donny Wise.' He swallowed, staring at me. 'Am I in some kind of trouble?'

I narrowed my eyes at him and sneered, 'We'll see about that. Do you have identification?'

'Sure, yeah.'

'Let me see it.' I speared him with a glance, and added, 'Slowly.'

He goggled at me and reached for his hip pocket with exaggerated slowness. With one hand, he drew out his wallet and flipped it open to his driver's license. I stalked toward him, snatched it, and studied it. His license and picture agreed with the name he'd given me.

'Well, Mr Wise,' I began, 'this is an ongoing investigation. So long as you give me your cooperation, I don't think that we—'

I looked up to see him peering at my name badge, and my voice trailed off. He jerked his wallet back, and accused, 'You're not a cop!'

I tilted my head back at an arrogant angle. 'Okay. Maybe not. But I work with the cops. And I've got your film.'

He cursed again and started stuffing his camera back into his bag, clearly meaning to leave. 'No. You got nothing. Nothing that connects any of this to me. I'm out of here.'

I watched him start past me, toward the door. 'Don't be so hasty, Mr Wise. I really think you and I have things to discuss. Like a dropped film canister underneath the deck of a house in Lake Providence, last Wednesday night.'

He flicked a quick glance up at me. 'I have nothing to say to you,' he mumbled, 'whoever the hell you are.' He reached for the door and started to open it.

I gestured curtly to my staff in the corner, and hissed, in my best dramatic voice, *'Vento servitas,'* jerking my hand at the doorway. My staff, driven by tightly controlled channels of air moving in response to my evocation, leapt across the room and slammed the door shut in front of Donny Wise's nose. He went stiff as a board. He turned to face me, his eyes wide.

'My God. You're one of them. Don't kill me,' he said. 'Oh God. You've got the pictures. I don't know anything. Nothing. I'm no danger to you.' He tried to keep his voice calm, but it was shaking. I saw him tilt his eyes at the glass sliding doors to the little patio, as though calculating his chances of making it there before I could stop him.

'Relax, Mr Wise,' I told him. 'I'm not here to hurt you. I'm after the man who killed Linda. Help me. Tell me what you know. I'll take care of the rest.'

He let out a harsh little laugh, and eased a half step toward the glass windows. 'And get myself killed? Like Linda, like those other people? No way.'

'No, Mr Wise. Tell me what you know. I'll put a stop to the killings. I'll bring Linda's murderer to justice.' I tried to keep my voice soothing, even, fighting against the frustration I felt. Hell, I'd wanted to rattle him, but I hadn't meant to scare him so badly that he wanted to jump through a plate-glass sliding door. 'I want these people stopped just as badly as you do.'

'Why?' he demanded. I saw a little contempt in his eyes,

now. 'What was she to you? Were you sleeping with her, too?'

I shook my head. 'No. No, she's just one more dead person who shouldn't be.'

'You're not a cop. Why risk your ass to do this? Why go up against these people? Haven't you seen what they can do?'

I shrugged. 'Who else is going to?' He didn't answer me, so I held up the film canister. 'What are these pictures, Mr Wise? What is on this film that was worth killing Linda Randall for?'

Donny Wise rubbed his palms over his thighs. His ponytail twitched as he looked about the room. 'I'll make you a deal. Give me the film, and I'll tell you what I know.'

I shook my head. 'I might need what's on here.'

'What's there isn't any good to you if you don't know what you're looking at,' he pointed out. 'I don't know you from Adam. I don't want any trouble. All I want is to get my ass out of this alive and in one piece.'

I stared at him for a moment. If I traded him, I'd lose the film, and whatever was on it. If I didn't, and if he was telling me the truth, the film wouldn't do me any good. The trail had led me here, to him. If I didn't dig up a lead to somewhere else, I was dead.

So I snapped my fingers, letting my staff rattle to the floor. Then I tossed him the film, underhand. He dropped it, and stooped to recover it, studying me warily.

'After I get out of here,' he said, 'we're quits. I've never seen you before.'

I nodded. 'Fine. Let's have it.'

Donny swallowed and ran a hand back over his hair, giving his ponytail a nervous little tug at the end of the motion.

'I knew Linda from around. I'd taken some pictures of her, for a portfolio. I do shoots for some of the girls around town. They want to make it into magazines, most of them.'

'Adult magazines?' I asked.

'No,' he snapped, nervous still, 'Uncle Abner's magazine for children. Of course adult mags. Nothing really classy, but you can make some good money even if you're not Hugh Hefner's type.

'So on Wednesday, Linda comes to me. She says she's got a deal for me. I shoot some pictures for her and give her the film, and I get – and she's real nice to me. All I have to do is show up where she says, shoot a roll through the windows, and go. Deliver to her the next day. So I did it. And now she's dead.'

'Out in Lake Providence,' I said.

'Yeah.'

'What did you see there?' I asked.

Donny Wise shook his head, his eyes drawn past me to the bed again. 'Linda. Some other people. No one I knew. They were having some kind of party. All candles and stuff. It was storming like hell, a lot of thunder and lightning, so I couldn't really hear them. I worried for a while about someone looking up and seeing me in the lightning, but I guess they were too busy.'

'They were having sex,' I said.

'No,' he snapped. 'They was playing canasta. Yeah, sex. The real thing, not fake stuff on a set. The real thing don't look as good. Linda, some other woman, three men. I shot my roll and got out.'

I grinned, but he didn't seem to have noticed the double entendre. You just don't get quality lowlife often enough anymore. 'Can you describe any of these other people?'

He shook his head. 'I wasn't looking. But they wasn't being too particular, if you take my meaning. Turned my stomach.'

'Did you know what Linda wanted with the pictures?'

He looked at me and then snickered, as though I were extremely simple. 'Jesus, buddy. What do you think someone wants with pictures like that? She wanted to get leverage on somebody. Hell, it wouldn't hurt her reputation any if pictures of her in the middle of an orgy got out. But it might have, some of the people with her. What kind of simp, wanna-be cop are you?'

I ignored the question. 'What are you going to do with the film, Donny?'

He shrugged. 'Trash it, probably.' I saw his eyes flick from side to side, and I knew that he was lying to me. He'd keep the film, find out who was in the pictures, and if he thought he could get away with it, he'd try to weasel whatever profit he could out of it. He seemed the type, and I trusted my instincts.

'Allow me,' I said, and snapped my fingers. '*Fuego.*'

The canister's grey lid flew off in a little whoosh of flame, and Donny Wise yelped, drawing his hand back sharply. The red canister burst into flame on its way to the ground and landed there in a crumpled, smoking lump.

He stared at the film, then up at me, his mouth gaping.

'I hope I don't find out you've lied to me, Donny,' I told him. He went white as a sheet, assured me that he hadn't, then turned and fled out of the apartment, knocking loose two bits of police tape on the way out. He didn't close the door behind him.

I let him go. I believed him. He didn't seem bright enough to make up a story on the fly, as rattled as he'd been. I felt a ferocious surge of triumph, of anger, and of the desire to find this person, whoever it was, who was taking the raw forces of life and creation and turning them to the ends of destruction, and to put him in the trash with the rest of the garbage. Whoever he was, murdering with magic and killing people by degrees with the ThreeEye drug, he was someone I wanted to put down. My brain lurched into gear, now that there was something to work with, some other possibility for tomorrow morning than me dying in a variety of gruesome ways.

Linda Randall had been planning on blackmailing someone. I took a staggering mental leap and figured it was Victor, or someone out at his house during the party. But why? I didn't have any pictures now, only the information I'd gotten from Donny Wise. I couldn't afford to wait around. I *had* to pursue the lead he'd given me if I was to get to the bottom of this, and find out who had killed Linda.

How had I managed to get into all of this trouble in only a few days? And how in the world had I managed to stumble across what appeared to be a complex and treacherous little plot by chance, out at the house in Lake Providence, on a separate investigation entirely?

Simple answer — it hadn't been an accident. It had all been by design. I had been directed there. Someone had wanted me out at the lake house, had wanted me to get involved and to find out what was going on out there. Someone who was nervous as hell around wizards, who refused to give out her name, who had carefully dropped phrases that would make me believe her ignorance, who had to rush out quickly from her appointment and who was willing to let five hundred dollars go, just to get me off the phone a few seconds faster. Someone had drawn me out and forced me into the open, where I had attracted all sorts of hostile attention.

That was the key.

I gathered up my staff and rod and stalked out the door. It was time to talk to Monica Sells.

20

The cabby dropped me off a block away from Monica Sells's house in the suburbs. I was running out of time, out of Murphy's loan, and out of patience, so I didn't waste any daylight in walking down the street toward her place.

It was a cute little house, two stories, a couple of young trees in the front yard, just now starting to rival the house for height. There was a minivan in the driveway, and a basketball goal, well used. The lawn was grown rather long, but all the recent rains left a good excuse for that. The street was a quiet one, and it took me a moment to realize that most of the houses on it were not occupied. FOR SALE signs stood in many of the yards. Sparse curtains draped over empty, gaping windows, like cobwebs. There wasn't a lot of birdsong, for a street with so many trees, and I couldn't hear any dogs barking as I walked along the sidewalk. Overhead, clouds were thickening, building up for another thunderstorm.

Taken all together, it had the feel of someplace blighted, a place where a black wizard had set up shop. I swung up through the Sells yard and to the front door.

I rang the bell, and waited.

There was no answer.

I knocked. I leaned on the doorbell.

Still no answer.

I tightened my jaw and looked around. I didn't see anyone, so I turned back to the door, preparing to use a spell to open it.

Instead, the door swung open, maybe six inches. Monica Sells stood inside, peering out at me with her green eyes. She was dressed in jeans, a plain flannel shirt with the sleeves rolled up, and her hair was covered by a bandana. She wore no makeup. She looked both older and more appealing that way – I think maybe because it was a more natural look for her, something that was closer to the sort of person she really was, rather than the nicer clothes and jewelry she'd worn when she visited my office. Her face went pale, her lips bloodless.

'I don't have anything to say to you, Mr Dresden,' she said. 'Go away.'

'I can't do that,' I said. She started to swing the door shut, but I jammed the end of my staff into the doorway, keeping it from closing.

'I'll call the police,' she said, voice strained. She leaned against the door, trying to keep me from coming in.

'Do it,' I growled, and then I played a hunch, 'and I'll tell them about you and your husband.' I was taking a shot in the dark, but what the hell. She didn't know that I didn't know what the hell was going on.

My instincts paid off. I heard her suck in a breath and felt her resistance on the door sag a little. I put my shoulder to the door, leaned into it hard, and she stepped back from me in surprise. I don't think she'd expected me to physically force my way into her house. Hell, I hadn't expected me to do that. I hadn't realized how angry I was until I saw the look of panic on her face when she looked up at me. I don't know what I looked like, but it must not have been friendly.

I stopped. I closed my eyes. I took a deep breath, and tried to get a handle on my anger. It wouldn't profit me anything to lose control.

That was when she went for the stunner.

I heard her move, opened my eyes in time to see her snatch a black-plastic case the size of a cellular phone from the piano and lunge toward me. Her face was pale, frightened. Blue lightning danced between the two tines of the stunner as she shoved it at my stomach.

I swept my staff, upright, from right to left, and the buzzing device went past me, along with her lunge, striking the doorframe behind me. I slipped past her, into the living room, turning to face her as she recovered and turned around.

'I won't let you hurt them,' she snarled. 'Not you, not anyone. I'll *kill* you before I let you touch them, wizard.' And then she was coming at me again, fury replacing the terror in her eyes, a grim determination to succeed that made me think of Murphy for a second. For the first time, she was looking me in the face. For the first time she forgot to keep her eyes averted from mine, and in that second, I saw inside of her.

Things seemed to slow down for a moment. I had time to see the color of her eyes, the structure of her face. To recognize where I had seen them before, why she had looked familiar to me. I had time to see, behind her eyes, the fear and the love that motivated every move she made, every step she took. I saw what had moved her to come to me, why she was afraid. I saw her grief, and I saw her pain.

And the pieces all fell into place. Knowing the emotions that drove her, the terrible love that she was showing even now, it all seemed perfectly obvious, and I felt stupid for not figuring it out days ago.

'Stop,' I said, or tried to say, before she thrust the stunner at my chest. I dropped staff and rod alike in a clatter of falling wood, and caught her wrist in both of my hands. She pushed the stunner up at my face, and I let her do it.

It got to within about three inches of me, the light bright in my eyes. Then I drew in a breath and puffed it out onto the stunner, along with an effort of will. There was a spark, a little puff of smoke, and then it went dead in her hands, like every other electronic gizmo seemed to do whenever I came around. Hell, I was surprised it had taken as long as it did to stop working. And even if it hadn't, it wasn't any trouble for me to hex it into uselessness.

I continued holding her wrist, but the driving tension behind her arm had eased away to nothing. She was staring at my face, her eyes wide with shock from the meeting of our gazes. She started shaking and dropped the useless stunner from limp fingers. It clattered to the floor. I let go of her, and she just stared at me.

I was shaking, too. A soulgaze is never something pleasant or simple. God, sometimes I hated that I had to live with that. I hadn't wanted to know that she had been abused as a child. That she'd married a man who provided her with more of the same, as an adult. That the only hope or light that she saw in her life was in her two children. There hadn't been time to see all of her reasons, all of her logic. I still didn't know why she had drawn me into this entire business — but I knew that it was, ultimately, because she loved her two kids.

And that was all I really needed, that and one other connection, the nagging resemblance to someone that I had noticed in her at my office. The rest fell into place from there.

It took Monica Sells a moment to recover herself. She did it with remarkable speed, as though she were a woman used to drawing on a mask again after having it knocked off. 'I . . . I'm sorry, Mr Dresden.' She lifted her chin, and regarded me with a fragile, wounded pride. 'What do you want here?'

'A couple of things,' I told her. I stooped down to recover my staff, my rod. 'I want my lock of hair back. I want to know why you came to me last Thursday, why you dragged me into this mess. And I want to know who killed Tommy Tomm and Jennifer Stanton and Linda Randall.'

Monica's eyes grew even duller, and her face paled. 'Linda's dead?'

'Last night,' I told her. 'And someone's planning on taking me out the same way, the next chance they get.'

Outside, in the far distance, thunder rumbled. Another storm was in the works, slowly building. When it got to town, I was a dead man. It was as simple as that.

I looked back to Monica Sells, and it was all over her face — she knew about the storm just as well as I did. She knew about it, and there was a sort of sad and weary frustration in her eyes.

'You have to go, Mr Dresden,' she said. 'You can't be here when . . . You've got to go, before it's too late.'

I stepped toward her. 'You're the only chance I have, Monica. I asked you once before to trust me. You've got to do it again. You've got to know that I'm not here to hurt you or your—'

A door opened, in the hallway behind Monica. A girl, on the gawky end of preadolescence, with hair the color of her mother's, leaned out into the hallway. 'Mom?' she said in a quavering voice. 'Mom, are you okay? Do you want me to call the police?' A boy, perhaps a year or two younger than his sister, poked his head out, too. He was carrying a well-used basketball in his hands, turning it in nervous little gestures.

I looked back to Monica. Her eyes were closed. There were tears coming, trailing down her cheeks. It took her a moment, but she drew in a breath and spoke to the girl in a clear, calm voice, without turning around. 'I'm fine,' she told them. 'Jenny, Billy, get back into the room and lock the door. I mean it.'

'But Mom—' the boy began.

'Now,' Monica said. Her voice was strained.

Jenny put a hand on her brother's shoulder. 'C'mon, Billy.' She looked at me for just a moment. Her eyes were too old and too knowing for a child her age. 'C'mon.' The two vanished back into the room, closed the door, and locked it behind them.

Monica waited until they were gone, and then broke down into more tears. 'Please. Please, Mr Dresden. You have to go. If you're here when the storm comes, if he knows . . .' She buried her face in her hands and made a quiet, croaking sound.

I stepped closer to her. I had to have her help. No matter how much pain she was in, no matter what kind of agony she was going through, I had to have her help. And I thought I knew the names to invoke to get it.

I can be such a bastard sometimes.

'Monica. Please. I'm up against a wall. I'm out of options. Everything I have leads here. To you. And I don't have time to wait. I need your help, before I wind up just like Jennifer and Tommy and Linda.' I sought her eyes, and she looked up at me without turning her gaze away. 'Please. Help me.' I watched her eyes, saw the fear and the grief and the weariness there. I saw her look at me as I leaned on her, and demanded more out of her than she could afford to give.

'All right,' she whispered. She turned away and walked toward the kitchen. 'All right. I'll tell you what I know, wizard. But there's nothing I can do to help you.' She paused at the doorway and looked back at me. Her words fell with the weight of conviction, simple truth. 'There's nothing anyone can do, now.'

21

Monica Sells had a cheerful, brightly colored kitchen. She collected painted cartoon cows, and they ranged over the walls and cabinet doors of the room in a cheerful, bovine sort of indolence. The refrigerator was covered with crayon drawings and report cards. There was a row of colored glass bottles on the windowsill. I could hear wind chimes outside, restlessly stirred by a cool, rising wind. A big, friendly cow clock on the wall swung its tail back and forth, *tick, tick, tick*.

Monica sat down at the kitchen table. She drew up her legs beneath her, and seemed to relax by a few degrees. Her kitchen, I sensed, was her sanctuary, the place where she retreated when she was upset. It was lovingly maintained, sparkling clean.

I let her relax for as long as I could, which wasn't long. I could almost feel the air building up to greater tension, the storm brewing in the distance. I couldn't afford to play with kid gloves. I was just about to open my mouth, to start pushing, when she said, 'Ask questions, wizard. I'll answer them. I wouldn't even know where to start, myself.' She didn't look at me. She didn't look at anything.

'All right,' I said. I leaned against the kitchen counter. 'You know Jennifer Stanton, don't you? You're related to her.'

Her expression didn't change. 'We have our mother's eyes,' she confirmed. 'My little sister was always the rebel.

She ran away to become an actress, but became a whore instead. It suited her, in her own way. I always wanted her to stop, but I don't think she wanted to. I'm not sure she knew how.'

'Have the police contacted you yet, about her death?'

'No. They called my parents, down in St Louis. They haven't realized, yet, that I live in town. Someone will notice soon, I'm sure.'

I frowned. 'Why didn't you go to them? Why did you come to me?'

She looked over at me. 'The police can't help me, Mr Dresden. Do you think they would believe me? They'd look at me like I was some kind of lunatic, if I went to them babbling about magic spells and rituals.' She grimaced. 'Maybe they'd be right. Sometimes I wonder if I'm going crazy.'

'So you came to me,' I said. 'Why didn't you just tell me the truth?'

'How could I?' she asked. 'How could I walk into the office of someone I didn't even know, and tell him—' She swallowed, and squeezed her eyes shut over more tears.

'And tell me what, Monica?' I asked. I kept my voice soft. 'Who killed your sister?'

Wind chimes tinkled outside. The friendly cow clock went *tick, tick, tick*. Monica Sells drew in a long, shuddering breath and closed her eyes. I saw her gathering up the frayed threads of her courage, knotting them up as tightly as she could. I knew the answer, already, but I needed to hear it from her. I needed to be sure. I tried to tell myself that it would be good for her to face such a thing, just to say it out loud. I wasn't sure I bought that – like I said, I'm not a very good liar.

Monica squeezed her hands into tight fists, and said, 'God help me. God help me. It was my husband, Mr Dresden. It was Victor.' I thought she would dissolve into tears, but instead she just hunched tighter into her little defensive ball, as though she expected someone to start hitting her.

'That's why you wanted me to find him,' I heard myself say. 'That's why you sent me out to the lake house, to look for him. You knew he was there. You knew that if you sent me out there, he would see me.' My voice was quiet, not quite angry, but the words pounded around Monica Sells like sledgehammers throwing up chips of concrete. She flinched from each of them.

'I had to,' she moaned. 'God, Mr Dresden. You don't know what it was like. And he was getting worse. He didn't start as a bad man, really, but he kept getting worse and worse, and I was afraid.'

'For your kids,' I said.

She nodded, and rested her forehead on her knees. And then the words started spilling out of her, slowly at first, and then in a greater and greater rush, as if she couldn't hold back the immense weight of them any longer. I listened. I owed it to her, for walking all over her feelings, for forcing her to talk to me.

'He was never a bad man, Mr Dresden. You have to understand. He worked hard. He worked so hard for us, to give us something better. I think it was because he knew that my parents had been so wealthy. He wanted to give me just as much as they could have, and he couldn't. It would make him so frustrated, so angry. Sometimes he would lose his temper. But it wasn't always so bad. And he could be so kind, sometimes, too. I thought that maybe the children would help him to stabilize.

'It was when Billy was about four that Victor found the magic. I don't know where. But he started getting obsessed with it. He brought home books and books. Strange things. He put a lock on the door to the attic, and after dinner he'd vanish up there. Some nights, he wouldn't come to bed. Some nights, I thought I could hear things, up there. Voices. Or things that weren't voices.' She shuddered.

'He started to get worse. He'd get angry, and things would happen. Little things. The drapes would catch on fire at one edge. Or things would fly off the walls and break.' She turned her haunted gaze toward her cute, tacky cows for a moment, as though assuring herself that they were still there.

'He'd scream at us for no reason. Or burst out laughing for no reason. He . . . He saw things. Things I couldn't see. I thought he was going crazy.'

'But you never confronted him,' I said, quietly.

She shook her head. 'No. God forgive me. I couldn't. I had gotten used to being quiet, Mr Dresden. To not making a fuss.' She took a deep breath and continued. 'Then, one night, he came to me and woke me up. He made me drink something. He told me that it would make me see, make me understand him. That if I drank, I would see the things he saw. That he wanted me to understand him, that I was his wife.' This time, she did start crying, tears that coursed silently down her cheeks, the corners of her mouth.

Something else clicked solidly into place, where I'd already thought it would go. 'The ThreeEye,' I said.

She nodded. 'And . . . I saw things, Mr Dresden. I saw *him*.' Her face screwed up, and I thought she was going to vomit. I could sympathize. To have the Third Sight suddenly opened to you like that, not knowing what it was, what was happening to you; to look on the man you had wed, who had given you children, and to see him for what he truly was, obsessed with power, consumed by greed — it had to have been hell. And it would remain with her. Always. She would never find the memory fading, never find the comfort and solace of years putting a comfortable padding between her and the image of her husband as a monster.

She continued, speaking in a low, hurried rush. 'I wanted more. Even when it was over, even though it was horrible, I wanted more. I tried not to let it show, but he could tell. He looked into my eyes and he *knew*, Mr Dresden. Like you did just now. And he started to laugh. Like he'd just won the lottery. He kissed me, he was so happy. And it made me sick.

'He started making more of the drug. But he could never make enough. It drove him berserk, furious. And then he started to realize that when he was angry, he could do more. He'd look for excuses to be angry. He'd drive himself into rages. But it still wasn't enough.' She swallowed. 'That's when . . . when.'

I thought of frightened pizza drivers and faerie commentary on human 'sporting'. 'That's when he realized that he could touch other people's emotions, too,' I said. 'Use them to help power his magic.'

She nodded, and curled tighter in on herself. 'It was only me, at first. He'd frighten me. And afterward I would be so exhausted. Then he found out that for what he was doing, lust worked better. So he started looking around. For backers. Investors, he called them.' She looked up at me, her eyes pleading. 'Please, Mr Dresden. You have to understand. It wasn't always so bad. There were moments that I could almost see him again. That I thought he was going to come back to us.'

I tried to look on her with compassion. But I wasn't sure I felt anything but fury, that someone, *anyone* should treat his family that way – or anyone else, for that matter. My feelings must have showed on my face, because Monica quickly averted her eyes, and huddled down in fear. She spoke in a hurried voice, as though to put off my rage, in the voice of a woman who has put off rage with desperate words more than once.

'He found the Beckitts. They had money. And he told them that if they would help him, he would help them get their vengeance on Johnny Marcone. For their daughter. They put their trust in him. They gave him all the money he needed.'

I thought of the Beckitts, and their lean, hungry faces. I thought of Mrs Beckitt's dead eyes.

'And he started the rituals. The ceremony. He said he needed our lust.' Her eyes shifted left and right, and the sickened look on her face grew deeper. 'It wasn't so bad. He would close the circle, and all of a sudden, nothing mattered. Nothing but flesh. I could lose myself for a while. It was almost like an escape.' She rubbed her hand on the leg of her jeans, as if trying to wipe something foul off of it. 'But it wasn't enough. That's when he started talking to Jennifer. He knew what she did. That she would know the right kind of people. Like her, like Linda. Linda introduced him to Marcone's man. I don't know his name, but Victor promised him something that was enough to bring him into the circle.

'I didn't have to go all the time, then. Either Jenny or I would stay with the children. Victor made the drug. We started to make money. Things got better for a little while. As long as I didn't think too much.' Monica took a deep breath. 'That's when Victor started getting darker. He called demons. I saw them. And he said he needed more power. He was hungry for it. It was horrible, like watching a starving animal, forever pacing. And I saw him start . . . start *looking* at the children, Mr Dresden. It made me afraid. The way he looked at them, sometimes, I knew—' This time she buckled and doubled toward the floor with a groan. She shuddered and wept, out of control. 'Oh, God. My babies. My babies.'

I wanted to go over to her. To offer her my hand to hold, to put an arm over her shoulders and to tell her that it would be all right. But I knew her, now. I had looked inside. It would make her scream. God, Harry, I thought. Haven't you tortured this poor woman enough?

I rummaged in cabinets until I found a glass. I ran cold water from the sink, poured it into the glass, then went over and put it down by her. She straightened in her chair and took the glass between shaking hands. She took a sip, and spilled a little onto her chin.

'I'm sorry,' I said. It was all I could think of to say.

If she heard me, it didn't show. She sipped water, then continued, as if desperate to finish, to get the taste of the words out of her mouth. 'I wanted to leave him. I knew he'd be furious, but I couldn't let the children stay close to him. I tried to talk to Jenny about it. And she took matters into her own hands. My little sister, trying to protect me. She went to Victor and told him that if he didn't let me leave, she'd go to the police and to Johnny Marcone. She'd tell them all about him. And he . . . he . . .'

'He killed her,' I said. Hell. Victor hadn't needed any of

Jennifer Stanton's hair to kill her. Any kind of sample of bodily fluids would have worked. With the ceremonies of lust that he'd been holding, he'd have had ample opportunity to collect from poor Jennifer Stanton. Maybe he'd even had her bring him a sample from Tommy Tomm. Or maybe Jennifer and Tommy Tomm had just been too close, as they were making love, for the spell to affect just one of them when he killed them.

'He killed her,' Monica confirmed. Her shoulders slumped with a sudden weariness. 'That's when I came to you. Because I thought you might be able to see. Be able to do something, before he hurt my babies. Before he killed someone else. And now Linda's dead, too. And soon you, Mr Dresden. You can't stop him. No one can.'

'Monica,' I said.

She shook her head and curled up in a miserable little ball. 'Go,' she said. 'Oh God. Please go, Mr Dresden. I don't want to see it when he kills you, too.'

My heart felt like a lump of cold wax in my chest. I wanted so badly to tell her that everything would be all right. I wanted to dry her tears and tell her that there was still joy in the world, that there was still light and happiness. But I didn't think she would hear me. Where she was, there was nothing but an endless, hopeless darkness full of fear, pain, and defeat.

So I did the only thing I could. I withdrew in silence and left her to her weeping. Perhaps it would help her start to heal.

To me, it only sounded like pieces of glass falling from a shattered window.

As I walked toward the front door, a little motion to the left caught my eye. Jenny Sells stood in the hallway, a silent wraith. She regarded me with luminous green eyes, like her mother's, like the dead aunt whose namesake she was. I stopped and faced her. I'm not sure why.

'You're the wizard,' she said, quietly. 'You're Harry Dresden. I saw your picture in the newspaper, once. The *Arcane*.'

I nodded.

She studied my face for a long minute. 'Are you going to help my mom?'

It was a simple question. But how do you tell a child that things just aren't that simple, that some questions don't have simple answers – or any answer at all?

I looked back into her too-knowing eyes, and then quickly away. I didn't want her to see what sort of person I was, the things I had done. She didn't need that. 'I'm going to do everything I can to help your mom.'

She nodded. 'Do you promise?'

I promised her.

She thought that over for a moment, studying me. Then she nodded. 'My daddy used to be one of the good guys, Mr Dresden. But I don't think that he is anymore.' Her face looked sad. It was a sweet, unaffected expression. 'Are you going to kill him?'

Another simple question.

'I don't want to,' I told her. 'But he's trying to kill me. I might not have any choice.'

She swallowed and lifted her chin. 'I loved my Aunt Jenny,' she said. Her eyes brightened with tears. 'Momma won't say, and Billy's too little to figure it out, but I know what happened.' She turned, with more grace and dignity than I could have managed, and started to leave. Then said, quietly, 'I hope you're one of the good guys, Mr Dresden.

We really need a good guy. I hope you'll be all right.' Then she vanished down the hall on bare, silent feet.

I left the house in the suburbs as quickly as I could. My legs drove me down the oddly silent sidewalk, and back to the corner where the cabby was waiting, meter ticking away.

I got in the cab and told the cabby to drive me to the nearest pay phone. Then I closed my eyes and struggled to think. It was hard, through all the pain I felt. Maybe I'm stupid or something, but I hate to see people like Monica, like little Jenny, hurting like that. There shouldn't be pain like that in the world, and every time I run into it, it makes me furious. Furious and sad. I didn't know if I wanted to scream or to cry. I wanted to pound Victor Sells's face in, and I wanted to crawl into bed and hide under the covers. I wanted to give Jenny Sells a hug, and to tell her that everything would be all right. And I was still afraid, all tight and burning in my gut. Victor Sells, of the shadows and demons, was going to kill me as soon as the storm rolled in.

'Think, Harry,' I told myself. '*Think*, dammit.' The cabby gave me an odd look in the rearview mirror.

I stuffed down all the feelings, all the fear, all the anger into a tight little ball. I didn't have time to let those feelings blind me now. I needed clarity, focus, purpose. I needed a plan.

Murphy. Murphy might be able to help me. I could tip her off about the lake house and send in the cavalry. They might find a stockpile of ThreeEye there. They could then arrest Victor like any other dealer.

But there were too many holes in that plan. What if Victor wasn't keeping his stores at the lake house? What if he eluded the police? Monica and her children would be in danger, if he did. Not only that, what if Murphy didn't listen to me? Hell, the judge might not issue a warrant to search private property on the word of a man who probably had a warrant out for his own arrest, now. Not only that, but the bureaucracy involved in working with the authorities in Lake Providence, on a Sunday, no less, would slow things down. It might not happen in time to save me from having my heart torn out. No, I couldn't rely on the police.

If this was any other time, if I was held in less suspicion by the White Council, I would report Victor Sells to them and let them handle the whole thing. They're not exactly soft on people using magic like Victor used it, to call up demons, to kill, to produce drugs. He had probably broken every Law of Magic. The White Council would waste no time in sending someone like Morgan to wipe Victor out.

But I couldn't do that, either. I was already under suspicion, thanks to Morgan's narrow-minded blindness. The Council was already meeting at sunrise on Monday. Some of the other members of the Council might listen to me, but they would be traveling, now. I had no way of reaching any of those who were sympathetic to me, no way of asking for help. There wasn't time, in fact, to try to round up any of my usual allies.

So, I concluded. It was up to me. Alone.

It was a sobering thought.

I had to confront Victor Sells, as strong a practitioner as I had ever gone up against, in his own place of power – the lake house. Not only that, but I had to do it without breaking any of the Laws of Magic. I couldn't kill him with sorcery – but somehow, I had to stop him.

Odds seemed really good that I was going to get killed, whether I tried to face him or not. To hell with it, then. If I was going to go out, it wasn't going to be while I was lying around moaning and bitching about how useless it all was. If Victor Sells wanted to take out Harry Blackstone Copperfield Dresden, he was going to have to shove his magic right down my throat.

This decision cheered me somewhat. At least I knew what I was doing now, where I was going. What I needed was an edge, I decided. Something to pull on Victor, something he wouldn't expect.

Now that I knew who he was, I understood the magic I had run into outside of my apartment a little bit better. It had been potent, deadly, but not sophisticated, not well controlled. Victor was powerful, strong, a natural mage — but he wasn't practiced. He didn't have any training. If only I had something of his, something like his own hair, that I could use against him. Maybe I should have checked the bathroom at Monica's, but I had the feeling that he wouldn't have been that careless. Anyone who spends time thinking about how to use that sort of thing against people is going to be doubly paranoid that no one have the opportunity to use it against him.

And then it struck me — I did have something of Victor's. I had his scorpion talisman, back in the drawer of my desk at the office. It was one of his own devices, something close and familiar. I could use it to create a bond to him, to sort of judo his own power back against him and beat him with it, hands down, no questions asked.

I might have a chance, yet. I wasn't finished, not by a long shot.

The cabby pulled into a gas station and parked next to

the pay phone. I told him to wait for me a minute and got out, fumbling a quarter from my pocket to make the call. If it did turn out that I wouldn't live to see tomorrow, I wanted to make damn sure that the hounds of Hell would be growling at Victor Sells's heels.

I dialed Murphy's number, down at the station.

It rang several times, and finally someone answered. The line was scratchy, noisy, and I could barely make out who it was. 'Murphy's desk, this is Carmichael.'

'Carmichael,' I said loudly into the phone. 'It's Harry Dresden. I need to talk to Murphy.'

'What?' Carmichael said. There was a squeal of static. Dammit, the phones go to hell on me at the worst times. 'I can't hear you. Murphy? You want Murphy? Who is this? Anderson, is that you?'

'It's Harry Dresden,' I shouted. 'I need to talk to Murphy.'

'Eh,' Carmichael grunted. 'I can't hear you, Andy. Look, Murphy's out. She took that warrant down to Harry Dresden's office to take a look around.'

'She *what*?' I said.

'Harry Dresden's office,' Carmichael said. 'She said she'd be back soon. Look, this connection is awful, try to call back.' He hung up on me.

I fumbled for another quarter, my hands shaking, and dialed my own office number. The last thing I needed was for Murphy to go poking around in my office, maybe impounding things. If she stuck the scorpion in evidence, I was done for. I'd never be able to explain it to her in time. And if she saw me face-to-face, she might be furious enough with me to just have me slapped into holding and left there overnight. If that happened, I'd be dead by morning.

My phone rang a couple of times, then Murphy answered. The line was blissfully clear. 'Harry Dresden's office.'

'Murph,' I said. 'Thank God. Look, I need to talk to you.'

I could practically feel her anger. 'Too late for that now, Harry. You should have come to talk to me this morning.' I heard her moving around. She started opening drawers.

'Dammit, Murph,' I said, frustrated. 'I know who the killer is. Look, you've got to keep out of that desk. It could be dangerous.' I thought I had been going to tell her a lie, but I realized as I said it that I was telling the truth. I remembered seeing, or thinking I had seen, movement from the talisman when I had examined it before. Maybe I hadn't been imagining things.

'Dangerous,' Murphy growled. I heard her scattering pens out of the top drawer of my desk, moving things around. The talisman was in the drawer beneath. 'I'll tell you what's dangerous. Fucking with me is dangerous, Dresden. I'm not playing some kind of game here. And I can't trust what you say anymore.'

'Murphy,' I said, trying to keep my voice even, 'you've got to trust me, one more time. Stay out of my desk. Please.'

There was silence for a moment. I heard her draw in a breath, and let it out through her mouth. Then Murphy said, her voice hard, professional, 'Why, Dresden? What are you hiding?'

I heard her open the middle drawer.

There was a clicking sound, and a startled oath from Murphy. The receiver clattered to the floor. I heard gunshots, shockingly loud, whining ricochets, and then a scream.

'Dammit!' I shouted at the phone. 'Murphy!' I slammed the phone down and sprinted back to the cab.

The cabby blinked at me. 'Hey, buddy. Where's the fire?'

I slammed the door shut, and gave him the address to my office. Then I thrust all of my remaining cash at him, and said, 'Get me there five minutes ago.'

The cabby blinked at the money, shrugged, and said, 'Crazies. Cabbies get all the crazies.' Then he tore out into the street, leaving a cloud of smoke behind us.

22

The building was locked on Sunday. I jammed my key in the lock, twisted it hard to open it, and jerked the keys out again. I didn't bother with the elevator, just hurtled up the stairs as quickly as I could.

Five stories' worth of stairs. It took me less than a minute, but I begrudged every second of it. My lungs were burning and my mouth was dry as sand as I reached the fifth floor and sprinted down the hallway to my office. The halls were quiet, empty, dim. The only light came from the exit signs and from the overcast day outside. Shadows stretched and settled in the closed doorways.

The door to my office was ajar. I could hear my ceiling fan squeaking on its mounting, underneath the labored wheezing of my own breath. The overhead light wasn't on, but the reading light on my desk must have been, because yellow light outlined the doorway and laid a swath of gold across the floor of the hall. I stopped at the threshold. My hands were shaking so much I could hardly hold my staff and rod.

'Murphy?' I called out. 'Murphy, can you hear me?' My voice was hoarse, breathless.

I closed my eyes, and listened. I thought I heard two things.

The first was a labored breath, with a faint moan on the exhale. Murphy.

The second was a dry, scuttling sound.

I could smell gunpowder on the air.

I clenched my jaw in sudden anger. Victor Sells's little beastie, whatever it was, had hurt my friend. Like hell I was going to stand out here and give it the run of my office.

I shoved the door open with my staff and stalked into the office, my blasting rod extended before me and words of power upon my lips.

Directly in front of my office door is a table arranged with a series of pamphlets with titles like *Real Witches Don't Float So Good*, and *Magic in the Twenty-first Century*. I had written some of them myself. They were meant for the curious, for people who just wanted to know about witches and magic. I squatted for a moment, blasting rod aimed beneath the table, but saw nothing. I rose again, looking back and forth, rod still ready.

To the right of the door is a wall lined with filing cabinets and a couple of easy chairs. The cabinets were shut, but something could have been hiding beneath one of the chairs. I slid to my left, checked behind the door to the office, and pressed my shoulders to the wall, keeping my eyes on the room.

My desk is in the back corner, to the right as you come in the door, diagonal from it. It's a corner office. There are windows on either of the outside walls. My shades were, as usual, drawn. The overhead fan, in the center of the room, spun around with a tired little groan on every rotation.

I kept my eyes moving, my senses alert. I choked down my anger, ferociously, and made myself remain cautious. Whatever had happened to Murphy, I wouldn't do her any good by letting it happen to me, too. I moved slowly, carefully, my blasting rod held ready.

I could see Murphy's tennis shoes behind my desk. She looked like she was curled on her side, from the way her feet were angled, but I couldn't see the rest of her. I pushed forward, striding to the center of the back wall, keeping my blasting rod leveled like a gun at the floor behind the desk as it became visible.

Murphy lay there, curled on her side, her golden hair in an artless sprawl about her head, her eyes open and staring blindly. She was dressed in jeans, a button-down shirt, and a Cubs satin jacket. Her left shoulder was stained with a blot of blood. Her gun lay next to her, a couple of feet away. My heart stepped up into my throat. I heard her take a little breath and groan when she let it out.

'Murphy,' I said. Then, louder, 'Murphy.'

I saw her stir, a fitful little motion that was in response to my voice. 'Easy, easy,' I told her. 'Relax. Don't try to move. I'm going to try to help you.'

I knelt next to her, very slowly, watching the room all around. I didn't see anything. I set my staff aside, and felt her throat. Her pulse was racing, thready. There was not enough blood for it to be a serious injury, but I touched her shoulder. Even through the jacket, I could feel the swelling.

'Harry?' Murphy rasped. 'Is that you?'

'It's me, Murph,' I told her, setting my blasting rod aside and slowly reaching for the phone. The middle drawer of my desk, where the scorpion talisman had been, was open and empty. 'Just hang on. I'm going to call an ambulance to help you.'

'Can't believe it. You bastard,' Murphy wheezed. I felt her stir around a little. 'You set me up.'

I drew the phone down and dialed 911. 'Hush, Murph. You've been poisoned. You need help, fast.'

The 911 operator came on and took my name and address. I told her to send an ambulance prepared to treat someone for poisoning, and she told me to stay on the line. I didn't have time to stay on the line. Whatever had done this to Murphy, it was still around, somewhere. I had to get her out of there, and then I had to recover Victor's talisman, to be able to use it against him when I went out to the lake house.

Murphy stirred again, and then I felt something hard and cool flick around my wrist and *clicker-clack* shut. I blinked and looked down at her. Murphy's jaw was set in a stubborn line as she clicked the other end of the handcuffs shut around her own wrist.

'You're under arrest,' she wheezed. 'You son of a bitch. Wait till I get you in an interrogation room. You aren't going anywhere.'

I stared at her, stunned. 'Murph,' I stammered. 'My God. You don't know what you're doing.'

'Like hell,' she said, her lip lifting in a ghost of its usual snarl. She twisted her head around, grimacing in pain, and squinted at me. 'You should have talked to me this morning. Got you now, Dresden.' She broke off in a panting gasp, and added, 'You jerk.'

'You stubborn bitch from hell.' I felt at a loss for a second, then shook my head. 'I've got to get you out of here before it comes back,' I said, and I stooped forward to try to gather her up.

That was when the scorpion exploded toward me from the shadows beneath my desk, a harsh burst of dry, scuttling motion. It wasn't a bug I could squash with my fingers, anymore. It was the size of a large terrier, all brown and glinting, and it was almost too fast to see coming.

I convulsed away from it, and saw the flash of its tail, saw its stinger whip forward and miss my eye by a hairbreadth. Something cool and wet speckled my cheek, and my skin started to burn. Venom.

My startled motion made my leg jerk, and kicked my staff and rod away from me. I rolled after the latter desperately. Murphy's handcuffs brought me up short, and both of us made sounds of discomfort as the steel bands cut at the base of our hands. I stretched for the rod, felt the smooth roundness of it on my fingertips, and then there was another scuttling sound and the scorpion came at my back. The rod squirted out from beneath my grasping fingers and rolled away, out of reach.

I didn't have time for a spell, but I grabbed at the middle drawer of my desk, jerked it all the way out of its frame and barely managed to shove it between the scorpion and myself. There was a hiss of air and a smacking sound of breaking wood. The scorpion's stinger plunged through the bottom of the desk drawer and stuck fast. A crab-claw pincer gouged a hole through my sweatpants and into my leg.

I screamed and hurled the drawer away. The scorpion, its tail still stuck, went with it, and they both landed in a heap a few feet away.

'Won't do you any good, Dresden,' Murphy moaned incoherently. She must have been too far gone from the poison to understand what was going on. 'I've got you. Stop fighting it. Get some answers from you, now.'

'Sometimes, Murph,' I panted, 'you make things just a little harder than they need to be. Anyone ever tell you that?' I bent down to her, and slipped my cuffed wrist beneath her arm and around her back, drawing her own

arm back with me, my right arm and her left bound by
the handcuff.

'My ex-husbands,' she moaned. I strained and lifted us
both up off the ground, then started hobbling toward the
door. I could feel the blood on my leg, the pain where the
scorpion had ripped it, hot and hateful. 'What's happening?'
Confusion and fear trembled in Murphy's voice. 'Harry, I
can't see.'

Shit. The poison was getting to her. The poison of the
common brown scorpion found all over most of the United
States isn't much more venomous than the sting of a
bumblebee. Of course, most bumblebees aren't the size of
the family dog, either. And Murphy wasn't a big person.
If a lot of poison had been introduced into her system, the
odds were against her. She needed medical attention, and
she needed it immediately.

If my hands had been free, I would have taken up my
staff and rod and done battle, but I didn't like my odds
tied to Murphy – even if I could keep the thing off of me,
it might land on her, sting her again, and put an end to
her. I was at a bad angle to search for her keys, and I didn't
have time to go down the ring trying them on the handcuffs one by one. Any magic that I could work fast enough
to shatter the cuffs in time would probably kill me with
flying shrapnel, and there wasn't time to work out a gentler
escape spell. *Dammit, Dad*, I thought, *I wish you'd lived long
enough to show me how to slip out of a pair of handcuffs*.

'Harry,' Murphy repeated, her voice thready, 'what's
happening? I can't see.'

I saved my breath and lugged Murphy toward the door
without answering her. Behind me, there was a furious
scraping and clicking. I looked back over my shoulder. The

scorpion's stinger was stuck fast in the drawer, but the thing was rapidly ripping the wood to shreds with its pincers and legs.

I gulped, turned, and hobbled out of my office and down the hall with Murphy. I managed to swing the door to my office shut with one foot. Murphy's legs did little to support her, and the difference in our heights made the trip awkward as hell. I was straining to keep her upright and moving.

I reached the end of the hall, the door to the stairway on my right, the elevator on my left.

I stopped for a moment, panting, trying not to let the sounds of splintering wood down the hall rattle my judgment. Murphy sagged against me, speechless now, and if she was breathing, I couldn't tell. There was no way I was going to be able to carry her down the stairs. Neither one of us had enough left to manage that. The ambulance would be arriving in minutes, and if I didn't have Murphy down there when it arrived, I might as well just leave her on the floor to die.

I grimaced. I hated elevators. But I pushed the button and waited. Round lights over the elevator doors began counting up to five.

Down the hall from me, the splintering sounds stopped, and something crashed into my office door, rattling it on its frame.

'Hell's bells, Harry,' I said aloud. I looked up at the lights. Two. A pause approximately ten centuries long. Three. 'Hurry *up*,' I snarled, and jabbed the button a hundred more times.

Then I remembered the bracelet of shields around my left wrist. I tried to focus on it but couldn't, with it twisted awkwardly beneath Murphy, supporting her. So I laid her down as gently and quickly as I could, then lifted my left hand and focused on the bracelet.

The lower third of my office door exploded outward, and the brown, gleaming form of the scorpion bounded across the hallway and into the wall. It was bigger, now. The damn thing was growing. It bounced off of the wall with a scrabbling, horrible agility, oriented on me, and hurtled down the hall toward me as fast as a man can run, its legs clicking and scuttling furiously over the floor. It leapt at me, claws extended, stinger flashing. I focused my will on the defensive shield the bracelet helped me form and maintain, struggling to get it together before the scorpion hit me.

I did it, barely. The invisible shield of air met the scorpion a handsbreadth from my body and sent it rebounding back onto its back. There it struggled for a second, awkward and flailing.

Behind me, the elevator dinged, and the doors swooped graciously open.

Without time to be delicate, I grabbed Murphy's wrist and hauled her into the elevator with me, jabbing at the button for the lobby. In the hall, the scorpion thrashed its tail and righted itself, oriented on me again with an uncanny intelligence, and flew toward me. There wasn't time to get my shield together again. I screamed.

The elevator doors swooped shut. There was a sharp thud, and the car rattled, as the scorpion smashed into them.

The car started down, and I tried to regain my breath. What the hell *was* that thing?

It wasn't just an insect. It was too fast, too damn smart for that. It had ambushed me, waiting until I had set my weapons aside to come after me. It had to be something else, some kind of power construct, built small, but designed to draw in energy, to get bigger and stronger, an arthropod version of Frankenstein's monster. It wasn't really alive, just a golem, a robot, a programmed thing with a mission. Victor must have figured out where his talisman had gotten to, and set a spell on it to attack anyone it came in contact with, the crazy bastard. Murphy had stumbled right into it.

It was still growing, getting faster and stronger and more vicious. Getting Murphy out of danger wasn't enough. I had to find a way to deal with the scorpion. I didn't want to, but I was the only one on the block who could. There was too much potential danger involved. What if it didn't stop growing? I had to kill it before it got out of control.

The lights on the elevator panel kept counting down, four to three to two. And then the elevator shuddered and ground to a stop. The lights flickered and went out.

'Oh, crap,' I said. 'Not now. Not *now*.' Elevators hate me. I jabbed at the buttons, but nothing happened, and a second later there was a cough of smoke, and the lights behind the buttons went out, too, leaving me in darkness. The emergency lighting came on for just a second, but then there was the pop of a burning filament, and it went away too. Murphy and I were left huddling in the darkness on the floor.

Overhead, outside in the elevator shaft, there was the sound of shrieking metal. I looked up at the invisible roof of the elevator car in the darkness. 'You have got to be kidding me,' I muttered.

Then there was a rattling bang, and something the weight of a small gorilla landed on the roof of the elevator. There was a second's silence, and then something started a deafening tearing at the roof.

'You have got to be kidding me!' I shouted. But the scorpion wasn't. It was wrenching back the roof of the elevator, rattling the bolts and supports, making it groan. Dust rattled down in the darkness, unseen grit for my unseeing eyes. We were sardines in a can, waiting to be torn up and eaten. I got the feeling that if the thing stung me now, the poison would be redundant – I would bleed to death before it became an issue.

'Think, Harry,' I shouted at myself. 'Think, think, think!' I was stuck in a frozen elevator, handcuffed to my unconscious friend who was dying of poison while a magical scorpion the size of some French cars tried to tear its way into me and rip me apart. I didn't have my blasting rod or my staff, the other gizmos I'd brought with me to the Varsity were drained and useless, and my shield bracelet would only prolong the inevitable.

A long strip of metal ripped away in the roof, letting in a strip of dim light, and I looked up at the scorpion's underbelly, saw it wedge a claw into the breach and start to tear it open wider.

I should have smashed it when it was just a bug. I should have taken off my shoe and smashed it right there on my desk. My heart leapt into my throat as the thing tilted up, drove an exploratory pincer down into the upper third of the elevator, then started tearing the hole even larger.

I gritted my teeth and started drawing in every ounce of power that I had. I knew it was useless. I could direct a firestorm up at the thing, but it would slag the metal it was on and that would come raining back down on us and kill us, make the elevator shaft too hot for us to survive. But I wasn't just going to let the thing have me, either, by God. Maybe, if I did it just right, I could catch it as it leapt, minimize the damage that I did to the surrounding scenery. That was the problem with not being too great at evocation. Plenty of speed, plenty of power, not much refinement. That's what the staff did, and the blasting rod – they were designed to help me focus my power, give me pinpoint control. Without them I might as well have been a suicide soldier carrying a dozen grenades strapped to his belt and ready to jerk out the pin.

And then it occurred to me. I was thinking in the wrong direction.

I swung my eyes down from the ceiling, to the elevator's floor, pressed my palms against it. Bits of something rained down on my head and shoulders, and the clicking and scuttling of the scorpion got louder. I took all the power I'd drawn in and focused it beneath my palms. There was airspace beneath the elevator, in the elevator shaft, and that was what I reached for – air, instead of fire.

This was a simple spell, one I'd done hundreds of times, I told myself. It wasn't any different from calling my staff to my hand. Just . . . a little bigger.

'*Vento servitas!*' I shouted, pouring every bit of strength, every ounce of anger, every shred of fear I had into the spell.

And, beneath the elevator, the winds rose up at my call, a solid column of air that caught the bottom of the elevator like a giant's palm and hurled it upward, through the darkness of the elevator shaft. The brakes squealed, threw off sparks, and fell to pieces that dropped through the hole the scorpion had torn, to land next to me. The force of it pressed me down to the floor with a groan. There was a long and rising whine as the car accelerated up the elevator shaft.

I hadn't meant for there to be quite *that* much wind, I

thought, and prayed that I hadn't just killed me and Murphy both.

The elevator hurtled up and up and up, and I could feel my face sagging down with the speed of it. My office building is twelve stories high. We'd started at the second floor, so assuming an average of nine feet per story, it was almost a hundred feet to the building's roof.

The car shot up it in less than a half dozen of my frantic heartbeats, slammed past the blocks at the top of the line, and hammered into the roof of the shaft like the bell on the strongman's sledgehammer game at the amusement park. The impact crushed the scorpion into the concrete with a series of sharp popping sounds as chitinous plates cracked and splintered, flattening it into a shapeless brown splotch. Colorless goo, the ectoplasm of magically created mass, spattered out between the crushed plates and hide and down into the car.

At the same time, Murphy and I were hurled *up*, meeting the goo halfway. I kept Murphy in the shelter of my body, trying to stay between her and the roof, and my back hit it hard enough to make me see stars. We tumbled loosely back down to the elevator's floor in a sprawl of limbs, and Murphy groaned beneath me when I landed on her.

I lay still for a moment, stunned. The scorpion was dead. I'd killed it, crushed it between the elevator and the roof of the shaft, and drenched myself and Murphy in ichor, doing it. I'd saved our lives from the murderous device, against the odds.

But I just couldn't shake the nagging impression that I was forgetting something.

There was a little groan from the elevator, and then it shuddered, and started sliding back down the shaft, no longer supported by the powerful but short-lived pillar of wind that had driven it up there. We were falling back down the way we had come, and I had the feeling that we weren't going to have a much better time of it at the bottom than the scorpion had at the top.

Now was the time for the bracelet, and I didn't waste a heartbeat grabbing Murphy close to me, and bringing the shield into being around us. I only had a couple of seconds to focus, to think – I couldn't make the globe around us too brittle, too strong, or we'd just smash ourselves against the inside of it in the same way we would if we just rode the elevator down. There had to be some give to it, some flexibility, to distribute the tremendous force of the abrupt stop at the first floor.

It was dark, and there wasn't much time. Murphy and I rose up to the center of the space of the elevator while I pushed the shield out all around us, filled up the space with layer after layer of flexible shielding, semicohesive molecules of air, patterns of force meant to spread the impact around. There was a sense of pressure all around me, as though I had been abruptly stuffed in Styrofoam packing peanuts.

We fell, faster and faster. I sensed the bottom of the shaft coming. There was an enormous sound, and I held on to the shield with all of my might.

When I opened my eyes again, I was sitting on the floor of the shattered, devastated elevator, holding a sagging, unconscious Murphy. The elevator doors gave a warped, gasping little ding, then shuddered open.

A pair of EMTs with emergency kits in hand stood staring at the elevator, at Murphy and me, their jaws hanging open to their knees. Dust billowed everywhere.

I was alive.

I blinked at that, somewhat stunned. I was alive. I looked down at myself, at my arms and legs, and they were all there. Then I let my head fall back and howled out a defiant laugh, a great, gawping whoop of primal joy.

'Take *that*, Victor Shadowman!' I shouted. 'Hah! *Hah!* Give me your best shot, you murderous bastard! I'm going to take my staff and shove it down your *throat*!'

I was still laughing when the EMTs gathered me up and helped me and Murphy toward the ambulance, too stunned to ask any questions. I saw them both give me wary looks, though, and then trade a glance with one another that said they were going to sedate me with something as soon as they got the chance.

'The champion!' I howled, still on an adrenaline rush the size of the Colorado River, as they helped me out toward the ambulance. I thrust my fist into the air, scarcely noting or caring that my bracelet of silver shields had turned into a blackened ring of curled and wilted links, burned to uselessness by the energies I had forced through it. 'I am the *man*! Shadowman, you'd better put your head between your legs and kiss your—'

The EMTs helped me outside. Into the rain. The wet slaps of raindrops on my face shut me up, made me cold sober faster than anything else in the world could have done. I was suddenly acutely aware of the handcuffs around my wrist, still, of the fact that I did not have Victor's talisman to use to turn his own power against him. Victor was still out there, out at his lake house, he still had a hank of my hair, and he was still planning on ripping my heart out as soon as he possibly could, when the storm gave him the strength he needed.

I was alive, and Murphy was alive, but my elation was premature. I didn't have anything to be celebrating, yet. I lifted my face to the sky.

Thunder growled, near at hand. Lightning danced overhead, somewhere in the clouds, casting odd light and spectral shadows through the roiling overcast.

The storm had arrived.

23

Raindrops pelted down around me, the big, splashy kind you only really see in the spring. The air grew thicker, hotter, even with the rain falling. I had to think fast, use my head, be calm, hurry up. Murphy's handcuffs still held me fastened to her wrist. Both of us were coated in dust that was stuck to the stinking, colorless goo, the ectoplasm that magic called from somewhere else whenever generic mass was called for in a spell. The goo wouldn't last long – within a few more minutes, it would simply dissipate, vanish into thin air, return to wherever it had come from in the first place. For the moment, it was just a rather disgusting, slimy annoyance.

But maybe one that I could put to use.

My own hands were too broad, but Murphy had delicate little lady's hands, except where practice with her gun and her martial arts staff routines had left calluses. If she had heard me thinking that, and had been conscious, she would have punched me in the mouth for being a chauvinist pig.

One of the EMTs was babbling into a handset, while the other was on Murphy's other side, supporting her along with me. It was the only chance I was going to get. I hunched over beside Murphy's diminutive form and tried to shroud what I was doing with the dark folds of my black duster. I worked at her hand, squeezing her limp, slimy fingers together and trying to slip the steel loop of the handcuffs over her hand.

I took some skin off of her, and she groaned a lot, but
I managed to get the cuffs off of her wrist just as the EMT
and I sat her down on the curb next to the ambulance.
The other EMT ran to the back of the ambulance and
swung it open, rummaging around inside of it. I could
hear sirens, both police cars and fire engines, approaching
from all directions.

Nothing's ever simple when I'm around.

'She's been poisoned,' I told the EMT. 'The wound site
is on her right upper arm or shoulder. Check for a massive
dose of brown scorpion venom. There should be some
antivenin available somewhere. She'll need a tourniquet
and—'

'Buddy,' the EMT said, annoyed, 'I know my job. What
the hell happened in there?'

'Don't ask,' I said, glancing back at the building. The
rain came down more heavily by slow degrees. Was I too
late? Would I be dead before I could get to the lake house?

'You're bleeding,' the EMT told me, without looking
up from Murphy. I looked down at my leg, but it didn't
start hurting until I actually saw the injury and remembered I had it. The scorpion's claw had ripped me pretty
good, opening a six-inch tear in the leg of my sweats and
a comparable gash in the leg beneath, ragged and painful.
'Sit down,' the EMT said. 'I'll take care of it in a second.'
He wrinkled up his face. 'What the hell *is* this stinking
shit all over you?'

I wiped rain from my hair, slicking it back. The other
EMT came running with a bottle of oxygen and a stretcher,
and they both bent over their work with Murphy. Her face
had discolored, pale in parts, too brightly red in others.
She was as limp as a wet dollar, except for the occasional

shudder or flinch, quivers of her muscles that came from nowhere, pained her for a moment, and then apparently vanished.

It was my fault Murphy was there. It had been my decision to hold information away from her that had compelled her to take direct action, to search my office. If I'd just been more open, more honest, maybe she wouldn't be lying there right now, dying. I didn't want to walk away from her. I didn't want to turn my back on her again and leave her behind me, alone.

But I did. Before the support units arrived, before police started asking questions, before the EMT's began looking around for me and giving my description to police officers, I turned on my heel and walked away.

I hated myself every step. I hated leaving before I knew if Murphy would survive the scorpion's venomous sting. I hated that my apartment and my office building had been trashed, torn to pieces by demons and giant insects and my own clumsy power. I hated to close my eyes and see the twisted, mangled bodies of Jennifer Stanton and Tommy Tomm, and Linda Randall. I hated the sick twisting of fear in my guts when I imagined my own spare frame torn asunder by the same forces.

And, most of all, I hated the one responsible for all of it. Victor Sells. Victor, who was going to kill me as soon as this storm grew. I could be dead in another five minutes.

No. I couldn't. I got a little more excited as I thought about the problem and looked up at the clouds. The storm had come in from the west, and was only now going over the city. It wasn't moving fast; it was a ponderous roller of a thunderstorm that would hammer at the area for hours. The Sells's lake house was to the east, around the shore of

Lake Michigan, maybe thirty or forty miles away, as the crow flies. I could beat the storm to the lake house, if I was fast enough, if I could get a car. I could get out to the lake house and challenge Victor directly.

My rod and staff were gone, dropped when the scorpion attacked. I might have been able to call them down from my office with winds, but as worked up as I was, I might accidentally blow out the wall if I tried. I didn't care to be crushed by hundreds of pounds of flying brick, called to my outstretched hand by the strength of my magic and my fury. My shield bracelet was gone, too, burned out by countering the tremendous force of the impact of the falling elevator.

I still had my mother's pentacle talisman at my throat, the symbol of order, of the controlled patterns of power that were at the heart of white magic. I still had the advantage of years of formal training. I still had the edge in experience, in sorcerous confrontations. I still had my faith.

But that was about all. I was weary, battered, tired, hurt, and I had already pulled more magic out of the hat in one day than most wizards could in a week. I was pushing the edge already, in both mystic and physical terms. But that just didn't matter to me.

The pain in my leg didn't make me weaker, didn't discourage me, didn't distract me as I walked. It was like a fire in my thoughts, my concentration, burning ever more brightly, more pure, refining my anger, my hate, into something steel-hard, steel-sharp. I could feel it burning, and reached for it eagerly, shoving the pain inside to fuel my incandescent anger.

Victor Shadowman was going to pay for what he'd done to all those people, to me and to my friends. Dammit all,

I was not going out before I'd caught up to that man and shown him what a real wizard could do.

It didn't take me long to walk to McAnally's. I came through the door in a storm of long legs, rain, wind, flapping duster, and angry eyes.

The place was packed, people sitting at every one of the thirteen stools at the bar, at every one of the thirteen tables, leaning against most of the thirteen columns. Pipe smoke drifted through the air in a haze, stirred by the languidly spinning blades of the ceiling fans. The light was dim, candles burning at the tables and in sconces on the walls, plus a little grey storm light sliding in through the windows. The light made the carvings on the columns vague and mysterious, the shadows changing them in a subtle fashion. All of Mac's chessboards were out on the tables, but my sense of it was that those playing and watching the games were trying to keep their minds off of something that was disturbing them.

They all turned to stare at me as I came in the door and down the steps, dripping rainwater and a little blood onto the floor. The room got really quiet.

They were the have-nots of the magical community. Hedge magi without enough innate talent, motivation, or strength to be true wizards. Innately gifted people who knew what they were and tried to make as little of it as possible. Dabblers, herbalists, holistic healers, kitchen witches, troubled youngsters just touching their abilities and wondering what to do about it. Older men and women, younger people, faces impassive or concerned or fearful, they were all there. I knew them all by sight, if not by name.

I swept my gaze around the room. Every one of the people I looked at dropped their eyes, but I didn't need to look deep to see what was happening. Word has a way of getting around between practitioners of magic, and the arcane party line was working as it usually did. Word was out. There was a mark on my head, and they all knew it. Trouble was brewing between two wizards, white and black, and they had all come here, to the shelter offered by McAnally's winding spaces and disruptive configurations of tables and columns. They'd come here to shelter until it was over.

It didn't offer any shelter to me, though. McAnally's couldn't protect me against a sharply directed spell. It was an umbrella, not a bomb shelter. I couldn't get away from what Victor would do to me, unless I cared to flee to the Nevernever itself, and for me that was more dangerous, in some ways, than staying at Mac's.

I stood there in the silence for a moment, but said nothing. These people were associates, friends of a casual sort, but I couldn't ask them to stand beside me. Whatever Victor thought he was, he had the power of a real wizard, and he could crush any of these people like a boot could a cockroach. They weren't prepared to deal with this sort of thing.

'Mac,' I said, finally. My voice fell on the silence like a hammer on glass. 'I need to borrow your car.'

Mac hadn't quit polishing the bar with a clean white cloth when I entered, his spare frame gaunt in a white shirt and dark breeches. He hadn't stopped when the room had grown still. And he didn't stop when he pulled the keys out of his pocket and tossed them to me with one hand. I caught them, and said, 'Thanks, Mac.'

'Ungh,' Mac said. He glanced up at me, and then behind me. I took the gesture for the warning it was, and turned.

Lightning flashed outside. Morgan stood silhouetted in the doorway at the top of the little flight of stairs, his broad frame black against the grey sky. He came down the stairs toward me, and the thunder came in on his heels. Rain had made little difference in the lay of his dull brown and grey hair, except for changing the texture of curl in his warrior's ponytail. I could see the hilt of the sword he wore, beneath his black overcoat. He had a muscular, scarred hand on it.

'Harry Dresden,' he said. 'I finally figured it out. Using the storms to kill those people is insanely dangerous, but you are just the sort of ambitious fool who would do it.' He set his jaw in a hard line. 'Have a seat,' he said, gesturing at a table. The people sitting at it cleared away, fast. 'We're going to stay here, both of us. And I'm going to make sure that you don't have the chance to use this storm to hurt anyone else. I'm going to make sure you don't get to try your cowardly tricks until the Council decides your fate.' His grey eyes glittered with grim determination and certainty.

I stared at him. I swallowed my anger, the words I wanted to throw back at him, the spell I wanted to use to blast him out of my way, and spoke gently. 'Morgan, I know who the killer is. And he's after me, next. If I don't get to him and stop him, I'm as good as dead.'

His eyes hardened, a fanatic's gleam. He spoke in two sharp little explosions of single syllables. 'Sit. Down.' He drew the sword out from its scabbard by a couple of inches.

I let my shoulders sag. I turned toward the table. I leaned against the back of one of the chairs for a moment, taking a little weight off of my injured leg, and drew the chair out from the table.

Then I picked it up, spun in a half circle with it to

gather momentum, and smashed it into the Warden's stomach. Morgan tried to recoil, but I'd caught him off guard, and the blow struck home, hard and heavy with the weight of Mac's handmade wooden chair. In real life, the chair doesn't break when you slug somebody with it, the way it does in the movies. The person you hit is the one who breaks.

Morgan doubled forward, dropping to one hand and one knee. I didn't wait for him to recover. Instead, as the chair bounced off his ribs, I used the momentum of it to spin all the way around in a complete circle in the other direction, lifting the chair high, and brought it smiting down over the other man's back. The blow drove him hard into the floor, where he lay unmoving.

I set the chair back at the table and looked around the room. Everyone was staring, pale. They knew who Morgan was, what his relationship to me was. They knew about the Council, and my precarious stance with it. They knew that I had just assaulted a duly appointed representative of the Council in pursuit of the execution of his duty. I'd rolled the stone over my own grave. There wasn't a prayer that I could convince the Council that I wasn't a rogue wizard fleeing justice, now.

'Hell with him,' I said aloud, to no one in particular. 'I haven't got time for this.'

Mac came out from behind the bar, not moving in a hurry, but not with his usual laconic lack of concern, either. He knelt by Morgan and felt at his throat, then peeled back an eyelid and peered at the man. Mac squinted up at me and said, expressionless, 'Alive.'

I nodded, feeling some slight relief. However much of an ass Morgan was, he had good intentions. He and I wanted the same thing, really. He just didn't realize that. I didn't want to kill him.

But I had to admit in some gleeful little corner of my soul that the look of shocked surprise on his arrogant face as I hit him with the chair was a sight worth remembering.

Mac stooped and picked up the keys, where I'd dropped them on the floor as I swung the chair. I hadn't noticed that I had. Mac handed them back to me and said, 'Council will be pissed.'

'Let me worry about that.'

He nodded. 'Luck, Harry.' Mac offered me his hand, and I took it. The room was still silent. Fearful, worried eyes watched me.

I took the keys and walked up, out of the light and shelter of McAnally's and into the storm, my bridges burning behind me.

24

I drove for my life.

Mac's car was an '89 TransAm, pure white, with a big eight-cylinder engine. The speedometer goes to 130 miles an hour. In places, I went past that. The falling rain made the roads dangerous at the speed I was driving, but I had plenty of incentive to keep the car moving as quickly as possible. I was still riding the steel-hard edge of anger that had carried me away from the ruins of my office and through Morgan.

The sky grew darker, a combination of building banks of storm clouds and the approaching dusk. The light was strange, greenish, the leaves of the trees as I left the city standing out too sharply, too harshly, the yellows of the lines in the road too dim. Most of the cars I saw had their headlights on, and streetlights were clicking alight as I barreled down the highway.

Fortunately, Sunday evening isn't a busy one, as far as traffic goes. I'd have been dead any other night. I must also have been driving during the watch rotation for the highway patrol, because not one of them tried to pull me over.

I tried to tune in the weather station, on the radio, but gave it up. The storm, plus my own agitation, was creating a cloud of squealing feedback on the radio's speakers, but nothing intelligible about the storm. I could only pray that I was going to get over to Lake Providence before it did.

I won. The curtains of rain parted for me as I whipped past the city-limits sign for Lake Providence. I hit the brakes to slow for the turn onto the lakefront road that led to the Sells house, started hydroplaning, turned into the slide with more composure and ability than I really should have had, and got the vehicle back under control in time to slide onto the correct road.

I pulled into the Sells gravel drive, on the swampy little peninsula that stretched out into Lake Michigan. The TransAm slid to a halt in a shower of gravel and a roar of mighty engine, then sputtered and gasped into silence. I felt, for a giddy second and a half, like Magnum, P.I. Blue Beetle aside, I could get into this sports-car thing. At least it had lasted long enough for me to get to the Sells place. 'Thanks, Mac,' I grunted, and got out of the car.

The gravel driveway leading back to the lake house was half-sunk in water from the recent storms. My leg hurt me too much to run very fast, but I set off down the drive at a long-legged lope, rapidly eating the distance to the house. The storm loomed before me, rolling across the lake toward the shore – I could see columns of rain, dimly lit by the fading light, falling into its waters.

I raced the storm to the house, and as I did I drew in every bit of power and alertness that I could, keyed myself to a tighter level, tuned my senses to their sharpest pitch. I came to a halt twenty yards shy of the house and closed my eyes, panting. There could be magical traps or alarms strewn about, or spiritual or shrouded guardians invisible to the naked eye. There could be spells waiting, illusions meant to hide Victor Sells from anyone who came looking. I needed to be able to see past all that. I needed to have every scrap of knowledge I could get.

So I opened my Third Eye.

How can I explain what a wizard sees? It isn't something that lends itself readily to description. Describing something helps to define it, to give it limits, to set guardrails of understanding around it. Wizards have had the Sight since time began, and they still don't understand how it works, why it does what it does.

The only thing I can say is that I felt as though a veil of thick cloth had been lifted away from me as I opened my eyes again – and not only from my eyes, but from all of my senses. I could abruptly smell the mud and fish odor of the lake, the trees around the house, the fresh scent of the coming rain preceding the storm on the smoke-stained wind. I looked at the trees. Saw them, not just in the first green coat of spring, but in the full bloom of summer, the splendor of the fall, and the barren desolation of winter, all at the same time. I Saw the house, and each separate part of it as its own component, the timbers as parts of spectral trees, the windows as pieces of distant sandy shores. I could feel the heat of summer and the cold of winter in the wind coming off the lake. I Saw the house wreathed in ghostly flames, and knew that those were part of its possible future, that fire lay down several of the many paths of possibility that lay ahead in the next hour.

The house itself was a place of power. Dark emotions – greed, lust, hatred – all hung over it as visible things, molds and slimes that were strewn over it like Spanish moss with malevolent eyes. Ghostly things, restless spirits, moved around the place, drawn to the sense of fear, despair, and anger that hung over it, mindless shades that were always to be found in such places, like rats in granaries.

The other thing that I saw over the house was a grinning, empty skull. Skulls were everywhere, wherever I looked, just at the edge of my vision, silent and still and bleach-white, as solid and real as though a fetishist had scattered them around in anticipation of some bizarre holiday. Death. Death lay in the house's future, tangible, solid, unavoidable.

Maybe mine.

I shuddered and shoved the feeling away. No matter how strong the vision, how powerful the image gained with the Sight, the future was always mutable, always something that could be changed. No one had to die tonight. It didn't have to come to that, not for them and not for me.

But a sick feeling had settled into me, as I looked on this darkling house, with all of its stinking lust and fear, all of its horrid hate worn openly upon it to my Sight, like a mantle of flayed human skin on the shoulders of a pretty girl with gorgeous hair, luscious lips, sunken eyes, and rotting teeth. It repulsed me and it made me afraid.

And something about it, intangible, something I couldn't name, called to me. Beckoned. Here was power, power I had thrust aside once before, in the past. I had thrown away the only family I had ever known to turn away power exactly like this. This was the sort of strength that could reach out and change the world to my will, bend it and shape it to my desiring, could cut through all the petty trivialities of law and civilization and impose order where there was none, guarantee my security, my position, my future.

And what had been my reward for turning that power aside thus far? Suspicion and contempt from the very wizards I had acted to support and protect, condemnation from the White Council whose Law I had clung to when all the world had been laid at my feet.

I could kill the Shadowman, now, before he knew I was here. I could call down fury and flame on the house and kill everyone in it, not leave one stone upon another. I could reach out and embrace the dark energy he had gathered in this place, draw it in and use it for whatever I wanted, and the consequences be damned.

Why not kill him now? Violet light, visible to my Sight, throbbed and pulsed inside the windows, power being gathered and prepared and shaped. The Shadowman was inside, and he was gathering his might, preparing to unleash the spell that would kill me. What reason had I to let him go on breathing?

I clenched my fists in fury, and I could feel the air crackle with tension as I prepared to destroy the lake house, the Shadowman, and any of the pathetic underlings he had with him. With such power, I could cast my defiance at the Council itself, the gathering of white-bearded old fools without foresight, without imagination, without vision. The Council, and that pathetic watchdog Morgan, had no idea of the true depths of my strength. The energy was all there, gleeful within my anger, ready to reach out and reduce to ashes all that I hated and feared.

The silver pentacle that had been my mother's burned cold on my chest, a sudden weight that made me gasp. I sagged forward a little, and lifted a hand. My fingers were so tightly crushed into fists that it hurt to try to open them. My hand shook, wavered, and began to fall again.

Then something strange happened. Another hand took mine. The hand was slim, the fingers long and delicate. Feminine. The hand gently covered mine, and lifted it, like a small child's, until I held my mother's pentacle in my grasp.

I held it in my hand, felt its cool strength, its ordered

and rational geometry. The five-pointed star within the circle was the ancient sign of white wizardry, the only remembrance of my mother. The cold strength of the pentacle gave me a chance, a moment to think again, to clear my head.

I took deep breaths, struggling to see clear of the anger, the hate, the deep lust that burned within me for vengeance and retribution. That wasn't what magic was for. That wasn't what magic did. Magic came from life itself, from the interaction of nature and the elements, from the energy of all living beings, and especially of people. A man's magic demonstrates what sort of person he is, what is held most deeply inside of him. There is no truer gauge of a man's character than the way in which he employs his strength, his power.

I was not a murderer. I was not like Victor Sells. I was Harry Blackstone Copperfield Dresden. I was a wizard. Wizards control their power. They don't let it control them. And wizards don't use magic to kill people. They use it to discover, to protect, to mend, to help. Not to destroy.

The anger abruptly evaporated. The burning hate subsided, leaving my head clear enough to think again. The pain in my leg settled into a dull ache, and I shivered in the wind and the first droplets of rain. I didn't have my staff, and I didn't have my rod. The trinkets I did have with me were either expended or burned to uselessness. All I had was what was inside me.

I looked up, suddenly feeling smaller and very alone. There was no one near me. No hand was touching mine. No one stood close by. For just a moment, I thought I smelled a whiff of perfume, familiar and haunting. Then it was gone. And the only one I had to help me was myself.

I blew out a breath. 'Well, Harry,' I told myself, 'that's just going to have to be enough.'

And so I walked through a spectral landscape littered with skulls, into the teeth of the coming storm, to a house covered in malevolent power, throbbing with savage and feral mystic strength. I walked forward to face a murderous opponent who had all the advantages, and who stood prepared and willing to kill me from where he stood within the heart of his own destructive power, while I was armed with nothing more than my own skill and wit and experience.

Do I have a great job or what?

25

The Sight of Victor's lake house will always be with me. It was an abomination. It looked innocuous enough, physically. But on a deeper level, it was foul, rotten. It seethed with negative energy, anger and pride and lust. Especially lust. Lust for wealth, lust for power, more than physical desire.

Shadowy spirit-beings that weren't wholly real, only manifestations of the negative energy of the place, clung to the walls, the rain gutters, the porch, the windowsills, glutting themselves on the negative energy left over from Victor's spellcasting. I was guessing that there was a lot of it. He didn't strike me as someone who would be able to make sure that his spells were energy-efficient.

I limped up the front steps. My Sight revealed no alarms, no sorcerous trip wires. I might be giving Victor Shadowman too much credit. He was as powerful as a full-blown wizard, but he didn't have the education. Muscle, not brains, that was Victor Shadowman. I had to keep that in mind.

I tried the front door, just for the hell of it.

It opened.

I blinked. But I didn't question the good fortune, or the overconfidence that had seen to it that Victor left his front door standing unlocked. Instead, I took a breath, gathered up what will I had, and pressed inside.

I forget how the house was furnished or decorated. All I remember is what the Sight showed me. More of the same as the outside, but more concentrated, more noxious. *Things* clung everywhere, things with silent, glittering eyes and hungry expressions. Some reptilian, some more like rats, some insectoid. All of them were unpleasant, hostile, and shied away from me as I came in, as the aura of energy I held in readiness around me touched them. They made quiet noises, things I would never have heard with my ears – but the Sight encompasses all of that.

There was a long, dark hallway coated with the things. I advanced slowly, quietly, and they oozed and crept and slithered from my path. The dark purple light of magic that I had seen from the outside was ahead of me, and growing brighter. I could hear music playing, and recognized it as the same piece that had been playing on the CD player at the Madison in Tommy Tomm's suite when Murphy had asked me there on Thursday. Slow, sensuous music, steady rhythm.

I closed my eyes for a moment, listening. I heard sounds. A quiet whisper, being repeated over and over, a man's voice repeating an incantation, holding a spell in readiness for release. That would be Victor. I heard soft sighs of pleasure from a woman. The Beckitts? I could only assume so.

And, in a rumble that I could feel through the soles of my boots, I heard thunder over the lake. The low, chanting voice took on an edge of vicious, spiteful satisfaction, and continued the incantation.

I gathered up what energy I had and stepped around the corner, out of the hallway, into a spacious room that stretched up to the full height of the house without interruption, yards of open air. The room below was a living room. A spiral staircase wound its way up to what looked like a kitchen and dining room on a sort of platform or balcony above the rest of the room. The elevated deck on the back of the house must be accessible from the platform.

There was no one in the main room. The chanting, and the occasional sigh, came from the platform above. The CD player was down in the room beneath, music flowing from speakers that were covered with an image of fire and dozens of bloated, disgusting creature forms, feeding on the music as it came out. I could see the influence of the music as a faint, violet mist, in tune with the light coming from the platform above. This was a complex ritual spell, then, involving many base elements coordinated by the central wizard, Victor. Tricky. No wonder it was so effective. It must have taken Victor a lot of trial and error to figure it out.

I glanced up at the platform, then crossed the room, keeping as far away as I could from the CD player. I slipped under the platform without making any noise, and dozens upon dozens of slimy not-physical spirit things oozed from my path. Rain increased to a dull, steady rhythm outside, on the roof and on the wooden deck and against the windows.

There were boxes stacked all around me, plastic cases and cartons and cardboard boxes and wooden crates. I opened the nearest one, and saw, inside, at least a hundred slender vials like the ones I had seen before, full of the liquid ThreeEye. Beneath the vision of my Sight, it looked different, thick and cloudy with possibility, potential disaster lurking in every vial. Faces, twisted in horror and torment, swam through the liquid, ghostly images of what might be.

I looked at the other boxes. In one, ancient liquor bottles full of an almost luminescent green liquid. Absinthe? I leaned closer, sniffing, and could almost taste the madness that swam latent in the liquid. I leaned back from the boxes, stomach churning. I checked the other boxes, quickly. Ammonia, reminiscent of hospitals and mental wards. Peyote mushrooms in plastic Tupperware – I was familiar with them. Alum, white and powdery. Antifreeze. Glitter in a hundred metallic shades in a huge plastic bag. Other things, deeper in the shadows, that I didn't take the time to look at. I had already figured out what all the articles were for.

Potions.

Ingredients for potions. This was how Victor was making the ThreeEye. He was doing the same thing I did when I made my little potions, but on a grander scale, using energy he stole from other places, other people. He used absinthe as the base, and moved out from there. Victor was mass-producing what amounted to a magical poison, one that probably remained inert until it was inside someone, inter-acting with their emotions and desires. That would explain why I hadn't noticed anything about it, before. It wouldn't have been obvious to a cursory examination, or to anything short of fully opening up my Sight, and that wasn't some-thing I did very often.

I closed my eyes, shaking. The Sight was showing me too much. That was always the problem with it. I could look at these ingredients, the cases of the finished drug, and catch flash images of exactly how much suffering could be caused. There was too much. I was starting to get disoriented.

Thunder came again, more sharply, and above me, Victor's voice rose in pitch, to something audible. He was chanting in an ancient language. Egyptian? Babylonian? It didn't really matter. I could understand the sense of the words clearly enough. They were words of hate, malevolence. They were words that were meant to kill.

My shaking was becoming more pronounced. Was it only the effects of the Sight? The presence of so much negative energy, reacting with me?

No. I was simply afraid. Terrified to come out of my hiding place under the platform and to meet the master of the slithering horde that was draped over everything in sight. I could feel his strength from here, his confidence, the force of his will infusing the very air with a sort of hateful certainty. I was afraid with the same fear that a child feels when confronted with a large, angry dog, or with the neighborhood bully, the kind of fear that paralyzes, makes you want to make excuses and hide.

But there was no time for hiding. No time for excuses. I had to act. So I forced my Sight closed and gathered my courage as best I could

Thunder roared outside and there was a flash of lightning, the two happening close together. The lights flickered, and the music skipped a track. Victor screamed out the incantation in a kind of ecstasy above me. The woman's voice, presumably Mrs Beckitt's, rose to a fevered pitch.

'You pays your money, you takes your chances,' I muttered to myself.

I focused my will, extended my right arm and open palm to the stereo system, and shouted, '*Fuego!*' A rush of heat from my hand exploded into flame on the far side of the room and engulfed the stereo, which began to emit a sound more like a long, tortured scream than music. Murphy's handcuffs still dangled from my wrist, one loop swinging free.

Then I turned, extended my arms and roared, '*Veni che!*' Wind swept up beneath me, making my duster billow like

Batman's cloak, lifting me directly up to the platform above
and over its low railing into the suspended room.

Even expecting the sight, it rattled me. Victor was dressed
in black slacks, a black shirt, black shoes – very stylish,
especially compared to my sweatpants and cowboy boots.
His shaggy eyebrows and lean features were highlighted
eerily by the dark light flowing up from the circle around
him, where the implements of his ritual spell were ready
to complete the ceremony that would kill me. He had what
looked like a spoon, its edges sharpened to razor keenness,
a pair of candles, black and white, and a white rabbit, its
feet bound with red cord. One of its legs was bleeding
from a small tear, staining the white fur. And tied against
its head with a cord was the lock of my own dark, straight
hair. Over to one side was another circle, laid out in chalk
upon the carpeting, maybe fifteen feet across. The Beckitts
were inside, writhing together in mindless, sweating desire,
generating energy for Victor's spell.

Victor stared at me in shock as I landed upon the balcony,
wind whipping around me, roaring inside the small room
like a miniature cyclone, knocking over potted plants and
knickknacks.

'You!' he shouted.

'Me,' I confirmed. 'There's something I've been meaning
to talk to you about, Vic.'

His shock transformed into snarling anger in a heartbeat. He snatched up the sharpened spoon, raised it in
his right hand, and screamed out words of the incantation.
He dragged the rabbit in front of him, the ceremonial
representation of me, and prepared to gouge out its, and
therefore my, heart.

I didn't give him the chance to finish. I reached into a

pocket and hurled the empty plastic film canister at Victor Shadowman.

As a weapon, it wasn't much. But it was real, and it had been hurled by a real person, a mortal. It could shatter the integrity of a magic circle.

The canister went through the air above Victor's circle and broke it, just as he completed the incantation and drove the spoon's blade down at the poor rabbit. The energy of the storm came whipping down the cylinder of focus created by Victor's now-flawed circle.

Power shattered out into the room, wild, undirected, and unfocused, naked color and raw sound spewing everywhere with hurricane force. It sent objects flying, including Victor and me, and shattered the secondary circle the Beckitts were in, sending them rolling and bumping across the floor and into one wall.

I braced myself against the guardrail and held on as the power raged around me, charging the air with raw, dangerous magic, surging about like water under pressure, seeking an outlet.

'You bastard!' Victor screamed into the gale. 'Why don't you just die!' He lifted a hand and screamed something at me, and fire washed across the space between us, instant and hot.

I tapped some of the ample power now available in the room and formed a hard, high wall in front of me, squeezing my eyes shut in concentration. It was a dozen times harder to shield without my bracelet, but I blocked the flame, sent it swirling high and over me, huddling under a little quarter dome of hardened air that would not let Victor's magic past it. I opened my eyes in time to see the flames touch the ceiling beams and set them alight.

The air still thrummed with energy as the wash of flame passed. Victor snarled when he saw me rise, lifted a hand to one side, and snarled out words of summoning. A crooked stick that looked like it might be some kind of bone soared through the air toward him, and he caught it in one hand, turning to me with the attitude of a man holding a gun.

The problem with most wizards is that they get too used to thinking in terms of one venue: Magic. I don't think Victor expected me to rise, lurch across the trembling floor toward him, and drive my shoulder into his chest, slamming him back into the wall with a satisfying thud. I leaned back a little and drove a knee toward his gut, missed, and got him square between the legs instead. The breath went out of him in a rush, and he doubled over to the ground. By this time, I was screaming at him, senseless and incoherent. I started kicking at his head.

I heard a metallic, ratcheting sound behind me and spun my head in time to see Beckitt, naked, point an automatic weapon at me. I threw myself to one side, and heard a brief explosion of gunfire. Something hot tore at my hip, spinning me into a roll, and I kept going, into the kitchen. I heard Beckitt snarl a curse. There were a number of sharp clicking sounds. The automatic had jammed. Hell, with this much magic flying around the room, we were all lucky the thing hadn't just exploded.

Victor, meanwhile, shook the end of the bone tube he held, and a half dozen dried, brown scorpion husks fell out onto the carpeting. His whiter-than-white teeth flashed in his boater-brown face, and he snarled, 'Scorpis, scorpis, scorpis!' His eyes gleamed with lust and fury.

One of my legs wasn't answering my calls to action, so I crab-walked backward into the kitchen on the heels of my hands and one leg. Out on the dining section of the balcony, the scorpions shuddered to life and started to grow. First one, and then the others, oriented on the kitchen and started toward me in scuttling bursts of speed, getting larger as they came.

Victor howled his glee. The Beckitts rose, both naked, lean and savage-looking, both sporting guns, their eyes empty of everything but a wild sort of bloodlust.

I felt my shoulders press against a counter. There was a rattle, and then a broom fell down against me, its handle bouncing off of my head and landing on the tile floor beside me. I grabbed at it, my heart pounding somewhere around my throat.

A roomful of deadly drug. One evil sorcerer on his home turf. Two crazies with guns. One storm of wild magic looking for something to set it into explosive motion. And half a dozen scorpions like the one I had barely survived earlier, rapidly growing to movie-monster size. Less than a minute on the clock and no time-outs remaining for the quarterback.

All in all, it was looking like a bad evening for the home team.

26

I was so dead. There was no way out of the kitchen, no time to use an explosive evocation in close quarters, and the deadly scorpions would rip me to pieces well before Victor could blow me up with explosive magic or one of the blood-maddened Beckitts could get their guns working long enough to put a few more bullets in me. My hip was beginning to scream with pain, which I supposed was better than the deadly dull numbness of more serious injuries and shock, but at the moment it was the least of my worries. I clutched the broom to me, my only pitiful weapon. I didn't even have the mobility to use it.

And then something occurred to me, something so childish that I almost laughed. I plucked a straw from the broomstick and began a low and steady chant, a bobbing about in the air with the fingers that held the straw. I reached out and took hold of the immense amounts of untapped energy running rampant in the air and drew them into the spell. '*Pulitas!*' I shouted, bringing the chant to a crescendo. '*Pulitas, pulitas!*'

The broom twitched. It quivered. It jerked upright in my hands. And then it took off across the kitchen floor, its brush waving menacingly, to meet the scorpions' advance. The last thing I had expected to use that cleaning spell for when I had laboriously been forced to learn it was a tide of poisonous scorpion monsters, but any port in a storm. The broom swept into them with ferocious energy and started flicking them across the kitchen toward the rest of the balcony with tidy, efficient motions. Each time one of the scorpions would try to dodge around it, the broom would tilt out and catch the beastie before it could, flick it neatly onto its back and continue about its job.

I'm pretty sure it got all the dirt on the way, too. When I do a spell, I do it right.

Victor screeched in anger when he saw his pets, still too small to carry much mass, being so neatly corralled and ushered off the balcony. The Beckitts lifted their guns and opened fire on the broom, while I hunkered down behind the counter. They must have been using revolvers now, because they fired smoothly and in an ordered rhythm. Bullets smacked into the walls and the counters at the back of the kitchen, but none of them came through the counter that sheltered me.

I caught my breath, pressing my hand against the blood on my hip. It hurt like bloody hell. I thought the bullet was stuck, somewhere by the bone. I couldn't move my leg. There was a lot of blood, but not so much that I was sitting in a puddle. Out on the balcony, the fire was beginning to catch, spreading over the roof. The entire place was going to come crashing down before much longer.

'Stop shooting, stop shooting, damn you!' Victor screamed, as the gunfire came to a halt. I risked a peek over the counter. My broom had swept the scorpions off the edge of the balcony and to the floor of the room below. As I watched, Victor caught the broom by its handle and broke it over the balcony railing with a snarl. The straw I still held in my fingers broke with a sharp little *twang*, and I felt the energy fade from the spell.

Victor Shadowman snarled. 'A cute trick, Dresden,' he

said, 'but pathetic. There's no way you can survive this. Give up. I'll be willing to let you walk away.'

The Beckitts were reloading. I ducked my head back down before they got any funny ideas, and hoped that they didn't have heavier rounds that could penetrate the counters I hid behind and whatever contents they contained, to kill me.

'Sure, Vic,' I replied, keeping my voice as calm as I could. 'You're known for your mercy and sense of fair play, right?'

'All I have to do is keep you in there until the fire spreads enough to kill you,' Victor said.

'Sure. Let's all die together, Vic. Too bad about all your inventory down there, though, eh?'

Victor snarled and pitched another burst of flame into the kitchen. This time, it was much easier to cover myself, half-shielded as I already was by the counters. 'Oh, cute,' I said, my voice dripping scorn. 'Fire's the simplest thing you can do. All the real wizards learn that in the first couple of weeks and move on up from there.' I looked around the kitchen. There had to be something I could use, some way I could escape, but nothing presented itself.

'Shut up!' Victor snarled. 'Who's the real wizard here, huh? Who's the one with all the cards and who's the one bleeding on the kitchen floor? You're nothing, Dresden, *nothing*. You're a *loser*. And do you know why?'

'Gee,' I said. 'Let me think.'

He laughed, harshly. 'Because you're an idiot. You're an idealist. Open your eyes, man. You're in the jungle, now. It's survival of the fittest, and you've proved yourself unfit. The strong do as they wish, and the weak get trampled. When this is over, I'm going to wipe you off my shoe and keep going like you never existed.'

'Too late for that,' I told him. I was in the mood to tell a white lie. 'The police know all about you, Vic. I told them myself. And I told the White Council, too. You've never even heard of them, have you, Vic? They're like the Superfriends and the Inquisition all rolled up into one. You'll love them. They'll take you out like yesterday's garbage. God, you really *are* an ignorant bastard.'

There was a moment's silence. Then, 'No,' he said. 'You're lying. You're lying to me, Dresden.'

'If I'm lying I'm dying,' I told him. Hell, as far as I knew, I was. 'Oh. And Johnny Marcone, too. I made sure that he knew who and where you were.'

'Son of a bitch,' Victor said. 'You stupid son of a bitch. Who put you up to this, huh? Marcone? Is that why he pulled you off the street?'

I had to laugh, weakly. A bit of flaming cabinet fell off an upper shelf onto the tiles next to me. It was getting hot in there. The fire was spreading. 'You never figured it out, did you, Vic?'

'Who?' Victor screamed at me. 'Who was it, damn you? That whore, Linda? Her whore friend Jennifer?'

'Strike two, strike three, the other side gets a chance to steal,' I said back. Hell. At least if I could keep him talking, I might keep him in the house long enough to go down with me. And if I could make him mad enough, he might make a mistake.

'Stop talking to him,' Beckitt said. 'He's not armed. Let's kill him and get out of here before we all die.'

'Go ahead,' I said in a cheerful tone. 'Hell, I've got nothing to lose. I'll send this whole house up in a fireball that'll make Hiroshima look like a hibachi. Make my day.'

'Shut up,' Victor shouted. 'Who was it, Dresden? Who, damn you?'

If I gave him Monica, he might still be able to get to her if he got away. There was no sense in risking that. So all I said was, 'Go to hell, Vic.'

'Get the car started,' Victor snarled. 'Go out through the deck doors. The scorpions will kill anything on the first floor.'

I heard motion in the room, someone moving out the doors onto the elevated deck at the back of the house. The fire continued to spread. Smoke rode the air in a thick haze.

'I've got to go, Dresden,' Victor told me. His voice was gentle, almost a purr, 'but there's someone I want you to meet, first.'

I got a sick, twisty little feeling in the pit of my stomach.

'Kalshazzak,' Victor whispered.

Power thrummed. The air shimmered and shone, began to twist and spiral.

'Kalshazzak,' Victor whispered again, louder, more demanding. I heard something, a warbling hiss that seemed to come from a great distance, rushing closer. The black wizard called the name for the third and final time, his voice rising to a screech, 'Kalshazzak!'

There was a thundercrack in the house, a dull and sulfurous stench, and I craned my neck to see over the counter, risking a glance.

Victor stood by the sliding glass doors that led out onto the wooden deck. Red-orange flames wreathed the ceiling on that side of the house, and smoke was filling the room below, casting the whole place in a hellish glow.

Crouched down on the floor in front of Victor was the

toad-demon I had banished the night before. I had known that I hadn't killed it. You can't kill demons, as such, only destroy the physical vessels they create for themselves when they come to the mortal world. If called again, they can create a new vessel without difficulty.

I watched in fascination, stunned. I had seen only one person call a demon before – and I had killed my old master shortly after. The thing crouched in front of Victor, its lightning blue eyes whirling with shades of scarlet hate, staring up at the black-clad wizard, trembling with the need to tear into him, to rend and destroy the mortal being who had dared summon it forth.

Victor's eyes grew wider and more mad, glittering with fevered intensity. Sweat ran down his face, and he tilted his head slowly to one side, as though his vision were skewing along the horizontal and by the motion he would compensate for it. I gave silent thanks that I had closed my Third Eye when I did. I did not want to see what that thing really looked like – and I didn't want to get a good look at the real Victor Sells, either.

The demon finally gave a hiss of frustration and turned toward me with a croaking growl. Victor dropped his head back and laughed, his will triumphant over that of the being he had called from beyond. 'There, Dresden. Do you see? The strong survive, and the weak are torn to little pieces.' He flapped his hand at me and said, to the demon, 'Kill him.'

I struggled to my feet, supporting my weight on the counter, to face the demon as it rose and began its slow stalk toward me.

'My God, Victor,' I said. 'I can't get over how clumsy you are.'

Victor's smile immediately became a snarling sneer once again. I saw fear touch the corners of his eyes, uncertainty even though he was on top, and I felt a little smile quirk my lips. I moved my gaze to the demon's.

'You really shouldn't just hand someone else a demon's name,' I told him. Then I drew in a breath, and shouted out in a voice of command, 'Kalshazzak!'

The demon stopped in its tracks and gave a whistling howl of agony and rage as I called its name and drew my will up to hurl against it.

'Kalshazzak,' I snarled again. The demon's presence was suddenly *there*, in my head, raging slippery and slimy and wriggling like a venomous tadpole. It was a pressure, a horrible pressure on my temples that made me see stars and threatened to steal enough of my balance to send me falling to the floor.

I tried to speak again and the words stuck in my throat. The demon hissed in anticipation, and the pressure on my head redoubled, trying to force me down, to make me give up the struggle, at which point the demon would be free to act. The lightning blue of its eyes became glaringly bright, painful to look upon.

I thought of little Jenny Sells, oddly enough, and of Murphy, lying pale and unconscious on a stretcher in the rain, of Susan, crouched next to me, sick and unable to run.

I had beaten this frog once. I could do it again.

I cried out the demon's name for the third and final time, my throat burning and raw. The word came out garbled and imperfect, and for a sinking moment I feared the worst, but Kalshazzak howled again, and hurled itself furiously to the floor, thrashing its limbs about like a poisoned bug, raging and tearing great swaths out of the carpet. I sagged, the weariness that came over me threatening to make me black out.

'What are you doing?' Victor said, his voice rising to a high-pitched shriek. 'What are you doing?' He was staring at the demon in horror. 'Kill him! I am your master! Kill him, kill him!' The demon howled in rage, turned its burning glare to me and then Victor, as though trying to decide who to devour first. Its eyes settled on Victor, who went pale and ran for the doors.

'Oh no you don't,' I muttered, and I uttered the last spell I could manage. One final time, on the last gasps of my power, the winds rose and lifted me from the earth. I hurtled into Victor like an ungainly cannonball, driving him away from the doors, past the demon as it made an awkward lunge at us, and toward the railing of the balcony.

We fell in a confused heap at the edge of the balcony that overlooked the room beneath, full of dark smoke and the red glow of flame. The air had grown almost too hot to breathe. Pain jolted through my hip, more bright and blinding than anything I had ever imagined, and I sucked in a breath. The smoky air burned, made me choke and gasp.

I looked up. Fire was spreading everywhere. The demon was crouched between us and the only way out. Over the edge of the balcony was only chaos and flame and smoke – strange, dark smoke that should have been rising, but instead was mostly settled along the floor like London fog. The pain was too great. I simply couldn't move. I couldn't even take in enough breath to scream.

'Damn you,' Victor screamed. He regained his feet and hauled me up toward his face with berserk strength. 'Damn you,' he repeated. 'What happened? What did you do?'

'The Fourth Law of Magic forbids the binding of any being against its will,' I grated out. Pain was tight around my throat, making me fight to speak the words. 'So I stepped in and cut your control over it. And didn't establish any of my own.'

Victor's eyes widened, 'You mean . . .'

'It's free,' I confirmed. I glanced at the demon. 'Looks hungry.'

'What do we do?' Victor said. His voice was shaking, and he started shaking me, too. 'What do we do?'

'We die,' I said. 'Hell, I was going to do that anyway. But at least this way, I take you out with me.'

I saw him glance at the demon, then back to me, eyes terrified and calculating. 'Work with me,' he said. 'You stopped it before. You can stop it again. We can beat it, together, and leave.'

I studied him for a moment. I couldn't kill him with magic. I didn't want to. And it would only have brought a death sentence on my head in any case. But I could stand by and do nothing. And that's exactly what I did. I smiled at him, closed my eyes, and did nothing.

'Fuck you, then, Dresden,' Victor snarled. 'It can only eat one of us at a time. And I'm not going to be the one to get eaten today.' And he picked me up to hurl me toward the demon.

I objected with fragile tenacity. We grappled. Fire raged. Smoke billowed. The demon came closer, lightning eyes gleaming through the hell-lit gloom. Victor was shorter than me, stockier, better at wrestling, and he hadn't been shot in the hip. He levered me up and almost threw me, but I moved quicker, whipping my right arm at his head and catching him with the flailing free end of Murphy's handcuffs, breaking his motion. He tried to break away, but I held on to him, dragged him in a circle to slam against the guardrail of the balcony, and we both toppled over.

Desperation gives a man extraordinary resources. I flailed at the balcony railing and caught it at the base, keeping myself from going over into the roiling smoke below. I shot a glance below, and saw the glistening brown hide of one of the scorpions, its stinging tail held up like the mast of a ship cutting through smoke at least four feet deep. The room was filled with angry clicking, scuttling sounds. Even in a single desperate glance, I saw a couch torn to pieces by a pair of scorpions in less time than it took to take a breath. They loomed over it, their tails waving in the air like flags from the back of golf carts. Hell's bells.

Victor had grabbed on to the railing a little above me and to the left, and he stared at the oncoming demon with a face twisted with hatred. I saw him draw in a breath, and try to plant a foot firmly enough to free one hand to point at the oncoming demon in some sort of magical attack or defense.

I couldn't allow Victor to get out of this. He was still whole. If he could knock the demon down, he might still slip out. So I had to tell him something that would make him mad enough to try to take my head off. 'Hey, Vic,' I shouted. 'It was your wife. It was Monica that ratted on you.'

The words hit him like a physical blow, and his head whipped around toward me, his face contorting in fury. He started to say something to me, the words of a spell meant to blow me to bits, maybe, but the toad-demon interrupted him by rearing up with an angry hiss and snapping its jaws down over Victor's collar-bone and throat. Bone broke with audible snaps, and Victor squealed in pain, his arms and legs shuddering. He tried to push his way *down*, away from the demon, and the creature's balance wobbled.

I gritted my teeth and tried to hold on. A scorpion leapt at me, brown and gleaming, and I drew my legs up out of reach of its pincers, just barely.

'Bastard,' Victor cried, struggling uselessly in the demon's jaws. There was blood running down his body, fast and hot. The demon had hit an artery, and it was simply holding on, wavering at the edge of the balcony as Victor struggled and started kicking at my near hand. He hit me once, twice, and my balance wavered, my grip slipping. A quick glance below me showed me another scorpion, getting ready to jump at me, this one closer.

Murphy, I thought. *I should have listened to you*. If the scorpions didn't kill me, the demon would, and if the demon didn't, the fire was going to kill me. I was going to die.

There was a certain peace in thinking that, in knowing that it was all about to be over. I was going to die. It was as simple as that. I had fought as hard as I could, done everything I could think of, and it was over. I found myself, in my final seconds, idly wishing that I could have had time to apologize to Murphy, that I could apologize to Jenny Sells for killing her daddy, that I could apologize to Linda Randall for not figuring things out fast enough and saving her life. Murphy's handcuffs lay tight and cold against my forearm as monsters and demons and black wizards and smoke closed in all around me. I closed my eyes.

Murphy's handcuffs.

My eyes snapped open.

Murphy's handcuffs.

Victor swung his foot at my left hand again. I kicked with my legs and hauled with my shoulders to give me a second of lift, and grabbed Victor Sells's pant leg in my left hand. With my right, I flicked the free end of the handcuffs around one of the bars of the guardrail. The ring of metal cycled around on its hinge and locked into place.

Then, as I started to fall back down, I hauled hard on Victor's leg. He screamed, a horrible, high-pitched squeal, as he started to fall. Kalshazzak, finally overbalanced by the additional weight and leverage I had added to Victor's struggles, pitched over the balcony guardrail and into the smoke below, crashing down to the floor, carrying Victor with him.

There was a rush of scuttling, clicking sounds, a piercing whistle-hiss from the demon. Victor's screams rose to something high-pitched and horrible, until he sounded more like an animal, a pig squealing at slaughter, than a man.

I swung from the balcony, my feet several feet above the fray, held suspended in an acutely painful fashion by Murphy's handcuffs, one loop around my wrist, the other locked around the balcony railing. I looked down as my vision started to fade. I saw a sea of brown, gleaming plates of segmented, chitinous armor. I saw the scorpions' stinging tails flashing down, over and over again. I saw the lightning eyes of Kalshazzak's physical vessel, and I saw one of them pierced and put out by the flashing sting of one of the scorpions.

And I saw Victor Sells, struck over and over again by stingers the size of ice picks, the wounds foaming with poison. The demon ignored the pincers and the stingers of the scorpions to begin tearing him apart. His face contorted in the final agony of rage and fear.

The strong survive, and the weak get eaten. I guess Victor had invested in the wrong kind of strength.

I didn't want to watch what was happening below me. The fires consuming the ceiling above were rather beautiful, actually, rolling waves of flame, cherry red, sunset orange. I was too weak to try to get out of this mess, and the entire thing had become far too annoying and painful to even consider anymore. I just watched the flames, and waited and noticed, oddly, that I was simply *starving*. And no wonder. I hadn't eaten a decent meal since . . . Friday? Friday. You notice odd things in those final moments, they say.

And then you start seeing things. For instance, I saw Morgan come through the sliding glass doors leading in from the outside deck, the silver sword of the White Council's justice in his hands. I saw one of the scorpions, now the size of a German shepherd, figure out the stairs, scuttle up them, and hurtle at Morgan. I saw Morgan's silver sword slash, *snickersnack*, and leave the scorpion in writhing pieces on the floor.

Then I saw Morgan, his expression grim, his weight making the fire-chewed balcony shudder, come for me. His eyes narrowed when he saw me, and he lifted the sword, leaning far over the balcony railing. The blade flashed bright silver in the firelight as it started to come down.

Typical, was my last thought. *How perfectly typical, to survive everything the bad guys could do, and get taken down by the people for whose cause I had been fighting.*

27

I awoke somewhere cool and dark, in tremendous pain, coughing my lungs out. Rain was falling on my face, and it was the greatest feeling I'd ever known. Morgan's face was over mine, and I realized he'd been giving me CPR. Eww.

I coughed and spluttered and sat up, wheezing for breath. Morgan watched me for a moment, then scowled and stood up, eyes flickering around.

I managed to get enough wind to speak, and said, numbly, 'You saved me.'

He grimaced. 'Yes.'

'But why?'

He looked at me again, then stooped to pick up his sword and slip it into the scabbard at his side. 'Because I saw what happened in there. I saw you risk your life to stop the Shadowman. Without breaking any of the Laws. You weren't the killer.'

I coughed some more, and said, 'That doesn't mean you had to save me.'

He turned and blinked at me, as though puzzled. 'What do you mean?'

'You could have let me die.'

His hard expression never changed, but he said, 'You weren't guilty. You're a part of the White Council.' His mouth twisted as though the words were fresh lemons. 'Technically. I had an obligation to preserve your life. It was my duty.'

'I wasn't the killer,' I said.

'No.'

'So,' I wheezed, 'that would make me right. And then that would make *you*—'

Morgan scowled. 'More than ready to carry out the Doom if you cross the line, Dresden. Don't think this has gotten you off the hook, as far as I'm concerned.'

'So. If I remember correctly, as a Warden, it is your duty to report on my conduct to the Council, isn't it?'

His scowl darkened.

'So you're going to have to go to them on Monday and tell them all about what really happened. The whole truth and nothing but the truth.'

'Yes,' he snarled. 'It is even possible they will lift the Doom.'

I started laughing, weakly.

'You haven't won, Dresden. There are many on the Council who know full well that you have consorted with the powers of darkness. *We*, at least, will not relax our vigil on you. We will watch you day and night, we will *prove* that you are a danger who must be stopped.'

I kept laughing. I fell over on my side, I laughed so much.

Morgan arched an eyebrow and simply stared at me. 'Are you all right?'

'Give me about a gallon of Listerine,' I choked, 'and I'll be just fine.'

Morgan just stared at me, and I laughed harder. He rolled his eyes and growled something about the police being here any moment to provide medical care. Then he turned and stomped off into the woods, muttering to himself the whole way.

The police arrived in time to catch the Beckitts trying to leave and arrested them for, of all things, being naked. Later, they were implicated in the ThreeEye drug ring, and prosecuted on distribution charges. Just as well for them that they're in the Michigan justice system. They wouldn't have come out of a cell alive if they'd been in Chicago. It wouldn't have been good for Johnny Marcone's business.

The Varsity suffered a mysterious fire the night of my visit. I hear Marcone didn't have any trouble collecting the insurance money, in spite of all the odd rumors going around. Word hit the street that Marcone had hired Harry Dresden to take out the head of the ThreeEye gang, one of those rumors that you can't trace back to any one person. I didn't try to deny it. It was a cheap enough price to not have to worry about anyone bombing my car.

I was too hospitalized to show up at the meeting of the White Council, but it turned out that they decided to lift the Doom of Damocles (which I had always thought a rather pretentious name in any case) from me, due to 'valorous action above and beyond the call of duty'. I don't think Morgan ever forgave me for being a good guy. He had to eat crow in front of the whole Council, relentlessly driven by his anal-retentive sense of duty and honor. There's no love lost between us. But the guy was honest. I'll give him credit for that.

And hell. At least I don't have to look forward to him popping out from nowhere every time I cast a spell. I hope.

Murphy was in critical condition for nearly seventy-two hours, but she pulled through. They gave her a room right down the hall from me, in fact. I sent flowers to her hospital room, along with the surviving ring of her handcuffs. I told her, in a note, not to ask how the chain between the rings had been so neatly severed. I didn't think she'd buy that someone cut it with a magic sword. The flowers must have helped. The first time she got out of bed was to totter down the hall to my room, throw them in my face, and leave without saying a word.

She professed to have no memory of what had happened at my office, and maybe she didn't. But in any case, she got the warrant for my arrest rescinded, and a couple weeks later, when she went back to work, she called me in for advice the next day. And she sent a big check to cover my expenses in the murder investigations. I guess that means we're friends again, in a professional sense. But we don't joke anymore. Some wounds don't heal very quickly.

The police found the remains of the huge ThreeEye stash in what was left of the lake house, and Victor Sells eventually came up as the bad guy. Monica Sells and her children vanished into Witness Protection. I hope they've got a better life now than they had before. I suppose it couldn't be much worse.

Bob eventually came home again, more or less within the twenty-four-hour time limit, I suppose. I turned a deaf ear to rumors of a particularly wild party at the University of Chicago which lasted from Saturday night to Sunday night, and Bob wisely never mentioned it.

DATE WITH A DEMON was a headliner for the *Arcane* when it came out the following Monday, and Susan came by my hospital room to bring me a copy and to talk to me about it. She seemed greatly amused by the cast that held my hips immobilized until the docs could be sure that there wasn't too much fracturing (the X-ray machine kept fouling whenever they tried to use it on me, for some reason), and commented that it was a pity I wasn't more mobile. I used the sympathy factor to badger another date out of her, and she didn't seem to mind too much.

That time, we were *not* interrupted by a demon. And I didn't need any of Bob's love potions or advice, thank you very much.

Mac got his TransAm back. I got the Blue Beetle back. That didn't seem exactly equitable, but at least the Beetle still runs. Most of the time.

I made sure to send pizza out to Toot-toot and his faerie buddies every night for a week, and once a week ever since. I'm pretty sure the kid from Pizza 'Spress thought I was a loony, having him drop off pizza by the roadside. Heck with him. I make good on my promises.

Mister got a little shortchanged on the whole deal, but it is well beneath his dignity to notice such things.

And me? What did I get out of it? I'm not really sure. I escaped from something that had been following me for a long time. I'm just not sure what. I'm not sure who was more certain that I was a walking Antichrist waiting to happen — the conservative branch of the White Council, the men like Morgan, or me. For them, at least, the question has been partly laid to rest. For myself, though, I'm not so sure. The power is there. The temptation is there. That's just the way it's going to be.

I can live with that.

The world is getting weirder. Darker every single day. Things are spinning around faster and faster, and threatening to go completely awry. Falcons and falconers. The center cannot hold.

But in my corner of the country, I'm trying to nail things down. I don't want to live in Victor's jungle, even if it did eventually devour him. I don't want to live in a world where the strong rule and the weak cower. I'd rather make a place where things are a little quieter. Where trolls stay the hell under their bridges and where elves don't come swooping out to snatch children from their cradles. Where vampires respect the limits, and where the faeries mind their *p*'s and *q*'s.

My name is Harry Blackstone Copperfield Dresden. Conjure by it at your own risk. When things get strange, when what goes bump in the night flicks on the lights, when no one else can help you, give me a call.

I'm in the book.

extras

www.orbitbooks.net

about the author

A martial arts enthusiast whose resumé includes a long list of skills rendered obsolete at least two hundred years ago, **Jim Butcher** turned to writing as a career because anything else probably would have driven him insane. He lives in Independence, Missouri, with his wife, his son and a ferocious guard dog. You can visit Jim's website at www.jim-butcher.com

Find out more about Jim Butcher and other Orbit authors by registering for the free monthly newsletter at www.orbitbooks.net

interview

What made you become interested in writing?
Repeating 'may I help you' about a zillion times was a
part of the equation. But mostly, it was just something
that I had more or less always done in one sense or another.
I had been a voracious reader of science fiction and fantasy
since about the first grade, when my sisters got me boxed
sets of *The Lord of the Rings* and *The Adventures of Han
Solo*. The first movie I can clearly remember seeing was
Star Wars (also a sister-assisted venture). For most of my
life, if I wasn't watching science fiction, or reading it, I
was drawing pictures with that omnipresent Death Star
half circle in the bottom right hand corner or writing
stories.

I remember that I felt frustrated at not being able to
find that 'perfect' story – you know what I'm talking about.
That story that absolutely rings true in every sense as you
read it, that makes you laugh and cry and when it's over
leaves this glowy, satisfied feeling resounding inside you.
Nowadays, I have the feeling that everyone's perfect story
is a bit different, but in the effort to find mine, I eventually wrote my first novel when I was nineteen.

It wasn't perfect. In fact, it was terrible. But I tried to
hang in there and upon getting involved with the
Professional Writing program at OU, I wrote my second
novel in an effort to make the perfect story.

It wasn't, either. In fact, it was even worse. Ditto the

third novel. The fourth was at least a little bit better, but it still wasn't good, much less the Perfect Story.

The fifth novel I wrote, though, all the stuff my teacher had been teaching me seemed to fall together. The book was then called *The Dresden Chronicles, Book One: Semiautomagic*. After a fairly light round of editing, it became *The Dresden Files, Book One: Storm Front*.

(For the record, I still haven't gotten the Perfect Story written. But maybe it will be the next one. Or the one after that. Or the one after that. Or . . .)

How do you come up with the characters for your books?

Callous as it sounds, mostly it depends on what I need them to do in the story. I hear a lot of talk about plot-driven books versus character-driven books, but my own impression on the subject leans more towards the idea that plot and character cannot be usefully separated from one another. But from the aspect of a writer who has a deadline and who needs to be able to plan and reliably produce a reasonably good story, I tend to make things easy on myself whenever I can. I figure out what I need a character to do in my story, and then I build a character who would do it.

I needed someone to provide threat, motivation, and distraction for Harry in *Storm Front*, for example, and got two characters who could do those jobs. John Marcone got to show up as the negative criminal element in the story, the human face of lawlessness and crime. Karrin Murphy is his opposite number, representative of the law, society, and order.

Neither one of them seems to do much for Harry that

doesn't make his day worse and worse, nine times out of ten, but no one's perfect.

Bob the Skull came about in the same way. In fact, he's something of an in-joke for the writers in the program at OU. Debbie Chester, my writing teacher, often warned us about producing an old and worn-out trope for our stories, called 'talking heads'. Talking heads are characters with no real purpose in the story other than to show up and explain something so that the reader can get what's going on. I knew that I was going to need a character who could explain things about magic to Harry (and through him to the reader) so that the magic 'rules' would hold together and make sense. So just to be a smart alec to my teacher, I made a literal 'talking head' for Harry, who gets to serve as an advisor, an information source and an annoyance – I can't plan a character, these days, without figuring out how it's going to drive Harry nuts.

What kind of research did you have to do to create the story world for the Dresden Files? How much of your research has actually been used throughout the life of the series?

I raided my local bookstores and prowled their metaphysical sections. I read up on several systems of the practice of magic as embraced by various systems of faith who incorporate them into their belief. I read about magical practitioners in a historical perspective, throughout multiple centuries. I read books coming out against the practice of magic as well, and tried to gain a general understanding of the principles the various systems had in common. That's how I built the basic magic of the Dresden Files – by taking those common elements and combining them into a polyglot whole, based upon a skeleton of Newtonian physics.

I wanted the magic of the Dresden Files to be simply a part of the story universe, a source of energy just like heat or electricity, and one which obeyed certain universal laws that governed its interaction with reality. I didn't want Dresden to be a mystic, shamanistic wizard. I wanted him to be a plumber, a carpenter, an engineer. Only instead of working with water, wood or physics, he was working with magic.

It's all come in somewhere, though it's hard for me to point out exactly what has gone where. I had the whole thing formed in my head when I started writing, and it just kind of started breathing on its own as the first story got rolling.

Harry's world is a blend of traditional fairy-tales and biblical nightmares. Where did you come up with it?
Much of it from *Scooby Doo*. When I was a kid there were all kinds of things that I would watch on TV that would be interesting or intriguing to me or scary, like *Damian* and *The Omen*. When I was young, they were just the scariest thing ever. [Those movies] gave me nightmares.

Watching something like *Scooby Doo* was something that I thought was fun as a kid. You know, you get to the end and, ha ha ha, it's not actually a hideous bog monster, its Old Man Witherspoon. 'And I'd have gotten away with it too if it weren't for you meddling kids.'

But in the Dresden world it isn't Old Man Witherspoon, it is the hideous bog monster, and that very real monster is something that Harry has to face and deal with. I think in one of the early books I call science one of the most successful religions of the twentieth century because everybody believes that there's a rational explanation for everything. In Dresden's world there isn't one. Sometimes the thing underneath the mask might be even worse than you thought it was. And it's not usually an old man, and there are nasty evil things that are still out there and they're just as dangerous even if people don't want to believe that they're real.

Do you have a specific destination for Harry? Do you know where he's going?
Very much so. I set out and was sure I knew where he was going in the beginning and while my perceptions of his world and the kind of things that he faces have changed, Harry is pretty much on course. If I get to do what I want, I'll get to do about twenty case books. And then at the end I'll do a big old apocalyptic trilogy because big old apocalyptic trilogies are fun.

How far ahead have you plotted the Dresden Files? Have you plotted the entire arc or are you taking it book by book?
I've got a good idea where I want the overall story to go. I've got an over-story for the entire series. A lot of it is tied into Harry's origins – his parents and the kind of lives they led early on. I keep dropping small hints and stuff about what's been going on in the past. Which should become more important as the series goes on.

I've got sort of stepping stones – where I want the character to be at any given point in the story arc. So far I'm doing all right. So far he's on track. The thing I don't have planned out is his romance. His love life is something that is more organic. I don't really have anything blocked out for that. I like playing with it, I like having that as something that I don't know exactly what's going to happen and as a result I think I've got some good stuff to work with.

What do you hope people get from your books?
What I most hope people get out of the books is a good time. I should probably have a higher literary aspiration, but really, I just want people to read the books. I want the book to be so good that they stay up late reading it, and when they get to the end, they say, 'Oh, cool! That was a good book!' That's really what I'm looking for.

Finally, what interests do you have outside of writing?
Oh, the usual kind of thing. I play a little guitar, I work out. I like video games like *Left 4 Dead*, *City of Heroes*, *Rock Band* and *Halo*. I go to live role-playing events run by the fledgling organisation, Heroic Interactive Theatre, where I can run around hitting people with nerf swords. I watch bad fantasy and science fiction movies and occasionally get on the floor and play with the dog.

This interview is published with permission from BittenbyBooks.com, TotalSciFiOnline.com, absentwillow.com, www.crescentblues.com and www.wizardsharry.com

if you enjoyed
STORM FRONT

look out for

FOOL MOON

a Dresden Files novel

also by

Jim Butcher

1

I never used to keep close track of the phases of the moon.
So I didn't know that it was one night shy of being full
when a young woman sat down across from me in
McAnally's pub and asked me to tell her all about something that could get her killed.

'No,' I said. 'Absolutely not.' I folded the piece of paper,
with its drawings of three concentric rings of spidery
symbols, and slid it back over the polished oak-wood table.

Kim Delaney frowned at me, and brushed some of her
dark, shining hair back from her forehead. She was a tall
woman, buxom and lovely in an old-world way, with pale,
pretty skin and round cheeks well used to smiling. She
wasn't smiling now.

'Oh, come on, Harry,' she told me. 'You're Chicago's
only practicing professional wizard, and you're the only
one who can help me.' She leaned across the table toward
me, her eyes intent. 'I can't find the references for all of
these symbols. No one in local circles recognizes them
either. You're the only real wizard I've ever even heard of,
much less know. I just want to know what these others
are.'

'No,' I told her. 'You don't want to know. You're better
off forgetting this circle and concentrating on something
else.'

'But—'

Mac caught my attention from behind the bar by waving

a hand at me, and slid a couple of plates of steaming food onto the polished surface of the crooked oak bar. He added a couple of bottles of his homemade brown ale, and my mouth started watering.

My stomach made an unhappy noise. It was almost as empty as my wallet. I would never have been able to afford dinner tonight, except that Kim had offered to buy, if I'd talk to her about something during the meal. A steak dinner was less than my usual rate, but she was pleasant company, and a sometime apprentice of mine. I knew she didn't have much money, and I had even less.

Despite my rumbling stomach, I didn't rise immediately to pick up the food. (In McAnally's pub and grill, there aren't any service people. According to Mac, if you can't get up and walk over to pick up your own order, you don't need to be there at all.) I looked around the room for a moment, with its annoying combination of low ceilings and lazily spinning fans, its thirteen carved wooden columns and its thirteen windows, plus thirteen tables arranged haphazardly to defray and scatter the residual magical effects that sometimes surrounded hungry (in other words, angry) wizards. McAnally's was a haven in a town where no one believed in magic. A lot of the crowd ate there.

'Look, Harry,' Kim said. 'I'm not using this for anything serious, I promise. I'm not trying any summoning or binding. It's an academic interest only. Something that's been bothering me for a while.' She leaned forward and put her hand over mine, looking me in the face without looking me in the eyes, a trick that few nonpractitioners of the Art could master. She grinned and showed me the deep dimples in her cheeks.

My stomach growled again, and I glanced over at the food on the bar, waiting for me. 'You're sure?' I asked her. 'This is just you trying to scratch an itch? You're not using it for anything?'

'Cross my heart,' she said, doing so.

I frowned. 'I don't know . . .'

She laughed at me. 'Oh, come *on*, Harry. It's no big deal. Look, if you don't want to tell me, never mind. I'll buy you dinner anyway. I know you're tight for money lately. Since that thing last spring, I mean.'

I glowered, but not at Kim. It wasn't her fault that my main employer, Karrin Murphy, the director of Special Investigations at the Chicago Police Department, hadn't called me in for consulting work in more than a month. Most of my living for the past few years had come from serving as a special consultant to SI, but after a fracas last spring involving a dark wizard fighting a gang war for control of Chicago's drug trade, work with SI had slowly tapered off – and with it, my income.

I didn't know why Murphy hadn't been calling me in as often. I had my suspicions, but I hadn't gotten the chance to confront her about them yet. Maybe it wasn't anything I'd done. Maybe the monsters had gone on strike. Yeah, right.

The bottom line was I was strapped for cash. I'd been eating ramen noodles and soup for too many weeks. The steaks Mac had prepared smelled like heaven, even from across the room. My belly protested again, growling its neolithic craving for charred meat.

But I couldn't just go and eat the dinner without giving Kim the information she wanted. It's not that I've never welshed on a deal, but I've never done it with anyone human – and definitely not with someone who looked up to me.

Sometimes I hate having a conscience, and a stupidly thorough sense of honor.

'All right, all right,' I sighed. 'Let me get the dinner and I'll tell you what I know.'

Kim's round cheeks dimpled again. 'Thanks, Harry. This means a lot to me.'

'Yeah, yeah,' I told her, and got up to weave my way toward the bar, through columns and tables and so on. McAnally's had more people than usual tonight, and though Mac rarely smiled, there was a contentment to his manner that indicated that he was happy with the crowd. I snatched up the plates and bottles with a somewhat petulant attitude. It's hard to take much joy in a friend's prosperity when your own business is about to go under.

I took the food, steaks and potatoes and green beans, back to the table and sat down again, placing Kim's plate in front of her. We ate for a while, myself in sullen silence and she in hearty hunger.

'So,' Kim said, finally. 'What can you tell me about that?' She gestured toward the piece of paper with her fork.

I swallowed my food, took a sip of the rich ale, and picked up the paper again. 'All right. This is a figure of High magic. Three of them, really, one inside the other, like layered walls. Remember what I told you about magical circles?'

Kim nodded. 'They either hold something out or keep it in. Most work on magic energies or creatures of the Nevernever, but mortal creatures can cross the circles and break them.'

'Right,' I said. 'That's what this outermost circle of symbols is. It's a barrier against creatures of spirit and magical forces. These symbols here, here, here, are the key ones.' I pointed out the squiggles in question.

Kim nodded eagerly. 'I got the outer one. What's the next?'

'The second circle is more of a spell barrier to *mortal* flesh. It wouldn't work if all you used was a ring of symbols. You'd need something else, stones or gems or something, spaced between the drawings.' I took another bite of steak.

Kim frowned at the paper, and then at me. 'And then what would that do?'

'Invisible wall,' I told her. 'Like bricks. Spirits, magic, could go right through it, but mortal flesh couldn't. Neither could a thrown rock, bullets, anything purely physical.'

'I see,' she said, excited. 'Sort of a force field.'

I nodded. 'Something like that.'

Her cheeks glowed with excitement, and her eyes shone. 'I *knew* it. And what's this last one?'

I squinted at the innermost ring of symbols, frowning. 'A mistake.'

'What do you mean?'

'I mean that it's just gobbledygook. It doesn't mean anything useful. Are you sure you copied this correctly?'

Kim's mouth twisted into a frown. 'I'm sure, I'm sure. I was careful.'

I studied her face for a moment. 'If I read the symbols correctly, it's a third wall. Built to withhold creatures of flesh *and* spirit. Neither mortal nor spirit but somewhere in between.'

She frowned. 'What kind of creatures are like that?'

I shrugged. 'None,' I said, and officially, it was true. The White Council of wizards did not allow the discussion of demons that could be called to earth, beings of spirit that could gather flesh to themselves. Usually, a spirit-circle was enough to stop all but the most powerful demons or Elder Things of the outer reaches of the Nevernever. But this third circle was built to stop things that could transcend those kinds of boundaries. It was a cage for demonic demigods and archangels.

Kim wasn't buying my answer. 'I don't see why anyone would make a circle like this to contain nothing, Harry.'

I shrugged. 'People don't always do reasonable, sensible things. They're like that.'

She rolled her eyes at me. 'Come on, Harry. I'm not a baby. You don't have to shelter me.'

'And you,' I told her, 'don't need to know what kind of thing that third circle was built to contain. You don't want to know. Trust me.'

She glowered at me for a long moment, then sipped at her ale and shrugged. 'All right. Circles have to be empowered, right? You have to know how to switch them on, like lights?'

'Something like that. Sure.'

'How would a person turn this one on?'

I stared at her for a long time.

'Harry?' she asked.

'You don't need to know that, either. Not for an academic interest. I don't know what you've got in mind, Kim, but leave it alone. Forget it. Walk away, before you get hurt.'

'Harry, I am not—'

'Save it,' I told her. 'You're sitting on a tiger cage, Kim.' I thumped a finger on the paper for emphasis. 'And you wouldn't need it if you weren't planning on trying to stick a tiger in there.'

Her eyes glittered, and she lifted her chin. 'You don't think I'm strong enough.'

'Your strength's got nothing to do with it,' I said. 'You don't have the training. You don't have the knowledge. I wouldn't expect a kid in grade school to be able to sit down and figure out college calculus. And I don't expect it of you, either.' I leaned forward. 'You don't know enough yet to be toying with this sort of thing, Kim. And even if you did, even if you did manage to become a full-fledged wizard, I'd still tell you not to do it. You mess this up and you could get a lot of people hurt.'

'*If* I was planning to do that, it's my business, Harry.' Her eyes were bright with anger. 'You don't have the right to choose for me.'

'No,' I told her. 'I've got the responsibility to help you make the right choice.' I curled the paper in my fingers and crushed it, then tossed it aside, to the floor. She stabbed her fork into a cut of steak, a sharp, vicious gesture. 'Look, Kim,' I said. 'Give it some time. When you're older, when you've had more experience . . .'

'You aren't so much older than me,' Kim said.

I shifted uncomfortably in my seat. 'I've had a lot of training. And I started young.' My own ability with magic, far in excess of my years and education, wasn't a subject I wanted to explore. So I tried to shift the direction of the conversation. 'How is this fall's fund-raiser going?'